Praise for James Lee Burke

"James Lee Burke is the reigning champ of nostalgia noir."
—*The New York Times Book Review*

"A gorgeous prose stylist."
—Stephen King

"James Lee Burke is the heavyweight champ, a great American novelist whose work, taken individually or as a whole, is unsurpassed."
—Michael Connelly

"Burke's evocative prose remains a thing of reliably fierce wonder."
—*Entertainment Weekly*

"America's best novelist."
—*The Denver Post*

"Burke can touch you in ways few writers can."
—*The Washington Post*

"For five decades, Burke has created memorable novels that weave exquisite language, unforgettable characters, and social commentary into written tapestries that mirror the contemporary scene. His work transcends genre classification."
—*The Philadelphia Inquirer*

"Burke's writing [is] Faulkner-esque in its beauty, its feel on the ear like a southern breeze blowing through magnolia blossoms and oil fields."
—*Missoulian*

Jolie Blon's Bounce

A DAVE ROBICHEAUX NOVEL

JAMES LEE BURKE

SIMON & SCHUSTER PAPERBACKS

New York London Toronto Sydney New Delhi

Simon & Schuster Paperbacks
An Imprint of Simon & Schuster, Inc.
1230 Avenue of the Americas
New York, NY 10020

This Simon & Schuster trade paperback edition April 2018

SIMON & SCHUSTER PAPERBACKS and colophon are registered trademarks of Simon & Schuster, Inc.

For information about special discounts for bulk purchases, please contact Simon & Schuster Special Sales at 1-866-506-1949 or business@simonandschuster.com.

The Simon & Schuster Speakers Bureau can bring authors to your live event. For more information or to book an event, contact the Simon & Schuster Speakers Bureau at 1-866-248-3049 or visit our website at www.simonspeakers.com.

Manufactured in the United States of America

3   5   7   9   10   8   6   4

Library of Congress Control Number: 2003544892

ISBN 978-1-9821-0024-7
ISBN 978-0-7432-4462-6 (ebook)

For Rick and Carole DeMarinis

and

Paul and Elizabeth Zarzysk

ACKNOWLEDGMENTS

Many people are involved in the career of an author, just as many are involved in the editing and production of a book, but very few of their names appear on the book jacket. Hence, I would like to give thanks to some of the people who have been so helpful to me and supportive of my work over the last forty years:

My original agent, the late Kurt Hellmer; my first editor, Joyce Hartman, at Houghton Mifflin; Bruce Carrick at Scribner; Martha Lacy Hall, Les Phillabaum, John Easterly, and the late Michael Pinkston at Louisiana State University Press; Rob Cowley at Holt; Roger Donald and Bill Phillips at Little, Brown; Robert Mecoy at Avon; Robert Miller and Brian Defiore at Hyperion; Shawn Coyne at Doubleday; George Lucas at Pocket Books; Carolyn Reidy, Chuck Adams, Michael Korda, and David Rosenthal at Simon & Schuster; and Susan Lamb and Jane Wood at Orion in Great Britain.

I would also like to thank my agents, Philip Spitzer and Joel Gotler, for their many years of commitment to my work, and Patricia Mulcahy, who has edited my work and been a family friend for thirteen years.

Once again, I would like to express my gratitude to my family: my wife, Pearl, and our four children, Jim Jr., Andree, Pamala, and Alafair.

Finally, in the words of Dave Robicheaux, may God bless reference librarians everywhere.

JOLIE BLON'S BOUNCE

CHAPTER 1

Growing up during the 1940s in New Iberia, down on the Gulf Coast, I never doubted how the world worked. At dawn the antebellum homes along East Main loomed out of the mists, their columned porches and garden walkways and second-story verandas soaked with dew, the chimneys and slate roofs softly molded by the canopy of live oaks that arched over the entire street.

The stacks of sunken U.S. Navy ships lay sideways in Pearl Harbor and service stars hung inside front windows all over New Iberia. But on East Main, in the false dawn, the air was heavy with the smell of night-blooming flowers and lichen on damp stone and the fecund odor of Bayou Teche, and even though a gold service star may have hung in a window of a grand mansion, indicating the death of a serviceman in the family, the year could have been mistaken for 1861 rather than 1942.

Even when the sun broke above the horizon and the ice wagons and the milk delivery came down the street on iron-rimmed wheels and the Negro help began reporting for work at their employers' back doors, the light was never harsh, never superheated or smelling of tar roads and dust as it was in other neighborhoods. Instead it filtered through Spanish moss and bamboo and philodendron that dripped with beads of moisture as big as marbles, so that even in the midst of summer the morning came to those who lived here with a blue softness that daily told them the earth was a grand place, its design vouchsafed in heaven and not to be questioned.

Down the street was the old Frederic Hotel, a lovely pink building with marble columns and potted palms inside, a ballroom, an elevator that looked like a brass birdcage, and a saloon with wood-bladed fans and an elevated, scrolled-iron shoeshine chair and a long, hand-carved mahogany bar. Amid the palm fronds and the blue and gray swirls of color in the marble columns were the slot and racehorse machines, ringing with light, their dull pewterlike coin trays offering silent promise to the glad at heart.

Farther down Main were Hopkins and Railroad Avenues, like ancillary conduits into part of the town's history and geography that people did not talk about publicly. When I went to the icehouse on Saturday afternoons with my father, I would look furtively down Railroad at the rows of paintless cribs on each side of the train tracks and at the blowsy women who sat on the stoops, hung over, their knees apart under their loose cotton dresses, perhaps dipping beer out of a bucket two

Negro boys carried on a broom handle from Hattie
Fontenot's bar.

I came to learn early on that no venal or meretricious
enterprise existed without a community's consent. I
thought I understood the nature of evil. I learned at age
twelve I did not.

My half brother, who was fifteen months younger than
I, was named Jimmie Robicheaux. His mother was a
prostitute in Abbeville, but he and I were raised together,
largely by our father, known as Big Aldous, who was a
trapper and commercial fisherman and offshore derrick
man. As children Jimmie and I were inseparable. On
summer evenings we used to go to the lighted ball games
at City Park and slip into the serving lines at barbecues
and crab boils at the open-air pavilions. Our larceny was
of an innocent kind, I suppose, and we were quite proud
of ourselves when we thought we had outsmarted the
adult world.

On a hot August night, with lightning rippling
through the thunderheads over the Gulf of Mexico,
Jimmie and I were walking through a cluster of oak trees
on the edge of the park when we saw an old Ford automobile with two couples inside, one in the front seat, one
in the back. We heard a woman moan, then her voice
mount in volume and intensity. We stared openmouthed
as we saw the woman's top half arch backward, her naked
breasts lit by the glow from a picnic pavilion, her mouth
wide with orgasm.

We started to change direction, but the woman was
laughing now, her face sweaty and bright at the open
window.

"Hey, boy, you know what we been doin'? It make my pussy feel so good. Hey, come here, you. We been fuckin', boy," she said.

It should have been over, a bad encounter with white trash, probably drunk, caught in barnyard copulation. But the real moment was just beginning. The man behind the steering wheel lit a cigarette, his face flaring like paste in the flame, then stepped out on the gravel. There were tattoos, like dark blue smears, inside his forearms. He used two fingers to lift the blade out of a pocketknife.

"You like to look t'rew people's windows?" he asked.

"No, sir," I said.

"They're just kids, Legion," the woman in back said, putting on her shirt.

"Maybe that's what they gonna always be," the man said.

I had thought his words were intended simply to frighten us. But I could see his face clearly now, the hair combed back like black pitch, the narrow white face with vertical lines in it, the eyes that could look upon a child as the source of his rage against the universe.

Then Jimmie and I were running in the darkness, our hearts pounding, forever changed by the knowledge that the world contains pockets of evil that are as dark as the inside of a leather bag.

Because my father was out of town, we ran all the way to the icehouse on Railroad Avenue, behind which was the lit and neatly tended house of Ciro Shanahan, the only man my father ever spoke of with total admiration and trust.

Later in life I would learn why my father had such

great respect for his friend. Ciro Shanahan was one of those rare individuals who would suffer in silence and let the world do him severe injury in order to protect those whom he loved.

On a spring night in 1931, Ciro and my father cut their boat engines south of Point Au Fer and stared at the black-green outline of the Louisiana coast in the moonlight. The waves were capping, the wind blowing hard, puffing and snapping the tarp that was stretched over the cases of Mexican whiskey and Cuban rum that my father and Ciro had off-loaded from a trawler ten miles out. My father looked through his field glasses and watched two searchlights sweeping the tops of the waves to the south. Then he rested the glasses on top of the small pilothouse that was built out of raw pine on the stern of the boat and wiped the salt spray off his face with his sleeve and studied the coastline. The running lights of three vessels pitched in the swells between himself and the safety of the shore.

"Moon's up. I done tole you, bad night to do it," he said.

"We done it before. We still here, ain't we?" Ciro said.

"Them boats off the bow? That's state men, Ciro," my father said.

"We don't know that," Ciro said.

"We can go east. Hide the load at Grand Chenier and come back for it later. You listen, you. Don't nobody make a living in jail," my father said.

Ciro was short, built like a dockworker, with red hair and green eyes and a small, down-hooked Irish mouth.

He wore a canvas coat and a fedora that was tied onto his head with a scarf. It was unseasonably cold and his face was windburned and knotted with thought inside his scarf.

"The man got his trucks up there, Aldous. I promised we was coming in tonight. Ain't right to leave them people waiting," he said.

"Sitting in an empty truck ain't gonna put nobody in Angola," my father said.

Ciro's eyes drifted off from my father's and looked out at the southern horizon.

"It don't matter now. Here come the Coast Guard. Hang on," he said.

The boat Ciro and my father owned together was long and narrow, like a World War I torpedo vessel, and had been built to service offshore drilling rigs, with no wasted space on board. The pilothouse sat like a matchbox on the stern, and even when the deck was stacked with drill pipe the big Chrysler engines could power through twelve-foot seas. When Ciro pushed the throttle forward, the screws scoured a trough across the swell and the bow arched out of the water and burst a wave into a horsetail spray across the moon.

But the searchlights on the Coast Guard cutter were unrelenting. They dissected my father's boat, burned red circles into his eyes, turned the waves a sandy green and robbed them of all their mystery, illuminating the bait fish and stingrays that toppled out of the crests. The boat's hull pounded across the water, the liquor bottles shaking violently under the tarp, the searchlights spearing through the pilothouse windows far out into the darkness. All the while the moored boats that lay between my father and the safety of the coastline waited, their cabin windows glowing now, their engines silent.

My father leaned close to Ciro's ear. "You going right into them agents," he said.

"Mr. Julian taken care of them people," Ciro said.

"Mr. Julian taken care of Mr. Julian," my father said.

"I don't want to hear it, Aldous."

Suddenly the boats of the state liquor agents came to life, lurching out over the waves, their own searchlights now vectoring Ciro and my father. Ciro swung the wheel hard to starboard, veering around a sandbar, moving over shallow water, the bow hammering against the out-going tide.

Up ahead was the mouth of the Atchafalaya River. My father watched the coastline draw nearer, the moss straightening on the dead cypress trunks, the flooded willows and gum trees and sawgrass denting and swaying in the wind. The tarp on the cases of whiskey and rum tore loose and flapped back against the pilothouse, blocking any view out the front window. My father cut the other ropes on the tarp and peeled it off the stacked cases of liquor and heaved it over the gunnel. When he looked at the shore again, he saw a series of sandbars ridging out of the bay like the backs of misplaced whales.

"Oh, Ciro, what you gone and did?" he said.

The boat rocketed between two sandbars, just as someone began firing an automatic weapon in short bursts from one of the state boats. Whiskey and rum and broken glass fountained in the air, then a tracer round landed on the deck like a phosphorous match and a huge handkerchief of flame enveloped the pilothouse.

But Ciro never cut the throttle, never considered giving up. The glass in the windows blackened and snapped in half; blue and yellow and red fire streamed off the deck into the water.

"Head into them leafs!" my father yelled, and pointed at a cove whose surface was layered with dead leaves.

The boat's bow crashed into the trees, setting the canopy aflame. Then my father and Ciro were over-board, splashing through the swamp, their bodies mar-bled with firelight.

They ran and trudged and stumbled for two miles through chest-deep water, sloughs, air vines, and sand bogs that were black with insects feeding off cows or wild animals that had suffocated or starved in them.

Three hours later the two of them sat on a dry levee and watched the light go out of the sky and the moon fade into a thin white wafer. Ciro's left ankle was the size of a cantaloupe.

"I'm gonna get my car. Then we ain't touching the liquor bidness again," my father said.

"We ain't got a boat to *touch* it wit'," Ciro said.

"T'ank you for telling me that. The next time I work for Mr. Julian LaSalle, go buy a gun and shoot me."

"He paid my daughter's hospital bills. You too hard on people, Aldous," Ciro said.

"He gonna pay for our boat?"

My father walked five miles to the grove of swamp maples where he had parked his automobile. When he returned to pick Ciro up, the sky was blue, the wild-flowers blooming along the levee, the air bright with the smell of salt. He came around a stand of willows and stared through the windshield at the scene he had blundered into.

Three men in fedora hats and ill-fitting suits, two of them carrying Browning automatic rifles, were escorting Ciro in wrist manacles to the back of a caged wagon, one with iron plates in the floor. The wagon was hooked to the back of a state truck and two Negroes who worked for Julian LaSalle were already sitting inside it.

My father shoved his transmission in reverse and backed all the way down the levee until he hit a board road that led through the swamp. As he splashed through the flooded dips in the road and mud splattered over his windshield, he tried not to think of Ciro limping in manacles toward the jail wagon. He hit a deer, a doe, and saw her carom off the fender into a tree, her body broken. But my father did not slow down until he was in Morgan City, where he entered the back of a Negro café and bought a glass of whiskey that he drank with both hands.

Then he put his big head down on his arms and fell asleep and dreamed of birds trapped inside the foliage of burning trees.

CHAPTER 2

Cops, street reporters, and hard-core caseworkers usually hang around with their own kind and form few intimate friendships with people outside their own vocation. They are not reclusive or elitist or self-anointed. They simply do not share the truth of their experience with outsiders. If they did, they would probably be shunned.

In one of the Feliciana parishes, I knew a black man who had been a sergeant in Lt. William Calley's platoon at My Lai. He had stood above the ditch at My Lai and machine-gunned children and women and old men while they begged for their lives. Years later the sergeant's son died of a drug overdose in his front yard. The sergeant believed his son's death was payback for the ditch at My Lai. He covered the walls of his home with pictures and news articles that detailed the atrocity he had participated in and relived his deeds at My Lai twenty-four hours a day.

But the politicians who sent my friend the sergeant into that Third World village would never have to carry his burden, nor would any civil or military authority ever hold them accountable.

That's the way it is. The right people seldom go down. Closure is a word that does not work well with the victims of violent crime. If you're a cop and you're lucky, you won't let your point of view put you in late-hour bars.

On a spring Saturday afternoon last year, I answered the phone on my desk at the Iberia Parish Sheriff's Department and knew I had just caught one of those cases that would never have an adequate resolution, that would involve a perfectly innocent, decent family whose injury would never heal.

The father was a cane farmer, the mother a nurse at Iberia General. Their sixteen-year-old daughter was an honor student at the local Catholic high school. That morning she had gone for a ride across a fallow cane field on a four-wheeler with her boyfriend. A black man who had been sitting on his back porch nearby said the four-wheeler had scoured a rooster tail of brown dust out of the field and disappeared in a grove of gum trees, then had rumbled across a wooden bridge into another field, one that was filled with new cane. A low-roofed gray gas-guzzler was parked by the coulee with three people inside. The black man said the driver tossed a beer can out the window and started up his automobile and drove in the same direction as the four-wheeler.

My partner was Helen Soileau. She had begun her career as a meter maid at NOPD, then had worked as a patrolwoman in the Garden District before she returned to her hometown and began her career over again. She had a masculine physique and was martial and often abrasive in her manner, but outside of Clete Purcel, my old Homicide partner at NOPD, she was the best police officer I had ever known.

Helen drove the cruiser past the grove of gum trees and crossed the bridge over the coulee and followed a dirt track through blades of cane that were pale green with the spring drought and whispering drily in the wind. Up ahead was a second grove of gum trees, one that was wrapped with yellow crime scene tape.

"You know the family?" Helen asked.

"A little bit," I replied.

"They have any other kids?"

"No," I said.

"Too bad. Do they know yet?"

"They're in Lafayette today. The sheriff hasn't been able to reach them," I said.

She turned and looked at me. Her face was lumpy, her blond hair thick on her shoulders. She chewed her gum methodically, a question in her eyes.

"We have to inform them?" she said.

"It looks like it," I replied.

"On this kind, I'd like to have the perp there and let the family put one in his ear."

"Bad thoughts, Helen."

"I'll feel as guilty about it as I can," she said.

Two deputies and the black man who had called in the "shots fired" and the teenage boy who had been the driver of the four-wheeler were waiting for us outside the crime scene tape that was wound around the grove of gum trees. The boy was sitting on the ground, in an unplanned lotus position, staring dejectedly into space.

Through the back window of the cruiser I saw an ambulance crossing the wooden bridge over the coulee.

Helen parked the cruiser and we walked into the lee of the trees. The sun was low in the west, pink from the dust drifting across the sky. I could smell a salty stench, like a dead animal, in the coulee.

"Where is she?" I asked a deputy.

He took a cigarette out of his mouth and stepped on it. "The other side of the blackberry bushes," he said.

"Pick up the butt, please, and don't light another one," I said.

Helen and I stooped under the yellow tape and walked to the center of the grove. A gray cloud of insects swarmed above a broken depression in the weeds. Helen looked down at the body and blew out her breath.

"Two wounds. One in the chest, the other in the side. Probably a shotgun," she said. Her eyes automatically began to search the ground for an ejected shell.

I squatted down next to the body. The girl's wrists had been pulled over her head and tied with a child's jump rope around the base of a tree trunk. Her skin was gray from massive loss of blood. Her eyes were still open and seemed to be focused on a solitary wildflower three feet away. A pair of panties hung around one of her ankles.

I stood up and felt my knees pop. For just a moment the trees in the clearing seemed to go in and out of focus.

"You all right?" Helen asked.

"They put one of her socks in her mouth," I said.

Helen's eyes moved over my face. "Let's talk to the boy," she said.

His skin was filmed with dust and lines of sweat had

run out of his hair and dried on his face. His T-shirt was grimed with dirt and looked as though it had been tied in knots before he had put it on. When he looked up at us, his eyes were heated with resentment.

"There were two black guys?" I said.

"Yes. I mean yes, sir," he replied.

"Only two?"

"That's all I saw."

"You say they had ski masks on? One of them wore gloves?"

"That's what I said," he replied.

Even in the shade it was hot. I blotted the sweat off my forehead with my sleeve.

"They tied you up?" I said.

"Yes," he replied.

"With your T-shirt?" I asked.

"Yes, sir."

I squatted down next to him and gave the deputies a deliberate look. They walked to their cruiser with the black man and got inside and left the doors open to catch the breeze.

"Let's see if I understand," I said to the boy. "They tied you up with your shirt and belt and left you in the coulee and took Amanda into the trees? Guys in ski masks, like knitted ones?"

"That's what happened," he replied.

"You couldn't get loose?"

"No. It was real tight."

"I have a problem with what you're telling me. It doesn't flush, partner," I said.

"Flush?"

"T-shirts aren't handcuffs," I said.

His eyes became moist. He laced his fingers in his hair.

"You were pretty scared?" I said.

"I guess. Yes, sir," he replied.

"I'd be scared, too. There's nothing wrong in that," I said. I patted him on the shoulder and stood up.

"You gonna catch those damned niggers or not?" he asked.

I joined Helen by our cruiser. The sun was low on the horizon now, bloodred above a distant line of trees. Helen had just gotten off the radio.

"How do you read the kid?" she asked.

"Hard to say. He's not his own best advocate."

"The girl's parents just got back from Lafayette. This one's a pile of shit, bwana," she said.

The family home was a one-story, wood-frame white building that stood between the state road and a cane field in back. A water oak that was bare of leaves in winter shaded one side of the house during the hot months. The numbered rural mailbox on the road and a carport built on the side of the house, like an afterthought, were the only means we could use to distinguish the house from any other on the same road.

The blinds were drawn inside the house. Plastic holy-water receptacles were tacked on the doorjambs and a church calendar and a hand-stitched Serenity Prayer hung on the living room walls. The father was Quentin Boudreau, a sunburned, sandy-haired man who wore wire-rim glasses and a plain blue tie and a starched white shirt that must have felt like an iron prison on his body. His eyes seemed to have no emotion, no focus in them, as though he were experiencing thoughts he had not yet allowed himself to feel.

He held his wife's hand on his knee. She was a small, dark-haired Cajun woman whose face was devastated. Neither she nor her husband spoke or attempted to ask a question while Helen and I explained, as euphemistically as we could, what had happened to their daughter. I wanted them to be angry with us, to hurl insults, to make racial remarks, to do anything that would relieve me of the feelings I had when I looked into their faces.

But they didn't. They were humble and undemanding and probably, at the moment, incapable of hearing everything that was being said to them.

I put my business card on the coffee table and stood up to go. "We're sorry for what's happened to your family," I said.

The woman's hands were folded in her lap now. She looked at them, then lifted her eyes to mine.

"Amanda was raped?" she said.

"That's a conclusion that has to come from the coroner. But, yes, I think she was," I said.

"Did they use condoms?" she asked.

"We didn't find any," I replied.

"Then you'll have their DNA," she said. Her eyes were black and hard now and fixed on mine.

Helen and I let ourselves out and crossed the yard to the cruiser. The wind, even full of dust, seemed cool after the long hot day and smelled of salt off the Gulf. Then I heard Mr. Boudreau behind me. He was a heavy man and he walked as though he had gout in one foot. A wing on his shirt collar was bent at an upward angle, like a spear point touching his throat.

"What kind of weapon did they use?" he asked.

"A shotgun," I said.

His eyes blinked behind his glasses. "Did they shoot my little girl in the face?" he asked.

"No, sir," I replied.

"'Cause those sons of bitches just better not have hurt her face," he said, and began to weep in his front yard.

By the next morning the fingerprints lifted from the beer can thrown out of the automobile window at the crime scene gave us the name of Tee Bobby Hulin, a twenty-five-year-old black hustler and full-time smart-ass whose diminutive size saved him on many occasions from being bodily torn apart. His case file was four inches thick and included arrests for shoplifting at age nine, auto theft at thirteen, dealing reefer in the halls of his high school, and driving off from the back of the local Wal-Mart with a truckload of toilet paper.

For years Tee Bobby had skated on the edge of the system, shining people on, getting by on rebop and charm and convincing others he was more trickster than miscreant. Also, Tee Bobby possessed another, more serious gift, one he seemed totally undeserving of, as though the finger of God had pointed at him arbitrarily one day and bestowed on him a musical talent that was like none since the sad, lyrical beauty in the recordings of Guitar Slim.

When Helen and I walked up to Tee Bobby's gas-guzzler that evening at a drive-in restaurant not far from City Park, his accordion was propped up in the backseat, its surfaces like ivory and the speckled insides of a pomegranate.

"Hey, Dave, what it is?" he said.

"Don't call your betters by their first name," Helen said.

"I gots you, Miss Helen. I ain't done nothing wrong, huh?" he said, his eyebrows climbing.

"You tell us," I said.

He feigned a serious concentration. "Nope. I'm a blank. Y'all want part of my crab burger?" he said.

His skin had the dull gold hue of worn saddle leather, his eyes blue-green, his hair lightly oiled and curly and cut short and boxed behind the neck. He continued to look at us with an idiot's grin on his mouth.

"Put your car keys under the seat and get in the cruiser," Helen said.

"This don't sound too good. I think I better call my lawyer," he said.

"I didn't say you were under arrest. We'd just like a little information from you. Is that a problem?" Helen said.

"I gots it again. White folks is just axing for hep. Don't need to read no Miranda rights to nobody. Sho' now, I wants to hep out the po-lice," he said.

"You're a walking charm school, Tee Bobby," Helen said.

Twenty minutes later Tee Bobby sat alone in an interview room at the Iberia Parish Sheriff's Department while Helen and I talked in my office. Outside, the sky was ribbed with maroon strips of cloud and the train crossing guards were lowered on the railway tracks and a freight was wobbling down the rails between clumps of trees and shacks where black people lived.

"What's your feeling?" I asked.

"I have a hard time making this clown for a shotgun murder," she said.

"He was there."

"This case has a smell to it, Streak. Amanda's boyfriend just doesn't ring right," she said.

"Neither does Tee Bobby. He's too disconnected about it."

"Give me a minute before you come in," she said.

She went into the interview room and left the door slightly ajar so I could hear her words to Tee Bobby. She leaned on the table, one of her muscular arms slightly touching his, her mouth lowered toward his ear. A rolled-up magazine protruded from the back pocket of her jeans.

"We've got you at the crime scene. That won't go away. I'd meet this head-on," she said.

"Good. Bring me a lawyer. Then I bees meeting it head-on."

"You want us to get your grandmother down here?"

"Miss Helen gonna make me feel guilty now. 'Cause you a big family friend. 'Cause my gran'mama used to wash your daddy's clothes when he wasn't trying to put his hands up her dress."

Helen pulled the rolled-up paper cylinder from her back pocket. "How would you like it if I just slapped the shit out of you?" she said.

"I bees likin' that."

She looked at him thoughtfully a moment, then touched him lightly on the forehead with the cusp of the magazine.

His eyelids fluttered mockingly, like butterflies.

Helen walked out the door past me. "I hope the D.A. buries that little prick," she said.

I went into the interview room and closed the door.

"Right now your car is being torn apart and two detectives are on their way to your house with a search warrant," I said. "If they find a ski mask, a shotgun that's been fired in the last two days, any physical evidence from that girl on your clothes, even a strand of hair, you're going to be injected. The way I see it, you've got about a ten-minute window of opportunity to tell your side of things."

Tee Bobby removed a comb from his back pocket and ran it up and down the hair on his arm and looked into space. Then he put his head down on his folded arms and tapped his feet rhythmically, as though he were keeping time with a tune inside his head.

"You're just going to act the fool?" I said.

"I ain't raped nobody. Leave me be."

I sat down across from him and watched the way his eyes glanced innocuously around the walls, his boredom with my presence, the beginnings of a grin on his mouth as he looked at the growing anger in my face.

"What's wrong?" he said.

"She was sixteen. She had holes in her chest and side you could put your fist into. You get that silly-ass look off your face," I said.

"I got a right to look like I want. You bring me a lawyer or you kick me loose. You ain't got no evidence or you would have already printed me and had me in lockup."

"I'm a half-inch from knocking you across this room, Tee Bobby."

"Yassir, I knows that. This nigger's bones is shakin', Cap'n," he replied.

I locked him in the interview room and went down to my office. A half hour later a phone call came in from the detectives who had been sent to Tee Bobby's home on Poinciana Island.

"Nothing so far," one of them said.

"What do you mean 'so far'?" I asked.

"It's night. We'll start over again in the morning. Feel free to join us. I just sorted through a garbage can loaded with week-old shrimp," he replied.

At dawn Helen and I drove across the wooden bridge that spanned the freshwater bay on the north side of Poinciana Island. The early sun was red on the horizon, promising another scorching day, but the water in the bay was black and smelled of spawning fish, and the elephant ears and the cypress and flowering trees on the banks riffled coolly in the breeze off the Gulf of Mexico.

I showed my badge to the security guard in the wooden booth on the bridge, and we drove through the settlement of tree-shaded frame houses where the employees of the LaSalle family lived, then followed a paved road that wound among hillocks and clumps of live oaks and pine and gum trees and red-dirt acreage, where black men were hoeing out the rows in lines that moved across the field as precisely as military formations.

The log-and-brick slave cabins from the original LaSalle plantation were still standing, except they had been reconstructed and modernized by Perry LaSalle and were now used by either the family's guests or life-time employees whom the LaSalles took care of until the day of their deaths.

Ladice Hulin, Tee Bobby's grandmother, sat in a

wicker chair on her gallery, her thick gray hair hanging below her shoulders, her hands folded on the crook of a walking cane.

I got out of the cruiser and walked into the yard. Three uniformed deputies and a plainclothes detective were in back, raking garbage out of an old trash pit. As a young woman, Ladice had been absolutely beautiful, and even though age had robbed her in many ways, it had not diminished her femininity, and her skin still had the smoothness and luster of chocolate. She didn't ask me onto the gallery.

"They tear up your house, Miss Ladice?" I said.

She continued to look at me without speaking. Her eyes had the clarity, the deepness, the unblinking fixed stare of a deer's.

"Is your grandson inside?" I asked.

"He didn't come home after y'all turned him loose. Y'all put the fear of God in him, if that make you feel good," she replied.

"We tried to help him. He chose not to cooperate. He also showed no feeling at all over the rape and murder of an innocent young girl," I said.

She wore a white cotton dress with a gold chain and religious medal around her neck. A perforated gold-plated dime hung from another chain on her anklebone.

"No feeling, huh?" Then she brushed at the air and said, "Go on, go on, take care of your bidness and be done. The grave's waiting for me. I just wish I didn't have to deal with so many fools befo' I get there."

"I always respected you, Miss Ladice," I said.

She put one hand on the arm of her chair and pushed herself erect.

"He's gonna run from you. He's gonna sass you. It's 'cause he's a scared li'l boy inside. Don't hurt him just 'cause he's scared, no," she said.

I started to speak, but Helen touched me on the arm. The plainclothes in back was waving at us, a dirty black watch cap on a stick in his right hand.

CHAPTER 3

One week later an assistant district attorney, Barbara Shanahan, sometimes known as Battering Ram Shanahan, came into my office without knocking. She was a statuesque, handsome woman, over six feet tall, with white skin and red hair and green eyes. She wore white hose and horn-rim glasses and a pale orange suit and a white blouse, and she seldom passed men anywhere that they did not turn and look at her. But her face always seemed enameled with anger, without cause, her manner as sharp as razor wire. Her dedication to destroying criminals and defense attorneys was legendary. However, the reason for that dedication was a matter of conjecture.

I looked up from the newspaper that was spread on my desk.

"Excuse me for not getting up. I didn't hear you knock," I said.

"I need everything you have on the Amanda Boudreau investigation," she said.

"It's not complete."

"Then give me what you have and update me on a daily basis."

"You caught the case?" I asked.

She sat down across from me. She looked at the tiny gold watch on her wrist, then back at me. "Is it always necessary that I say everything twice to you?" she said.

"The forensics just came in on the watch cap we dug up at Tee Bobby's place. The rouge and skin oils came off Amanda Boudreau," I said.

"Good, let's cut the warrant." As she got up to go, her eyes paused on mine. "Something wrong?"

"This one doesn't hang together."

"The victim's DNA is on the suspect's clothes? His prints are on a beer can at the murder scene? But you have doubts about what occurred?"

"The semen on the girl wasn't Tee Bobby's. The man who called in the 'shots fired' said there were three people in the car. But Amanda's boyfriend said only two men accosted him. Where was the other one? The boyfriend said he was tied up with a T-shirt. Why didn't he try to get away?"

"I have no idea. Why don't you find out?" she said.

I hesitated before I spoke again. "I have another problem. I can't see Tee Bobby as a killer."

"Maybe it's because you want it both ways," she said.

"Excuse me?"

"Some people always need to feel good about themselves, usually at the expense of others. In this case at the expense of a dead girl who was raped while she had a sock stuffed down her throat."

I folded my newspaper and dropped it in the trash can.

"Perry LaSalle is representing Tee Bobby," I said.

"So?"

I got up from my chair and closed the Venetian blinds on the corridor windows.

"You hate the LaSalles, Barbara. I think you asked for this case," I said.

"I don't have any feeling about the LaSalle family one way or another."

"Your grandfather went to prison for old man Julian. That's how he got his job as a security guard on LaSalle's bridge."

"Have the paperwork in my office by close of business. In the meantime, if you ever impugn my motives as a prosecutor again, I'll take you into civil court and fry your sorry ass for slander."

She threw the door open and marched down the corridor toward the sheriff's office. A uniformed cop watched her sideways while he drank from the water fountain, his eyes glued on her posterior. He grinned sheepishly when he saw me looking at him.

It was Friday afternoon and I didn't want to think anymore about Barbara Shanahan or a young girl who had probably been forced to stare into the barrel of a shotgun and wait helplessly while her executioner decided whether or not to pull the trigger.

I drove south of town, down a dusty road, along a tree-lined waterway, to the house built by my father during the Depression. The sunlight looked like yellow smoke in the canopy of the live oaks, and up ahead I saw the dock and bait shop that I operated as a part-time business and a lavender Cadillac convertible parked by the boat ramp, which meant that my old Homicide partner, the bane of NOPD, the good-natured, totally irresponsible, fiercely loyal Clete Purcel, was back in New Iberia.

He had dumped his cooler on a bait table at the end of the dock and was gutting a stringer of ice-flecked sac-a-lait and bream and big-mouth bass with a long, razor-edged knife that had no guard on the handle. He wore only a pair of baggy shorts and flip-flops and a Marine Corps utility cap. His whole body was oily with lotion and baked with sunburn, his body hair matted in gold curlicues on his massive arms and shoulders.

I parked my pickup truck in the driveway to the house and walked across the road and down the dock, where Clete was now scaling his fish with a tablespoon and washing them under a faucet and placing them on a clean layer of ice in his cooler.

"It looks like you had a pretty good day," I said.

"If I can use your shower, I'll take you and Bootsie and Alafair to Bon Creole." He picked up a salted can of beer off the dock rail and watched me over the bottom of it while he drank. His hair was bleached by the sun, his green eyes happy, one eyebrow cut by a scar that ran across the bridge of his nose.

"You just here for a fishing trip?" I asked.

"I got a shitload of bail skips to pick up for Nig and Willie. Plus Nig may have written a bond on a serial killer."

I was tired and didn't want to hear about Clete's ongoing grief as a bounty hunter for Nig Rosewater and Wee Willie Bimstine. I tried to look attentive, but my gaze started to wander toward the house, the baskets of impatiens swaying under the eaves of the gallery, my wife, Bootsie, weeding the hydrangea bed in the shade.

"You listening?" Clete said.

"Sure," I replied.

"So this is how we heard about the serial sex predator or killer or whatever the hell he is. No Duh Dolowitz got nailed trying to creep Fat Sammy Figorelli's skin parlor, but this time Nig says he's had it with No Duh and his half-baked capers, like putting dog shit in the sandwiches at a Teamsters convention or impersonating a chauffeur and driving away with the Calucci family's limo.

"So No Duh calls up from central lockup and says Nig and Wee Willie are hypocrites because they wrote the bond on some dude who killed a couple of hookers in Seattle and Portland.

"Nig asks No Duh how he knows this and No Duh goes, ' 'Cause one year ago I was sitting in a cell next to this perverted fuck while he was pissing and moaning about how he dumped these broads along riverbanks on the West Coast. This same pervert was also talking about two dumb New Orleans Jews who bought his alias and were writing his bond without running his sheet.'

"But Nig's got scruples and doesn't like the idea he might have put a predator back on the street. So he has me start going over every dirtbag he's written paper on for the last two years. So far I've checked out one hundred twenty or one hundred thirty names and I can't come up with anyone who fits the profile."

"Why believe anything Dolowitz says? One of the

Giacanos put dents in his head with a ball peen hammer years ago," I said.

"That's the point. He's got something wrong with his brain. No Duh is a thief who never lies. That's why he's always doing time."

"You're going to take us to Bon Creole?" I asked.

"I said I was, didn't I?"

"I'd really enjoy that," I said.

But I would not be able to free myself that evening from the murder of Amanda Boudreau. I had just showered and changed clothes and was waiting on the gallery for Clete and Bootsie and Alafair to join me when Perry LaSalle's cream-yellow Gazelle, a replica of a 1929 Mercedes, turned off the road into our driveway.

Before he could get out of his automobile, I walked down through the trees to meet him. The top was down on his automobile, and his sun-browned skin looked dark in the shade, his brownish-black hair tousled by the wind, his eyes bright blue, his cheeks pooled with color.

He had given up his studies at a Jesuit seminary when he was twenty-one, for no reason he was ever willing to provide. He had lived among street people in the Bowery and wandered the West, working lettuce and beet fields, riding on freight cars with derelicts and fruit tramps, then had returned like the prodigal son to his family and studied law at Tulane.

I liked Perry and the dignified manner and generosity of spirit with which he always conducted himself. He was a big man, at least six feet two, but he was never grandiose or assuming and was always kind to those less fortunate than he. But like many of us I felt Perry's story was infinitely more complex than his benign demeanor would indicate.

"Out for a drive?" I said, knowing better.

"I hear Battering Ram Shanahan thinks you're soft on the Amanda Boudreau investigation. I hear she wants to use a nail gun on your cojones," he said.

"News to me," I replied.

"Her case sucks and she knows it."

"Seen any good movies lately?" I asked.

"Tee Bobby's innocent. He wasn't even at the murder scene."

"His beer can was."

"Littering isn't a capital crime."

"It was good seeing you, Perry."

"Come out to the island and try my bass pond. Bring Bootsie and Alafair. We'll have dinner."

"I will. After the trial," I said.

He winked at me, then drove down the road, the sunlight through the trees flicking like gold coins across the waxed surfaces of his automobile.

I heard Clete walking through the leaves behind me. His hair was wet and freshly combed, the top buttons of his tropical shirt open on his chest.

"Isn't that the guy who wrote the book about the Death House in Louisiana? The one the movie was based on?" he said.

"That's the guy," I replied.

Clete looked at my expression. "You didn't like the book?" he asked.

"Two kids were murdered in a neckers' area up the Loreauville Road. Perry made the prosecutor's office look bad."

"Why?"

"I guess some people need to feel good about themselves," I answered.

The next morning there was fog in the trees when Alafair and I walked down the slope and opened up the bait shop and hosed down the dock and fired up the barbecue pit on which we prepared links and chicken and sometimes pork chops for our midday customers. I went into the storage room and began slicing open cartons of canned beer and soda to stock the coolers while Alafair made coffee and wiped down the counter. I heard the tiny bell on the screen door ring and someone come into the shop.

He was a young man and wore a white straw hat coned up on the sides, a pale blue sports coat, a wide, plum-colored tie, gray pants, and shined cordovan cowboy boots. His hair was ash-blond, cut short, shaved on the neck, his skin a deep olive. He carried a suitcase whose weight made his face sweat and his wrist cord with veins.

"Howdy do," he said, and sat down on a counter stool, his back to me. "Could I have a glass of water, please?"

Alafair was a senior in high school now, although she looked older than her years. She stood up on her tiptoes and took down a glass from a shelf, her thighs and rump flexing against her shorts. But the young man turned his head and gazed out the screen at the trees on the far side of the bayou.

"You want ice in it?" she asked.

"No, ma'am, I dint want to cause no trouble. Out of the tap is fine," the young man replied.

She filled the glass and put it before him. Her eyes glanced at the suitcase on the floor and the leather belt that was cinched around the weight that bulged against its sides.

"Can I help you with something?" she asked.

He removed a paper napkin from the dispenser and folded it and blotted the perspiration on his brow. He grinned at her.

"There's days I don't think the likes of me is meant to sell sno'balls in Hades. Is there people up at that house?" he said.

"What are you selling?" she asked.

"Encyclopedias, Bibles, family-type magazines. But Bibles is what I like to sell most of. I aim to go into the ministry or law enforcement. I been taking criminal justice courses over at the university. Could I have one of them fried pies?"

She reached up on the shelf again, and this time his gaze wandered over her body, lingering on the backs of her thighs. When I stepped out of the storage room, his head jerked toward me, the skin tightening around his eyes.

"You want to rent a boat?" I asked.

"No, sir. I was just taking a little rest break on my route. My name's Marvin Oates. Actually I'm from herebouts," he said.

"I know who are you. I'm a detective with the Iberia Parish Sheriff's Department."

"Well, I reckon that cuts through it," he said.

My memory of him was hazy, an arrest four or five years back on a bad check charge, a P.O.'s recommendation for leniency, Barbara Shanahan acting with the charity that she was occasionally capable of, allowing him to plead out on time served.

"We'll be seeing you," I said.

"Yes, sir, you got it," he replied, cutting his head.

He tipped his hat to Alafair and hefted up his suitcase and labored out the door as though he were carrying a load of bricks.

"Why do you have to be so hard, Dave?" Alafair said.

I started to reply, then thought better of it and went outside and began laying out split chickens on the grill.

Marvin Oates paused at the end of the dock, set his suitcase down, and walked back toward me. He gazed reflectively at an outboard plowing a foamy yellow trough down the bayou.

"Is that your daughter, sir?" he asked.

"Yep."

He nodded. "You saw me looking at her figure when her back was turned. But she's good-looking and the way of the flesh is weak, at least it is with me. You're her father and I offended you. I apologize for that."

He waited for me to speak. When I continued to stare into his face, he cut his head again and walked back to his suitcase and hefted it up and crossed the dirt road and started up my driveway.

"Wrong house, partner," I called.

He lifted his hat in salute and changed direction and headed toward my neighbor's.

Monday morning I called before I drove out to the LaSalles' island to see Tee Bobby's grandmother. When she let me in, she was wearing a beige dress and white shoes that had been recently polished and her hair was brushed and fastened in back with a comb. Her living room had throw rugs on the floor and a wood-bladed fan that turned overhead, and the slipcovers on the upholstery were printed with flowery designs. The wind was blowing off the bay, and the red bloom of mimosa and poinciana trees flattened softly against the screens. From the couch Ladice looked at me and waited, her face cautionary, her chest rising and falling.

"Tee Bobby doesn't have an alibi. Or at least not one he'll give me," I said.

"What if I say he was here when that girl died?" she said.

"Your neighbors say he wasn't."

"Then why you bother me, Mr. Dave?"

"People around here are in a bad mood about that girl's death. Tee Bobby is a perfect dartboard for their anger."

"This all started way befo' he was born. Ain't none of this that boy's fault."

"You're going to have to explain that to me."

I heard the back screen door open and saw a young woman walk across the kitchen. She wore pink tennis shoes and an oversize blue dress that hung on her like a sack. She took a soda pop that was already opened from the icebox, a paper straw floating in the bottle's neck. She stood in the doorway, sucking on the straw, her face the twin of Tee Bobby's, her expression vacuous, her eyes tangled with thoughts that probably no one could ever guess at.

"We going to the doctor in a li'l bit, Rosebud. Wait on the back porch and don't be coming back in till I tell you," Ladice said.

The young woman's eyes held on mine a moment, then she pulled the drinking straw off her lips and turned and went out the back screen door and let it slam behind her.

"You look like you got somet'ing to say," Ladice said.

"What happened to Tee Bobby and Rosebud's mother?"

"Run off wit' a white man when she was sixteen. Left them two in a crib wit'out no food."

"That's what you meant when you said none of this was Tee Bobby's fault?"

"No. That ain't what I meant at all."

"I see." I stood up to leave. "Some people say old man Julian was the father of your daughter."

"You come into the house of a white lady and ax a question like that? Like you was talking to livestock?" she said.

"Your grandson may end up in the Death House, Ladice. The only friend he seems to have is Perry LaSalle. Maybe that's good. Maybe it isn't. Thanks for your time."

I walked outside, into the yard and the smell of flowers and the sun-heated salty hint of rain out on the Gulf. Across the road I could see peacocks on the lawn of the scorched three-story stucco ruins that had been Julian LaSalle's home. I heard Ladice open the screen door behind me.

"What you mean, it ain't good Perry LaSalle's the only friend Tee Bobby got?" she said.

"A man who's driven by guilt eventually turns on those who make him feel guilty. That's just one guy's observation," I said.

The breeze blew a strand of her hair down on her forehead. She brushed it back into place and stared at me for a long time, then went back into her house and latched the screen door behind her.

At sunset an elderly black man named Batist helped me close up the bait shop and chain-lock our rental boats to the pilings under the dock. Heat lightning flickered over the Gulf and I could hear the distant rumble of thunder, but the air was dry, the trees along the road coated with dust, and a column of acrid smoke blew from a neighbor's trash fire and flattened in a gray haze on the bayou.

This was the third year of the worst drought in Louisiana's history.

I pressure-hosed the dried fish blood and scales off the cleaning boards, then folded the Cinzano umbrellas that protruded from the spool tables on the dock and went inside the shop.

A few years ago a friend had given me a replica of the classic Wurlitzer jukebox, one whose domed plastic casing swirled with color, like liquid candy that had not been poured into the mold. He had stocked it with 45 rpm records from the 1950s, and I had never replaced them. I dropped in a quarter painted with red nail polish and played Guitar Slim's "The Things That I Used to Do."

I had never heard a voice filled with as much sorrow as his. There was no self-pity in the song, only acceptance of the terrible conclusion that what he loved most in the world, his wife, had become profligate and had not only rejected his love but had given herself to an evil man.

Guitar Slim was thirty-two when he died of his alcoholism.

"That's old-time blues there, ain't it?" Batist said.

Batist was well into his seventies now, his attitudes intractable, his hair the color of smoke, the backs of his broad hands flecked with pink scars from a lifetime of working on fishing boats and shucking oysters at one of the LaSalle canneries. But he was still a powerful, large man who was confident in himself and took pride in his skill as a boatmate and fisherman and was proud of the fact that all of his children had graduated from high school.

He had grown up in a time when people of color were not so much physically abused as taken for granted, used as a cheap source of labor, and deliberately kept uneducated and poor. Perhaps an even greater injury done to them came in the form of the white man's lie when they sought redress. On those occasions they were usually treated as children, given promises and assurances that would never be kept, and sent on their way with the feeling that their problems were of their own manufacture.

But I never saw Batist show bitterness or anger about his upbringing. For that reason alone I considered him perhaps the most remarkable man I had ever known.

The lyrics and the bell-like reverberation of Guitar Slim's rolling chords haunted me. Without ever using words to describe either the locale or the era in which he had lived, his song re-created the Louisiana I had been raised in: the endless fields of sugarcane thrashing in the wind under a darkening sky, yellow dirt roads and the Hadacol and Jax beer signs nailed on the sides of general stores, horse-drawn buggies that people tethered in stands of gum trees during Sunday Mass, clapboard juke joints where Gatemouth Brown and Smiley Lewis and Lloyd Price played, and the brothel districts that flourished from sunset to dawn and somehow became invisible in the morning light.

"You t'inking about Tee Bobby Hulin?" Batist asked.

"Not really," I said.

"Boy got a bad seed in him, Dave."

"Julian LaSalle's?"

"I say let evil stay buried in the graveyard."

A half hour later I turned off the outside floodlamps and the string of electric lights that ran the length of the dock. Just as I locked the front door of the shop I heard the phone inside ring. I started to let it go, but instead I went back in and reached over the counter and picked up the receiver.

"Dave?" the sheriff's voice said.

"Yeah."

"You'd better get over to the jail. Tee Bobby just hung himself."

CHAPTER 4

When the jailer had walked past Tee Bobby's cell and seen his silhouette suspended in midair, he had thrown open the cell door and burst inside with a chair, wrapping one arm around Tee Bobby's waist, lifting him upward while he sawed loose the belt that was wrapped around an overhead pipe.

After he dropped Tee Bobby like a sack of grain on his bunk, he yelled down the hall, "Find the son of a bitch who put this man in a cell with his belt!"

When I went to see Tee Bobby the next morning in Iberia General, one of his wrists was handcuffed to the bed rail. The capillaries had burst in the whites of his eyes and his tongue looked like cardboard. He put a pillow over his head and drew his knees up to his chest in an embryonic position. I pulled the pillow out of his hands and tossed it at the foot of the bed.

"You might as well plead out," I said.

"What you talking about?" he said.

"Attempted suicide in custody reads just like a confession. You just shafted yourself."

"I'll finish it next time."

"Your grandmother's outside. So is your sister."

"What you up to, Robicheaux?"

"Not much. Outside of Perry LaSalle, I'm probably the only guy on the planet who wants to save you from the injection table."

"My sister don't have nothing to do wit' this. You leave her alone. She cain't take no kind of stress."

"I'm letting go of you, Tee Bobby. I hope Perry gets you some slack. I think Barbara Shanahan is going to put a freight train up your ass."

He raised himself up on one elbow, the handcuffs clanking tight against the bed rail. His breath was bilious.

"I hear you, boss man. Nigger boy got to swim in his own shit now," he said.

"Run the Step 'n' Fetch It routine on somebody else, kid," I said.

I passed Ladice and Rosebud in the waiting room. Rosebud had a cheap drawing tablet open on her thighs and was coloring in it with crayons, her face bent down almost to the paper.

At noon the sheriff buzzed my extension. "You know that black juke joint by the Olivia Bridge?"

"The one with the garbage piled outside?" I said.

"I want Clete Purcel out of there."

"What's the problem?"

"Not much. He's probably setting civil rights back thirty years."

I drove down Bayou Teche and crossed the drawbridge into the little black settlement of Olivia and parked by a ramshackle bar named the Boom Boom Room, owned by a mulatto ex-boxer named Jimmy Dean Styles, who was also known as Jimmy Style or just Jimmy Sty.

Clete sat in his lavender Cadillac, the top down, listening to his radio, drinking from a long-necked bottle of beer.

"What's the haps, Streak?" he said.

"What are you doing out here?"

"Checking on a dude named Styles. Nig and Willie wrote a bond on him about the time No Duh was in central lockup."

"No Duh said the serial killer was using an alias."

"Styles used just his first and middle names—Jimmy Dean."

Clete drank out of the beer bottle and squinted up at me in the sunlight. There was an alcoholic shine in his eyes, a bloom in his cheeks.

"Styles is a music promoter. He's also the business manager for a kid named Tee Bobby Hulin, who's in custody right now for rape and murder. I think maybe you should leave Styles alone until we've finished our investigation."

Clete peeled a stick of gum and slipped it into his mouth. "No problem," he said.

"Did you have trouble inside?"

"Not me. Everything's copacetic, big mon." Clete's eyes smiled at me while he snapped his gum wetly in his jaw.

A black Lexus pulled into the lot and Jimmy Dean Styles pulled the keys from the ignition and got out and looked at us, flipping the keys back and forth over his knuckles. He had close-set eyes and a nose like a sheep's and the flat chest and trim physique of the middleweight boxer he'd been in Angola, where he'd busted up all comers in the improvised ring out on the yard.

"You're looking good, Jimmy," I said.

"Yeah, we all be lookin' good these days," he replied.

"Saw your picture in *People* magazine. A guy from the Teche doesn't make it in rap every day," I said.

"I'd like to talk wit' y'all, but I got a call from my bartender. Some big fat cracker was inside, being obnoxious, rollin' the gold on my customers like he was a real cop 'stead of maybe a P.I. does scut work for a bondsman. I better check to see he took his fat ass somewhere else."

"Hey, that's no kidding? You're a rapper? You've been in *People* magazine?" Clete said, turning around in the car seat to get a better look at Styles, his mouth grinning.

"You right on top of it, Marse Charlie," Styles said.

Clete opened the Cadillac's door and put one loafered foot out on the dirt, then rose to his full height, like an elephant standing up after sunning itself on a riverbank, his grin still in place, the skin on the back of his neck peeling like fish scales. A slapjack protruded from the side pocket of his slacks.

"Being in entertainment, you must get out on the Coast a lot," Clete said.

I gave Clete a hard look, but he didn't let it register.

"See, I travel to promote a couple of groups. That's the way the bidness work. But right now I got to hep my man inside. So I'm cutting this short and telling you I ain't shook nobody's tree. That means they don't be needing to shake mine." Styles placed the flat of his hand on his chest to show his sincerity, then went inside.

"I'm going to join the Klan," Clete said.

I followed Styles inside. The interior was dark, lit only by a jukebox and a neon beer sign over the bar. A woman sat slumped over at the bar, her head on her arms, her eyes closed, her open mouth filled with gold teeth.

She wore pink stretch pants and her black underwear was bunched out over the elastic waistband. Styles pinched her on the rump, hard, his thumb and forefinger catching a thick fold of skin on one buttock.

"This ain't Motel 6, mama. You done fried your tab, too," he said.

"Oh, hi, Jimmy. What's happenin'?" she said lazily, as though waking from a delirium to a friendly face.

"Let's go, baby," he replied, and took her under one arm and walked her to the back door and pushed her out into the whiteness of the day and slammed and latched the door behind her.

He turned around and saw me.

"Sorry about my friend Clete Purcel out there," I said. "But a word of caution. Don't mess with him again. He'll rip your wiring out."

Styles took a bottle of carbonated water from the cooler and cracked off the cap and dropped it between the duckboards and drank from the bottle.

"What you want wit' me, man?" he asked.

"Tee Bobby may go down on a bad beef. He could use some help."

"I cut Tee Bobby loose. Zydeco and blues ain't my gig no more."

"You cut loose a talent like Tee Bobby Hulin?"

"Big shit in South Lou'sana don't make you big shit in L.A. I got to piss. You want anything else?"

"Yeah, I'm going to ask you not to manhandle a woman like that again, at least not when I'm around."

"She puked all over the toilet seat. You want to take care of her? Hep me clean it up. I'll drop her by your crib," he replied.

Two weeks later Perry LaSalle went bail for Tee Bobby Hulin. Virtually everyone in town agreed that Perry LaSalle was a charitable and good man, although some were beginning to complain about a suspected rapist and murderer being set free, perhaps to repeat his crimes. With time, their sentiments would grow.

That same day a white woman named Linda Zeroski had a shouting argument with her pimp, a black man, on her pickup corner in New Iberia's old brothel district. On the corner was an ancient general store shaded by an enormous oak. In a happier time the store's owner had sold sno'balls to children on their way home from school. Now the apron of dirt yard around the store was occupied each afternoon and evening and all day Saturday and Sunday by young black men with jailhouse art on their arms and inverted ball caps on their heads. If you slowed the car by the corner, they would turn up their palms and raise their eyebrows, which was their way of asking you what you wanted, simultaneously indicating they could supply it—rock, weed, tar, China white, leapers, downers, almost any street drug except crystal meth, which was just starting its odyssey from Arizona to the rural South.

Linda Zeroski did not have to pay for the crack she smoked daily or the tar she injected into her veins. Or the fines she paid in city court or the bonds she posted for the incremental privilege of dismantling her own life. Her financial affairs were all handled by her pimp, a pragmatic, emotionless man by the name of Washington Trahan, who viewed women as he would bars of soap. Except for Linda Zeroski, who knew how to put slivers of bamboo under his fingernails and ridicule and demean him in public. Washington would have loved to slap her cross-eyed, to drag her by her hair into a car and dump her naked and stoned on a highway, but Linda's background was different from that of his other whores.

She had attended college for three years and was the daughter of Joe Zeroski, an ex–button man for the Giacano crime family.

I used to see Linda on her corner, her body heavy with beer fat, her hair bleached and full of snarls, wearing jeans and a shirt without a bra, a cigarette always between her fingers, the smoke crawling up her wrist. Sometimes her father would come to New Iberia and haul her off to a treatment center, but in a week or two she would be back on the corner, offering herself up for whatever use her johns wished to extract from her.

Sometimes I would pull the cruiser or my truck over and talk to her. She was always pleasant to me and appeared to take pride in the fact she had a friendly relationship with a law officer. In fact, except for Perry LaSalle, who sometimes helped her out at the court, I was probably the only white-collar man she knew on a first-name basis in New Iberia other than johns. On one occasion I took her to a drive-in for a root beer and a hamburger. I started to ask her straight out why she allowed men not only to exploit her for their sexual pleasure but, worse, in many instances to use her womb as the depository of their racial anger and their own self-loathing.

But that is the one question you never present to a sad woman like Linda Zeroski. The answer is one she knows, but she will never share it, and she will forever despise the man who asks it of her.

It was hot and dry the day Tee Bobby bonded out of the parish prison. Across town Linda Zeroski was picked up on her corner by a white man, taken to a motel out on the four-lane, and driven back to her corner. She drank beer in the shade of the live oak with the teenage crack dealers who were all her friends, shouted down her pimp when he accused her of shorting him on his forty percent, then had sex in the back of a black man's car and ate her supper under the tree and tied off her arm in a crack house up the street and cooked a tablespoon of brown tar over a candle flame and shot it into a vein that was as purple and swollen as a tumor.

Just after sunset a gas-guzzler pulled to the curb on Linda's corner and parked under the spreading branches of the live oak. A man in a hat, his face and the color of his hands obscured by shadow, smoked a cigarette behind the wheel while Linda leaned into the passenger-side window and read off her list of prices.

Then she turned and waved good-bye to the crack dealers in front of the store and got into the automobile.

Two hours later Linda Zeroski, the girl who had attended Louisiana State University for three years, sat very still in a straight-back wood chair next to a beached houseboat off Bayou Benoit, her forearms taped to the chair's arms, a paper sack placed loosely over her head, while a man who wore leather gloves paced in a circle around her.

She tried to make sense of the man's words, to somehow find reason inside the blood rage he was working himself into. If only the brown skag she had shot up would stop hammering in her ears, if only she did not have to breathe through her nose because of the dirty sock he had stuffed in her mouth.

Then, just as the man wearing leather gloves suddenly ripped into her with both fists, she thought she heard the voice of a little girl inside her. The little girl was calling out her father's name.

Her body was found just before dawn the next morning by a black man who was running his trotlines in the swamp. The sun was still low on the horizon, veiled in mist, when Helen Soileau and I boarded a St. Martin Parish Sheriff's Department boat with two detectives and the coroner and a uniformed deputy from St. Martinville. We headed up Bayou Benoit in the coolness of the early morning, between flooded woods and through bays that were absolutely silent, undimpled by rain or ruffled by wind, the willows and gum trees and moss-hung cypress as still in the green light as if they had been painted against the sky.

The uniformed deputy turned the boat out of the main channel and cut back the throttle and took us through a stand of tupelo gums that were hollowed out by dry rot and whose trunks resonated like drums when the boat's hull scraped against them. Then we saw the desiccated remains of a houseboat that had lain twisted inside the trees since Hurricane Audrey had struck south Louisiana in 1957, its gray sides strung with blooming morning glories.

Up on a sand spit that looked like the humped back of a whale, Linda Zeroski sat in the wood chair, her head slumped forward, as though she had nodded off to sleep. At her feet were the bloodied pieces of brown paper that had been the bag covering her head. The coroner, who was a decent elderly man known for his planter's hats and firehouse suspenders and bow ties, pulled polyethylene gloves on his hands and lifted Linda's chin, then gingerly rotated her head from side to side. A breeze suddenly came up and the leaves in the canopy fluttered with sunlight, and I looked into Linda's destroyed face and felt myself swallow.

The coroner stepped back and pulled off his gloves with popping sounds and dropped them in a garbage bag.

"How do you read it, Doc?" Helen asked.

"I'd say she was beaten with fists, probably by somebody who's as powerful with one hand as with the other," he said. "There are fragments of what looks like leather in a couple of the wounds. My guess is he was wearing gloves. Of course, he could have been using a leather-covered instrument, but in that case there would probably be lesions on the top of the skull, where the skin would split more easily."

A St. Martin Parish detective named Lemoyne was writing in a notepad. He was an overweight man and wore a rain hat and tie and long-sleeved white shirt and galoshes over his street shoes. He kept swiping mosquitoes out of his face.

"What kind of guy are we looking for, Doc?" he asked.

"You ever get drunk and do something you wished you hadn't?" the coroner asked.

The detective seemed to study his notepad. "Yeah, once or twice," he replied.

"The man who did this wasn't drunk. He beat her for a very long time. He enjoyed it immensely. He crushed every bone in her face. One eye is knocked all the way back into the skull. She may have strangled to death on her own blood. The beating may have gone on after she was dead. What kind of man is he? The kind who looks just like your next-door neighbor," the coroner said.

The next afternoon Clete Purcel dropped by my office. He was living in a lovely old stucco motor court, shaded by live oaks, on Bayou Teche, and he was trying to convince me to go fishing with him that evening. Then something out the window caught his attention.

"Is that Joe Zeroski coming up the walk?" he asked.

"Probably."

"What's he doing around here?"

"The prostitute who was killed on Bayou Benoit yesterday? That was his daughter," I said.

"I didn't make the connection. I'll wait for you outside."

"What's wrong?"

"He and I have a history."

"Over what?"

"When I was at the First District, I had to clock him once with a flashlight. Actually, I had to clock him five or six times. He wouldn't stay down. The guy's nuts, Streak. I'd lose him."

Then Clete grinned with self-irony, as he always did when he knew his advice was of no use, and left my office and went into the men's room across the corridor.

Joe Zeroski grew up in the Irish Channel of New Orleans and quit high school when he was sixteen in order to become a high-rise steelworker. Even as a kid Joe was wrapped so tight his fellow workers treated him as they would gasoline fumes around an open flame. When he was twenty, a notoriously violent and cruel Texas oilman and his bodyguard came into Tony Bacino's club in the French Quarter and arbitrarily decided to pulverize someone at the bar. The oilman chose a laconic, seemingly innocuous working-class kid who was hunched over a draft beer. The kid was Joe Zeroski. Fifteen minutes later the oilman and his bodyguard were in an ambulance on their way to Charity Hospital.

Two Detroit wrestlers were hired by a construction company to escort scabs through a union picket line. One of them stiff-armed Joe aside. Before the wrestler ever knew what hit him, he was on the ground and Joe was astraddle his chest, packing handfuls of gravel into his mouth while the strikers cheered.

But Joe's first big score was one he could never claim official recognition for. At twenty-two he made his bones with the Giacano family by taking out a cop killer who had tried to clip Didoni Giacano's son. Wiseguys and off-duty cops all across New Orleans bought Joe a beer and a shot whenever they saw him.

Joe came into my office like a man who had just

clawed his way out of a tomb. He stood flat-footed in the center of the room, slightly hunched, his nostrils white-edged, his hands balling and unballing by his sides.

"Sorry about your daughter, Joe. I hope to be of some help in finding the guy who did this," I said.

His hair was steel-gray, parted in the middle, sheep-sheared on the sides, and his gray eyes were filled with an analytical glare that seemed to dissect both people and objects with the same level of suspicion. He wore a tweed sports coat, gray slacks, loafers with white socks, and a pink shirt with a charcoal-colored tennis racquet above the pocket. When he stepped closer to my desk, I smelled an odor like heat and stale antiperspirant trapped in his clothes.

"There's a black kid just made bond. He raped and snuffed a white girl with a shotgun. Why ain't he in here?" His speech was like most New Orleans working-class people of his generation, an accent and dialect that sounded much more like Brooklyn than the Deep South.

"Because he's not connected with your daughter's death," I replied.

"Yeah? How many people you got around here could do these kinds of things?" he said. When he spoke, he tilted his face upward so that his bottom teeth were exposed in the way a fish's might.

"We're working on it, partner," I said.

"The black kid's name is Hulin. Bobby Hulin. He lives on an island somewhere."

"Right. You stay away from him, too."

He leaned down on my desk, his fists denting my ink

blotter. His breath was moist, sour, rife with funk, like the smell a freshly opened grease trap might give off.

"My wife died of leukemia last year. Linda was my only child. I ain't got a lot to lose. You reading me on this?" he said.

"Wrong way to talk to people who are on your side, Joe," I said.

"Y'all are lucky I ain't who I used to be."

"I'll walk you to the front door," I said.

"Flog your joint," he replied.

So instead I got a drink from the watercooler in the corridor and watched Joe walk toward the front of the courthouse, then I went to check my mail.

But it was not over.

Perry LaSalle had just walked into the department. Joe Zeroski's head jerked around when he heard Perry give his name to the dispatcher.

"You're the lawyer for that Hulin kid?" he asked.

"That's right," Perry replied.

"It makes you feel good putting a degenerate kills young girls back on the street?" Joe asked.

"Looks like I wandered in at the wrong time," Perry said.

"My daughter was Linda Zeroski. I find out some shitbag you sprung beat her to death . . ."

He couldn't finish his sentence. His eyes watered briefly, then he brushed his wrist across his mouth, staring disjointedly into space. Outside, the bells on the railway crossing clanged senselessly in an empty street.

Wally, our three-hundred-pound, hypertensive dispatcher, stopped his work and slipped his horn-rimmed glasses into their leather case and placed the case on his desk and stepped out into the foyer. Clete Purcel stood at the reception counter, motionless, his damp comb clipped inside the pocket of his Hawaiian shirt, his pale blue porkpie hat slanted on his head. He inserted a Lucky Strike in the corner of his mouth and opened the cap on his Zippo but never struck the flint.

"You all right, Joe?" Clete asked.

Joe stared at Clete, his temples pulsing with tiny veins.

"What the fuck *you* doing here?" he asked.

Then Perry LaSalle decided to continue on his way to the sheriff's office. "I'm sorry for your loss, sir," he said.

He accidentally brushed against Joe's arm.

Joe blindsided him and hooked him murderously in the jaw, the blow whipping Perry's face sideways, flinging spittle against the wall. Then Joe hit him below the eye and a third time in the mouth before Clete caught him from behind and wrapped his huge arms around Joe's chest and lifted him off the ground and slammed his face down on a desk.

But Joe freed one arm and ripped an elbow into Clete's nose, splattering blood across Clete's cheek. The dispatcher and I both grabbed Joe and threw him against the desk again and kicked his legs apart and pushed the side of his face down on a dirty ashtray.

"Put your wrists behind you! Do it now, Joe!" I said.

Then Joe Zeroski, who had killed perhaps nine men, sank to one knee, the backs of his thighs trembling, his arms forming a tent over his head as he tried to hide the shame and grief in his face.

CHAPTER 5

I walked with Perry LaSalle into the men's room and held his coat for him while he washed his face with cold water. There was a cluster of red bumps under his right eye and blood in his saliva when he spit.

"You cutting that guy loose?" he asked.

"Unless you want to press charges," I replied.

He felt his mouth and looked in the mirror. His eyes were still angry. Then, as though realizing his expression was uncharacteristic of the Perry LaSalle we all knew, he blew out his breath and grinned.

"Maybe I'll catch him down the road," he said.

"I wouldn't. Joe Zeroski was a hit man for the Giacano family," I said.

His eyes became neutral, as though he did not want me to read them. He took his coat from my hand and put it on and combed his hair in the mirror. Then he stopped.

"Are you staring at me for some reason, Dave?" he asked.

"No."

"You think I'm bothered because this guy was a meatball for the Giacanos?" he said.

"On my best day I can't even take my own inventory, Perry," I said.

"Save the Twelve Step stuff for a meeting, old pard," he replied.

A few minutes later I walked with Clete Purcel to his car. The top was down and a half-dozen fishing rods were propped against the backseat. We watched Perry LaSalle's Gazelle pull out of the parking lot and cross the train tracks and turn onto St. Peter Street.

"He's not going to file on Zeroski?" Clete asked.

"Perry's grandfather ran rum with the Giacanos during Prohibition. I don't think Perry wants to be reminded of the association," I said.

"Everybody ran rum back then," Clete said.

"Somebody else did his grandfather's time. You're not going to try to square that elbow in the nose, are you?"

Clete thought about it. "It wasn't personal. For a button man Joe's not a bad guy."

"Great standards."

"This is Louisiana, Dave. Guatemala North. Quit pretending it's the United States. Life will make a lot more sense," he said.

I worked late at the office that evening. The eight-by-ten death photos of Linda Zeroski and Amanda Boudreau were spread on my desk. The body postures and faces of the dead always tell a story. Sometimes the jaw is slack, the mouth robbed of words, as though the dying person has suddenly discovered the fraudulent nature of the world. Perhaps the gaze is focused on a shaft of sunlight through a tree, or a tear is sealed in the corner of the eye, or the palms lie open as though surrendering the spirit. I would like to believe that those who die violently are consoled by presences that care for and protect them in a special way. But the eyes of Linda Zeroski and Amanda Boudreau haunted me, and I wanted to find their killers and do something horrible to them.

On the way home I drove to the pickup corner where Linda Zeroski had gotten into an automobile under a spreading oak and driven off, without concern, into a sunset that looked like purple and red smoke against the western sky. The teenage crack dealers who had supposedly been her friends were bored with my questions, then irritated that I was interrupting the flow of business on the corner. When I did not leave, they glanced at one another, formulating a different response, as though I were not there. Their voices became unctuous, their faces sincere, and they indicated to a man they would certainly call my office if they heard any information that might be helpful.

I started to get back into my truck. Then I stopped and walked back under the oak tree.

"Does Tee Bobby Hulin ever swing by the corner?" I asked.

"Tee Bobby likes them when they sweet, white, and sixteen. I don't see nothing like that 'round here, suh," one kid said. The others snickered.

"What are you telling me?" I asked.

"Tee Bobby got his own thing. It just ain't got nothing to do wit' us," the same kid said.

They lowered their heads in the shadows, suppressing their grins, kicking at the dust, their eyes flicking with amusement at one another. I walked back to my truck and got in. The heat lightning in the south pulsed like quicksilver in the clouds.

Joe Zeroski had asked how many individuals in our area were capable of the crimes committed against the persons of his daughter and Amanda Boudreau. Could Tee Bobby have been involved in the abduction of Linda Zeroski? Tee Bobby's grandmother had said that Tee Bobby's present trouble had started before he was born. Maybe it was time to find out what she had meant.

I drove home and parked in the drive and went into the bait shop. Batist was by himself, eating a sandwich at the counter.

"How well do you know Tee Bobby?" I asked.

"Good enough so's I don't want to know him," he answered.

"You think he could rape and murder a young girl?"

"What I t'ink don't count."

"What do you know about Ladice Hulin's relationship to the LaSalle family?"

He finished his coffee and stared out the screen at the bream night-feeding on the moths that fried themselves on the floodlamps and fell into the water.

"Stories about white men and black field women ain't never good, Dave. You want to hear it, my sister growed up with Ladice," he said.

I told my wife, Bootsie, I'd eat supper late, and Batist

and I drove to his sister's small house outside Loreauville, where I listened to a tale that took me back into the Louisiana of my boyhood.

But actually, even before Batist's sister began her account, I already knew much of the LaSalle family's history, not because I necessarily admired them or even found them interesting, but because their lives had become the mirror and measure of our own. In one fashion or another the town had been a participant in all their deeds, all their reversals of fortune, for good or bad, from the time the first cabins were hewn and notched out of cypress on the banks of Bayou Teche, to the federal occupation in 1863 and later the restoration of the old oligarchy by the White League and the Knights of the White Camellia during Reconstruction, into modern times when Cajuns and people of color were deliberately kept uneducated and poor in order to ensure the availability of a huge and easily manipulated labor pool.

The LaSalles had believed colonial Louisiana would allow them to realize all the grandiose dreams that Robespierre's guillotine had denied some of their family members. But they soon learned that revolutionary France had not quite finished paying back their kind for centuries of royal arrogance. In fact, they were the bunch Napoleon Bonaparte selected as the target for his most successful large-scale swindle. They paid large sums to obtain land grants in Louisiana from his government, only to discover in 1803 that Napoleon had sold the land from under their feet to the Americans in order to finance his wars.

But the LaSalles were a resilient group, not to be undone by a Corsican usurper or their new egalitarian neighbors. They bought slaves whom James Bowie and his business partner, Jean Lafitte, were smuggling into Louisiana from the West Indies after the prohibition of 1809. They drained swamps and felled forests and later laid log roads and railway tracks for steam engines across acreage that was so black and rich with sediment from the alluvial fan of the Mississippi that any kind of seed would grow on it if the seed were simply thrown on the ground and stepped upon.

Like his predecessors, Julian LaSalle was a practical man who did not argue or contend with the world. Perhaps his family had built its wealth upon the backs of slave labor, but that had been the ethos of the times and he felt no guilt about it. He paid what was considered a fair wage to his field hands, saw to their medical care, always kept his word, and during the Great Depression never turned a man in need from his door.

As a little boy I saw him when my father took me with him to Provost's Bar and Pool Room. Mr. Julian, as we called him, was a dark-haired, handsome man with a cleft chin, who wore suspenders and linen suits and Panama hats and two-tone shoes, like an American you might see at a Havana racetrack. He never sat at the bar but always stood, a cigar in one hand, a tumbler of bourbon and ice in the other. On Saturday afternoons Provost's was always filled with both business and blue-collar men, the floor spread with green sawdust, sometimes littered with football betting cards. Mr. Julian treated all the patrons there with equal respect, bought drinks for the old men at the domino and bouree tables, and walked away when other men used racist language or told bawdy jokes. He was wealthy and educated, but his graciousness and good nature inspired in others admiration rather than envy.

There were stories about his involvement with black women, one in particular, but someone was always quick to offer that Mr. Julian's wife suffered from cancer and other illnesses and had been in a sanitarium in the North, that her hysterical behavior at Mass was such that even a sympathetic priest had reluctantly asked her not to attend. Who could expect Mr. Julian to abide what even the church could not?

But Batist's sister did not begin her story with Mr. Julian. Instead she told of an overseer on Poinciana Island, a lean, rough-grained, angular man who wore sunglasses, western boots, a straw cowboy hat, and khaki clothes when he sat atop his horse and rode among the black workers in the fields. The year was 1953, a time when the white overseer on a Louisiana plantation had the same powers over those in his charge as his antebellum antecedents did. No one knew his origins, but his name was Legion, and the first day he appeared in the field one worker, who had been a convict on Angola Farm, looked into Legion's face and at first opportunity leaned his hoe against a fence rail and walked seven miles back to New Iberia and never returned to ask for his pay.

"You say his name was Legion?" I asked Batist's sister.

"That's the name he give us. Didn't have no first name, didn't have no last name. We didn't even have to call him 'Mister.' Just 'Legion,'" she replied.

He believed clothes kept the heat off the body, and he buttoned his shirt at the throat and wrists, no matter how humid and hot the weather became. The back of his shirt was peppered with sweat by midday, and while the blacks ate their sandwiches of company-store balogna and potted meat in a grove of gum trees, he tethered his horse under a solitary live oak in the middle of a pepper field and sat in a folding chair a black man hand-carried to him for that purpose. He ate the boudin or pork chops and dirty rice the blacks said a prostitute at Hattie Fontenot's bar prepared and wrapped in wax paper for him each morning.

He took the girls and women he wanted from the field, indicating with a nod of the head for one of them to follow his horse into a canebrake or pine thicket, where he dismounted from the saddle and stripped nude and told the girl or woman to remove her underpants and lie down and open her legs, his language as mechanical and dehumanized as the violence of his copulation and the release of his animus as he plunged inside the girl or woman, his upper torso propped up stiffly on his arms, as though he did not want to touch any more of her body than was necessary.

Afterward the girl or woman had to wash him. His body was as rough as animal hide, they said, welted with knife scars, the insides of his forearms blue with tattoos that looked like the crudely drawn figures in old black-and-white movie cartoons.

Then the day came when his eyes settled on Ladice Hulin.

"Go up yonder in them gum trees and sit in the shade," he said.

"I got to pick to the end of the row, suh. Then I got the other row. Or I'm gonna come up short," she said.

He reached down and lifted the cloth sack out of her hand and tied its loose end to his saddle pommel.

"The pepper juice giving you blisters. You need to soak your hands in milk at night. It gonna take the sting right out," he said.

"They don't be hurting, Legion. I promise. I got to get my row," Ladice said.

This time he didn't reply. He turned his horse in a circle and came up behind her and let the horse's forequarters knock against her.

"Legion, my daddy expecting to see me this afternoon. He coming down from the quarters. I got to be out here in the row where he can see me," she said.

"You ain't got a daddy, girl. Don't make me ax you again, no," Legion said.

The other workers, bent over in the pepper bushes, never looked up from their own fear and grief with the sun and heat and blistered fingers and the ball of pain that grew steadily in the small of the back through the long afternoon. Ladice wiped the dust and sweat off her face with her dress and began the walk to the gum trees in whose midst was a thorn bush, one with deep green leaves and red flowers that looked like drops of blood in the hot shade.

She heard a car honk on the road. She turned and saw Mr. Julian in his Lincoln Continental, its whitewall tires and wirewheels gleaming in the sunlight, like a shining invention that had appeared out of a cloud. He got out in the road, wearing a long-sleeved white shirt with purple garters on the sleeves and seersucker pants and a Panama hat on the back of his head. His smile was wonderful, and he was looking at her, his face filled with goodness, the influence of his presence so immediate that Legion dropped her sack to the ground and dismounted from the saddle and led his horse toward the road, so his employer would not be forced to look up at him and address him on horseback.

The easy smile never left Mr. Julian's face, but she could hear his words drifting across the rows on the wind.

"I'm surprised to see you bump a young woman with your horse like that, Legion. I suspect that was an accident, wasn't it?" he said.

"Yes, sir. I tole her I was sorry about that," Legion said.

"That's good. 'Cause you're a good man. Let's don't have a conversation like this again."

Ladice picked up her sack and got back in the row and stooped over and began picking the peppers whose juice sometimes caused her hands to swell as though they had been stung by bumblebees. She glanced sideways at Mr. Julian, at the way he held himself, the cleft in his chin, the sheen on his hair when he removed his hat, his red tie blowing over his shoulder in the wind. Physically, Legion towered over Mr. Julian, but Legion stood in silence, like a chastised child, motionless, while Mr. Julian unsnapped the cover on his gold vest watch and looked at the time and snapped the cover shut again, then began discussing a deep-sea fishing trip he wanted to take.

While he talked his eyes remained fastened on Ladice.

"Don't be t'inking you special, girl. Don't be that kind of fool," an old woman in the next row said.

A week later Mr. Julian gave Ladice a job in the big house and new dresses to wear to work and the apartment over the garage to live in. She knew the price he would extract but did not think less of him for it. In fact, his obvious need, his male dependency, the fact that he wanted her, that he had chosen her out of all the women in the quarters, that any night he would come for her, all his weaknesses exposed, these thoughts made her cheeks burn and her breath rise like a shard of glass in her chest.

She entertained herself with fantasies as she worked in the ornate silence of his house, dusting the antique chairs that were never sat in, placing cut flowers in a large silver bowl on a dining room table that was never used, listening for the little bell by Mrs. LaSalle's bedside, the only lifeline the old woman had to the world beyond her bedroom. The Negro boys who had courted Ladice only a week earlier seemed part of a distant memory now, one of parked cars behind juke joints and insects humming in the hot darkness or a hurried coupling on a stale-smelling mattress in a corncrib.

She sensed a new power in herself among all those who lived by the rules and strange parameters that governed life on Poinciana Island. On her first visit to the plantation store after moving up to the big house, the clerk called her "Miss Ladice," and Legion and another white man stepped aside when she crossed the gallery to the parking lot.

It was during her second week at the big house, just after sunset, when she was fresh from her bath and dressed in clean clothes, that she heard the weight of Mr. Julian's footsteps on the garage apartment stairs. Her hand moved to the switch for the outside light.

"There's no need to turn that on. It's only I," he said through the screen door.

She stood still, her hands folded demurely in front of her, unsure whether she should act first by pushing open the door for him, wondering if even that small a courtesy would indicate a foreknowledge about his behavior that he would find insulting and presumptuous.

When she didn't speak, he said, "Am I disturbing you, Ladice?"

"No, suh, you ain't. I mean, you aren't." She held the door open. "Would you like to come in, suh?"

"Yes, I couldn't sleep. I left Miz LaSalle's window open so I could listen for her bell. I understand you've graduated from high school."

"Yes, suh. I went t'ree years at plantation school and one at St. Edward's."

"Have you thought about college?"

"The closest for colored is Southern in Baton Rouge. I ain't got the money for that."

"There're scholarships. I could help with one," he said.

But he was not hearing his own words now. His eyes lingered on her mouth, the thickness of her hair, her skin that was as smooth as melted chocolate, the lovely heart shape of her face. She saw him swallow and an expression like both shame and lust suffuse his face. His hands cupped her shoulders, then he bent toward her and kissed her cheek and let his hands slip down her arms and over her waist and onto the small of her back.

"I'm a foolish old man who has little in the way of a married life, Ladice. If you wish, I'll leave," he said.

"No, suh. You ain't got to go. I mean, you don't got to go," she replied.

He kissed her neck and touched the points of her breasts with his fingers and unbuttoned her shirt and blue jeans. He helped her slip her shirt off her arms and held one of her hands while she stepped out of her jeans, then walked her to the narrow bed in the room off the kitchen and unhooked her bra and laid her down on the bed and removed her panties.

"Mr. Julian, ain't you gonna use somet'ing?" she asked.

"Yes," he said, his voice hoarse, the folds of flesh in his throat red and bewhiskered in the moonglow through the window.

There was a sadness in his eyes she had never seen in a white person's before.

"You feel bad about somet'ing, Mr. Julian?"

"What I do is a sin. I've made you part of it, too."

She took his hand and flattened it on her breast. "Feel my heart beating? It ain't a sin when a woman's heart beats like that," she said, and held him with her eyes.

He sat on the edge of the mattress and kissed her stomach and the insides of her thighs and put her nipples in his mouth, then he entered her and came within seconds, his back shaking while she stroked the curly locks of hair on the back of his neck.

"I'm sorry. I didn't give you satisfaction," he said.

"It's all right, suh. Lie on your back. Let me show you somet'ing," she said.

Then she mounted him and lifted his sex and placed it inside her and closed her knees and thighs tightly against him. She looked into his eyes in a way she had never dared look at a white man, probing his thoughts, controlling his sensations with the movements of her loins, leaning down to kiss him as she might a child. She came at the same time as he and she felt a surge of power and electricity in her thighs and genitalia and breasts that made her cry out involuntarily, not as much in pleasure as with a sense of triumph she never thought she could experience.

Through the window she heard the tiny bell ring in Mrs. LaSalle's bedroom.

"I always fix Mrs. LaSalle a sandwich and a glass of milk at this time of night," he said.

"I can do it, suh."

"No, your duties are in the downstairs of the house. That's where you work and remain, Ladice, unless I'm away and Mrs. LaSalle calls you."

There was a sharpness in his voice that made her blink. She covered herself with the sheet and pulled her knees up in front of her. She had only to look into his eyes for a second to realize that a transformation had taken place in him since his moment of need had passed. He began dressing, his face composed now, his chin pointed upward while he buttoned his shirt. Ladice stared into the shadows and removed a strand of hair from her forehead, her lips slightly pursed, her eyes veiled.

Then she lay back on the pillow with one arm behind her head and watched him prepare to leave.

"Good night, Ladice," he said.

She looked at him indifferently and did not answer.

You gonna be back. Won't be long, either. See who talks down to who next time, she said to herself.

The following week the tiny bell on Mrs. LaSalle's nightstand rang when Mr. Julian was in town. Ladice climbed the stairs and stood in Mrs. LaSalle's doorway in her maid's black dress and frilled apron.

"Yes, ma'am?" she said.

Mrs. LaSalle had forced her husband to put iron grill-work over the windows, although there had never been a burglary on the island, and she never allowed the windows to be unlocked or opened. The air in the room was oppressive and smelled of camphor and urine. Mrs. LaSalle's skin looked like candle wax, her hair like a tangled red flame on the pillow of her tester bed. Her eyes were dark, larger than they should have been, luminous with either the cancer in her body or the fits of insanity that took possession of her mind.

"What happened to the other nigra girl?" she asked.

"Mr. Julian said you wanted her sent away, ma'am," Ladice replied.

"That sounds like someone's fabrication. Why would I want to do that? Never mind. Come here. Let me look at you."

Ladice walked closer to the tester bed. Mrs. LaSalle's pink nightgown was sunken into her chest, where her breasts had been removed.

"Why, you're a juicy little thing, aren't you?" she said.

"Ma'am?"

"I'm incontinent. I want you to rinse my panties."

"Excuse me?"

"Are you deaf? Remove my panties and rinse them. I've soiled them."

"I cain't be doing that, ma'am."

"You impudent thing."

"Yessum," Ladice said. She turned and left the room.

That night Mr. Julian was at her door.

"My wife says you sassed her," he said.

"I don't see it that way," Ladice replied.

He opened the screen door and stepped inside without being invited. He was much taller than she, his shadow blocking out the evening light that shone through the trees outside. But she didn't move. She wore jeans and sandals and a blue V-necked T-shirt and a gold-plated chain with a small purple stone around her throat. Her body felt cool and fresh from the cold bath she had just taken, and she had put perfume behind her ears, and one lock of her hair hung down over her eye.

"I need to know what happened today, Ladice," he said.

"If Miz LaSalle want her clothes laundered, I'll be glad to carry them on down to the washing machine. I'll iron them, too," Ladice said.

"I see. I think maybe this was just a miscommunication in language," he said.

She didn't reply. His eyes softened and moved over her face and studied her mouth. His hand touched her arm.

"My momma and uncle are picking me up to go to town," she said.

"Will you be back later?"

She moved the lock of hair from her eyebrow. "I t'ink my momma want me to stay over wit' her tonight," she said.

"Yes, I'm sure she's lonely sometimes. I'm very fond of you, Ladice."

"Good night, Mr. Julian."

"Yes, well, I guess good night it is, then," he said.

But his words did not coincide with his immobility

and the longing in his face. She held her eyes steadily on his until he actually blinked and color came into his throat. Then his jawbone flexed and he let himself out the door.

She watched him through the window as he crossed his yard to the back of his house, tearing angrily at the knot in his necktie.

Maybe your wife will let you rinse her panties, she said to herself, and felt surprise at the vitriolic nature of her thoughts.

In her naïveté she thought their arrangement, love affair, whatever people wished to call it, would aim itself at a dramatic denouement, like a sulfurous match suddenly igniting the dryness of her life, bringing it to an end in some fashion, perhaps even a destructive one, that would set her free from the world she had grown up in.

But the long, humid days of summer blended one into another, as did Mr. Julian's nocturnal visits and the depression and sleeplessness they engendered in her. She no longer thought about control or power or her status among the other blacks on Poinciana Island. Her familiarity with Mr. Julian made her think of him with pity, when she thought of him at all, and his visits for her were simply a biological matter, in the same way her other bodily functions were, and she wondered if this wasn't indeed the attitude that all women developed when they coupled out of necessity. It wasn't a sin; it was just boring.

Then it was fall and she could smell gas from the swamp at night and the faint, salty odor of dead fish that had been trapped in tidal pools by the bay. Sometimes she would lie awake in her bed and listen to the moths hitting on her screens, destroying their wings as they tried to reach the nightlight in the bathroom. She wondered why they were created in such a way, why they would destroy themselves in order to fly onto an electrically heated white orb that eventually killed them. When she had these thoughts, she covered her head with a pillow so she could not hear the soft thudding of the moths' bodies against the screens.

But the venal and pernicious nature of her relationship with Julian LaSalle and his family and Poinciana Island, and its cost to her, would reveal itself in a way she had never guessed.

In November she boarded a Greyhound bus and rode across the Atchafalaya Swamp to Baton Rouge. She stayed in the old Negro district called Catfish Town, where juke joints and shotgun shacks left over from the days of slavery still lined both sides of the streets. Her first morning in the city she took a cab to the campus of Southern University and entered the administration building and told a white-haired black woman in a business suit she wanted to pre-enroll in the nursing program for the spring semester.

"Did you graduate from high school?" the woman asked.

"Yessum."

"Where?"

"In New Iberia."

"No, I mean what was the name of the school?"

"I got a certificate from plantation school. I went to St. Edward's, too."

"I see," the woman said. Her eyes seemed to cloud. "Fill out this application and return it with your transcripts. You could have done this through the mail, you know."

"Ma'am, is there somet'ing you ain't telling me?"

"I didn't mean to give that impression," the woman replied.

When Ladice walked outside, the air was sunlit and cool and smelled of burning leaves. A marching band was practicing beyond a grove of trees, the notes of a martial song rising off the brass and silver instruments into a hard blue sky. For some reason she could not explain, the expectation of football games and Saturday-night dances and corsages made of chrysanthemums and gin fizzes in the back of a coupe had become the province of others, one she would not share in.

One month later the mail carrier told Ladice he had left a letter from Southern University for her at the plantation post office. She walked down the dirt road in the dusk, between woods that smelled of pine sap and dust on the leaves and fish heads that raccoons had strewn among the trunks. The sun burned like a flare on a marshy horizon that was gray with winterkill.

She took the envelope from the hand of the postal clerk and walked back to the garage apartment and put it on her breakfast table under a salt shaker and lay down on her bed and went to sleep without opening the letter.

It was dark when she awoke. She turned on the kitchen light and washed her face in the bathroom, then sat down at the table and read the two brief paragraphs that had been written to her by the registrar. When she had finished, she refolded the letter and placed it back in the envelope and walked down to Julian LaSalle's front door, not the back, and knocked.

He was in slippers and a red silk bathrobe when he opened the door, his reading glasses tilted down on his nose.

"Is something wrong?" he asked.

"My credits from plantation school ain't no good."

"Beg your pardon?"

"Southern will take my credits from St. Edward's. The ones from plantation school don't count. You must have knowed that when you said you would get me a scholarship to Southern. Did you know that, Mr. Julian?"

"We provide a free school on Poinciana. Most people would find that generous. I'm not familiar with the accreditation system at Southern University."

"I t'ink I'm gonna be moving back to the quarters."

"Now, listen," he said. He looked over his shoulder, up the curved stairs that led to the second floor. "We'll talk about this tomorrow."

She wadded up the envelope and the letter and threw it over his shoulder onto his living room rug.

The following Thursday, the one night he always spent playing gin rummy with his wife, Mr. Julian drove to Ladice's house, where she now lived with her mother on a dead-end, isolated road lined with slash pines. It was cold and smoke from wood fires hung as thick as cotton in the trees. She watched him through the front window as he studied her vegetable garden, thumb and forefinger pinched on his chin, his eyes busy with thoughts that had nothing to do with her garden.

When he entered the house, he removed his hat.

"There's a Catholic college for colored students in

New Orleans. I had a talk with the dean's office this morning. Would you be willing to take some preparatory courses?" he said.

She had been ironing when he had driven up to the house, and she picked up the iron from the pie pan it sat in and sprinkled a shirt with water from a soda bottle and ran the iron hissing across the cloth. She hadn't bathed that day, and she could smell her own odor in her clothes.

"If I take these courses, how I know I'm gonna get in?" she asked.

"You have my word," he replied.

She nodded and touched at the moisture on her forehead with her wrist. She wanted to tell him to leave, to take his promises and manipulations and mercurial moods back to his home, back to the wife whose cancer of the spirit was greater than the disease that attacked her body. But she thought about New Orleans, the streetcars clattering down the oak- and palm-lined avenues, the parades during Mardi Gras, the music that rose from the French Quarter into the sky at sunset.

"You ain't fooling me, Mr. Julian?" she said.

Then she knew how weak she actually was, how much she wanted what he could give her, and consequently, when all was said and done, how easily she would always be used either by him or someone like him. She felt a sense of shame about herself, her life, and most of all her self-delusion that she had ever been in control of Julian LaSalle.

"I passed your mother and uncle on the road. Will they be back soon?" he said, and rubbed her arm with his palm.

"No. They gone to Lafayette," she said, wondering at

how easy it was to become complicitous in her own exploitation.

He removed the iron from her hand and put his arms around her and rubbed his face in her hair and pressed her tightly against his body.

"I'm dirty. I been on my feet all day," she said.

"You're lovely anytime, Ladice," he said. He led her to her bedroom, which was lit only by a bedside lamp, and pulled her T-shirt over her head and pushed her jeans down over her hips.

"It's Thursday. You don't have a sitter for Miz LaSalle on Thursday night," she said.

"She's taking a nap. She'll be fine," he replied. Then he was on top of her, his body trembling, his lips on her breasts.

She fixed her eyes on the smoke in the slash pines outside, the fireflies that lit like sparks in the limbs, the moon that was orange with dust from the fields. She thought she heard a pickup truck clanking by on the road, but the sound of its engine was absorbed by the distant whistle of a Southern Pacific freight rumbling through the wetlands toward New Orleans. She closed her eyes and thought of New Orleans, where the mornings always smelled of mint and flowers and chicory coffee and beignets frying in someone's kitchen.

She felt his body constrict and tighten and his loins shudder, then his weight left her and he was lying next to her, his breath short, his hair damp against her cheek. After a moment he widened his eyes, like a man returning to the world that constituted his ordinary life. He sat on the side of the mattress, his pale back sweaty and etched by vertebrae.

Then he did something he had never done in the aftermath of their lovemaking. He patted her on top of the hand and said, "In another time and place we might have made quite a pair, you and I. You're an extraordinary woman. Don't let anybody ever tell you otherwise."

The inside of the room seemed filled with mist or smoke, and the fireflies in the tops of the trees seemed brighter than they should have been. She wondered if she was coming down with a cold or if she had lost a part of her soul and no longer knew who she was. She rose from the bed, still naked, and went to the window.

"Turn out the light," she said.

He clicked off the lamp on the bedside table and the room dropped into darkness. She looked out the window and realized it was too late in the year for fireflies, that the red pinpoints of light in the pines were sparks tumbling out of the sky.

But it was not the threat of fire to her own house that made her heart stop. The narrow, grained face of Legion the overseer suddenly moved into her vision, no more than three feet on the other side of the glass. His eyes raked her nude body even as he was tipping his hat.

CHAPTER 6

The fire at the LaSalle home had started in the kitchen, probably by a dish towel that had been left near an open flame. The fire climbed up the wall and flattened on the ceiling, then spread through a hallway and was sucked by a draft up the staircase onto the second story. Mr. Julian had removed the phone from Mrs. LaSalle's bedroom long ago, after a judge in Opelousas and a U.S. attorney in Baton Rouge complained she was calling them in the middle of the night, claiming that Huey Long had been murdered by agents of Franklin Roosevelt.

The clerk from the plantation store was passing on the road when he saw the windows of the house fill with pink light. He was an excitable man, given to belief in demonic possession and the gift of tongues, and after the heat of the front doorknob seared his hand, he began shouting at the house and throwing dirt clods on the roof to alert those who might be sleeping upstairs.

He picked up a garden rake and broke the glass out of a living room window. The flames mushroomed up through the second and third stories like cold oxygen igniting in a chimney.

The store clerk and the black people from up the road tried to soak the roof with a lawn hose. They scooped dirt with their hands and threw it through the windows into the smoke and hand-carried water buckets from the bay but were finally driven back from the house by the heat radiating from the walls. They heard glass break in Mrs. LaSalle's bedroom and saw her hands on the iron grillwork, like the yellow talons of a bird extended through a cage. They never saw more of her physical person than her hands; the rest of her body disappeared in an envelope of flame.

An obese black woman grabbed her daughter and held her tightly against her stomach, smothering her daughter's head with her arms so she would not hear the sounds that came from Mrs. LaSalle's window.

But at Ladice Hulin's house, neither she nor Mr. Julian knew of these events. Legion waited outside for her and Mr. Julian to emerge. There was ash on his khaki clothes, a smear of soot on his cheek and one shirtsleeve.

"You were watching us through the window? You were spying on me?" Mr. Julian said incredulously.

"No, sir, I wouldn't say that. I come here to tell you somet'ing else. It's sad news, yeah. Miz LaSalle got burned up in a fire."

Legion turned his face away, but he watched Mr. Julian out of the corner of his eye to see the reaction his words would cause.

"What? What did you say?" Mr. Julian said.

"Your home's gone, too. I hate to be the one to tell you, Mr. Julian."

Mr. Julian's face was bloodless, popping with sweat, even though the temperature was still dropping.

"We'll go back wit' you, Mr. Julian," Ladice said.

"I was the first one in her room. The deadbolt was locked from the outside. I took the key out and stuck it in the other side of the lock, so nobody ain't gonna get the wrong idea, no," Legion said.

"You did what? Say that again?" Mr. Julian said as though he could not sort through Legion's words.

"The key was almost melted. But I moved it to the other side of the lock, me. You ain't got to worry," Legion replied.

But Mr. Julian wasn't listening now. He walked to his car and started the engine and backed one tire into Ladice's garden, then drove down the road under an orange moon toward the smoke that rose from the ruins of his home.

Ladice looked up into Legion's face. He had removed his hat and was running a comb through his hair. His hair was black, like tar from a barrel, the vertical lines in his narrow face like those in a prune.

"You going in the field tomorrow, Ladice. It ain't gonna hep you to sass me about it, either," he said.

She started to speak, but he placed his thumb on her mouth.

What did Legion do to her?" I asked Batist's sister.

She was a heavy woman, with a big head and wide shoulders and knees that looked like hubcaps. She sat in an overstuffed chair in a gloomy corner of her living room, her large hands squeezing each other in the cone of light from a floor lamp.

"Did Ladice have a child by Mr. Julian?" I asked.

"I ain't said that," she answered.

"Why won't you tell me the rest of the story? Mr. Julian and his wife are both dead," I said.

Batist's sister was silent a moment.

"He still out there. Maybe in St. Mary Parish. Maybe down by New Orleans. Some of the old people say he killed a man in Morgan City," she said.

"Who?" I said.

"Legion. He out there, in the dark. He don't like the sun. His face is pale, like it don't have no blood. I seen him once. It was Legion," she said.

She looked at the tops of her folded hands and would not raise her eyes to mine.

It was late when I got home and Bootsie was asleep. I ate a ham and onion sandwich in the kitchen, then brushed my teeth and lay down by her side and stared at the ceiling in the darkness. I could hear the cries of nutrias out in the swamp, an alligator rolling its tail in the flooded trees, the echo of distant thunder that gave no rain.

The moon was up and Bootsie's hair was the color of honey on the pillow. She was the only woman I had ever known who had a natural fragrance, like night-blooming gardenias. Her eyes opened and she smiled and turned on her side and put her arm across my chest, one knee over my leg. Her body had the curvature and undulations of a classical Greek sculpture, but her skin was always smooth and soft under my hand, virtually without a wrinkle, as though age had decided to pass her by.

"Anything wrong?" she said.

"No."

"You can't sleep?"

"I'm fine. I didn't mean to wake you."

She touched me under the sheet. "It's all right," she said.

I awoke at dawn and made coffee on the stove. The light was gray in the trees, the Spanish moss motionless in the silence.

"Did you ever hear of an overseer at Poinciana Island by the name of Legion?" I asked Bootsie.

"No, why?"

"When I was twelve, my brother, Jimmie, and I had a bad encounter with some low-rent people in City Park. A man opened a knife on us. One of the women with him called him Legion."

"Why do you ask about him now?"

"His name came up when I was checking out some background material on Tee Bobby. It may not be important."

"By the way, Perry LaSalle came by last night," she said.

"Perry is becoming a pain in the ass," I said.

"He told me you'd say that."

Before I went to the office I drove out to Ladice Hulin's house on Poinciana Island and asked her about the overseer named Legion and the death of Mrs. LaSalle in the fire.

"Mind your own bidness. No, I take that back. Get

out of my life altogether," she said, and closed the door in my face.

The next day Perry was at my office door. Before he could speak, I said, "Why were you at my house the other night?"

"One of Barbara Shanahan's colleagues got drunk and shot off his mouth at the country club. Barbara and the D.A. think you're not a team player. I'm calling you as a witness for the defense, Dave. I thought I ought to warn you in advance," he replied.

I went back to the paperwork on my desk and tried to pretend he was not there.

"On another subject, you care to explain to me why you're bothering Ladice Hulin about my grandfather?" he asked.

I put the cap on my pen and looked up at him. "She told me Amanda Boudreau's death was related to events that happened before Tee Bobby was born. What do you think she meant by that?" I said.

"I wouldn't know. But stay out of my family's private life," he replied.

"Your book on capital punishment didn't spare people in the Iberia prosecutor's office. What makes the LaSalles sacrosanct? The fact y'all own some canneries?"

He shook his head and went out the door. I thought he had gone and I got up from my desk to go down the corridor for my mail. But he came back through the door, the blood pooled in his cheeks.

"Where do you get off indicting my family?" he said.

"That case you used in your book, the murder of those teenagers up on the Loreauville Road? The mother of that girl those two fuckheads killed said she heard her daughter's voice out in the front yard at the same hour her daughter died. Her daughter was saying, 'Please help me, Momma.' I don't remember seeing that in either your book or the movie."

"You make a remark about my family again, and cop or no cop, I'm going to bust your jaw, Dave."

"Give your grief to Barbara Shanahan. I think you two deserve each other," I said.

My hands were shaking when I brushed past him.

That night Clete Purcel called the house. I could hear an electric guitar and saxophones and laughter and people talking loudly in the background.

"I can hardly hear you," I said.

"I thought I'd have another run at Jimmy Dean Styles. I'm at a joint he owns in St. Martinville. I thought you'd like to know who's parked across the street."

"It's late, Clete."

"Joe Zeroski. He's got a P.I. with him, his niece, Zerelda Calucci. Her old man was one of the Calucci brothers."

"Tell me about it tomorrow."

"The kid you're looking at for the murder of the girl in the cane field? He's playing here."

"Say again?"

"What's his name? Hulin? He's up there on the bandstand. Anyway, I'd better hit the road. The only other thing white in this place is the toilet bowl. Sorry I bothered you."

"Give me a half hour," I said.

I drove up the Teche, under the long canopy of live oaks on the St. Martinville highway, the same road that federal soldiers had marched in 1863, the same road that Evangeline and her lover had walked almost a century before the federals came.

Jimmy Dean Styles owned only a half-interest in the nightclub Clete had called from. His business partner was a black bondsman named Little Albert Babineau who had recently made the state news wires after he threw packages of condoms off a Mardi Gras float. Each package was printed with the words "Be Sure You 'Bond' Right. Be Safe with Little Albert. 24-Hour Bail Bonds. Little Albert Will Not Let You Down."

The club was built of plywood that had been painted blue and strung with yellow and purple lights. The window glass and walls literally shook from the noise inside. I pulled in at the back, where Clete waited for me next to his Cadillac. Through the trees below the club I could see a glaze of yellow light on Bayou Teche and the wake of a large boat slapping into the elephant ears along the banks.

"You're not pissed off because I took another run at Styles?" Clete said.

"Why should I be? You never listen to anything I say, anyway."

"How you want to play it?" he asked.

"We need to get Joe Zeroski out of here. What was that you said about a P.I.?"

"It's his niece. I'd like to develop a more intimate relationship with her, except I always get the feeling she'd like to blow my equipment off. Wait till you see the bongos on that broad."

"Will you stop talking like that? I'm not kidding you, Clete. It's an illness."

He put two sticks of gum in his mouth and chewed them loudly, his eyes full of mirth, his head seeming to turn in all directions at once.

"I tell you what. I'll handle Joe, you deal with Zerelda," he said.

Joe Zeroski's car was parked down the block, across the street, in front of a small grocery store. A woman was behind the wheel. Her hair was black and long, the neckline of her blouse plunging, her nails and mouth painted arterial red. I opened my badge holder and lifted it into the light so she could see it. A holstered revolver sat on the seat between the woman and Joe Zeroski.

"We need you to move your car out of here," I said.

"Pull your pud on somebody else's time," she said. I heard Clete snicker behind me.

"Sorry?" I said.

"You're out of your jurisdiction. Go screw yourself," she said.

"You have a permit for that gun?"

"I don't need one. In Louisiana the automobile is an extension of the home. But in answer to your question, yes, I do have a permit. Now, how about moving yourself out of my view?"

I looked across the seat at Joe Zeroski. His stolid face and wide-set eyes had all the malleability of a cinder block.

"She's doing her job," he said.

"Tee Bobby didn't kill your daughter, Joe," I said.

"Then why were you asking about him down at that pickup corner, the one my little girl was abducted from?" he replied.

I blew out my breath and recrossed the street with Clete.

"Lighten up, Streak. I think Zerelda likes you. Notice how she squeezed her .357 when she told you to fuck off?" he said, his eyes beaming.

We went through the side entrance of the nightclub. It was loud and hot inside, the air hazy with cigarette smoke, dense with the smells of whiskey and boiled crabs and beer sweat. Tee Bobby was at the microphone, his long-sleeved lavender shirt plastered against his skin, a red electric guitar hanging from his neck. He drank from a long-necked bottle of Dixie beer and wiped the moisture out of his eyes on his sleeve and stumbled slightly against the microphone, then began singing "Breaking Up Is Hard to Do." His eyes were closed while he sang, his face suffused with a level of emotion that at first glance might have seemed manufactured until you heard the irrevocable sense of loss in his voice.

"Guitar Slim didn't have anything on this guy. Too bad he's a rag nose," Clete said.

"How do you know he is?" I asked.

"He was snorting lines off the toilet tank. I thought that might be a clue."

We found Jimmy Dean Styles in his office at the rear of the club. He sat at a cluttered desk, above which was a framed autographed photo of Sugar Ray Robinson. He was counting money, his fingers clicking on a calculator. His eyes lifted to mine.

"See, I went out of Angola max-time. That means I ain't got my umbilical cord thumbtacked to some P.O.'s desk. How about respecting that?" he said.

"Where'd you get the autographed photo of Sugar Ray?" I said.

"My grandfather was his sparring partner. You probably don't know that 'cause when you growed up most niggers around here picked peppers or cut cane," he replied.

"You told me you cut Tee Bobby loose. Now I see him up on your bandstand," I said.

"Little Albert Babineau own half this club. He feel sorry for Tee Bobby. I don't. Tee Bobby got a way of stuffing everything he make up his nose. So when he finish his gig tonight, he packing his shit." His eyes shifted to Clete. "Marse Charlie, don't be sitting on my desk."

"There's a guy outside named Joe Zeroski. I hope he comes in here," Clete said.

"Why's that, Marse Charlie?" Styles said.

"He was a mechanic for the Giacanos. Nine or so hits. Your kind of guy," Clete said.

"I'll be worried about that the rest of the night," Styles replied.

Clete stuck a matchstick in the corner of his mouth and stared at Styles, who had gone back to counting a stack of currency, his fingers dancing on the calculator.

I touched Clete on the arm and we walked back through the crowd and out the side door. The parking lot smelled of dust and tar, and the stars were hot and bright above the trees. Clete stared back into the club, his face perplexed.

"That guy's dirty. I don't know what for, but he's dirty." Then he said, "You think his grandfather really sparred with Sugar Ray Robinson?"

"Maybe. I remember he was a boxer."

"What happened to him?"

"He was lynched in Mississippi," I said.

But our evening at the club owned by Jimmy Dean Styles and Little Albert Babineau wasn't over. As Clete and I walked toward my truck, we heard the angry voices of two men behind us, the voices of others trying to restrain or pacify them. Then Tee Bobby and Jimmy Dean Styles burst out the back door into the parking lot, with a balloon of people following them.

There was a smear of blood and saliva on Tee Bobby's mouth. He swung at Styles's face and missed, and Styles pushed him down on the oyster shells.

"Touch me again, I'm gonna mess you up. Now haul your freight down the road," Styles said.

Tee Bobby got to his feet. His slacks were torn, his knees lacerated. He ran at Styles, his arms flailing. Styles set himself and hooked Tee Bobby in the jaw and dropped him as though he had used a baseball bat.

Tee Bobby got to his feet again and stumbled toward the crowd, swinging at anyone who tried to help him. One of his shoes was gone and his belt had come loose, exposing the elastic of his underwear.

"You're one sorry-ass, pitiful nigger," Styles said, and fitted his hand over Tee Bobby's face and shoved him backward into the crowd.

Tee Bobby reached in his pocket and flicked open a switchblade knife, but I doubted he had any idea whom he was going to use it on or even where he was. I started toward him.

"Mistake, Dave," I heard Clete say.

I came up behind Tee Bobby and grabbed him around the neck and twisted his wrist. There was little strength in his arm and the knife tinkled on the oyster shells. Then he began to fight, as a girl might, with his elbows and nails and feet. I locked my arms around him and carried him down the bank, through the trees, onto a dock, and flung him as far as I could into the bayou.

He went under, then burst to the surface in a cloud of mud and slapped at the water with both hands until his feet gained the bottom. He slipped and splashed through the shallows, grabbing the stems of elephant ears for purchase, his hair and body strung with dead vegetation.

Then, as the crowd from the nightclub flowed down the bank, someone switched on a flood lamp in the trees, burning away the darkness like a phosphorous flare, lighting me and Tee Bobby Hulin like figures frozen in a photograph of a waterside baptism.

At the edge of the crowd I saw Joe Zeroski and his niece Zerelda. Joe's face was incredulous, as though he had just walked into an open-air mental asylum. Clete lit a cigarette and rubbed the heel of his hand on his temple.

"*I* don't listen to you? Dave, you just threw a black man in the bayou while two hundred of his relatives watched. Way to go, big mon," he said.

I sat in the sheriff's office early the next morning. He was generally a quiet, avuncular man, looking forward to his retirement and the free time he would have to spend with his grandchildren. He did not contend with either the world or mortality, did not grieve upon the wrongs of his fellowman, and possessed a Rotarian view of both charity and business and saw one as a natural enhancement of the other. But sometimes on a wintry day I would catch him gazing out the window, a liquid glimmer in his eyes, and I knew he was back in his youth, on a long, white road that wound between white hills that were rounded like women's breasts, the road lined with chained-up Marine Corps six-bys and marching men whose coats and boots and steel pots were sheathed with snow.

He had just finished a phone conversation with the chief of police in St. Martinville. He opened the blinds on the window and stared at the crypts in St. Peter's Cemetery for a long time, his shoulders erect to compensate for the way his stomach protruded over his belt. His face was slightly flushed, his small mouth pinched. He removed his suit coat and placed it on the back of his chair, then brushed at the fabric as an afterthought but did not sit down. His cheeks were flecked with tiny blue and red veins. I could hear him breathing in the silence.

"You went out of your jurisdiction and made a bunch of people mad in St. Martinville. I can live with that. But you've deliberately involved Clete Purcel in department business. That's something I won't put up with, my friend," he said.

"Clete gave me a lead I didn't have."

"I got a call earlier from Joe Zeroski. You know what he said? 'This is how you guys solve cases? Fire up the cannibals?' I couldn't think of an adequate reply. Why are you still following Tee Bobby Hulin around?"

"I'm not convinced of his guilt."

"Who died and made you God, Dave? Tell Purcel he's not welcome in Iberia Parish."

I focused my gaze on a neutral space, my face empty.

"You AA guys have an expression, don't you, something about not carrying another person's load? How's it go? You'll break your own back without making the other person's burden lighter?" the sheriff said.

"Something like that."

"Why go to meetings if you don't listen to what people say at them?" he said.

"Clete thinks Jimmy Dean Styles might be a predator," I said.

"Go back to your office, Dave. One of us has a thinking disorder."

Later in the morning I passed the district attorney's office and saw Barbara Shanahan inside, talking to the young salesman who had dragged a suitcase filled with Bibles and encyclopedias and what he termed "family-type magazines" into my bait shop. What was the name? Oates? That was it, Marvin Oates. He was sitting in a wood chair, bending forward attentively, his eyes crinkling at something Barbara was saying.

I saw him again at noon when I was stopped by the traffic light at the four corners up on the Loreauville Road; this time he was pulling his suitcase on a roller skate up a street in a rural black slum by Bayou Teche. He tapped on the screen door of a clapboard shack that was propped up on cinder blocks. A meaty black woman in a purple dress opened the door for him, and he stepped inside and left his suitcase on the gallery. A moment later he opened the door again and took the suitcase inside with him. I parked in the convenience store at the four corners and bought a soft drink from the machine and drank it in the shade and waited for Marvin Oates to come out of the shack.

Thirty minutes later he walked back out in the sunlight and fitted his bleached cowboy straw hat on his
head and began pulling his suitcase down the street. I
drove up behind him and rolled down the window. He
wore a tie and a navy-blue sports coat in spite of the heat
and breathed with the slow inhalation of someone in a
steam room. But his face managed to fill with a grin
before he even knew whose vehicle had drawn abreast of
him.

"Why, howdy do, Mr. Robicheaux," he said.

"I see you and Barbara Shanahan are pretty good
friends," I said.

His grin remained on his face, as though incised in
clay, his eyes full of speculative light. He removed his hat
and fanned himself. His ash-blond hair was soggy with
sweat and there were gray strands in his sideburns, and I
realized he was older than he looked.

"I don't quite follow," he said. For just a second his
gaze lit on the shack he had just left.

"I saw you in Barbara's office this morning," I replied.

He nodded agreeably, as though a humorous mystery
had just been solved. He wiped the back of his neck with
a handkerchief and twisted his head and looked down
toward the end of the street, although nothing of particular interest was there.

"It's flat burning up, ain't it?" he said.

"In traveling through some of the other southern
parishes, have you run across a man by the name of
Legion? No first name, no last name, just Legion," I
said.

He raised his eyebrows thoughtfully. "An old man?
He worked in Angola at one time? Black folks walk

around him. He lives behind the old sugar mill down by
Baldwin. Know why I remember his name?" he said. His
face lit as he spoke the last sentence.

"No, why's that?" I said.

"'Cause when Jesus was fixing to heal this possessed
man, he asked the demon his name first. The demon said
his name was Legion. Jesus cast the demon into a herd of
hogs and the hogs run into the sea and drowned."

"Thanks for your help, Marvin. Did you sell a Bible to
the woman in that last house you were in?"

"Not really."

"I imagine it'd be a hard sell. She hooks in a joint on
Hopkins."

He looked guardedly up and down the road, his
expression cautionary now, one white man to another.
"The Mormons believe black people is descended from
the lost tribe of Ham. You think that's true?"

"Got me. You want a ride?"

"If you work in the fields of the Lord, you're suppose
to walk it, not just talk it."

His face was full of self-irony and boyish good cheer.
Even the streaks of sweat on his shirt, like the stripes a
flagellum would make on the chest of its victim, excited
sympathy for his plight and the humble role he had chosen for himself. If his smile could be translated into
words, it was perhaps the old adage that goodness is its
own reward.

I gave him the thumbs-up sign and made a mental
note to run his name through the computer at the
National Crime Information Center in Washington,
D.C., at the first opportunity.

CHAPTER 7

The next night Batist's sister banged down the dirt road in a dilapidated pickup that sounded like a dying animal when she parked it by the bait shop and turned off the ignition.

She sat down heavily at the counter and fished in her purse for a Kleenex and blew her nose, then stared at me as though it were I rather than she who was expected to explain her mission to my bait shop.

"Ain't nobody ever known the true story of what happened on Julian LaSalle's plantation," she said.

I nodded and remained silent.

"I had bad dreams about Legion since I was a girl. I been afraid that long," she said.

"Lots of us have bad memories from childhood. We shouldn't think less of ourselves for it, Clemmie," I said.

"I always tole myself God would punish Legion. Send him to hell where he belong."

"Maybe that'll happen."

"It ain't enough," she said.

Then she told me of the events following the death by fire of Julian LaSalle's wife.

Ladice went back to work in the fields but was not molested by Legion. In fact, he didn't bother any of the black girls or women and seemed preoccupied with other things. Vendors and servicepeople drove out to see him, rather than Julian LaSalle, with their deliveries or work orders for electrical or plumbing repairs on the plantation. Legion sometimes tethered his horse in the shade and went away with the vendors and servicepeople and did not return for hours, as though his duties in the fields had been reduced to a much lower level of priority and status.

Mr. Julian stayed in a guest cottage by the freshwater bay and was rarely seen except when he might emerge at evening in a robe and stand in the gloom of the trees next to the water's edge, unshaved, staring at the wooden bridge that led to the mainland and the community of small houses where most of his employees lived.

Sometimes his employees, perhaps washing their cars in the yard or barbecuing over a pit fashioned from a washing machine, would wave to him in the waning light, but Mr. Julian would not acknowledge the gesture, which would cause his employees to round up their children and go inside rather than let the happiness of their world contrast so visibly with the sorrow of his.

But to most of the black people on the plantation the die was cast three weeks after Mrs. LaSalle's death by an event that to outsiders would seem of little importance.

A bull alligator, one that was at least twelve feet long, had come out of the bay in the early dawn and caught a terrapin in its jaws. Down the bank, a black woman had left her diapered child momentarily unattended in the backyard. When the child began crying, the alligator lumbered out of the mist into the yard, rheumy-eyed, pieces of sinew and broken terrapin shell hanging from its teeth, its green-black hide slick with mud and strung incongruously with blooming water hyacinths.

The mother bolted hysterically into the yard and scooped her child into her arms and ran all the way down the road to the plantation store, screaming Mr. Julian's name.

Mr. Julian knew every alligator nesting hole on or near the island, the sandbars where they fed on raccoons, the corners and cuts in the channels where they hung in the current waiting for nutria and muskrat to swim across their vision.

Mr. Julian hunted rogue alligators in his canoe. He'd paddle quietly along the bank, then stand suddenly, his balance perfect, lift his deer rifle to his shoulder, and drill a solitary .30–06 round between the alligator's eyes.

Mr. Julian had his faults, but neglecting the safety of a child was not one of them.

The woman who had run to the plantation store was told by the clerk to return home, that someone would take care of the gator that had strayed into her yard.

"Mr. Julian gonna bring his gun down to my house?" she said.

"Legion is handling things right now," the clerk said.

"Mr. Julian always say tell him when a gator come up

in the yard. He say go right on up to the house and bang on the do'," the woman said.

The clerk removed a pencil from behind his ear and wet the point in his mouth and wrote something on a pad. Then he took a peppermint cane out of a glass case and gave it to the woman's child.

"I'm putting a note for Legion in his mailbox. You seen me do hit. Now you take your baby on home and don't be bothering folks about this no more," he said.

But three days passed and no one hunted the rogue alligator.

The same black woman returned to the store. "You promised Legion gonna get rid of that gator. Where Mr. Julian at?" she said.

"Send your husband down here," the clerk said.

"Suh?" the woman said.

"Send your man here. I want to know if y'all plan to keep working on Poinciana Island," the clerk said.

Two days later Legion and another white man showed up behind the black woman's house and flung a cable and a barbed steel hook through the fork of a cypress tree on the water's edge. They spiked one end of the cable into the cypress trunk and baited the hook with a plucked chicken carcass and a dead blackbird and threw the hook out into the lily pads.

That night, under a full moon, the gator slipped through the reeds and the hyacinths and the layer of algae that floated in the shallows and struck the bait. Its tail threw water onto the bank for fifteen feet.

In the morning the gator lay in the shallows, exhausted, hooked solidly through the top of the snout, through sinew and bone, so that its struggle was useless, no matter how often it wrenched against the cable or thrashed the water with its tail.

Legion left the gator on the hook until dusk, when he and two other white men backed a truck up to the cypress tree and looped the free end of the cable through the truck's bumper. Then they pulled the cable through the fork of the tree, grinding off the bark, hoisting the gator halfway out of the water, its pale yellow stomach spinning in the last red glow of sunlight in the west.

Legion slipped on a pair of rubber boots and waded into the shallows and swung an ax into the gator's head. But the angle was bad and the gator was only stunned. Legion swung again, whacking the blade into its neck, then he hit it again and again, like a man who knows the strength and courage and ferocity of his adversary is greater than his own and that his own efforts would be worthless on an equal playing field. Finally the gator's stubby legs quivered stiffly and its tail knotted over and became motionless in the hyacinths below.

Legion and his two workmen skinned out the carcass and left the meat to rot and took the hide to a tanner in Morgan City.

The next afternoon Ladice's mother received a call from a white woman who ran a laundry in New Iberia. The white woman said one of her regular girls was sick and she needed Ladice's mother to fill in. That evening. Not the next day. That evening or not at all.

Just after dark Legion came to Ladice's house. He didn't knock; he simply opened the front door and walked into the front room. His khakis were starched and pressed, his jaws freshly shaved. The top of a thick silver watch, with a Lima construction fob on it, protruded from the watch pocket in his trousers. He removed a toothpick from his mouth.

"You getting along all right?" he asked.

She was cutting bread that she had just baked and her face was hot from the oven, her T-shirt damp with perspiration against her breasts.

"My mother gonna be back soon, Legion."

"Your mother's working at the laundry tonight. I give her name to Miz Delcambre. I thought y'all could use the money." He cupped his hand on her shoulder.

"Don't mess wit' me," she said.

His hand left her person, but she could feel his breath on her skin, his loins an inch from one of her buttocks.

"You gonna tell Mr. Julian on me?" he asked.

"If you make me."

"I wonder what it was like for Mr. Julian's wife to be locked in that burning room, grabbing that hot grillwork with her bare hands, trying to pull open the do' he locked from the outside. Don't nobody else know how that po' woman died, no," Legion said.

Ladice drew the butcher knife through the loaf of bread. The knife was thick at the top, the color of an old five-cent piece, wood-handled, the cutting edge ground on an emery wheel. She felt the knife snick into the chopping board. Legion touched her cheek with the ball of his finger.

"Mr. Julian sold me a quarter hoss for ten dollars. I liked that hoss so much, me, I went back and bought four more, same price," he said.

"What I care?" she said.

"Them hoss worth a hunnerd-fifty apiece. Why you t'ink he give me such a good price?" Legion said.

She concentrated on her work and tried to hide the expression on her face, but he could see the recognition grow in the corner of her eye. He stroked her hair and the callused edges of his fingers brushed lightly against her skin. Then he slipped his hand down her back and she felt his sex swelling against her. "You t'ink you worth more than them hoss, Ladice?" he asked.

His words were like an obscene presence on her skin, as though Legion knew her in a way that no one else did, knew the truth about her real worth, as though all her self-deception and vanity and her attempt to manipulate Mr. Julian's carnality for her own ends had made her deserving of anything Legion wished to do to her. He placed his hand loosely on her wrist, then removed the knife from her grasp and set it in a pan of greasy water and picked her up against his chest, locking his arms around her rib cage, squeezing until her head reared back in pain and her knees opened and clenched his hips and her hands fought to find purchase around his neck.

"A colored man ever hold you that tight, Ladice?" he said.

He carried her in that position through the curtained entrance to her bedroom.

After he dropped her on top of the quilt, her eyes brimming with water, he sat on the side of the bed and formed a triangle over her with his arms and sternum and stared into her face. "I ain't a bad man, no. I'm gonna treat you a whole lot better than that old man. You gonna see, you," he said.

*   *   *

Perhaps she tried to report Legion to Mr. Julian. No one ever knew. Mr. Julian received no visitors and was often unwashed and drunk. He forgot to feed his Labrador retriever and the animal had to beg food scraps from the back doors of Negro homes along the bay. To people on East Main, where most of his peers lived, he was an object of pity when they saw him escorted by his elderly black chauffeur into the doctor's office for his medical appointments. On one occasion an old friend, a man who had been a recipient of the Medal of Honor in the Great War, persuaded Mr. Julian to join him at the Frederic Hotel for a meal. At the table Mr. Julian became very still and his face filled with shame. The elderly ex-soldier did not understand and wondered what he could have said to hurt his friend, then realized that Mr. Julian had soiled himself.

But one fine morning Mr. Julian awoke before dawn, seemingly a new man, and worked in his flower garden and bathed in a great iron tub in the washhouse behind the cottage and watched the sun rise and the mullet fly on the bay. He packed a suitcase and whistled a song and dressed in a white linen suit and put on his Panama hat and had his driver take him to the train depot in New Iberia, where he caught the Sunset Limited for New Orleans. From the club car, a drink in his hand, he watched the familiar world he had grown up in, one of columned homes and oak-lined streets and gentle people, slip past the window.

In New Orleans he checked into a luxury hotel on Canal and while unpacking he heard a woman weeping through the wall. When he knocked on her door, she told him her husband had left her and their ten-year-old daughter and she was sorry for her emotional behavior.

He drank whiskey sours in the bar and danced with the cocktail waitress. That evening he dined at the Court of Two Sisters and strolled through the French Quarter and attended a religious service in a storefront church whose congregation was composed mostly of black people. In front of St. Louis Cemetery he talked about baseball with a beat cop and put a twenty-dollar bill in the begging can of a blind woman.

A formal dance was being held at his hotel, and he stood in the entrance of the ballroom and watched the dancers and listened to the orchestra, his hat held loosely on his fingers, his face marked with a wistfulness that caused the hostess to invite him inside. Then he stopped for a cup of coffee in the bar and asked that a dozen roses and a dish of ice cream, with cinnamon sprinkled on it, be sent up to his room. When the tray was delivered on a cart, he instructed the waiter to leave it in the corridor.

A few moments later Mr. Julian moved the cart in front of the door of the woman whose husband had abandoned her and their daughter. He tapped with the brass knocker on her door and went back inside his room and opened the French doors that gave onto the balcony and looked out at the pink glow of the sky over Lake Pontchartrain while the curtains puffed in the breeze around his head. Then Julian LaSalle mounted the rail on the balcony and like a giant white crane sailed out over the streetcars and the flow of traffic and the neon-lit palm trees along the neutral ground twelve stories below.

CHAPTER 8

In the morning I ran the name of Marvin Oates, the Bible salesman, through the NCIC computer.

But the sheet I got back contained no surprises. Besides his arrest on a bad check charge, he had been picked up for nothing more serious than petty theft and failure to appear, panhandling in New Orleans, and causing a disturbance at a homeless shelter in Los Angeles.

"You know a guy named Marvin Oates?" I asked Helen.

She was gazing out my office window, her hands in her back pockets.

"His mother was a drunk who used to drift in and out of town?" she asked.

"I'm not sure."

"She was from Mississippi or Alabama. They used to live by the train tracks. What about him?"

"He was trying to sell door-to-door out by my house. I didn't like the way he looked at Alafair."

"Get used to it."

"Pardon?"

"Your daughter's beautiful. What do you expect?"

She laughed to herself as she walked out the door.

I waited five minutes, then went down the corridor to her office.

"You ever hear of an overseer on Poinciana Island by the name of Legion?" I asked.

"No. Who is he?" she replied.

"This character Oates says 'Legion' is the name of a demon in the New Testament. Oates believes people of color are descended from the lost tribe of Ham. Think Oates might be unusual in any way?"

She brushed at her nose with a Kleenex and went back to reading an open file on her desk.

"Take a ride with me down to Baldwin," I said.

"What for?"

"I thought I might check out a guy from my boyhood."

We drove south on the four-lane, through sugarcane acreage that had been created out of the alluvial floodplain of Bayou Teche. The sky was sealed with clouds that had the bright sheen of silk or steam but offered no rain, and I could see cracks in the baked rows of the cane fields and dust devils spinning across the road and breaking apart on the asphalt. The air smelled like salt and the odor a streetcar gives off when it scotches across an electrical connection. Up ahead was the gray outline of an abandoned sugar mill.

When we are injured emotionally or systematically

humiliated or made to feel base about ourselves in our youth, we are seldom given the opportunity later to confront our persecutors on equal terms and to show them up for the cowards they are. So we often create a surrogate scenario in which the vices of our tormentors, the fears that fed their cruelty, the self-loathing that drove them to hurt the innocent, eventually consume them and make them worthy of pity and in effect drive them from our lives.

But sometimes the dark fate that should have been theirs just does not shake properly out of the box.

Helen pulled off the road and stopped at a small grocery store in front of a cluster of shacks. In the distance the rectangular tin outline of the sugar mill was silhouetted against the sky. On the side of the grocery was a crude porte cochere and under it sat a thin, black-haired man in a blood-smeared butcher's apron, peeling potatoes and onions into a stainless-steel cauldron that was boiling on a grated butane burner that rested on the ground. Close by, a gunnysack crackling with live crawfish lay on top of a wood worktable.

I opened my badge holder. "I was looking for a fellow by the name of Legion," I said.

"Legion Guidry?" the man said. He dropped the peeled onions and potatoes into the cauldron and dumped a bowl of artichokes and husked yellow corn on top of them.

"I only know him by the name Legion," I said.

"He don't come in here," the man said.

"Where's he live?" I asked.

The man shook his head and didn't reply. He turned his back on me and began cutting open a box of seasoning.

"Sir, I asked you a question," I said.

"He works at the casino. Go ax up there. He don't come in here," the man replied. He raised his finger for added emphasis.

Helen and I drove to the casino on the Indian reservation, a garish obscenity of a building that had been constructed in what was once a rural Indian slum overgrown with persimmons and gum trees and swamp maples. Now the poor whites and blacks, the trusting and the naive, the working-class pensioners and the welfare recipients and those who signed their names with an *X*, crowded the gaming tables inside an air-conditioned, hermetically sealed, sunless environment, where cigarette smoke clung to the skin like damp cellophane. Collectively they managed to feed enormous sums of money into an apparatus that funneled most of it to Las Vegas and Chicago, all with the blessing of the State of Louisiana and the United States government.

A St. Mary Parish deputy sheriff, directing traffic in the casino parking lot, told us where we could find the man named Legion. The man who had once lived in my childhood dreams was down the road, under a picnic shelter, eating a barbecue sandwich on top of a paper towel that he had spread neatly on the table to catch his crumbs. He wore a starched gray uniform, with dark blue flaps on the pockets, and a polished brass name tag on his shirt, with his title, Head of Security, under the engraved letters of his name. His hair was still black, with white streaks in it, his face creased vertically with furrows like those in dried fruit. A crude caricature of a naked woman was tattooed with blue ink on the underside of each of his forearms.

I looked at him a long time without speaking.

"Can I hep you wit' somet'ing?" he said.

"You were an overseer at Poinciana Island?" I asked.

He folded the paper towel around his sandwich and pitched it toward the trash barrel. It struck the side of the barrel and fell apart on the ground.

"Who want to know?" he asked.

I opened my badge holder in my palm.

"I used to be. A long time ago," he said.

"You rape a black woman by the name of Ladice Hulin?" I asked.

He put an unfiltered cigarette in his mouth and lit it and exhaled the smoke across the tops of his cupped fingers. Then he removed a piece of tobacco from his tongue and looked at it.

"That bitch still spreadin' them rumor, huh?" he said.

"Let me run something else by you, Legion. That's the name you go by, right? Legion? No first name, no last name?" I said.

"I know you?" he asked.

"Yeah, you do. My brother and I walked up on you and some other white trash while y'all were copulating in an automobile. You opened a knife on me. I was twelve years old."

His eyes shifted on mine and stayed there. "You're a goddamn liar," he said.

"I see," I said. I looked at my feet and thought about the mindless animus in his stare, the arrogance and stupidity and insult in his words, the ignorance that he and his kind used like a weapon against their adversaries. I heard Helen shift her weight on the gravel. "What I wanted to run by you, Legion, is the fact there's no statute of limitations on a homicide. Nor on complicity in a homicide. You getting my drift on this?"

"No."

"Julian LaSalle's wife was locked in her room the night she burned to death. That's called negligent homicide. You removed the key from the deadbolt and inserted it on the inside of the door in order to protect Mr. Julian. Then you blackmailed him."

He stood up from the picnic table and put his pack of cigarettes in his shirt pocket and buttoned the flap.

"You t'ink I care what some nigger done tole you?" He cleared his throat and spat a glob of phlegm two inches from my shoe. A trace of splatter, like strands of cobweb, clung to the cuff of my trouser leg.

"How old are you, sir?" I asked.

"Seventy-four."

"I'm going to stick it to you. For all the black women you molested and raped, for all the defenseless people you humiliated and degraded. That's a promise, partner."

He lifted his chin and rubbed the whiskers on his throat, the cast in his green eyes as ancient and devoid of moral light as those in a prehistoric, scale-covered creature breaking from the egg.

A week passed. Clete Purcel went back to New Orleans, then returned to New Iberia to hunt down more of Nig Rosewater and Wee Willie Bimstine's bail skips. On Monday Clete and I went to Victor's, a cafeteria located on Main Street in a refurbished nineteenth-century building with a high, stamped ceiling, where cops and businesspeople and attorneys often ate lunch.

"Check out the pair by the cashier," Clete said.

I turned around and saw Zerelda Calucci and Perry LaSalle at a small table, their heads bent toward each other, a solitary rose in a small vase between them.

But Clete and I were not the only ones who had taken notice of them. Barbara Shanahan was eating at another table, her muted anger growing in her face.

When Clete and I walked outside, Zerelda and Perry were across the street in the parking lot. Perry opened the passenger door of his Gazelle for Zerelda to get inside. Barbara Shanahan stood on the sidewalk in a white suit, staring at them, her eyes smoldering.

"What's the deal with Zerelda Calucci and Perry?" I asked.

"Ask *him*," she replied.

"I'm asking you."

"She was always one of his on-again, off-again groupies. Perry likes to think of himself as the great benefactor of the underclass. It's part of his mystical persona."

"She's Joe Zeroski's niece. Zeroski thinks Tee Bobby Hulin killed both the Boudreau girl and his daughter. Why's Zerelda hanging with Tee Bobby's defense attorney?"

"Duh, I don't know, Dave. Why don't you research the LaSalle family history? Are you sure you're in the right line of work?" Barbara said.

"What's that supposed to mean?" I asked.

"God, you're stupid," she replied.

She crossed the street and walked down to the bayou, where she lived by herself in a waterfront apartment surrounded by banana trees.

"That broad gives me a boner just watching her walk," Clete said.

"Clete, will you—" I began.

"How long ago was she LaSalle's punch?" he said.

"Why do you always have to ask questions that offer a presumption as a truth? Why don't you show a little humility about other people once in a while?"

"Right," he said, sticking a cigarette in the corner of his mouth, his face thoughtful. "You think she might dig an older guy?"

That afternoon I was visited by the parents of Amanda Boudreau. They sat side by side in front of my desk, their faces impassive, their eyes never lingering on any particular object, as though they were sitting in a vacuum and addressing voices and concerns that were alien to all their prior experience. They wore their best clothes, probably purchased at a discount store in Lafayette, but they looked like people who might have recently drowned and not become aware of their fate.

"We don't know what's going on," the father said.

"I'm sorry, I don't understand," I said.

"A woman came to our house yesterday. She told us she was a detective," he said.

"Her name was Calucci. Zerelda Calucci," the mother said.

"She asked how long Amanda was seeing Tee Bobby Hulin," the father said.

"What?" I said.

"She said our daughter was seeing Bobby Hulin," the mother said.

"Why's she saying this about our daughter? Why you

sending out people like this to our house?" the father said.

"Zerelda Calucci is not a police officer. She's a private investigator from New Orleans. I suspect she's now working for the defense," I said.

They were both silent for several moments, their faces pinched with the knowledge that they had been deceived, that again someone had stolen something from their lives.

"People are saying you don't believe Bobby Hulin killed Amanda," the mother said.

I tried to return her and her husband's stare, but I felt my eyes break.

"I guess I'm not sure what happened out there," I said.

"This morning we took flowers out to the spot where Amanda died. Her blood is still on the grass. You can come out there with me and look at our daughter's blood and maybe that'll hep you see what happened," the father said.

"Call me if the Calucci woman bothers you again," I said.

"What for?" the mother asked.

"Pardon?" I said.

"I said, 'What for?' I don't think you're on our side, Mr. Robicheaux. I saw the man who killed our daughter in the grocery store this morning, buying coffee and doughnuts and orange juice, laughing with the cashier. Now people are saying Amanda was his girlfriend, the man who tied her up with a jump rope and killed her with a shotgun. I think y'all ought to be ashamed, you most of all," she said.

I looked out the window of my office until she and her husband were gone.

That evening, after work, I drove south of town and crossed the freshwater bay onto Poinciana Island. As I followed the winding road through hillocks and cypress and gum trees and live oaks that were almost two centuries old, I could feel the attraction that had probably kept the LaSalles and their vision of themselves intact for so many generations. The island was as close to Eden as the earth got. The evening sky was ribbed with purple and red clouds. In the trees I could see deer and out on the bay flying fish that were bronze and scarlet in the sunset. The lichen on the oaks, the lacy canopy overhead, the pooled water and the mushrooms and layers of blackened leaves and pecan husks back in the shade, all created a sense of botanical insularity that had not been tainted by the clank of engines and the smells of gasoline and diesel or the heat that rose from city cement. In effect, Poinciana Island had successfully avoided the twentieth century.

If I owned this place, would I willingly give it up? If I had to deal in slaves to keep it, would I not be tempted to allow the Prince of Darkness to have his way with my business affairs once in a while?

These were thoughts I didn't care to dwell on.

Perry lived in a two-story house constructed of soft, variegated brick that had been recovered from torn-down antebellum homes in South Carolina. The royal palms that towered over the house had been transported by boat from Key West, their enormous root balls wrapped in canvas that was wet down constantly with buckets of fresh water. The one-acre pond in back, which had a dock with a pirogue moored to it (no motorized boats were allowed on the island), had been stocked years ago with fingerling bass, and now some of them had grown to fifteen pounds, their backs as dark green and thick across as moss-slick logs when they roiled the surface among the lily pads.

And that's where I saw Perry, on a scrolled-iron bench by the waterside, casting a lure in a long arc out over the dimpled stillness of the pond's surface.

But he was lost in his own thoughts, and they did not seem happy ones, when I walked up behind him.

"Having any luck?" I asked.

"Oh, Dave, how you doin'? No, it's slow tonight."

"Try a telephone crank. It works every time," I said.

He smiled at my joke.

"Amanda Boudreau's parents were in to see me today," I said. "It wasn't a good experience. Zerelda Calucci went to their house and gave them the impression she was a police officer."

"Maybe it was a misunderstanding," Perry said.

"She's working for you?"

"You could say that."

"What's Joe Zeroski have to say about that?"

"I don't know. He's back in New Orleans. Listen, Dave, Zee is a good P.I. She's found two people who say they saw Amanda Boudreau and Tee Bobby together. The Boudreau girl's DNA was on his watch cap, all right, but it didn't get there at the crime scene."

"Tee Bobby is almost fourteen years older than Amanda Boudreau was. She was a straight-A, traditional Catholic girl who didn't hang around juke joints or petty criminal wiseasses."

"What you mean is she didn't hang around black musicians."

"Read it any way you want. I get the sense you're using this Calucci woman for your own ends."

"You come out to my house without calling, then you insult me. You're too much, Dave."

"A friend of mine thinks you and Barbara Shanahan were an item at one time."

"I suspect you're talking about that trained rhino who follows you around, what's his name, Purcel? He's an interesting guy. Tell him to keep his mouth off me and Barbara Shanahan."

Through the trees I could see the sun glimmering on the bay like points of fire.

"When I walked down to the pond and saw you on the bench here, I was put in mind of Captain Dreyfus. It's a foolish comparison, I guess," I said.

He reeled in his lure until it was snug against the tip of his rod, then idly flicked drops of water off it onto the pond's surface.

"I like you, Dave. I really do. Just cut me a little slack, will you?" he said.

"By the way, I ran down a guy named Legion, one of your old overseers. He raped Ladice Hulin. Can you figure out how a guy like that became head of security at the casino? Something else, too. Zerelda Calucci comes from a Mafia family. Is that how you know her, through your grandfather's old connections?" I said.

Perry's lips parted and the blood drained out of his cheeks. He clenched his fishing rod in his hand and walked up the embankment toward his house, the azaleas and four-o'clocks in his yard rippling with color in the shade.

Then he flung the fishing rod against a porch column and walked back down the slope and faced me, his hands balled into fists.

"Get this straight. Barbara might hate my guts, but I respect her. Number two, I'm not my grandfather, you self-righteous son of a bitch. But that doesn't mean he was a bad man. Now get off my property," he said.

CHAPTER 9

The next Saturday was a festive day for New Iberia, featuring a citywide cleaning of the streets by volunteers, a free crawfish boil in City Park, and a sixteen-mile foot race that began with a grand assemblage of the runners under the trees by the recreation center. At 8 A.M. they took off, jogging down an asphalt road that meandered through the live oaks and out onto the street, their bodies hard and sinewy inside a golden tunnel of mist and sunlight that seemed to have been created especially for the young at heart.

They thundered past an art class that was sketching on the tables under the picnic shelters. Among the runners was every kind of person, the narcissistic and passionately athletic, the lonely and inept who loved any community ritual, and those who humbly ignored their limitations and were content simply to finish the race, even if last.

There was another group, too, whose psychology was less easily defined, whose normal pursuits separated them from their fellowmen but who sought membership in the crowd, perhaps to convince both others and themselves that they were made of the same stuff as the rest of us. On a gold-green morning, under oaks hung with Spanish moss, who would begrudge them their participation in a fine event that ultimately celebrated what was best in ourselves?

Jimmy Dean Styles wore a black spandex gym suit that looked like a shiny plastic graft on his skin. Three of his rappers ran at his side, their hair dyed orange or blue and purple, their eyebrows and noses pierced with jeweled rings. Behind them I saw the door-to-door magazine-and-encyclopedia-and-Bible salesman, Marvin Oates, a soggy sweatband crimped around his hair, his olive skin stretched as tightly as a lampshade on his ribs and vertebrae, his scarlet running shorts wrapped wetly on his loins, emphasizing the crack in his buttocks.

After the runners had streamed by the old brick firehouse onto a neighborhood side street, one member of the art class began to draw furiously on her sketch pad, her face bent almost to the paper, a grinding sound emanating from her throat.

"What's wrong, Rosebud?" the art teacher asked.

But the young black woman, whose name was Rosebud Hulin, didn't reply. Her charcoal pencil filled the page, then she dropped the pencil to the ground and began to hit the table with her fists, trembling all over.

After the race I drove home and showered, then returned to City Park with Alafair and Bootsie for the

crawfish boil. The art teacher, who was a nun and a volunteer at the city library, found me at the picnic pavilion
by the National Guard Armory, not far from the spot
where years ago the man named Legion had opened a
knife on a twelve-year-old boy.

"Would you take a walk with me?" she asked, motion-
ing toward a stand of trees by the armory.

She was an attractive, self-contained woman in her
sixties and not one to burden others with her concerns or
to look for complexities that in the final analysis she
believed human beings held no sway over. A large piece
of art paper was rolled up in her hands. She smiled awk-
wardly. "What is it, Sister?" I said when we were alone.

"You know Rosebud Hulin?" she asked.

"Tee Bobby's twin sister?" I replied.

"She's an autistic savant. She can reproduce in exact
detail a photograph or painting she's seen only once,
maybe one she saw years ago. But she's never been able
to create images out of her imagination. It's as though
light goes from her eye through her arm onto the page."

"I'm not following you."

"This morning she drew this figure," the art teacher
said, unrolling the charcoal drawing for me to see.

I stared down at a reclining female nude, the wrists
crossed above the head, a crown of thorns fastened on
the brow. The woman's mouth was open in a silent
scream, like the figure in the famous painting by Munch.
The eyes were oversize, elongated, wrapped around the
head, filled with despair.

Two skeletal trees stood in the foreground, with
branches that looked like sharpened pikes.

"The eyes are a little like a Modigliani, but Rosebud

didn't re-create this from any painting or picture I ever saw," the art teacher said.

"Why are you bringing me this, Sister?"

She gazed at the smoke from cook fires drifting into the trees.

"I'm not sure. Or maybe I'm not sure I want to say. I had to take Rosebud into the rest room and wash her face. That gentle girl tried to hit me."

"Did she tell you why she drew the picture?"

"She always says the pictures she draws are put in her head by God. I think maybe this one came from somewhere else," the art teacher said.

"Can I keep this?" I asked.

On Monday I called Ladice Hulin's house on Poinciana Island and asked to speak to Tee Bobby.

"He's at work," she said.

"Where?" I asked.

"The Carousel Club in St. Martinville."

"That's Jimmy Dean Styles's place. Styles told me he wasn't going to let Tee Bobby play there again."

"You ax where he work. I tole you. I said anyt'ing about music?"

I drove up the bayou to St. Martinville and parked in the lot behind the Carousel Club. The garbage piled against the back wall hummed with flies and reeked of dead shrimp. Tee Bobby was using a wide-bladed shovel to scoop up the rotted matter and slugs that oozed from a mound of split vinyl bags.

He was sweating profusely, his eyes like BBs when he looked at me.

"You're doing scut work for Jimmy Sty?" I said.

"Ain't no clubs want to hire me. Jimmy give me a job."

He slung a shovel-load of garbage into the back of a pickup truck. His eyes were filled with a peculiar light, the irises jittering.

"You looked like you cooked your head, podna," I said.

"Cain't you leave me be, man?"

"I want to show you something."

I started to unroll his sister's drawing, but he speared his shovel into a swollen bag of garbage and went through the side door of the club. I used a pay phone at the grocery down the street and called the St. Martin Parish Sheriff's Department to let them know I was on their turf, then went inside the club. The chairs were stacked on the tables and a fat black woman was mopping the floor. Tee Bobby sat at the bar, his face in his hands, the streamers from an air-conditioning unit blowing above his head.

I flattened the sketch of the reclining nude on the bar.

"Rosebud drew this. Look at the crossed wrists, the fear and despair in the woman's eyes, the scream that's about to come from her mouth. What's that make you think of, Tee Bobby?" I said.

He stared down at the drawing and took a breath and wet his lips. Then he blew his nose on a handkerchief to hide the expression on his face.

"Perry LaSalle say I ain't got to talk wit' you," he said.

I clenched his wrist and flattened his hand on the paper.

"For just a second feel the pain and terror in that drawing, Tee Bobby. Look at me and tell me you don't know what we're talking about," I said.

He pressed his head down on his fists. His T-shirt was gray with sweat; his pulse was leaping in his throat.

"Why don't you just put a bullet in me?" he said.

"You got a meth problem, Tee Bobby? Somebody giving you crystal to straighten out the kinks?" I said.

He started to speak, then he saw a silhouette out of the corner of his eye. I didn't think his face could look sicker than it did, but I was wrong.

Jimmy Dean Styles walked from his office and crossed the dance floor and went behind the bar. He wore a maroon silk shirt unbuttoned on his chest and gray slacks that hung low on the smooth taper of his stomach. He opened a small refrigerator behind the bar and removed a container of coleslaw, then began eating it with a plastic fork, his eyes drifting casually to Rosebud's drawing. He tilted his head curiously.

"What you got, my man?" he asked.

"This is a police matter. I'd appreciate your not intruding," I said.

Styles chewed his food thoughtfully, his eyes focused out the open front door.

"Tee Bobby ain't did you nothing. Let the cat have some peace," he said.

"For a guy who busted him up on the oyster shells, you're a funny advocate," I said.

"Maybe we got our disagreements, but he's still my friend. Look, the man's coming down wit' the flu. Ain't he got enough misery?" Styles said.

I rolled up Rosebud's drawing. "I'll be around," I said.

"Oh, yeah, I know. I got a broken toilet that's the same way. No matter what I do, it just keep running out on the flo'," Styles said.

When I got back to the department, I went into the office of a plainclothes detective who worked Narcotics. His name was Kevin Dartez and he wore long-sleeved white shirts and narrow, knit ties and a pencil-thin black mustache. His younger sister had been what is called a rock queen, or crack whore, and had died of her addiction. Dartez's ferocity toward black dealers who pimped for white girls was a legend in south Louisiana law enforcement.

"You seen any crystal meth around?" I asked.

"Out-of-towners bring it into the French Quarter. That's about it so far," he replied, tilted back in his swivel chair, hands clasped behind his head.

"The Carousel Club in St. Martinville? I wonder if anyone's ever tossed that place. Who owns the Carousel, anyway?" I said.

"Say again?" Dartez said, sitting up straight in his chair.

That afternoon Helen came into my office and sat on the corner of my desk and looked down at a yellow legal pad she had propped on her thigh.

"I've found three or four people who say they saw Tee Bobby with Amanda Boudreau. But it was always in a public place, like he'd see her and try to strike up a conversation," she said.

"You think they had some kind of secret relationship?" I asked.

"None I could find. I get the sense Tee Bobby was just a routine pain in the ass Amanda tried to avoid."

I dropped a paper clip I had been fiddling with on my desk blotter and rubbed my forehead.

"How do you think it's going to go?" I asked.

"The fact Tee Bobby and Amanda were seen together provides another explanation for Amanda's DNA being on Tee Bobby's watch cap. The right jury, he might skate."

"I think we need to start over," I said.

"Where?"

"Amanda's boyfriend," I replied.

After school hours we drove up the Teche to the little town of Loreauville. The pecan trees were in new leaf; a priest was watering his flowers in front of the Catholic church; kids were playing softball in a schoolyard. The moderate-size brick grocery that advertised itself as a supermarket, the saloon on the corner by the town's only traffic signal, the humped dark green shapes of the oaks along the bayou were out of a Norman Rockwell world of years ago. Down the main thoroughfare was an independently owned drive-in hamburger joint, the parking lot sprinkled with teenagers.

In their midst was Amanda's boyfriend, whose name was Roland Chatlin, in starched khakis and a green and white Tulane T-shirt, bouncing a golf ball off the side of the building. When Helen and I approached him, he was drinking a soda pop and talking to a friend and, amazingly, seemed not to recognize us. All the kids in the parking lot were white.

"Remember us?" I asked.

"Oh, yeah, you," he said, chewing gum, his eyes lighting now.

"Step over here, please," I said.

"Sure," he replied, blowing out his breath, slipping his hands into his pockets.

"Your inability to help us is causing us all kinds of problems, Roland. You tell us two black guys in ski masks murdered Amanda, but that's as far as we get," I said.

"Sir?" he said.

"You've got no idea who they were. You can't tell us what their voices sounded like. You can't even tell us how tall they were. I've got the feeling maybe you don't want us to catch them," I said.

"Look at us, not at the ground," Helen said.

"Your hands were tied with nothing but your shirt. You could have gotten loose if you'd wanted to, couldn't you? But you were too scared. Maybe you even begged. Maybe you told these guys their identity was safe. When people fear for their lives, they do all kinds of things they're ashamed of later, Roland. But it was pretty hard to just lie there and listen to them rape your girl, wasn't it?" I said.

"Maybe it's time to get it off your chest, kid," Helen said.

"Have you ever seen Tee Bobby Hulin play in a local club?" I asked.

"Yes, sir. I mean, I don't remember."

He had dark hair and light skin, arms without muscular definition, narrow hips, and a feminine mouth. Involuntarily he felt for a religious medal through the cloth of his shirt.

"Out at the crime scene you called them niggers. You don't care for black people, Roland?" I said.

"I was mad when I said that."

"I don't blame you. Which guy shot her?" I said.

"I don't know. I didn't think they were gonna—"

"They weren't gonna what?" I said.

"Nothing. You got me mixed up. That's why you're here. My daddy says I don't have to talk to y'all anymore."

Then his face darkened, as though the politeness toward adults that was mandatory in his world had been replaced by other instincts.

"They shove people around at school. They take the little kids' lunch money. They carry guns in their cars. Why don't you go after *them?*" he said vaguely, sweeping his hand at the air.

"Hear this, Roland," Helen said. "If you know who these guys are and you're lying to us, I'm going to find the shotgun that killed Amanda and jam it up your ass and pull the trigger myself. Tell *that* to your old man."

Two nights later the air was cool and dry, and the cypress trees in the swamp bloomed with heat lightning. Clete came into the bait shop as I was closing up. I smelled him before I saw him.

He helped himself to a water glass off a wall shelf and sat down heavily at the counter and unscrewed the cap from a pint bottle of bourbon wrapped in a brown-paper sack. A noxious fog, an odor of suntan lotion and cigarette smoke and beer sweat, begin to fill the shop like a living presence. Clete poured four fingers of whiskey in his glass and drank it slowly, watching me turn the electric fan on an overhead shelf in his direction. The lid of his left eye was swollen, a bruise like a small blue mouse in the crow's-feet at the corner.

"You got a reason for trying to blow me out the door?" he asked.

"Nope. How you doin', Cletus?"

"Joe Zeroski is back in town. At my motor court with Zerelda Calucci and half the greaseballs in New Orleans. Last night I'm trying to take a nap and this collection of shitbags are cooking sausages on a hibachi ten feet from my window and playing a Tony Bennett tape loud enough to be heard in Palermo. So I make the mistake of talking to them like they're human beings, asking them politely to dial it down a few notches so I can get some sleep.

"What do I get? Nothing, like I'm not there. I go, 'Look, just face your stereo the other way, okay?' One guy says, 'Hey, Purcel, I got your ten-inch frank right here. You want it with mustard?' and grabs his flopper while the other greaseballs laugh.

"So I go back inside, take a shower, put on fresh clothes, comb my hair, give these assholes every chance to go somewhere else. When I go outside, they're still there, except now Zerelda Calucci is sitting at the picnic table with them, the tops of her ta-tas sticking out like beach balls, her shorts rolled up so tight they almost split when she crosses her legs.

"So I walk over and ask her out for a late dinner, figuring that ought to put the lasagna through the fan if nothing else won't. She sits there, scraping the label off a beer bottle with her thumbnail, rolling it into little balls, then goes, 'I don't mind.'

"I try to use the wet dream of the Mafia to provoke these guys, and instead she agrees to have dinner with me. The greaseballs know better than to say dick about it, either. I put on my sports coat and back my convertible around to pick her up. Except here comes Perry LaSalle in his Gazelle. Zerelda gets this look on her face like she's creaming in her pants and I'm back in my room, watching TV, dinner date canceled, LaSalle and Zerelda over in her room, blinds drawn."

He finished his glass of whiskey and opened a can of beer and broke a raw egg in the glass and poured the beer on top of it. He took a drink and stared out the window into the darkness, an unfocused light in his eyes.

"So good riddance," I said.

"I did some checking on that dude. You know why he didn't finish at the Jesuit seminary? He couldn't keep it in his pants."

"What are you talking about, Clete?"

"He belongs to Sexaholics Anonymous. The guy's a gash hound. Why is it everybody in this town has some kind of problem? I don't know why I keep coming over here."

I turned off the outside floodlamps, and the bayou went dark and the tops of the cypresses were green and ruffling in the moonlight.

"Where'd you get the mouse?" I asked.

"I got up at four in the morning and walked into a door," he replied.

At the office the next morning I glanced at the state news section of the *Times Picayune* and saw an Associated Press article describing the homicide of a waitress outside Franklin, Louisiana. Her name was Ruby Gravano, a member of that group of marginal miscreants I had known for years in New Orleans, what I called the walking wounded, whose criminal deeds became a kind of incremental suicide, as though they were doing penance for sins committed in a previous incarnation. The body had been found by a roadside, not far from the banks of Bayou Teche, the clothes torn off her back. The article described her injuries as massive, which usually meant the details could not be published in a family newspaper.

I started out my door toward Helen's office and almost collided into Clete Purcel. He was dressed in a tan suit and a powder-blue shirt with a rolled collar and a tie with a horse painted on it and shined cordovan loafers. His cheeks were shiny with aftershave lotion.

"Have a cup of coffee with me. I'm a little wired right now," he said.

"Got a lot of work to do, Cletus," I said.

"Fill me in on this Shanahan broad."

"What?"

"I asked her out to lunch. I told her I had some helpful information on an armed robber she's prosecuting."

"Can't you let one day go by without stirring something up?"

He snuffed down in his nose and nodded to a uniformed deputy passing in the corridor. The deputy did not acknowledge him.

"I'm sorry. I'll catch you another time," Clete said.

"Come inside," I said.

I closed the office door behind us. Before he could speak, I said, "Remember Ruby Gravano?"

"A hooker, used to live in a flophouse by Lee Circle?"

"She was killed last night. Maybe beaten to death."

"I heard she was out of the life. You talk to her pimp?" he said.

"Beeler something?"

"Beeler Grissum. I think she married him," Clete said.

"Thanks, Cletus."

He opened the office door. "I'll let you know how my lunch came out. This is a class broad, Dave." He blew his breath on his palm and sniffed it. "Oh, man, I smell like puke. I got to brush my teeth."

The sheriff's wife, who was a mild and genteel woman, happened to be passing in the corridor. She shut and opened her eyes, as though she were riding in an airplane that had just hit an air pocket.

Helen Soileau and I checked out a cruiser and drove the thirty miles down to Franklin, then stopped by the sheriff's department and got directions to Ruby Gravano's, which turned out to be a one-story, weathered, late-Victorian frame house, with ventilated window shutters and high windows and a wide gallery hung with flower baskets. An oak tree that must have been two hundred years old grew in the side yard, a broken rope swing dangling in the dust.

Ruby's husband, Beeler Grissum, who was from north Georgia or South Carolina, sat on the steps, cracking peanuts and flicking them to a turkey in the yard. Two or three years ago, in a Murphy scam gone bad, a john had delivered a martial-arts kick into Beeler's face that had broken his neck. Today his body had the contours of a sack of potatoes, his chin held erect by a leather and steel neck brace, so that his head looked like a separate part of his anatomy positioned inside a cage. His hair was dyed platinum, like a professional wrestler's, combed straight back on his scalp. He rotated his upper torso as we approached the steps, a vague recognition swimming into his face.

"Sorry about your wife, Beeler," I said.

He removed a peanut from the sack in his hand, then offered the sack to us.

"No, thanks," I said. "The sheriff thinks maybe Ruby was thrown from a car."

"He wasn't there. But if that's what he says," Beeler said.

As I remembered him, he had been a carnival man before he was a pimp and had lived most of his life off the computer. His speech was flat, adenoidal, laconic, so lacking in joy or passion or remorse or emotion of any kind that the listener felt Beeler did not care enough about others or the world or even his own fate to lie.

"Two women have been murdered recently in Iberia Parish. Maybe Ruby's death is connected to them," I said.

He looked into space and seemed to think about my words. He scratched a place under his eye with one fingernail.

"It ain't her death brought you here then. It's the cases you ain't been able to solve?" he said.

"I wouldn't put it that way," I said.

"Don't matter. It's my fault," he said.

"I don't follow you," I said.

"We had a fight. She took off in my truck. Sometimes she'd go to a colored blues joint, sometimes to the casino on the reservation. She kept all her tips in a fruit jar. She had a thing for poker machines."

"Was she involved with another man?" Helen asked.

"She was out of the life. She been a one-man woman since. Most ex-whores are. Don't be talking about her like that," he replied.

"Can you let us have a picture of your wife?" Helen asked.

"I reckon."

He went into the house and returned with a photograph of Ruby and himself that was tucked with several others inside a gold-embossed Bible. He handed it to Helen. Ruby's hair was full and black, but the gauntness of her face made her hair look like a wig on a mannequin.

"Ruby hooked for eleven years. Curbside, motels, truck stops. She seen it all, every kind of pervert and geek they is. The guy who got next to her? You ain't gonna catch him," he said.

"You want to explain that?" Helen said.

"I just did," Beeler replied.

He shook the peanuts from his sack onto the ground for the turkey to eat and went back inside the gloom of his house without saying good-bye.

That night I hosed down the dock and threaded a chain through the steel eyelet screwed into the bow of each of our rental boats and wrapped the chain around a dock piling and snapped a heavy padlock on it, then tallied up the receipts in the bait shop and turned off the lights and locked the door and walked up the dock toward the house.

A brown and gray pickup truck, dented and work-scratched from bumper to bumper, was parked under the overhang of a live oak. A tall man in khaki clothes and a western straw hat stood by the tailgate, smoking a cigarette. The cigarette sparked in an arc when he tossed it into the road.

"You looking for somebody?" I asked.

"You," he said. "The man hepping that black bitch spread them rumor."

He walked out of the shadows into the moonlight. The skin of his face was white, furrowed in vertical lines. One oily strand of black hair hung from under his hat, across his ear.

"Mistake to come around my house, Legion," I said.

"That's what you t'ink," he replied, and swung a blackjack down on my head, clipping the crown of the skull.

I fell on the side of the road, against the embankment of my yard. I could smell leaves and grass and the moist dirt on my hands as he walked toward me. His blackjack hung from his fingers, like a large, leather-sheathed darning sock.

"I'm a police officer," I heard myself say.

"Don't matter what you are, no. When I get finish here, you ain't gonna want to tell nobody about it," he replied.

He backstroked me across the side of the head, and when I tried to curl into a ball, he beat my arms and spine and kneecaps and shins, then pulled me by my shirt onto the road and laid into my buttocks and the backs of my thighs. The lead weight inside the stitched leather sock was mounted on a spring and wood handle, and with each blow I could feel the pain sink all the way to the bone, like a dentist's drill hollowing into marrow.

He stopped and stood erect, and all I could see of him were his khaki-clad legs and loins and the western belt buckle on his flat stomach and the blackjack hanging motionlessly from his hand.

I was sitting up now, my legs bent under me, my ears ringing with sound, my stomach and bowels like wet newspaper torn in half. If he had hit me again, I couldn't have raised my arms to ward off the blow.

He lifted me by the front of my shirt and dropped me in a sitting position on the embankment of my yard. He slipped the blackjack into his side pocket and looked down at me.

"How you feel?" he asked.

He waited in the silence for my reply.

"I'll ax you again," he said.

"Go fuck yourself," I whispered.

He knotted my hair in his fist and wrenched back my head and kissed me hard on the mouth, pushing his tongue inside. I could taste tobacco and decayed food and bile in his saliva and smell the road dust and body heat and dried sweat in his shirt.

"Go tell them all what I done to you. How I whipped you like a dog and used you for my bitch. How it feel, boy? How it feel?" he said.

CHAPTER 10

The sunrise in the morning was pink and misty, like the colors and textures inside a morphine dream, and through the window at Iberia General I could see palm trees and oaks hung with moss along the Old Spanish Trail and a white crane lifting on extended wings off the surface of the bayou.

The sheriff sat hunched in a chair at the foot of my bed, staring at the steam rising from his paper coffee cup, his face angry, conflicted with thought.

Clete stood silently against one wall, rolling a matchstick from side to side in his mouth, his massive arms folded on his chest. Through the open door I saw Bootsie in the hall, talking to a physician in green scrubs.

"The guy comes out of nowhere, beats the shit out of you with a sap, gives no explanation, and drives off?" the sheriff said.

"That's about it," I said.

"You didn't get a license number?" he asked.

"The lights were off on the dock. There was mud on the tag."

The sheriff started to look at Clete, then forced his eyes back on me, not wanting to recognize Clete as a legitimate presence in the room.

"So I'm to conclude maybe one of our clientele got discharged from Angola and decided to square an old beef? Except the cop he clocked, one with thirty years' experience, didn't recognize him. That makes sense to you?" he said.

"It happens," I said.

"No, it doesn't," he replied.

I kept my eyes flat, my expression empty. My face felt out of round, my forehead as large as a muskmelon. When I moved any part of my body, the pain telegraphed all the way through my system and a wave of nausea rose into my mouth.

"You mind if we have a minute alone?" the sheriff said to Clete.

Clete removed the matchstick from his mouth and flipped it into the wastebasket.

"No, I don't mind. You might check the walls for bugs, though. You can never tell in a place like this," he said.

The sheriff stared at Clete's back as he went out the door, then turned back toward me. "What's with that guy?" he asked.

"Everybody wants respect, Sheriff. There're times Clete doesn't get it. He was a good cop. Why not give credit where it's due?"

The sheriff leaned forward in his chair.

"I learned in the Corps a good officer takes care of his people first. Everything else is second. But you don't allow that to happen, Dave. You think you operate in your own time zone and zip code. And every time you get in trouble, your friend out there seems to be belly-deep in it with you."

"Sorry to hear you feel that way."

The sheriff stood up from his chair and pulled at his coat sleeves until they were even on his wrists. "You know why the world's run by clerks? It's because our best people flame out across the sky and never leave anything behind but a good light show. Is that what you want to be, Dave? A light show? Damn, if you don't piss me off."

After he was gone, Clete put ice in a water glass and inserted a straw in the ice and held the glass for me to drink.

"What happened out there?" he asked.

I told him of the systematic beating from head to foot, the contempt shown my person, the sense that I no longer possessed control over my life, that my confidence in myself, my ability to deal with the world, had always been the stuff of vanity.

Then I told him about the kiss, a male tongue rife with nicotine pushed inside my mouth, over the teeth, into the throat, his saliva like an obscene burn on my chin.

I looked up into Clete's face. His green eyes were filled with a mixture of pity and the kind of latent thoughts that made his enemies back out of rooms when they recognized them.

"You're not going to file on this guy?" he asked.

"No."

"You feel ashamed because of what he did to you?" he asked.

When I didn't reply, he walked to the window and looked at the trees out on the road and the moss on the limbs lifting in the wind.

"I can set it up. He'll never know what hit him. I've got the throw-down, too, all numbers acid-burned and ground on an emery wheel," he said.

"I'll let you know."

"Yeah, I bet," he said, turning from the window. He picked his porkpie hat off the sill and slanted it on his brow. "I'll see you this afternoon, Streak. But with or without you, that cocksucker is going to get blown out of his socks."

Bootsie came through the door with a vase of flowers and a box of doughnuts. She had slept all night in a chair under a rough woolen blanket, but her face, even without makeup, was as pink and lovely as the morning.

"What's going on?" she said, looking from me to Clete.

Two days later I left the hospital, limping on a cane, my head spinning with painkillers, one eye swollen almost shut, the side of my face inflated with a large yellow and purple bruise. It was Friday, a workday, but I did not go back to the office. Instead, I sat for a long time in the living room by myself, the blinds drawn, and listened to a strange whirring sound in my head. I found myself at the kitchen sink, first pouring a glass of iced tea and a second later opening the bottle of painkillers the doctor had given me.

One or two to get back to normal can't hurt, I thought. Right.

I poured the pills down the drain, then ran water on top of them and dropped the bottle in the garbage sack under the counter.

Bootsie and I ate lunch on the redwood table under the mimosa tree in the backyard. It was shady and cool in the yard, and a gust of wind ruffled the periwinkles and bamboo that grew along the coulee, but there was no hint of rain in the air and dust blew in brown clouds out of my neighbor's cane field.

Bootsie was talking about a college baseball game scheduled for that night in Lafayette. I tried to follow what she was saying, but the whirring sound began again in my head.

"Do you?" she said.

"Excuse me?" I said.

"Do you want to go to the game tonight?"

"Tonight? Who did you say was playing?"

She set her fork down on her plate. "You have to get your mind off it. The sheriff will find this guy," she said.

My eyes avoided hers. I felt her gaze sharpen and fix on the side of my face.

"Right?" she said.

"Not necessarily."

"Take the marbles out of your mouth, Streak."

"The sheriff doesn't know what to look for. I didn't tell him everything."

"Oh?"

"It was the man called Legion, the overseer from Poinciana Island. He put his tongue in my mouth. He called me his bitch."

She was quiet a long time.

"That's why you kept the sheriff in the dark?"

"This guy Legion is seventy-four years old. Nobody would believe my story. Legion knew that. He really pushed the hook in deep."

Bootsie got up from her bench and walked around the table and put her fingers in my hair and brushed her nails back and forth on my scalp. Then she kissed the top of my head.

"Why didn't you tell me?" she said.

"It wouldn't change anything."

"Come inside, soldier," she said.

We went into the bedroom. She closed the curtains on the window that looked out on the front yard, then disconnected the telephone cord from the jack in the wall and removed her blouse.

"Unhook me, big guy," she said, turning her back to me while she unbuttoned her blue jeans and let them drop to her ankles.

She put her arms around my neck and kissed me on the mouth.

"You all right?" she said.

"Fine."

"Then how about getting undressed?"

I took off my clothes and lay down gingerly on the bed. Bootsie slipped her fingers down inside the elastic of her panties and pushed them over her thighs and lay beside me, her head propped up on her elbow.

"You told Clete about all this?" she asked.

"Yes."

"Before you told me?"

"Yes."

"You don't trust me? You believed I'd think less of you?"

"It wasn't my proudest moment out there."

"Oh, Dave, you're so crazy," she said, and put her face close to mine and touched my sex with her fingers.

"The doc loaded me up on downers. I don't know if I'm up to it, Boots," I said.

"That's what you think, bubba," she replied.

She raised herself up and stroked my sex, then kissed it and placed it in her mouth.

"Boots, you don't need to—" I began.

A moment later she spread her knees and sat on top of me and held me between her hands. As I looked up at her, the light from the side window woven in her hair, all the goodness and beauty in the world seemed to gather in her face. She placed me inside her, then leaned down and kissed me on the mouth again and brushed a strand of hair out of my eyes.

I ran my hands over her back and pressed her down on top of me and kissed her hair and bit her neck. Then, for just a moment, all the pain and solitary rage, all the ugly images that the man called Legion had tried to leave forever in my memory, seemed to become as dross. The only sound in the room was the rise and fall of Bootsie's breath against my chest and the squeak of the bedsprings under our weight and occasionally a small moist, popping noise when her stomach formed a suction against mine. Then her body began to stiffen, the muscles in her back hardening, her thighs tightening on mine. Her eyes were closed now, her face growing small and soft and tense at the same time. I held her as close as I could, as though we were both balanced on the tip of a precipice, then I felt my sex harden and swell and burn in a way it never had, to a degree that made me cry out involuntarily, more like a woman than a man, and the entirety of my life, my identity itself, seemed to dissolve and break and then burst from my loins in a white glow, and in that moment I was joined with her, the two of us locked inseparably together inside the heat of her thighs, the mystery of her womb, the beating of her heart, the sweat on her skin, the flush of blood in her cheeks, the odor of crushed gardenias that rose from her hair when I buried my face in it.

After I showered and put on a fresh pair of khakis and a Hawaiian shirt, I took my holstered 1911-model .45 automatic from the dresser and placed it on the rail of the gallery, then went into the kitchen and rubbed Bootsie on the back and kissed her neck.

"You're special, kid," I said.

"I know," she replied.

"I'll be gone for a little while. But I'll be back in time to go to the game."

"What are you about to do, Dave?"

"There's not a perp or lowlife or shitbag in Louisiana who would come after a cop with a blackjack unless he thought he was protected."

"You and Clete are going to settle things on your own?"

"I wouldn't say that."

"Why not?"

"Because Clete's out of it," I replied, and went out the front door and backed the truck down the drive. Through the windshield I saw Bootsie come out on the porch. I waved, but she didn't respond.

*   *   *

I crossed the freshwater bay onto Poinciana Island and followed the winding paved road through red-dirt acreage and hummocks and oaks green with lichen to Ladice Hulin's house, where she sat on the gallery, absorbed in a magazine, directly across from the scorched stucco shell of the place in which Julian LaSalle's wife had burned to death like a bird caught inside a cage.

I got out of my truck and limped toward her with my cane. "May I sit down?" I asked.

"Looks like you better. A train hit you?" she said.

I eased myself down on the top step and propped my cane across the inside of my leg and looked at the peacocks picking in the grass across the road. In the distance I could see the sunlight on the bay, like thousands of coppery lights, and a boat with a sky-blue sail turning about in the wind. Neither of us spoke for a long time.

"I want to take Legion down. Maybe blow up his shit," I said.

"You use that kind of language in front of white ladies?" she asked.

"Sometimes. With the ones I respect."

Her eyes roved over my face. "Legion done this to you?" she asked.

I nodded, my gaze fixed across the road. I heard her close her magazine and set it down on the gallery.

"It ain't just the beating that bother you, though, is it?" she said.

"I really don't know what I feel right now, Ladice," I lied.

"He done somet'ing to you right befo' he finished, somet'ing that makes you feel dirty inside. You wash yourself all over, but it don't do no good. Every place you go, you feel his hand on you. He always in your thoughts. That's what Legion know how to do to people. Every black woman on this plantation learned that," she said.

I snuffed down in my nose and cleared my throat. I put on my sunglasses, even though there was no glare in the yard, and rubbed my palms on my knees.

"Maybe I should go," I said.

"Legion killed a man in Morgan City. A man from up Nort' who was down here writin' a book."

"He was never arrested?"

"The people in the bar said the man threatened Legion with a gun and Legion took it from him and shot him. It ain't true, though."

"How do you know?" I asked.

"A black man in the kitchen seen Legion get the gun from under the bar and follow him out in the parking lot. Legion shot the man so close his coat caught on fire. Then he shot him again on the ground. This was maybe t'urty or t'urty-five years ago."

"Thanks for you help, Ladice."

"Jimmy Dean Styles was out here."

"When?"

"Yesterday. He axed about my granddaughter, Rosebud, how's she doin' and all. Why would he come out here axing about Rosebud?"

I remembered taking Rosebud's sketch of the reclining nude to the Carousel, the nightclub half-owned by Styles, and Styles stealing a look at it, his head tilted curiously.

"Let me know if he comes around again," I said.

I took off my sunglasses and folded them and replaced them in my shirt pocket and tried to seem casual.

"You tell me only what you feel like I should know, huh? That's the way it's always been, Mr. Dave. Ain't changed. The little people ain't got the same rights as everybody else. That's how come Legion could take any black girl he wanted into the trees or the canebrake, make them carry his baby and never tell who the father was. When you talk down to me like you just done? You're no different from Legion, no."

Late that night a huge rental moving van lumbered down a state road outside town, followed by two big cars filled with men who looked straight ahead, somber, not talking to one another, their faces marked with purpose. The caravan passed through a black slum far out in the parish, crossed a bridge over a coulee, and turned down a shell road that led to a cluster of burial crypts in a cemetery by the bayou.

The men piled out of the cars and unwound a firehose that had been stolen from an apartment building in Lafayette, then screwed the hose onto a fire hydrant by the side of the shell road. One man fitted a wrench on top of the hydrant and revolved it around and around until the hose was hard and stiff with pressurized water.

They unlocked the back doors of the van and threw them back on the hinges, and the high-beam headlights from the cars lit up ten terrified black men inside. Two of the men from the cars, all of whom were white, pushed open the valve on the firehose and directed a skin-blistering jet of water inside the van, skittering the black men across the floor, blowing them against the walls, knocking them back down when they tried to rise, bursting against their faces and groins with the force of huge fists.

The men from the cars gathered in a semicircle to watch, lighting up cigarettes now, laughing in the iridescent spray that floated in the headlights.

Then a man with a body as compact as a stack of bricks, with dead gray eyes and a haircut like a 1930s convict, walked into the light. He wore a suit with suspenders and only a formfitting, ribbed undershirt beneath the coat.

"Get 'em out of there and line 'em up," he said.

"Hey, Joe, some fun, huh?" one of the men on the hose said, then looked at the man with dead eyes and went silent and shut off the valve on the nozzle.

The men who had ridden in the two cars pulled the black men tumbling out of the van and shoved them through the cemetery to the edge of the bayou. When a black man looked back over his shoulder, he was hit with either a sap or a baton or kicked so hard between his buttocks, he had to fight to gain control of his sphincter.

A few minutes later all of the black men stood in a row, most of them trembling uncontrollably now, looking across the water, their clothes molded wetly against their bodies, their fingers laced on top of their heads.

The man with dead eyes walked up and down behind the row, staring at the back of each black man's head.

"My name is Joe Zeroski. I got nothing against you personally. But you're pimps and rock dealers, and that means nobody cares what happens to you. You're gonna tell me what I want to know about my little girl. Her name was Linda, Linda Zeroski," he said.

He pointed at the back of a huge black kid nicknamed Baby Huey, who had played football at Grambling before he had gone to prison for statutory rape. One of Joe's crew stepped forward with a stun gun cupped in his hand, an electrical thread of light crackling between the extended prongs. He touched the prongs to Baby Huey's back, which left Baby Huey writhing in the grass, his eyes bulging with shock.

Joe looked down at him. "Who picked up my daughter on the corner?" he asked.

"Washington Trahan was her manager. I didn't know nothing about her," Baby Huey said.

"The piece of shit you call a manager blew town. That means you take his weight. You think about that the next time you see him," Joe said, and nodded to the man with the stun gun.

When the man with the stun gun was finished, Baby Huey was curled in an embryonic ball, begging for his mother, shivering like a dog trying to pass glass.

Joe Zeroski walked farther down the line, then paused behind a slender, light-skinned man with moles on his face and a mustache and hair that was buzzed on the temples and cut long in back. Joe nodded to the man with the stun gun, but suddenly the intended victim dropped his arms and shook his head violently, his eyes squeezed shut, crying out, "It was Tee Bobby Hulin. He did at least one white chick already. He always lookin' for white bread. Everybody on the corner know it. It's him, man."

"I already checked him out. Four people put him in a club in St. Martinville," Joe said.

"I got a pacemaker. Please don't do it, suh," the light-

skinned man said, his voice and accent reverting to a sub-
servient identity he had probably thought was no longer
part of his life.

The man with the stun gun waited. "Joe?" he said. He
had an unshaved, morose face, with big jowls and eyebrows that were like shaggy hemp. His stomach was so
large his shirt wouldn't tuck into his belt.

"I'm thinking," Joe replied.

"They're niggers, Joe. They start lying the day they
come out of the womb," the man said.

Joe Zeroski shook his head. "They got no percentage
in standing up for a guy is hurting their business. Y'all
wait for me at the cars," he said.

Joe Zeroski's crew drifted back through the crypts to
their cars and the rented moving van. Joe stepped out in
front of the black men and pulled a .45 automatic from
his belt. He racked a round into the chamber and set the
safety.

"You guys kneel down. Don't move your hands from
your head," he said.

Joe waited until they were all on their knees, their
faces popping with sweat now, mosquitoes buzzing about
their ears and nostrils, their eyes avoiding any contact
with his.

"You ever hear why some guys use a .22?" he said.
"Because the bullet bounces around inside the skull and
makes a mess in there. That story is shit. The guys use a
.22 just don't like noise. So they got to put one through
the temple, one in the ear, and one through the mouth.
That's supposed to be a Mob hit. But it gets done that
way just because some guys don't like noise. No other
reason.

"I carry ear plugs and use a gun that makes an exit hole like a half-dollar. See?"

Joe screwed a rubber plug into his ear, then removed it and put it back in his coat pocket.

"There's a building with a steeple on it across the bayou. You keep looking at it and don't turn around till sunrise. If you want your brains running out your nose, turn around while I'm still here. Remember my name. Joe Zeroski. You want to make yourself some cash, come see me with the name of the man killed my daughter. You want to lose your life, fuck with me just once."

Minutes later the moving van and the two cars drove away.

At dawn the pastor of a ramshackle fundamentalist church, with a wood cross and a facsimile of a bell tower nailed on the roof, walked down the sloping green lawn of his rectory to take his wash off the clothesline. He stopped in the mist drifting off the bayou and stared openmouthed at a row of black men kneeling on the opposite bank, their hands clasped on the crowns of their skulls like prisoners of war in a grainy black-and-white news film.

CHAPTER 11

The sheriff was surprisingly calm and reflective as he sat down in my office Monday morning.

"For years I've been trying to put these pimps and drug dealers out of business. Then the goddamn Mafia comes in and does it in one night," he said.

"They'll be back," I said.

"What do you know about this guy Zeroski?"

"He's an old-time mechanic. Supposedly, he hung it up after he accidentally shot a child by the St. Thomas Project."

"Eventually we've got to run him out of town. You know that, huh?"

"Easier said than done," I replied.

The sheriff got up from his chair and gazed out the window at the old crypts in St. Peter's Cemetery. "Who beat you up, Dave?" he said.

* * *

At noon I signed out of the office to interview a woman in St. Mary Parish, down the bayou, who claimed to have awakened in the middle of the night to find a man standing over her. She said the man had worn leather gloves and a rubber mask made in the image of Alfred E. Neuman, the grinning idiot on the cover of *Mad* magazine. The man had tried to suffocate her by pressing his hands down on her mouth and nose, then had fled when the woman's dog attacked him.

Unfortunately for her, she was uneducated and poor, a cleaning woman at a motel behind a truck stop, and had filed reports of attempted rape twice in the past. The city police had blown off her claims, and I was about to do the same when she said, "He smelled sweet inside his mask, like there was mint on his breath. He was trembling all over." Then her work-worn face creased with shame. "He touched me in private places."

It wasn't the kind of detail that people imagined or manufactured. But if the intruder at her home had any connection to the death of either Linda Zeroski or Amanda Boudreau, I couldn't find it. I handed her my business card.

"You coming back to hep me?" she said, looking up at me from a kitchen chair.

"I work in Iberia Parish. I don't have any authority here," I said.

"Then why you got me to tell you all them personal t'ings?" she asked.

I had no answer. I left my card on her kitchen table.

An hour later I asked a cop at the entrance of the casino on the Indian reservation where I could find the man named Legion, then walked inside, into the smell of refrigerated cigarette smoke and rug cleaner, through banks of slot and video-poker machines, past crap and blackjack tables and a fast-food bar and an artificial pond with a painted backdrop that was meant to look like a cypress swamp, a stone alligator half submerged in the water, its mouth yawning open among the coins that had been thrown at it.

The man named Legion was at the bar in a darkened cocktail lounge, drinking coffee, smoking a cigarette in front of a mirror that was trimmed with red and purple neon. His eyes looked at me indifferently in the mirror when I sat down on the stool next to him and hung my cane from the edge of the bar. A waitress in a short black skirt and fishnet stockings set a napkin down in front of me and smiled.

"What will you have?" she asked.

"A Dr Pepper on ice with some cherries in it. Mr. Legion here knows me. He comes around to my house sometimes. Put it on his tab," I said.

At first she thought she was listening to a private joke between Legion and me, then she glanced at his face and her smile went away and she made my drink without looking up from the drainboard.

I hooked my coat behind the butt of the .45 automatic I carried in a clip-on holster.

"*T'es un pédéraste, Legion?*" I asked.

His eyes locked on mine in the mirror. Then he brought his cigarette up to his mouth and exhaled smoke through his nose and tipped the ash into his coffee saucer, his eyes following the woman behind the bar now.

"You don't talk French?" I said.

"Not wit' just anybody."

"I'll ask you in English. You a homosexual, Legion?"

"I know what you doin'. It ain't gonna work, no," he replied.

"Because that's the impression you left me with. Maybe raping those black women convinced you there's not a girl buried down inside you."

He rotated the burning tip of his cigarette in his coffee saucer until the fire was dead. Then he fastened a button on his shirt pocket and straightened his tie and looked at his reflection in the mirror.

"Go back to the kitchen and see if they got my dinner ready," he said to the barmaid.

I turned on my stool so I was looking at his profile.

"I'm a superstitious man, so I went to see a *traiture* about you," I lied. "My *traiture* friend says you got a *gris-gris* on you. Those women you forced yourself on, Mr. Julian, his poor wife who burned up in the fire, a man you murdered outside a bar in Morgan City? Their spirits all follow you around, Legion, everywhere you go."

The skin wrinkled under his right eye. He turned his head slowly and stared into my face.

"What man in Morgan City?"

"He was a writer. From somewhere up North. You shot him outside a bar."

"You found that in an old newspaper. It don't mean anyt'ing."

"You shot him twice. His coat caught fire from the muzzle flash. The second time you shot him on the ground."

His mouth parted and his eyes narrowed and stayed fixed on mine.

From my shirt pocket I removed a dime I had drilled a hole through early that morning, then strung on a piece of looped red string. I pushed the dime across the bar toward his coffee cup.

"The *traiture* said you should carry this on your ankle, Legion."

"Like a nigger woman, huh?" he said, and pitched the dime into the bottles behind the bar.

The barmaid came out of the kitchen with a tray. She took a plate of rice and gravy and stewed chicken and string beans off the tray and set it in front of Legion with a napkin and knife and fork.

"Anything wrong here, Legion?" she asked.

"Not wit' me," he replied, and tucked his napkin into his shirt and picked up his silverware.

"Why would you kill a writer from up North?" I said.

He leaned over his plate and opened his mouth to shovel in a fork piled with food. His face suddenly slanted sideways.

Then I would have sworn his voice and accent actually changed, that it seemed to rumble and echo out of a cavern that was far larger in circumference and depth than his size.

"You'd better leave me the fuck alone," it said.

I felt my scalp recede against my skull. I got up from my stool, my face suddenly cold and moist in the air-conditioning.

I wiped my forehead on my coat sleeve and picked up my cane. When I did, the man called Legion looked ordinary again, a workingman bent over his dinner, his lips smacking his food.

But my heart was still racing. As I stared at his back, I

was determined that whatever fear he had engendered in me would not be one I walked out of the room with.

"This time I'll give *you* something to remember. Just so you'll know what it's going to be like every time we meet," I said, and pulled his plate sideways and spit in it.

Clete came into the bait shop on Wednesday afternoon, his hair and eyebrows freshly trimmed, wearing new slacks and a starched shirt and a gold neck chain and religious medal I'd never seen before.

"Want to wet a line?" I asked.

"No, not really. Just thought I'd drop by."

"I see," I said.

"I took Barbara Shanahan to a luncheon on Monday," he said.

"A luncheon?"

"Yeah, at the country club. It was full of lawyers. Last night we went to a lawn party on Spanish Lake. The governor was there."

"No kidding? Who else?"

"Perry LaSalle."

"Was he at the luncheon, too?"

"Yeah, I guess." Clete was sitting on one of the counter stools now, drumming his nails on the Formica. He looked up at me. "You saying Barbara's using me to jerk LaSalle around?"

The phone rang and I didn't have to answer his question. After I hung up, I turned around and Clete was staring out the screened window at the bream popping the surface among the lily pads on the far side of the bayou. Three long lines, like strands of wire, were stretched across his forehead.

"What's wrong, podna?" I asked.

"Last night I told Barbara I liked her a lot. I also told her maybe she was carrying a torch for a guy I don't have much respect for, but if that was her choice, I could boogie on down the road."

"How'd she take it?"

"She got mad."

"Her loss. Blow it off."

"That's not all of it. She lives in this apartment on the bayou. I'm downstairs, on my way to the parking lot, and here she comes down the staircase. She apologizes. The moon's up, the azaleas and the bougainvillea and wisteria are blooming. She's standing there in her hose, her shoes off, her face like a little girl's. She takes me by the arm and leads back up the stairs again. Dave, stuff like this doesn't happen to guys like me with women like that. I kissed her in the living room and rockets went off in my head."

"Uh, maybe you don't need to tell me any more, Cletus."

"There's a knock at the door."

"LaSalle?"

"No, some peckerwood who sells magazines and Bibles. His name is Marvin something or another."

"Marvin Oates?"

"Yeah, that's the guy. A real con man. He's got this hush-puppy accent and pitiful look on his face, like the orphanage just slammed the door on his nose. But Barbara laps it up, fixing him a sandwich and pouring a glass of milk for him, asking him if he wants some ice cream and melted chocolate to go with it. It was sickening. She said she'd forgotten she'd told Marvin to drop by, which meant I was supposed to leave."

I picked up two freshwater rods that were propped in the corner, the Mepps spinners on the lines snugged into the cork handles. I tossed one to Clete.

"Let's entertain the bass," I said.

"There's more," he said. His green eyes flicked sideways at me. His face was pink and oily with perspiration under the light, his fresh haircut like a little boy's.

I sat down next to him and tried not to look at my watch. "So what's the rest of it?" I asked, feigning as much interest as I could.

"I was back at my motel, just about asleep, when a car pulls up in front of Zerelda Calucci's cottage. Guess who?" he said. "Perry LaSalle again. Like everywhere I go I see Perry LaSalle. Like any broad around here I'm interested in has got a thing with Perry LaSalle. Except this time he's getting his genitalia ripped out.

"Zerelda calls him a douche bag and a brain-dead horse dick, then picks up a flowerpot off the walk and smashes it on the dashboard of his convertible.

"I hear his car leave and I think, Ah, I can get some sleep. Ten minutes later Zerelda taps on my door. Man, she was drop-dead beautiful, with those big ta-tas and pale skin and black hair full of lights and fire-alarm lipstick, and she's holding this big, sweaty bottle of cold duck, and she says, 'Hey, Irish. I've just had the worst fucking night of my life. Feel like hearing about it?'

"And I'm telling myself, Go back to sleep, Clete. Barbara Shanahan waits for you in the morning. Wet dream of the Mafia or not, no Sicilian skivvy runs tonight.

"Those thoughts lasted about two seconds. Guess which podjo of yours got fucked on the ceiling last night and fucked on the ceiling and floor and in the shower and every other surface of the room this morning?"

"I don't believe it."

"I don't, either. Except I'm having dinner with her this evening."

"With Joe Zeroski's niece?" I said.

"Yeah. I think I just took Perry LaSalle's place. You and Bootsie want to join us?" He looked at me expectantly.

"I think we're supposed to go to the PTA tonight," I replied.

"Right. I forgot you were tight with the PTA," he said. He stood up and put on his hat. "By the way, I found out where that guy Legion lives. I let him know the Bobbsey twins from Homicide are a factor in his life."

"You did what?"

On Thursday morning the sheriff called me down to his office.

"You know a fellow named Legion Guidry?" he asked.

"I know a man named Legion. I'm not sure if that's his first or last name, though. He used to be an overseer on Poinciana Island."

"I got a call from the sheriff in St. Mary Parish. A couple of his deputies work at the casino in their off hours. One of them says you went into the lounge and spit in this fellow's food."

There was a long silence.

"I guess I was having a bad day," I said.

The skin seemed to shrink on the sheriff's face. "You're telling me you actually did this?" he said.

"This is a bad guy, Sheriff. A real bucket of shit left behind by the LaSalle family."

"You want a lawyer in here?"

"What for?"

"Two nights ago somebody slashed all four of this fellow's truck tires. A filling-station operator saw a man in a rattletrap Cadillac convertible leaving the neighborhood." The sheriff picked up a yellow legal pad that he had written some notes on. "The filling-station operator said the driver looked like an albino ape with a little hat perched on his head. Sound like anybody you know?"

"No, I don't know any albino apes," I replied.

"You think this is funny?"

"No, I don't."

"I think your real beef is with the LaSalle family, Dave. You blame the rich for all our racial and economic problems. You forget the other canneries have shipped their jobs to Latin America. The LaSalles still take care of all their employees, all the way to the grave, no matter what it costs them."

"This man Legion is a sexual predator. He was given free rein to sexually exploit black women on the LaSalle plantation. That doesn't seem like a protective attitude to me."

"Then maybe they should have gotten jobs somewhere else." He stared hard at me, a piece of cartilage knotted in his jaw. "You got something you want to add?"

I let my eyes slip off his face. "No, sir," I said.

The sheriff bit a piece of loose skin on the ball of his thumb, then rose from his chair and put on his suit coat and picked up his Stetson.

"You and Helen Soileau check out shotguns," he said.

"What?"

"We're going out to have a talk with Joe Zeroski and his friends. Doesn't Purcel live in that same motor court?"

"Yes."

"Sounds like he made a good choice."

The motor court was out on East Main in a grove of live oak trees. The cottages were made of tan stucco and stayed in shade from morning to sunset, and each evening the smoke from meat fires drifted through the trees and bamboo onto Bayou Teche.

Our caravan of six cruisers and a jail van slowed and turned into the motor court drive, passing a cottage at the entrance that had been converted into a barbershop, complete with a striped barber pole. At the end of the drive I saw Clete's lavender Cadillac convertible parked across from Zerelda Calucci's cottage.

In a dry, brittle place inside my head I could hear a persistent humming sound, like an electrical short buzzing in the rain, the same sound I'd heard when I came home from Iberia General, wired to the eyes on painkillers.

Helen parked the cruiser and looked at me. My walking cane and two sawed-down Remington pump twelve-gauge shotguns were propped on the seat between us.

"You got something eating you?" she asked.

"This is a dumb move. You don't 'front Joe Zeroski."

"Maybe you should tell the skipper."

"I already did. Waste of time," I said.

"Try to enjoy it. Come on, Streak, time to rock 'n' roll, lock and load," she said, opening her door.

JAMES LEE BURKE   *160*

I got out on the driveway with my cane in one hand
and a shotgun propped over my shoulder with the
other. The sheriff, three plainclothes, and at least ten
uniformed sheriff's deputies and a dozen city policemen
were walking toward me. The wind had started to gust
and leaves from the oaks spun in circles on the drive.

"You got a second, Skipper?" I said.

"What is it?" he asked, his eyes fixed on the cottages
at the end of the row. A bullhorn hung from his right
hand.

"Let me talk with Joe."

"No."

"That's it?"

"Get with the program, Dave."

My gaze went through the crowd of police officers
and focused on a man with ash-blond hair in jeans and a
sports coat and a golf shirt and a white straw hat coned
up on the sides who was getting out of a cruiser, his face
filled with expectation, like a kid entering an amusement
park.

"What's that guy doing here?" I asked.

"Which guy?" the sheriff said.

"Marvin Oates. He's got a sheet. What's he doing
here?"

"He's a criminal justice student. We're letting them
ride with us. Dave, I think maybe you should go sit
down, take it easy a while, maybe go up to the barbershop and get a haircut. We'll pick you up on the way
out," the sheriff said.

His words hung in the silence like the sound of a
slap. He and everyone around him walked past me
toward the end of the motor court as though I were

not there. I could hear dead leaves blowing in a vortex around me.

Helen looked over her shoulder, then walked back toward me. Her shirtsleeves were rolled in cuffs, her arms pumped. She squeezed my wrist.

"He just found out his wife has cancer. He's not himself, bwana," she said.

"This is a mistake."

"Forget I said anything."

She followed the others, her shotgun held in two hands, canted at an upward angle, her jeans tight on her rump, her handcuffs drawn through the back of her belt.

A moment later the sheriff was on the bullhorn, his voice echoing off the trees and cottages. But I couldn't hear his words. My ears were ringing now, my scalp cold in the wind. Joe Zeroski came out of his cottage, barechested, wearing sweatpants and a pair of snow-white tennis shoes, a piece of fried chicken in his hand, his face like that of a man who might have been working in front of a blast furnace.

"What is this?" he said.

"Tell all your people to get out here," the sheriff said.

"I don't got to tell them. They go where I go. I asked you what this is. We got the Mickey Mouse show here?" Joe said.

"You kidnapped a bunch of black men. They won't file charges on you, but I know what you did. Here's the search warrant if you care to look at it, Mr. Zeroski," the sheriff said.

"Wipe your ass with it," Joe replied.

Uniformed deputies and city police were now pulling

Joe's people out of their cottages, lining them up, pushing them into search positions against trees and cars.

"Turn around and place your hands on that tree, please," the sheriff said to Joe.

Nests of veins rippled through Joe's chest and shoulders; rose petals of color bloomed in his throat. He threw his chicken bone into the bushes.

"Somebody beat my daughter so bad her face didn't look human. But you're out here, knocking around blue-collar guys ain't done you nothing. You know why that is? Because I bother you. You can't do nothing about the degenerates you got in this town, so you lean on people you think are easy. Hey, you're as old as I am. I look easy to you?" Joe said.

Joe saw two uniformed deputies shove a man with a leviathan stomach and melancholy face and jowls like a St. Bernard's over a car fender. "Hey, that's Frankie Dogs they're rousting," Joe said. "You know who Frankie Dogs is? Even in a shithole like this they got to know who that is. Hey, you get your fucking hands off me."

But two deputies already had Joe against the tree and were feeling inside his thighs.

Just then a city cop escorted Clete Purcel and Zerelda Calucci out of Zerelda's cottage. It was all moving fast now.

"What do you want to do with *him?*" the city cop asked, indicating Clete.

"He goes down with the rest," the sheriff replied.

Clete and Zerelda propped their arms against the side of Clete's Cadillac, waiting to be searched. Clete looked at me over his shoulder, then raised his eyebrows and looked away and watched a tugboat passing on the bayou, his sandy hair blowing in the wind.

Cletus, Cletus, I thought.

Joe Zeroski began to fight with the deputies who were shaking him down. A half-dozen cops swarmed him, including the city cop who had been about to search Clete and Zerelda.

Marvin Oates was standing right behind Zerelda now, his face transfixed, a strange, almost ethereal light in his eyes. He stepped closer to her, as though drawing near a presence from another world, leaves crackling under the soles of his shoes. He leaned down toward her shoulders, perhaps trying to breathe in the heat from her body or the perfume in her hair. Then his hands slid down the muscles in her back, under her arms and on her sides. I saw her body jerk, as though she were being sexually violated, but Oates whispered something in her ear and his hand went to her blue jeans pocket and came away with a small bag, which he pushed up into his coat sleeve.

I headed toward him with my cane, the shotgun still propped on my shoulder.

"What do you think you're doing?" I asked.

His face drained.

"Trying to hep out," he replied.

"You're not a police officer. You don't have the right to put your hand on anybody here. You understand that?" I said.

"You're right, sir. I dint have no bidness coming here. I'm just a simple student at the university. You ain't gonna have no trouble with the likes of me," he said.

He hurried through the trees toward the bayou, pushing through bamboo and underbrush, his sports coat tearing on a thorn bush.

"Come back here," I said.

But he was gone. I limped down to the bank and amid a tangle of morning glory vines saw a Ziploc bag that was fat with a greenish-brown substance inside. I poked at the bag with my cane, then picked it up and shook out the marijuana inside it and put the bag in my pocket.

When I got back up to the driveway, Joe Zeroski and all of his men were hooked up on a long wrist chain, and so were Clete and Zerelda.

"How about some slack on Purcel, Skipper?" I said.

"Let him sit in his own mess for a change," the sheriff replied.

"Earlier today you made a remark about the women who were raped on the LaSalles' plantation. You said maybe they should have gotten jobs somewhere else. I believe that's the filthiest fucking thing I've ever heard you say, sir," I said.

I pumped open the breech on my shotgun and threw the shotgun in the backseat of the sheriff's cruiser. Then I hooked my walking cane on the limb of a persimmon tree, like a misplaced Christmas ornament, and limped unassisted toward the front of the motor court.

"Where you going, Dave?" Helen asked.

"To get a haircut," I said, and gave her the thumbs-up sign.

Late that night, after Joe Zeroski and all of his men were released from jail, a car pulled into the motor court and stopped in front of Zerelda Calucci's cottage. A young man in a white straw hat and pale blue cowboy shirt with flowers stitched on it got out of the car and walked to the cottage door, bending down briefly, then got back in the car and drove away.

The next morning, when Zerelda Calucci opened her door, she found a dozen red roses, wrapped in green tissue paper, lying across a gold-embossed copy of the Bible.

CHAPTER 12

Friday night I experienced what recovering alcoholics refer to as drunk dreams, nocturnal excursions into the past that represent either a desire to get back on the dirty boogie or a fear of it. In my dream I visited a saloon on Magazine Street in New Orleans, where I stood at a mirrored bar with two inches of Beam in a glass and a long-necked Jax on the side. I drank as I did before I entered Alcoholics Anonymous, knocking back doubles with the careless disregard of a man eating a razor blade, confident that this time I would not wake trembling in the morning, filled with rage and self-hatred and an insatiable desire for more drink.

Then I was in another saloon, this one located in an old colonial hotel in Saigon, one with wood-bladed ceiling fans and ventilated shutters on the windows and marble columns and potted palms set between tables that were covered with white linen. I wore a freshly pressed uniform and sat in a tall chair at a teakwood bar next to a friend, an Englishman who owned an export-import company there and who had been an intelligence agent in Hanoi when the Viet Minh, later named the Viet Cong, were America's allies. He wore a white suit and a Panama hat and a trimmed white mustache, and was always kind and deferential toward those who thought they could succeed as colonials where he could not. Aside from his flushed complexion, the enormous quantities of scotch he drank seemed to have little influence on him.

He tapped my glass with his, his blue eyes sorrowful, and said, "You're such a nice young officer. A shame you and your chaps have to die here. Oh, well, give the little buggers hell."

Then it was night and I was looking out on a sea of windswept elephant grass lit by the phosphorous halos of pistol flares. Inside the grass toy men in conical straw hats and black pajamas, armed with captured American ordnance and French and Japanese junk, tripped a wire strung with C-rat cans. The Zippo-tracks cut loose, with a mewing sound like a kitten's, arcing liquid flame over the grass, filling the sky with voices and a smell that no amount of whiskey ever rinses from the soul.

I sat up on the edge of the bed and pushed the sleep out of my eyes. The window curtains were blowing in the wind, and the clouds above the swamp were as black as soot, heat lightning ballooning inside them, and I could smell a trash fire in a coulee and hear the hysterical shrieking sound of a nutria calling to its mate.

I went into the bathroom and opened a bottle of aspirin and poured eight into my hand, then ate them off my palm, biting down on the acidic taste of each, cup-

JAMES LEE BURKE 168

ping water into my mouth, taking the rush just as if I had
eaten a handful of white speed.

I lay back down on top of the sheets, a pillow over my
face, but did not sleep again until dawn.

It was Saturday morning and I drove to Morgan City
and searched the city newspaper's morgue for an account
of a homicide involving the man some called Legion
Guidry. It wasn't hard to find. On a weekday night in
December of 1966 a freelance writer named William
O'Reilly, age thirty-nine, of New York City, had acted
belligerent in a bar down by the shrimp docks. When
asked to leave, he had pulled a pistol on the bartender.
The bartender, one Legion Guidry, had tried to disarm
him. William O'Reilly was shot twice, then had stag-
gered into the parking lot, where he died.

The story did not run until two days after the death of
the victim and appeared on the second page of the newspaper. The story stated that William O'Reilly had been
unemployed for several years and had been dismissed
from both a newspaper and a university teaching job for
alcohol-related problems.

I turned off the microfilm scanner and looked out the
window at the palm trees and rooftops of Morgan City. I
could see the bridges over the wide sweep of the
Atchafalaya River and the shrimp boats and bust-head
saloons down by the waterfront and the dead cypresses
in the chain of bays that formed a deep-water channel
into the Gulf of Mexico. But to the denizens of America's
criminal subculture, Morgan City was more than a piece
of Jamaica sawed loose from the Caribbean. It had
always been the place to go to if you were on the run and

needed a new identity, access to dope, whores, foreign ports, and money that was not on the record. What better place to murder a worrisome alcoholic writer from New York and get away with it, I thought.

That afternoon Clete Purcel came into the bait shop and rented a boat. I had not seen him since he had been released from jail.

"You want to talk about anything?" I asked.

"About getting put in the bag with psychopaths like Frankie Dogs? Not really," he said.

"I was going to ask you if you'd had any contact with Legion Guidry."

His face became vague, then he yawned and looked at his watch. "Wow, the fish are waiting," he said.

He loaded his tackle box and cooler and spinning rod and himself into a narrow aluminum outboard and roared down the bayou, splitting the water in a yellow trough behind him. He returned just before dark, sunburned, his face dilated from drinking beer all afternoon, an eleven-pound large-mouth bass iced down in the cooler, the treble hooks of the Rapala still buried deep in its throat.

I heard him scaling and scraping out his fish under a faucet on the dock, then he entered the bait shop and washed his hands and face with soap at a sink in back and helped himself to a sandwich off the shelf and a cup of coffee and sat down at the counter, his eyes clear now. He counted the money out of his wallet for the sandwich and coffee, then lost his concentration and knitted his fingers in front of him.

"I need to put my schlong in a lockbox," he said.

"You're talking about your involvement with Zerelda?"

"I can't believe I was in a cell with Frankie Dogs. He was a bodyguard for one of the guys who probably killed John Kennedy. It's like standing next to a disease."

"Go back to New Orleans for a while."

"That's where all these guys live."

"So pull the plug with Zerelda."

"Yeah," he said vaguely, looking into space, puffing out the air in one cheek, then the other. "I think she's still got the hots for Perry LaSalle, anyway. I guess he poked her a few times, then decided to zip up his equipment. Zerelda says he did the same thing with Barbara Shanahan."

I busied myself at the cash register, then carried out a bucket of water that had drained from the pop cooler and threw it across one of the bait tables. When I came back inside, Clete was looking at me, his face flat.

"You don't want to hear about other people's sex lives?" he said.

"Not particularly."

"Well, you'd better hear this, because this guy LaSalle has thumbtacks in his head and makes a full-time career of finding reasons to jam boards up everybody's ass except his own.

"Barbara and Zerelda used to know each other when Barbara and LaSalle were at Tulane together. Barbara wouldn't have anything to do with LaSalle, because LaSalle's family let Barbara's grandfather do time that should have been theirs. Then one night outside a law-school party on St. Charles, LaSalle saw these gang-bangers tearing up two Vietnamese kids. LaSalle waded into about six of them, so they stomped him into marmalade instead of the Vietnamese.

"Barbara took LaSalle home and cleaned up his cuts and fed him soup and, guess what, they end up doing the horizontal bop.

"Guess what again? LaSalle comes around a few more times for some more boom-boom, then turns her off like she doesn't exist."

"This means he has thumbtacks in his head?" I asked.

"A guy who dumps a woman like Barbara Shanahan? Either he's got shit for brains or he's a closet bone-smoker."

"You called her a woman instead of a broad," I said.

Clete raised his eyebrows. "Yeah, I guess I did," he said.

The phone rang. When I got finished with the call, Clete was gone. I caught him at his car, out by the boat ramp.

"The other day the sheriff told me somebody slashed Legion Guidry's truck tires. You were seen in the neighborhood," I said.

"That's a heartbreaking story," he said.

"Stay out of it, Cletus."

"The show is just getting started, big mon," he replied, and drove away.

The following Monday I drove down East Main, past the antebellum and gingerbread homes along the Teche and the shady lawns scattered with the bloom of azalea bushes. I parked by the Shadows, where a tourist bus was unloading, and crossed the street and entered a two-story Victorian house that had been remodeled into the law offices of Perry LaSalle. It was like entering a monument to the past.

Three secretaries sat behind computers in the front office, phones ringing, a fax machine pumping laser-printed correspondence into a basket, but these concessions to modern times were clearly overwhelmed in significance by an enormous glass-encased, sun-faded Confederate battle flag that had been carried by members of the 8th Louisiana Volunteers, its cloth rent by grapeshot or minnie balls, the names Manassas Junction, Fredericksburg, Antietam, Cross Keys, Malvern Hill, Chantilly, and Gettysburg inked into brown patches that were hand-stitched along the flag's border. Oil paintings of LaSalles hung over the fireplace and between the high windows. A Brown Bess musket used by one of them at the Battle of New Orleans was propped on the mantel-piece, a framed letter of gratitude written to Perry's ancestor by Andrew Jackson resting on the flintlock mechanism.

But it was not the LaSalles' historical memorabilia that captured my attention. Through the window I saw a tall man backing a fire-engine-red pickup truck out the driveway. He wore a flower-print shirt and a straw hat, with the brim slanted over his forehead, but I could see the vertical furrows in his face, like those on a prune.

The secretary told me I could go upstairs to Perry's office.

"You look a little battered. What happened?" Perry said from behind his desk.

"Bad day on the job. You know how it is. Who was that backing his truck out your driveway?"

Perry gazed out the window at the traffic passing

on the street. "Oh, that fellow?" he said casually. "That's Legion, the guy you were asking about once before."

"He's your client?"

"I didn't say that."

"Then what's he doing here?"

"None of your business."

I sat down without being asked.

"You know the name William O'Reilly?" I asked.

"No."

"He was a writer from New York. Legion shot him to death outside a bar in Morgan City."

Perry picked up a pen and rotated it in his fingers, then dropped it back on his desk. His office shelves were filled with law and historical books and leather-bound biographies of the classical world. A photograph of the legendary Cajun musician Iry LeJeune hung on the wall. An old canvas golf bag stuffed with mahogany drivers stood in the corner like a reminder of an earlier, more leisurely time.

"Legion's a leftover from a bygone era. I can't change what he is or what he's done," Perry said. "Sometimes he needs money. I give it to him."

"I had a recent encounter with this man. I think he's evil. I don't mean bad. I mean evil, in the strictest theological sense."

Perry shook his head. His brownish-black hair was untrimmed and curly at the back of his neck, his eyes deeply blue inside his tanned face. "I thought I'd heard it all," he said.

"Beg your pardon?"

"Here's an old man, an illiterate Cajun, who is as

much victim as he is victimizer, and you make him out to be the acolyte of Satan."

"Why is it I always have the sense you glow with blue fire, while the rest of us bumble our way through the moral wilderness?" I said.

"You really know how to go for the throat, Dave."

"Next time you see Legion, ask him why a police officer would spit in his food," I said, and got up to go.

"Somebody *spit* in his food? You?" Perry put a breath mint in his mouth and cracked it between his molars. He laughed to himself. "You're a heck of a guy, Dave. By the way, Tee Bobby Hulin passed a lie detector test. He didn't rape or shoot Amanda Boudreau."

That afternoon I met Clete Purcel for coffee at McDonald's on East Main.

"So what?" he said. "You get the right polygraph expert, you get the right answers. No Duh Dolowitz always said he could throw the machine off by scrunching his toes."

"Maybe I've helped set up an innocent man."

"If they're not guilty for one caper, they're guilty for another. Innocent people don't leave their DNA on the person of a murder victim. That kid probably should have been poured out with the afterbirth, anyway."

I finished my coffee and watched a group of black kids dribbling a basketball down the sidewalk under an oak tree. Clete began to relate another detailed account of his ongoing problems with Zerelda Calucci. He caught the look on my face.

"What, you got to be someplace?" he asked.

"To tell you the truth—"

"I'll make it fast. Last night I'm grilling a steak with her on the little patio by her cottage, trying to find the right words to use, you know, so I can kind of ease on out of what I've gotten myself into without getting hit with a flowerpot. But she keeps brushing against me, pulling the meat fork out of my hand and flipping the steak like I'm a big kid who doesn't know what he's doing, smoothing my shirt on my shoulders, humming a little tune under her breath.

"Then for no reason she puts her arms around my neck and pushes her stomach up against me and plants one on my mouth, and suddenly I'm sort of in an awkward manly state again and I'm thinking maybe there's no need to toss our situation over the gunnels all at once.

"Just when I'm about to suggest we move our operation indoors I hear somebody behind us and I turn around and there's that hillbilly Bible salesman again, dressed in a white sports coat with a red carnation and his hat in his hand. He goes, 'I dint know if you found the Bible and the rose I left for you.'

"Zerelda goes, 'Oh, *that* was so sweet.'

"So of course I step in my own shit and say, 'Yeah, thanks for coming around. We'd invite you to have supper with us, but you've probably already eaten, so why don't you come back another time?'

"Zerelda goes, 'Clete, I don't believe your rudeness.'

"I say, 'Sorry. Stay and eat. Maybe if I roast some potatoes there'll be enough for three.'

"She says, 'Well, just eat by yourself, Clete Purcel.' And the two of them walk on down the street to the ice cream parlor. I've gotten blown out of the water twice by a meltdown who pulls a suitcase full of magazines and Bibles around town on a roller skate. My self-esteem is on a level with spit on the sidewalk."

"It sounds like you're off the hook with Zerelda. Count your blessings," I said.

He rubbed his face against his hand. I could hear his whiskers against his skin.

"After Zerelda and Gomer are gone, Frankie Dogs comes up to me and says, 'I seen that guy before.'

"I ask him where, like at that point I really care.

"Frankie Dogs says, 'He used to sell vacuum cleaners to the niggers up Tchoupitoulas. The vacuum cleaners cost four hundred dollars, but they were Korean junk. He'd talk the niggers into signing a loan they'd never get out of.'

"I say, 'Thanks for telling me that, Frankie.'

"Frankie goes, 'He was around three or four times looking for Zerelda. Joe don't want him here. You ain't got to worry about him kicking you out of the sack.'"

Clete blew air out his nose and picked up his coffee cup and stared out the window, as though he couldn't believe the implication that the success of his love life was dependent upon the Mafia's intercession.

"What did you say?" I asked.

"Nothing. I moved out of the motor court. Why is stuff like this always happening to me?" he said.

Search me, I thought.

The next day I tried to concentrate on the investigation into the murder of Linda Zeroski. But the pimps and crack dealers and street whores who had been Linda's friends all stonewalled me and I got absolutely nowhere. I had another problem, too. I could not get the man named Legion off my mind. In the midst of a conversation or a meal, I would see his mouth leaning down to mine and smell the tobacco odor of his breath, the dried testosterone on his clothes, and I would have to break from whatever I was doing and walk away from the curious stares I received from others.

The first story I had heard about Legion had been told to me by Batist's sister. I remembered her describing Legion's arrival on Poinciana Island and the ex-convict who had taken one look at the new overseer and leaned his hoe against a fence rail and walked seven miles into New Iberia, never to return, even for his pay.

I made a phone call to a retired Angola gunbull by the name of Buttermilk Strunk, then signed out of the office and drove to a small pepper farm and tin-roofed white frame house not far from the entrance of the prison. Buttermilk was not a rotund, happy, doughlike creature, as his name might suggest. Instead, he was one of those for whom psychiatrists and theologians do not have an adequate category.

It is difficult to describe in a convincing way the kind of place Angola was in the Louisiana of my youth, primarily because no society wishes to believe itself capable of the kinds of abuse that occur when we allow our worst members, usually psychopaths themselves, to have sway over the powerless.

For the inmates on the Red Hat gang, which was assigned to the levee along the river, it was double time and hit-it-and-git-it from sunrise to sunset, or what the guards called "cain't-see to cain't-see." The guards on the Red Hat gang arbitrarily shot and killed and buried troublesome convicts without ever missing a beat in the work schedule. The bones of those inmates still rest, unmarked, under the buttercups and the long green roll of the Mississippi levee.

The sweatboxes were iron cauldrons of human pain set in concrete on Camp A, where Leadbelly, Robert Pete Williams, Hogman Matthew Maxey, and Guitar Welch did their time. Convicts who passed out on work details were stretched on anthills. Trusty guards, mounted on horseback and armed with chopped-down double-barreled shotguns, had to serve the time of any inmate they let escape. There was a high attrition rate among convicts who tried to run.

I sat at the kitchen table with Buttermilk Strunk, the curtains puffing in the breeze. His face was like a pie plate, his skin almost hairless, his eyes baby-blue, so pure in color they seemed incapable of moral doubt. His breath wheezed inside his massive chest, and he smelled of soap and talcum powder and the whiskey he drank from a jelly glass. His shirt was scissored off below his nipples, and the place where his liver was located looked as if a football had been sewn beneath the skin there. After he had retired from the prison, he had worked for five years for the state police. Whenever a convict ran, the state always called upon Buttermilk Strunk to bring him back. Buttermilk killed eight men and never returned a living convict to the prison system.

"Remember a guard named Legion, Cap? Maybe last name of Guidry?" I asked.

His eyes left mine uncertainly, then came back. "He worked at Camp I. That's when it was half female," he replied.

"Know much about him?"

"They run him off. Some of the colored girls said he was molesting them."

"That's all you recall about him?"

"Why you want to know?"

"I've had trouble with him."

He started to take a drink from his jelly glass, then set it down. He got up from the table and poured his glass in the sink and rinsed it under the faucet.

"Did I say something wrong?" I asked.

"You read much of Scripture?"

"A bit."

"Then you seen his name before. Don't you drag that man into my life and don't you tell nobody I was talking about him, either. You best be on your way, Mr. Robicheaux," he said, his mouth puckered, his eyes steadfastly avoiding mine.

The next day Barbara Shanahan showed me a side to her character that made me reconsider all my impressions about her.

CHAPTER 13

She had gone to bed early, then had been awakened near midnight by a dream of a hard-bodied bird thudding against her window glass. She sat up in bed and looked out the back window but saw only the tops of banana trees and the green slope of her yard that dead-ended against the rear wall of a nineteenth-century brick warehouse. Then she heard the sound again.

She put on a robe and looked out the front window on Bayou Teche and the dark cluster of oaks and the gray stone presence of the ancient convent across the water. She realized the sound came from below her feet, down in the garage, where she parked her car.

She pulled out the drawer to her desk and removed a .25-caliber automatic. In the kitchen she opened the door to the enclosed stairwell that led downstairs and switched on the light. The garage door was shut, locked electronically from the inside, and her tan Honda four-door gleamed softly under the overhead light, its surfaces waxed and immaculately clean. Her ten-speed bicycle, her snow skis and alpine rock-climbing equipment she took to Colorado and Montana on vacation were all placed neatly on hooks and wall shelves, her nylon backpacks and winter jackets glowing with all the colors of the rainbow.

But as she descended the stairs she could feel a presence that didn't belong there, a violation of the fresh white paint on the garage walls, the cement floor that did not have a drop of oil on it, the cleanliness and order that always seemed to define the environment Barbara chose to live in. She smelled an odor, like unwashed hair, bayou water, clothing that had started to rot. A window on the side wall had been pried open, the wall marked with black scuffs from someone's shoes or boots.

She moved around the front of her car and under the window saw a shape curled inside the tarp she used to cover her vegetable garden when there was frost.

She pulled back the slide on the .25 and released it, snicking the small round off the top of the magazine into the chamber.

"If you like, I can just shoot through the canvas. Tell us what your decision is," she said.

Tee Bobby Hulin uncovered his face and pushed himself up on his palms, his back against the wall. His eyes looked scalded; his hair was like dirty string. He wore a pullover, a moth-holed black sweater that emanated an eye-watering stench.

"What in the world do you think you're doing?" Barbara asked.

"I ain't got no place to go. You got to hep me, Miss Barbara," he said.

"Are you retarded? I'm the prosecutor in your case. I'm going to ask that you be sentenced to death."

He covered his head with his arms and pressed his face down on the tops of his knees. His left forearm was perforated with needle tracks that had become infected and looked like a tangle of knotted red wire under his skin.

"What are you shooting?" she asked.

"Speedballs, smack straight up, sometimes smack and whiskey, sometimes I ain't sure. There's a bunch of us cook with the same spoon, shoot with the same works sometimes."

"I'm going to have you picked up. I suggest when you're allowed to use the phone, you contact your attorney. Then you have him call me."

"I used to cut your grass. I run errands for your granddaddy. Perry LaSalle don't care about black people, Miss Barbara. He care about hisself. They gonna kill my gran'mama. They'll kill my sister, too."

"Who's going to kill them?"

He balled both his fists and squeezed them into his temples. "The day I say that, that's the day my gran'mama and sister die. Ain't no place to go wit' it, Miss Barbara," Tee Bobby said.

Barbara released the magazine from the butt of her .25, ejected the round from the chamber, and dropped the magazine and the pistol into the pocket of her robe.

"How many times did you fix today?" she asked.

"T'ree. No, four."

"Get up," she said.

"What for?"

"You're going to take a shower. You stink."

She lifted him by one arm from the floor, then pushed him ahead of her up the stairs.

"You gonna dime me?" he asked.

"Right now I recommend you shut your mouth." She shoved him inside the bathroom door. "I have some of my brother's clothes here. I'm going to throw them and a paper bag inside. When you finish showering, put your dirty things in the paper bag. Then wipe down the shower and the floor and put the soiled towel in the basket. If you ever break into my house again, I'm going to blow your head off."

She shut the bathroom door and punched in a number on the telephone.

"This is Barbara Shanahan. Here's your chance to prove what a great guy you are," she said into the receiver.

"It's one in the morning," I said.

"You want to pick up Tee Bobby at my apartment or would you like him to sweat out a four-balloon load in a jail cell?" she asked.

When I got to Barbara's, Tee Bobby was sitting in the living room, dressed in oversize khakis and a gold and purple LSU T-shirt with the sleeves cut off. He kept sniffling and wiping his nose with the back of his wrist.

"They sent *you?*" he said.

"Go down to my truck and wait there," I said.

"Detox ain't open. What you up to?" he said.

"I'm about to throw you down the stairs," Barbara said.

After Tee Bobby was gone, she told me everything that had happened.

"Why didn't you have the city cops pick him up?" I asked.

"This case has too many question marks in it," she replied.

"You have doubts about his guilt?"

"I didn't say that. Others were involved. That dead girl deserves better than what she's getting."

Her terry-cloth robe was cinched above her hips. Even in her slippers she was slightly taller than I. In the soft light her freckles looked like they had been feather-dusted on her skin. Her hair was dark red, and she lifted a lock of it off her brow and for just a moment reminded me of a high school girl caught unawares in a camera's lens.

"Why are you staring at me like that?" she asked.

"No reason."

"You taking Tee Bobby to his grandmother's?"

"I thought I'd cuff him to a train track," I said.

A grin started to break at the corner of her mouth.

Tee Bobby was sitting in the passenger seat of my truck when I got downstairs. He had vomited on the gravel and the foulness and density of his breath filled the cab of the truck. His hands were pressed between his legs, his back shivering.

"Are your grandmother and sister in harm's way, Tee Bobby?" I asked before starting the engine.

"I ain't saying no more. I was sick up there. I couldn't keep my thoughts straight."

"Even if you beat the charges, where do you think all this will end?"

"Gonna be back playing my gig."

"You want me to drop you somewhere you can fix?"

We were on the drawbridge over the Teche. I could hear the tires on the steel grid in the silence.

"I ain't got no money," he answered.

"What if I gave you some?"

"You'd do that? I'd really appreciate that. I'll pay you back, too. There's a joint off Loreauville Road. I just need to flatten out the kinks, then maybe join some kind of program."

"I don't think there's a lot of real hope for you, Tee Bobby."

"Oh, man, what you doin' to me?"

"I can't get Amanda Boudreau out of my mind. I see her in my sleep. Does she bother you at all?" I said.

"Amanda hurt me, man, but it wasn't me shot her." His voice was squeezed in his throat, his eyes wet.

"Hurt you how?"

"Made like we couldn't have no kind of relationship. She say it was 'cause I was so much older. But I knowed it was 'cause I'm black."

"You want to come down to the department and make a statement?"

He tried to open the truck door, even though I was up on the Loreauville Road now, speeding past a rural slum by the four corners. I reached across the seat and pulled the door shut, then hit him on the side of the face with my elbow.

"You want to kill yourself, do it on your own time," I said.

He cupped one hand over his ear and cheek, then he began to shake, as though his bones were disconnected.

"I'm gonna be sick. I got to fix, man," he said.

I drove him out in the country to the home of a black minister who ran a shelter for alcoholics and homeless men. When I left, heading up the dirt track toward the highway, the sky was still black, bursting with all the constellations, the pastures sweet with the smell of grass and horses and night-blooming flowers.

It was one of those moments when you truly thank all the spiritual powers of the universe you were spared the fate that could have been yours.

My partner, Helen Soileau, was eating outside at the McDonald's on East Main later the same day when she saw Marvin Oates towing his suitcase filled with his wares up East Main, his powder-blue, long-sleeved shirt damp at the armpits. He paused in the shade of a live oak in front of the old Trappey's bottling plant and wiped his face, then continued on to the McDonald's, took his sack lunch and a thermos out of his suitcase, and began eating at a stone table, outside, under the trees.

An unshaved man with jowls like a St. Bernard was eating at another table a few feet away. He picked up his hamburger and fries and sat down next to Marvin without being invited, sweeping crumbs off the table, flattening a napkin on the stone, knocking over Marvin's thermos. Marvin righted his thermos but remained hunched over his sandwich, his eyes riveted on a neutral spot ten inches in front of his nose.

"You bring your own lunch to a restaurant?" the unshaved man asked.

"I don't know you," Marvin said.

"Yeah, you do. They call me Frankie Dogs. Some

people say it's because I look like a dog. But that ain't true. I used to race greyhounds at Biscayne Dog Track. So the people I worked for started calling me Frankie Dogs. You like greyhound racing?"

"I don't gamble."

"Yeah, you do. You're trying to put moves on Zerelda Calucci. That's a big gamble, my friend. One you ain't gonna win. Look at me when I'm talking to you."

"I dint hear Miss Zerelda say that."

"Take the shit out of your mouth. You got a speech defect? Here, I'll give you the short version. Joe Zeroski don't want no peckerwood magazine salesman coming around his niece. You do it again, I'll be paying you a visit."

Marvin nodded solemnly, as though agreeing.

"Good man," Frankie said, and got up from the table and patted Marvin on the back. "I'll tell Joe we don't got no problem. You have a good day."

Frankie started to walk away.

"You forgotta your Bigga Mac," Marvin said into the dead space in front of him.

Frankie stopped, straightening his shoulders above the enormous breadth of his stomach. He walked back to the table and propped one arm on it and leaned down toward Marvin's face.

"What'd you say?" he asked.

"You lefta a bigga mess. It don'ta looka good."

"That's what I thought you said. Check you out later. Say, I like your tie," Frankie said.

"Later" turned out to be a passage of five minutes, when Marvin finished eating and went into the men's room. Frankie Dogs came through the door right behind him and drove Marvin's face into the tile wall above the urinal, then wheeled him around and buried his fist in Marvin's stomach.

A middle-aged man was exiting the toilet stall, belting his trousers.

"Out of the way! We got an emergency here!" Frankie said, shoving the man aside and plunging Marvin's head into the toilet bowl.

Then Frankie repeatedly flushed the toilet, pressing Marvin's face deeper into the vortex swirling about his ears. When the manager burst through the door, Frankie pulled Marvin out of the bowl by his collar, a curtain of water cascading onto the floor. Marvin lay half unconscious against the wall, a long strand of wet toilet paper hanging from one ear.

"You people need to clean this place up. It ain't sanitary," Frankie said to the manager, gesturing at the paper towels someone had left scattered on the washbasin.

That evening I drove to Baron's, our local health club, and worked out on the machines, lightly at first, then increasing the weight incrementally as the pain and the stiffness from the beating Legion had given me gradually dissipated in my muscles and bones. Then I went into the aerobics room, which was empty now, and did a series of leg-lifts and push-ups and curls with thirty-pound dumbbells. I could feel the blood swell in my arms, my palms ring with the tremolo of the dumbbells when I clanged them down on the steel rack. I wasn't out of the woods yet, but at least I didn't feel as though I had been rope-drug down a staircase.

I sat in a folding chair, a towel draped over my head, and touched the floor with my hands, constricting the muscles in my stomach at the same time. When I glanced up, I saw Jimmy Dean Styles enter at the far end of the room and begin pounding the heavy bag with a pair of dull red slip-on gloves, smacking the bag so hard, sweat showered from his head.

He used the classic stance of Sugar Ray Robinson, his weight forward, raised on the balls of his feet, his chin tucked into his shoulder, his left jab aimed eye-level at an opponent, his right hook a blur of light. A row of stitches was ridged across one cheek, like a centipede embedded in the skin. With his sheep's nose and close-set eyes, a ragged line of beard along his jawbones, his profile could have been lifted from a mural depicting an Etruscan gladiator.

But Jimmy Dean Styles was not one who performed or forfeited his own well-being for the entertainment of the upper classes.

A college girl and her boyfriend had just entered the room. The girl was rich, a well-known loud presence at the club, vacuous, obtuse, spoiled, protected by her family's wealth, totally unaware of the tolerance that other people extended to her. Her blond hair was moist with sweat, tied up on her head, her white shorts rolled up high on her tanned thighs. She plugged a tape into the stereo and began an aerobic dance routine, kicking at the air, chewing gum, the stereo's speakers loud enough to rattle glass.

"Like, I don't want to create no problem here, but I don't need my eardrums blown out," Styles shouted, lowering his gloves to his sides.

But she kept up her routine, her hands on hips now, her breasts bouncing, her mouth counting *one-two, one-*

two, her eyes shifting to Jimmy Dean Styles for a moment, then looking straight ahead again, *one-two*, *one-two*, her attention now concentrated on her reflection in the floor-to-ceiling mirror.

"Say, maybe you ain't heard me, but there ain't no aerobic class in here right now. That means I didn't come in here for no Excedrin headache," Styles tried to yell above the music.

She paused and blotted her face with a towel, then wiped her arms and the top of her chest and threw the towel on the carpet. I thought she was going to pull the tape from the stereo, but instead she did a cartwheel all the way across the room, exhaled a self-congratulatory deep breath, then filled a paper cone with water at the cooler and brushed strands of hair off her forehead in the mirror.

Styles dialed down the volume of the music and picked up a second pair of heavy-bag gloves from a chair and tossed them to the girl's boyfriend.

"Here, I'll show you how to float like a butterfly, sting like a bee," he said.

"I don't box," the boy replied, his eyes looking away from Styles. There was a flush in his cheeks, like the color of a window-ripened peach. The softness in his arms, his narrow chest, the insularity he tried to wrap himself in, had probably made him the target of bullies all his life. "I mean, I probably would be just wasting your time," he added, wondering which excuse would be acceptable.

"Better put 'em on, my man," Styles said, then threw a left-right combination that stopped a half-inch from the boy's nose.

"Okay, you showed me. Thanks."

"Here, I'll do it again. You ready? Tell me if you're not ready. Don't blink. I told you not to blink," Styles said.

"I'm no good at this," the boy said.

Styles's fists flashed, zipping by the boy's eyes and chin, causing him to flinch and cower, the old stain of fear and shame and failure creeping into his face.

Styles smiled, pulled the glove from his right hand.

"Hey, didn't mean nothing by it. Right coaching, you could kick some ass. Ax your lady over there. She know a killer when she see one," he said. He put his finger in his mouth and then placed a glob of spit inside the boy's ear.

Ten minutes later I was alone in the steam room when Styles came in, naked, a towel tied around his neck. He sat down on the ledge, his buttocks splaying on the moist tiles.

"You don't like white people much, do you?" I said.

He felt the hard row of stitches in his cheek and untied the towel from his neck and spread it across his thighs and phallus.

"A couple of cops rousted me outside my crib. Tore the carpet out of my car. I heard them say your name. Like maybe you tole them I was dealing," Styles said.

"They gave you those stitches?" I asked.

"I ain't done you nothing, man. Why you always on my case?"

"You make life hard for people of your own race."

He studied the drops of water running down the wall. His skin was gold, dripping in the clouds of steam. He bit down softly on the corner of his lip.

"You ax if I like white people. My grandfather use to

say just a few white folks was bad. No matter how bad he got treated, he always say that. They chained him to a tree and burned him to death wit' a blowtorch. Now, I'm gonna do my steam," he said.

"You were out at Poinciana Island, asking about Tee Bobby's sister. Why are you so interested in the welfare of an autistic girl?"

"'Cause Tee Bobby's grandmother and Rosebud got nobody to care for them. That don't fit in your head, that's your motherfucking problem, man."

He glared into my face, his nostrils flaring with a visceral hatred of me or the authority I represented or perhaps a lifetime of dealing with the worst members of the white race.

"You don't got nothing more clever to say?" he asked.

"No," I replied.

"That's good, man." He cupped his palm on his sex and massaged his shoulders against the hot tiles, his eyes closed, his face oily in the heat.

"Your grandfather was the victim of Klansmen and misanthropes. But you're not. You use the suffering of others to justify your own evil. It's the mark of a coward," I said.

He leaned forward, his forearms propped on his thighs, closing and opening his hands, as though considering a reckless course of action. He stood up, the towel dropping from his loins. His body was networked with rivulets of sweat. He scratched a place below his stitches, his eyes taking my measure.

"I seen you earlier in the dressing room. Eating some pills out of a li'l vial. Them ain't M&M's. You was taking the rush, man. You call me a coward? You used other cops to do this to my face, kick my feet out from under me while my wrists was cuffed behind my back. You got a problem, man, but it ain't me."

He went out of the door, past the big window on the steam room, his flip-flops slapping, a smile at the corner of his mouth.

I showered and changed into my street clothes and stuffed my gym shorts and soiled T-shirt and socks into my workout bag. Bootsie's diet pills, which I had taken from our medicine cabinet, lay in the bottom of the bag. I thought of Jimmy Dean Styles, the sneer on his face, the calculated insult of his words, and I felt my bowels slide in and out, a pang of anger rip through my chest as bright and sharp as a piece of scissored tin. I dropped two of the diet pills in my mouth and cupped a handful of water from the faucet and swallowed. The rush went through my system with the warm and soft glow of an old-fashioned, like the caress of a destructive ex-girlfriend reentering your life.

Outside, the wind was blowing hard, the palms whipping on the neutral ground, the sky bursting with trees of lightning. Garbage cans and newspapers bounced through the streets, the air smelling of dust and distant rain. Jimmy Dean Styles was putting up the top on a red convertible. A short, heavyset white woman, with bleached hair that looked as if it had been electrified in a microwave, stood behind Styles and watched him clamp down the convertible's top, patiently holding a yogurt cone wrapped in a napkin. I couldn't place her at first, then I remembered seeing her with Linda Zeroski, hanging on the same corner where Linda had been picked up the night she died.

Styles took the cone from her hand and hugged her close and licked a huge swath out of the yogurt, then fed the cone to the woman as he would a pet, her neck snugged tightly in his bare armpit.

"How you like it, my man? I'm talking about my car. You could use a 'sheen like this. Put a li'l boom-boom in yo' bam-bam, know what I mean?" Styles said, laughing openly at me now.

CHAPTER 14

Frankie Dogs was a private man who shared little about himself with other people. He and his wife had not been able to have children, and after she died of colon cancer many years ago, his only family had become the Mob. Frankie was a made guy and stand-up soldier in the old tradition. He went down twice, a three-bit in Raiford and a hard nickel in Angola. At Raiford he was kept in the Flat Top, maximum security, and the other inmates called him "mister." In Angola he was classified a big stripe and spent most of his sentence in twenty-three-hour lockdown. His neighbors were shank artists, snitches, gangbang yard bitches, and meltdowns who threw their feces through the bars at the guards.

Bad screws could jam him up, take away his privileges, leave him unwashed and foul in his cell. But Frankie Dogs never ratted anybody out, never used a punk, took on all comers in the showers or anywhere else, and would let his enemies rub salt in his wounds rather than complain or ask for help from a corrections officer.

Frankie grew up in the Irish Channel with Joe Zeroski and became a made guy the same week as Joe. But unlike Joe, who never gambled, Frankie loved racetracks in general and Miami's Biscayne Dog Track in particular. That's where he met Johnny (whose last name Frankie never used), silver-haired, handsome, profile like a Roman emperor's, connected in Hollywood, always dressed in fifteen-hundred-dollar tailored suits, a boyish grin on his mouth that was so congenial no one would later believe he helped to murder the president of the United States.

Johnny almost took out Fidel Castro with an exploding cigar. Frankie hand-waited on Johnny at his home in Ft. Lauderdale, played cards and swam with him in his pool, listened to Johnny talk about Benny Siegel and Meyer and how Albert died in the barbershop and who put the hit on him. Johnny not only had the keys to magic places in Phoenix and Beverly Hills and the Islands, he had the keys to history.

He might have been a greaseball from the slums of New York, but he had reinvented himself as a man of grace and charm in a world of palm trees, tile-roofed stucco mansions, and champagne lawn parties. Each morning the tropical sunrise came to Johnny as an absolution, not of sin but of poverty.

"What you brooding about, kid?" Johnny asked him one evening when they were playing cards and grilling steaks on the patio.

"These political people ain't no good for us," Frankie replied.

"It's a racket, just like unions or construction or any of our regular businesses."

"These guys got no loyalty, Johnny. They send their messages through Cuban street mutts 'cause they're ashamed to be seen with us. They'll use you and throw you away."

Johnny cupped his hand on the back of Frankie Dogs's neck, his eyes paternal, glistening with sentiment.

"You worry too much, kid. But that's why I like you. You don't never let a man down," he said.

The next day Frankie slept late in the pool house. When he went inside for breakfast, he asked the Puerto Rican cook where Johnny was.

"Is no here," the cook replied.

"I know that. That's why I'm asking you. Why don't you learn the English language?" Frankie said.

The cook said Johnny had walked to the shopping center for a pack of cigarettes.

"He ain't supposed to do that. Why didn't nobody wake me up? Which shopping center? Hey, I'm talking here," Frankie said.

"I don't know nozzing," the cook replied.

One week later a sealed oil drum floated to the surface in Biscayne Bay. The drum was wrapped with chains and sash weights and should have remained buried forever in the silt bottom of the bay. But the people who had shot Johnny through the head and sawed off his legs and stuffed them with his torso inside the drum, pausing to jab an ice pick into his abdomen to break the stomach lining, had botched the job, allowing Johnny's last meal on earth to form into gas and float his body parts back into the tropical sunrise.

Frankie Dogs never forgave himself for sleeping in the day Johnny died.

He left Miami on the Sunset Limited, broke and depressed, and found his old friend Joe Zeroski waiting for him on the platform in New Orleans. Joe moved him into his house and gave him a job collecting the vig for the Giacano family's Shylocks. Frankie found a stained form of redemption in devoting his life to Joe and Joe's sad, drug-addicted, profligate daughter, Linda.

But it was all going south again. If you were a button man, the only edge you had was *the* edge. You got high on it and wore your indifference like an unshaved man in a tailored suit. Your enemies looked into your eyes and knew that even if they blew out your lights you'd smoke them on the way down. But some guys out of Houston tried to cowboy Joe by the St. Thomas Project. Joe fired his .45 through the back window of his car and hit a kid on a bicycle.

Bad luck for everybody. But that's all it was, bad luck. It don't mean you're some kind of degenerate, Frankie told himself.

In Frankie's opinion everything about this New Iberia gig was wrong. Frankie's motto was: When in doubt, take 'em all out. For openers he told Joe to pop that black kid, Tee Bobby Whatever. Throw a pimp off a roof and make his friends watch. And tell Zerelda to stop complicating things by rolling down her panties at every opportunity. First she's pumping it with that animal Purcel, then she's messing around with a door-to-door salesman packs his own lunch into restaurants. It was disgusting.

Frankie shot nine-ball in a back-of-town bar in

Lafayette, where the beer was cold, the fried-oyster po'boys good, the green-felt table level, the pockets leather, the competition first-class. It was like the saloons on Magazine he and Joe had shot pool in when they were kids.

Lightning flickered on the banana trees outside the back window and he heard a few drops of rain ping against the tin roof like scattered birdshot. A man with silver hair came in and sat at the bar in front. He had a Roman nose and a broad forehead that caught the light. Frankie had to look at him twice to make sure it wasn't Johnny back from the grave. Frankie speared the cue ball into the rack and ran the string all the way to the nine ball. When he looked at the bar again, the man with silver hair was gone.

Besides the bartender, the only other person in the building was a guy playing a pinball machine in a side room, back in the shadows, a guy with his slacks tucked into red and green hand-tooled cowboy boots that came almost to the knee, his face obscured by a peaked cowboy hat.

Frankie had not heard the front door open or close, had felt no puff of wind or balloon of rain-scented air come into the room. Where had the man with silver hair gone?

"Bring me another beer," Frankie called to the bartender.

"You got a beer."

"It's flat. Bring me an oyster po'boy, too," Frankie said.

Ten minutes later Frankie glanced out the side window. The man with silver hair was standing by a black

Caddy, the wind blowing his raincoat. Lightning pulsed across the heavens and the reflection illuminated the parking lot. The man by the Caddy seemed to smile at him.

Frankie told himself he was coming down with something. His stomach was roiling; his bowels were on fire. He went into the rest room and entered the wooden stall and latched the stall door behind him. When he dropped his pants and sat down heavily on the toilet seat, he looked through a clear spot on the painted window glass and saw the silver-haired man enter the back of the tavern.

The door to the rest room opened and Frankie felt the cool rush of air from the outside and heard the rain ticking on the banana trees. Then, for a reason he could not explain, he knew he was going to die.

He had left his gun in his coat on the back of a chair by the pool table. But strangely he felt no fear. In fact, he even wondered if this wasn't the moment that he had always sought, the one that came to you like an old friend showing up unexpectedly at a train station.

"That you, Johnny? What's going on?" Frankie said.

His eyes dropped to a pair of green and red cowboy boots, just before four splintered swatches exploded out of the door into Frankie's face.

An hour later Helen Soileau and I joined a Lafayette Homicide detective and three uniformed cops at the back of the tavern where Frankie Dogs died and waited for the paramedics to load his elephantine weight onto a gurney that was spread with an unzipped black body bag.

The Homicide detective, whose name was Lloyd

Dronet, wore a rain-spotted tan suit and a tie with a palm tree and tropical sunset printed on it. He had picked up four nine-millimeter shell casings on the end of a pencil and dropped them into a Ziploc bag. A fifth shell casing lay inside the stall, glued to the floor by Frankie Dogs's blood.

"So this fits with what the bartender told us. Four quick pops, then a pause and another pop. The last round was close-up. The muzzle flash burned the hair above the ear," Dronet said.

"Meaning?" Helen said.

"The shooter was a pro. This guy Dogs was mobbed up, right? Another greaseball whacked him out," Dronet said.

The man with silver hair sat at the bar, waiting for us to interview him. He was a local liquor distributor and was watching a baseball game on the television mounted up on the wall.

"Both the bartender and the liquor salesman say the only other person in the building was the guy in cowboy boots. You know any cowboys in the Mob?" I said.

"Greaseballs don't go to western stores?" Dronet said.

"You've got a point," I said.

We talked to the liquor distributor. He kept looking at his watch and jiggling his car keys in his coat pocket.

"You got somewhere to go?" Helen asked.

"I'm taking my wife out tonight. I'm already late. I'm trying to get home before the storm breaks," he replied.

"You saw the guy in cowboy boots go out the back door?" I said.

"I didn't say that. I saw a man playing pinball. I didn't

pay any attention to him. I heard the shots, then I went into the rest room. I wish I hadn't gotten mixed up in this."

"You saw no one else?" Dronet asked.

"No. I feel sorry for the man who died. But I don't know anything. The guy with the cowboy boots, they were green and red. I remember that. Like a Mexican might wear. But I didn't see his face. Can't we do this tomorrow?"

"If you didn't bother to look at his face, why'd you look at his boots?" Helen asked.

"Because his pants were tucked inside them. Can I go now?"

"Yeah. You and your wife have a good time," Dronet said.

"Who's Johnny?" the liquor distributor asked.

"Say again?" I said.

"The man on the floor was still alive when I got to him. He said, 'Hey, Johnny, some guy took me down hard.' It was funny, because my first name is Johnny. My wife's not gonna believe this."

"Get out of here," Helen said.

The bartender was an over-the-hill ex-wrestler and competition weight lifter from New Orleans, with a walleye and a polished round head and strands of braided barbed wire tattooed around both his upper arms.

"You got a look at the cowboy?" I asked him.

"It's a dump. I don't concentrate on the faces that come in here. Short version, I failed Braille school. You guys finished back there? I got to mop out the shitter," he replied.

*   *   *

Helen was thoughtful and quiet on the way back into New Iberia. Rain was falling on Spanish Lake, and fog rolled off the water and hung in the trees and smudged the lit windows in the houses set back from the road.

"You think it was a Mob hit?" she asked.

"Nope. Frankie was a made guy, Joe Zeroski's number one man."

She yawned and steered the cruiser around a possum that was crossing the road in the headlights, the windshield wipers beating hard against the rain.

"Long day, bwana. You want to hang it up for tonight?" she said.

"How about a visit to our local Bible salesman first?"

"Surprise, surprise," she said.

Marvin Oates lived downtown on St. Peter Street in a rented shotgun house, one with ventilated shutters, left over from the 1890s. Banana trees were wedged in a cluster against one side of his gallery, and on the other side bougainvillea with stems as thick as broomsticks had tangled itself in the railings so that the front of the house looked like an impacted tooth.

An ancient Buick, one side burned black by a fire, the entire paint job encrusted with soot and rust, sat in the shell drive, the rain pinging on the metal. Helen placed her hand on the hood.

"Still ticking," she said.

Marvin Oates answered the door in pajama bottoms and a pajama shirt that was unbuttoned on his chest, barefoot, his face full of sleep, his breath sweet with mouthwash through the screen.

"Can we come in?" I asked.

"I was sleeping. I get up early."

"We'd sure like to come in. It's wet out here," I said.

He pushed open the door, then stepped back in the shadows and removed a pair of blue jeans from a hat rack and put them on with his back to us.

"I got to get my shirt. Excuse me," he said.

"Don't worry about it. We'll just be a minute. Have you been anywhere tonight?" Helen said.

"To the show. I come home just a little while ago," he replied.

"Then went right to sleep?" Helen said. She sniffed at the air. "You smell anything, Dave?"

"Smoke?" I said.

"Something burning in your house?" Helen said.

"No," Marvin replied.

"It sure smells like it," she said, and walked through the front room into the middle area of the house and opened his closet. "I'd swear it was coming from here. You want us to call the fire department?"

"No. What's going on?" Marvin said.

Helen picked up a pair of cordovan cowboy boots from the bottom of the closet. "These are sure nice. You got any others?" she said.

"I don't think y'all are s'pposed to come in my bedroom. You're s'pposed to have a warrant or something," Marvin said.

Helen set the boots back on the floor and casually glanced over the shelf above Marvin's row of hanging shirts. She turned around.

"A greaseball named Frankie Dogs got popped tonight, Marvin. You own a gun?" she said.

"No. Why you telling me this?"

"Because he used your head for a toilet brush in McDonald's," she replied.

Outside, the yard was flooded and rain blew in a mist through the window screen onto Marvin's bedsheets. He pushed the glass down and twisted the lock in the frame. His chest and stomach were flat, his nipples the size of dimes. He pulled the covers off his bed and sat on the dryness of the mattress and looked at nothing, his arms propped on the mattress, his eyes focused on thoughts inside his head.

"The Lord is my light, my sword, and my shield," he said.

"That's not a bad statement. If I were you, I'd get my side of the situation on record. In my opinion, nobody's going to be missing Frankie Dogs," I said.

But Marvin Oates was not easily manipulated. "I been bothering you since I looked the wrong way at your daughter, Mr. Robicheaux. That's my fault, not yours. But I ain't gonna hep y'all hurt me. And I don't want y'all treating me like I'm stupid, either."

"We're sorry we woke you up, partner," I said.

Outside, in the cruiser, Helen started the engine and clicked on the windshield wipers. The rain was sliding in torrents off Marvin's roof, the banana fronds whipping in the wind against the side of his porch. The inside of his house was absolutely dark now.

"When's the last time you saw somebody sleep in a damp bed?" Helen said.

"Marvin's an unusual guy," I replied.

Helen switched on the interior light and studied my face. I felt my eyes break.

"You're not tired at all?" she said.

"No, I feel fine."

"I saw you go into an aspirin bottle twice tonight. But I don't think those were aspirins in the bottle. You doing whites on the half shell, Dave?"

When the man called Legion was much younger, he hung in Hattie Fontenot's bar down on Railroad Avenue, a tin-roofed frame building that shook with nickelodeon music, the passing of trains, and the drunken shrieks of deranged whores. Cops hung in there, too, because the coffee and boudin and cracklings were free—sometimes the whores, too—and the bouree game at the big round green-felt table in back was in progress twenty-four hours a day.

Negro shoeshine boys brought their wood shine boxes inside and knelt in the tobacco spittle and sawdust and cleaned and polished shoes and boots for ten cents. The white women in the cribs were five dollars, the black ones three. A long-necked Jax or Regal was twenty cents, a shot of whiskey a quarter. A Negro shucked oysters out of the shell and slid them down the bar in a trail of melting ice, briny and cold, a nickel apiece, the sliced lemon free. All the pleasures of the earth were available to any white male who desired them.

Then the times changed, without visible cause or explanation, so rapidly the man the Negroes knew only by the name Legion guessed that forces far to the North, where he had never visited, were behind the events reshaping the Louisiana he had grown up in. The cribs closed and most of the prostitutes drifted away. The state police hauled off the slot machines and sunk them in a hundred feet of salt water. Cops no longer hung in

Hattie Fontenot's bar and the color line began to dissolve, then broke like a dam. Black men took the jobs white men had always considered theirs at birth and walked with white women on the street.

But the man named Legion did not change. He wore his starched khaki work shirts and trousers like a uniform, a Lima watch fob hanging from his watch pocket, his cuffs buttoned at the wrists, his straw hat slanted over one eye. He smoked his cigarettes unfiltered, drank his whiskey neat, disdained warnings about diet and lungs and liver, coerced a black girl into bed when he felt like it, and occasionally on a Friday afternoon sat at a back table in Hattie's old bar on Railroad Avenue, a saucer and tiny spoon and demitasse of French coffee by his elbow, a hand of solitaire spread out on the felt cover, as though forty years had not passed and the building still shook with music and the rumble of trains and the disconnected laughter of deranged prostitutes.

He pared out the detritus from each of his fingernails with a penknife and brushed it off the knife blade on the table and watched a loud black man at the bar, the black man knocking back shots, joking with the white barmaid, yelling at people out on the porch. The black man's hair was mowed into his scalp, his skin shiny, his face beaded with either sweat or rainwater. He went to the rest room and reemerged, an idiot's grin on his mouth, flicking his hands to the music playing on the jukebox.

"What's happenin', cap?" he said to Legion.

The black man went to the bar, picked up his shot glass, and was about to drink from it when he looked at the expression on the barmaid's face and saw her eyes riveted on someone behind him.

"You shook piss off your hands on my neck," Legion said.

"Say what?" the black man said.

"Don't you pretend wit' me, nigger."

"You out of line, man."

The black man turned to set down his shot glass, raising his eyebrows at the barmaid, as though she and he were both witness to an aberration from out of the past that had to be temporarily tolerated. Then the black man made a serious mistake. He grinned at Legion.

Legion seized the black man's throat with his left hand and drove him against the wall, shutting down his air, almost lifting him from the floor. Then he inserted the blade of a penknife into the black man's left nostril.

"Mr. Legion, he ain't meant you no harm," the barmaid said.

"Pick up that phone, I'll be back later," Legion said.

Ropes of spittle drained from the corners of the black man's mouth. Legion tightened his grip and pushed the black man's head and neck harder into the wall, then worked the knife blade higher into the nostril, wedging the sharpened edge against the rim.

"You ready for it? Tell people your girl closed her legs," he said.

Legion looked deeply into his victim's eyes, his own face tangled with a twisted light that caused the black man to lose control of his sphincter.

Legion hurled him into a chair.

"I'm gonna finish my coffee, me. You clean that chair befo' you go," he said.

*   *   *

Helen Soileau and I were at the city police station when the anonymous 911 call came in from a passerby who had witnessed the scene in Hattie's old bar through a window. We got in the cruiser and drove down Main toward Railroad, past the Shadows and Perry LaSalle's office.

"Why you want to take a city call?" she asked.

Rainwater was over the curbs now, rippling back from the tires of passing cars into the bamboo that bordered the Shadows.

"The assailant is that guy Legion Guidry we checked out at the casino," I replied.

"So what? Let the city guys pick him up. We have our own collection of assholes to worry about," she said.

"He's the guy who used a blackjack on me."

She turned, fixed her eyes on me. Water flew up under a fender. I heard her fingernails clicking on the steering wheel.

We drove down Railroad, bounced across the tracks, passed a crack house, clapboard bars, shacks without doors or glass in the windows, and yards that were covered with litter. Helen pulled under a spreading oak by a small general store with an ice locker in front that steamed in the rain.

"Why you stopping?" I asked.

"I'm tired of you deciding what I should know and not know. Or in this case when I should know it."

"He put his tongue in my mouth. He's an old man who took me apart in front of my own house. It's not a story many people would believe."

"We tell rape victims they have to meet it head-on if they ever want any peace. What makes you different?"

"Nothing," I said.

A swath of rainwater and leaves blew out of the tree across the windshield.

"You going to tell the old man?" she asked.

"Maybe."

She shook her head and shifted the transmission into drive.

"I always thought you got a bum deal when you were thrown off the force in New Orleans," she said.

"Finish your thought," I said.

"I guess there're two sides to every story," she said.

We parked by Hattie Fontenot's old bar and Helen got out first and slipped her baton into the ring on her gunbelt. We went inside and saw Legion sitting at a back table, playing solitaire, his attention concentrated on his game. The bar stools were all empty; our footsteps were loud on the wood floors that had been scrubbed gray with bleach. The barmaid sat on a stool, hiding behind the cigarette she smoked, her shoulders rounded, her lipsticked mouth as bright as a rose inside the wreaths of smoke and the dyed blond hair that framed her face.

"Where's the man Legion assaulted?" I asked.

She inhaled on her cigarette and tipped her ashes into a beer cap and watched a bottle fly crawl up the wall, her eyelids fluttering. Helen and I walked toward Legion's table, dividing as we approached him, Helen slipping her baton from its ring.

"Stand up," she said.

"A black boy call y'all?" he said, rising from his chair, his hat brim tilting up now, exposing the long, vertical creases in his face.

"That's a gun in your belt?" Helen said.

"Ain't nothing wrong with that. State man give me a permit," Legion said. His hand drifted toward the checkered grips on a chrome-plated .25.

Her baton whipped through the air and cracked across his wrist. The blow was of a bone-bruising kind, one that usually swelled into a plum-colored, blood-filled knot. But Legion showed no reaction other than a flinch in his face, a quiver along the jawline.

"You got me now, bitch. But wait till down the road," he said.

She shoved him into the wall and kicked his legs apart, pulled the .25 automatic from his belt, and tossed it to me. He started to turn around and she whacked him behind the knee with the baton, a blow that should have crumpled him to the floor. Instead he twisted his neck so she could look into his eyes and read the malevolence in them, his breath reaching out and touching her cheek. But Helen was all business. She hooked him up, crimping the cuffs hard into his wrists.

"You're under arrest for threatening a police officer," she said.

"I give a shit, me," he said. He jerked his head at me. "Pick up my hat, you."

"You want your hat? Here," Helen said, and stepped on the crown, then shoved it down on his ears. "I hear you like to put your tongue in men's mouths. We just ran a couple of black cross-dressers in. I'll see what I can arrange."

After we put Legion in the back of the cruiser and closed the door on him, I touched Helen on the arm.

"What?" she said, her eyes flashing.

"Don't let this bum put a letter in your jacket," I said.

Her brow was cut with furrows. She rubbed her palms on her jeans. "I feel like I touched something obscene," she said.

At the lockup Helen placed Legion in a cell occupied by two heavily perfumed transvestites in spiked heels, sequined blouses, shorts sewn with lace fringe, layers of makeup, auburn wigs, false eyelashes, and Dracula nail polish. They both leaned against the bars, a cant to one hip, flirtation and fuck-you pouts dancing on their faces.

I waited at the cell door until Helen was gone.

"You going to be all right in here, Legion?" I asked.

"Sho he is. We gonna take good care of li'l dookie-wookie here," one of the transvestites said. She pinched a fold of Legion's cheek between her thumb and forefinger and shook it gingerly, her lips pursed.

At sunrise the night jailer walked down to Legion's cell to inform him that his lawyer, Perry LaSalle, had just arranged his bail. The transvestites sat close together on a bench in a corner, holding hands, their faces downcast.

"What's wrong with them?" the jailer said.

"How the hell I know? Where my t'ings at?" Legion said.

Later in the morning the jailer called me at the bait shop.

"Sherenda the drag queen wants to see you," he said.

"It's Saturday."

"That's what I told her. She pissed her panties and dropped them out in the corridor for me to pick up. Is it okay if she comes out to your house when she makes bail?" he said.

I asked Batist to watch the shop and drove to the lockup. Sherenda, whose male name was Claude Walker, was washing her underarms in the tin sink attached to the top of the commode. She blotted her face with a lavender handkerchief and stuck it down in her bra. She folded her hands around the bars, her pointed red nails clicking against the hardness of the steel.

"Legion give you a bad time?" I asked.

She buckled her knees and perched out her rump and started to grin, then gave up the act.

"Man talk shit all night. Couldn't understand none of it. Ever hear a cat hissing inside a sewer pipe? Scare po' Cheyenne to det'. Why Miss Helen and you done that to us?"

"He's a Cajun. He was probably talking French," I said.

"Darlin', I know French when I hear it. I could have done 'French' for that boy on any level. But that ain't what we talking 'bout," Sherenda said.

Sherenda's friend, whose female name was Cheyenne Prejean, took a deep breath in the back of the cell and lifted up her head. Her eyes were puffy with sleeplessness, red along the rims, her lipstick smeared like a broken flower on her mouth.

"My mother was a preacher. That man was calling out names from Scripture. He was talking to demons, Mr. Dave," she said.

She stared into space, like a creature who heard sounds others did not.

CHAPTER 15

The sheriff lived in a rambling pale yellow house with steel-gray trim and a wide gallery up on Bayou Teche. The sky was rainwashed and blue when I pulled into his drive and he was raking leaves out of his coulee, stacking them in a black pile for burning.

"The cross-dressers told you Legion Guidry talks to demons?" he said, his palms propped on the upended handle of his rake.

"Yeah, I guess that sums it up," I replied.

"You drove out here on a Saturday to tell me this?"

"It's not an everyday event."

"Dave, you're a toe-curlin' delight. I never know when you're going to drop one on me a sane person couldn't think up in a lifetime. Let me call my mother-in-law out here. She's in Eckankar. She teleports herself to Venus through a third eye in her head to check the records on her former lives. I'm not making this up." His eyes were starting to brim with water. "Where you going?"

A moment of contrasts.

That same afternoon a gumbo cook-off was in progress at City Park. The manicured and sloping lawns along the bayou were dark green in the shade, scattered with azalea bloom, the sky strung with strips of pink cloud. Three shrimp boats festooned with flags blew their horns near the drawbridge. The shouts of children and the twang of a diving board resonated from the park's swimming pool like a collective announcement that this was indeed the first day of a verdant and joyous summer.

In the midst of the live oaks, the gaiety of the crowd, the smell of boudin and boiling shrimp and okra and pecan pie and keg beer swilled from paper cups, Tee Bobby Hulin mounted a knocked-together stage with his band, plugged the jack of his electric guitar into the sound system, and went into a re-created version of "Jolie Blon" I had never heard before.

It was like Charlie Barnet's 1939 recording of "Cherokee," a perfect moment in music that probably had no specific origin or plan, a deep rumbling of saxophones, a building percussion in the background, a melody and countermelody that were like a tongue-and-groove frame around the whole piece, and inside it all an innovative artist who took long rides on a score created extemporaneously in his own head without ever violating the musical intricacies at work around him.

Tee Bobby looked like a man back from the dead. Or maybe he was high again on meth or skag and had bought a temporary reprieve from the hunger that ate at his system twenty-four hours a day, but I couldn't say. He wore shades and a purple fedora and a long-sleeved black shirt with garters on the arms and beige suede boots and lavender slacks flared and sewn with flowers at the bottom. After the first piece, he did two more numbers, conventional rock 'n' roll pieces that he took no rides on and showed little interest in. Then he slipped off his guitar and went to the beer stand.

"What was that first piece you did?" I said behind him.

He turned around, lowering a beer cup from his mouth. " 'Jolie Blon's Bounce.' I just wrote it. Ain't tried it on an audience before. Didn't nobody seem real tuned in to it," he said.

"It's great."

He nodded, his shades mirroring the crowd around us, the thick overhang of the live oaks.

"Jimmy Dean say he might take a demo out to L.A. for me. Souped-up zydeco's hot in some clubs out there," he said.

"Jimmy Dean is a parasite. He couldn't shine your shoes."

"Least he ain't dumped me at a homeless shelter in the middle of the night."

"Have a good life," I said.

"Try to make me feel bad all you want. You don't bother me no more. I passed the lie detector," he said.

He faced the bandstand and upended his beer cup, the foam rilling down the sides of his mouth, the corner of his eye like a prosthetic implant. His self-satisfaction and stupidity made me want to hit him.

I started back through the crowd to find Bootsie and

Alafair and bumped against the father of Amanda Boudreau. His body was hard, his feet planted solidly, his gaze unblinking behind his wire-rim glasses. His wife's arm was tucked inside his, the two of them like an island of grief that no one saw.

"Excuse me. I wasn't watching where I was going," I said.

"That was Bobby Hulin you were talking to, wasn't it?" Mrs. Boudreau said.

"Yes, ma'am. That's correct," I said.

"He's here, playing at a concert, and the man who supposedly represents our daughter chats with him by the beer stand. I can't quite express my feelings. You'll have to forgive me," she said, and pulled her arm from her husband's and walked quickly toward the rim of the park, pulling a handkerchief from her purse.

"You got a daughter, Mr. Robicheaux?" her husband asked.

"Yes, sir. Her name's Alafair," I replied.

He fixed his glasses up on his nose with his thumb. "You have to pardon my wife. She's not doing too good. I probably don't make it any easier for her, either. I hope your daughter has a wonderful life. I truly do, sir."

And he walked away, limping like a man whose gout gave him no peace.

That night I had drunk dreams and woke at two in the morning, wired, my mouth dry, my ears filled with sounds that had no origin. I could not remember the images in the dreams, only the nameless feeling they left me with.

Like being slapped awake when no one else was in the room.

Like stepping unexpectedly off a ledge one hundred feet below the Gulf's surface and plummeting into a chasm filled with coldness and rough-skinned finned creatures whose faces flared at you out of the silt.

I went to the kitchen and sat in the dark, the luminous numbers of my watch glowing on my wrist. A bottle of vanilla extract sat on the windowsill in the moonlight, the curtains blowing around it. In the distance I heard a train and I thought of the old Southern Pacific, its lounge car lit, the passengers sipping highballs at the bar as the locomotive pulled them safely across the dark land to an improbable country of blue mountains and palm trees and pink sunrises where no one ever died.

I wanted to get in my truck and bang down corrugated roads, grind gears, thunder across plank bridges. I wanted to drive deep into the Atchafalaya Swamp, past the confines of reason, into the past, into a world of lost dialects, gator hunters, busthead whiskey, moss harvesters, Jax beer, trotline runners, moonshiners, muskrat trappers, cockfights, bloodred boudin, a jigger of Jim Beam lowered into a frosted schooner of draft, outlaw shrimpers, dirty rice black from the pot, hogmeat cooked in rum, Pearl and Regal and Grand Prize and Lone Star iced down in washtubs, crawfish boiled with cob corn and artichokes, all of it on the tree-flooded, alluvial rim of the world, where the tides and the course of the sun were the only measures of time.

All you had to do was release yourself from the prison of restraint, just snip loose the stitches that sewed your skin to the hairshirt of normalcy.

I got in the truck and drove full-bore down the four-lane, the frame shaking in the Gulf wind, until I saw the bridge spanning the Atchafalaya River at Morgan City and the network of adjoining bayous and canals and the shrimp and pleasure boats moored in the moss-green, softly muted tropical ambience that defines almost every unimpaired waterway in southern Louisiana. I turned into a clapboard bar that looked like it had floated out of the mist onto the road, one window scrolled with a green and gold Dixie beer sign.

I sat for five minutes in the false dawn, my hand trembling on the floor stick, my upper lip beaded with sweat. Then I drove back down the highway, fifteen miles under the speed limit, cars whizzing by me, their horns blowing, all the way back to New Iberia and the apartment where Clete Purcel was now living, wondering how in the name of a merciful God I could have a Sunday morning hangover without touching a drop of alcohol.

I sat at the counter in his small kitchen while Clete fixed coffee and stirred a skillet filled almost to the brim with a half-dozen eggs, strips of bacon, chunks of sausage and yellow cheese, and a sprinkling of chopped scallions to disguise enough cholesterol to clog a sewer main. He wore clacks and his Marine Corps utility cap and a pair of boxer undershorts, printed with fire engines, that hung on his hips like women's bloomers.

"But you didn't go in the bar?" he said, not looking at me.

"No."

"Helen thinks you're doing speed." When I didn't

reply, he said, "You got a hearing problem this morning?"

"I ate a few of Bootsie's diet pills."

"What else?"

"A few whites."

"Maybe you ought to go all out. Chop up some lines. Start hanging with the rag noses in north Lafayette," he said.

He filled a plate for me and clattered it down on the counter.

We ate in silence. Outside, the morning was taking hold, wind blowing in a sugarcane field, buzzards circling over a grove of trees. I put four teaspoons of sugar in my coffee and drank it black, in one long swallow.

"I'd better get going," I said.

"You've got a strange look on your face. Does Bootsie know where you are?"

"I called her from the highway."

"We're going to a meeting," he said.

"We?"

"I think you're figuring out ways to get loaded again. I'm not going to allow it. That's just the way it is, big mon." He cupped his huge hand on my neck and squeezed, his breath heavy with the booze he had drunk the night before.

I called the Alcoholics Anonymous hotline number and found a meeting in Lafayette. We drove up the old highway in Clete's convertible, with the top down, past Spanish Lake, through Broussard and tree-lined streets dotted with Victorian homes, people crossing through the traffic to Sunday Mass. After I had almost convinced myself that perhaps Clete enjoyed levels of reason and control in his life that I should envy, he described some of his activities of the last week or so, the Clete Purcel version of ecoterrorism.

"This guy Legion's not that smart. He hasn't figured out where it's coming from yet," he said.

Clete had put in a change of address for Legion at the post office, forwarding his mail to General Delivery, Bangor, Maine; called the utility companies and ordered the cutoff of his water, electricity, telephone, and gas service; hired neighborhood black kids to throw firecrackers on his roof, shoot out his windows with BB guns, and shove a burning sack of dog shit under his bedroom floor.

Then, in a finale that would have made even No Duh Dolowitz, the Mob's merry prankster, doff his hat, he got an exterminator to go to Legion's house, while Legion was at work, and tent the whole building and fumigate it with termicide, so that the building stank of noxious chemicals for days.

Clete casually sipped on a beer while he drove and told me these things, his face handsome with windburn and his aviator's sunglasses, his tropical shirt puffing, steering with two fingers at the bottom of the wheel, like an over-the-hill low rider cruising out of the 1950s.

"Have you lost your mind?" I said.

"You stoke 'em and smoke 'em, noble mon. I give this character about two weeks before he runs into a wrecking ball. Hey, I'm taking Barbara Shanahan to dinner tonight. You and Bootsie want to come along? Zerelda Calucci told me Perry LaSalle's schlong looks like a fifteen-inch nozzle on a firehose. She's exaggerating, right?"

I couldn't even begin to track his train of thought. We

were on University Avenue in Lafayette now, passing the old oak-shaded brick buildings and colonnaded walkways where I once attended college.

"Drop me in front of the meeting," I said.

"I'm going in with you."

"With a beer can?"

He pulled to the curb and tossed the can in an arc over his head, depositing it dead center in a trash barrel.

CHAPTER 16

A love affair with Louisiana is in some ways like falling in love with the biblical whore of Babylon. We try to smile at its carnival-like politics, its sweaty, whiskey-soaked demagogues, the ignorance bred by its poverty and the insularity of its Cajun and Afro-Caribbean culture. But our self-deprecating manner is a poor disguise for the realities that hover on the edges of one's vision like dirty smudges on a family portrait.

The state roadsides and parking lots of discount stores are strewn, if not actually layered, with mind-numbing amounts of litter, thrown there by the poor and the uneducated and the revelers for whom a self-congratulatory hedonism is a way of life. With regularity, land developers who are accountable to no one bulldoze out stands of virgin cypress and two-hundred-year-old live oaks, often at night, so the irrevocable nature of their work cannot be seen until daylight, when it is too late to stop it. The petrochemical industry poisons waterways with impunity and even trucks in waste from out of state and dumps it in open sludge pits, usually in rural black communities.

Rather than fight monied interests, most of the state's politicians give their constituency casinos and Powerball lotteries and drive-by daiquiri windows, along with low income taxes for the wealthy and an eight and one quarter percent sales tax on food for the poor.

Why meditate upon a depressing subject?

Because on occasion an attempt at redress can come from an unexpected source.

On Monday afternoon Marvin Oates was pulling his suitcase on wheels down a rural road that traversed cattle acreage and pecan orchards, across a bridge that spanned a coulee lined with hardwoods and palmettos, past neat cottages with screened porches and shade trees. Up ahead was the Boom Boom Room, the dilapidated Iberia Parish bar owned by Jimmy Dean Styles. A red convertible, the top down, roared past him, the stereo blaring. A bag of fast-food trash and beer cans sailed out of the backseat and exploded against the trunk of a pecan tree, showering litter in a yard.

Marvin Oates labored down the road, the roller skate affixed to the bottom of his suitcase grating against the road surface with the unrelieved intensity of marbles rolling down a corrugated tin roof. When he reached the Boom Boom Room, three of Jimmy Styles's rappers and two tattooed, peroxided white women in shorts were drinking long-necked beer and passing a joint by the side of the convertible.

A line of sweat leaked from Marvin's hat down his

cheek. He loosened his tie, craned his neck, blew out his breath, as though releasing the heat trapped inside his sports coat.

"Excuse me, but back yonder one of y'all threw a bag of trash out your car," he said.

"Say what?" said a tall man with orange and purple hair and rings through his eyebrows.

"There's some old colored folks living in that house where you flung your garbage. How'd you like it if you was them and you had to pick up lunch trash with mouth germs all over it?" Marvin said.

"Where you from, cracker?" the tall man with orange and purple hair said.

"Where folks ain't so ashamed of what they are they got to pay a couple of fat whores to take their dick out of their pants for them," Marvin said.

"Hey, Jimmy Sty, come out here! You got to check this out!" another black man called out. Then he turned back to Marvin. "Run all that by us again, man."

"Ain't my purpose to get nobody mad. I'm going back on my route now. Lessen one of y'all is interested in a magazine subscription or a discount Bible offer," Marvin said.

"You believe this motherfucker?" the man with orange and purple hair said, then balanced his beer bottle on the oyster shells.

"You ask me a question, I give you a straight answer. The Bible is my road map, sir. You don't like what you hear, that's your dadburn problem," Marvin said, and blotted his forehead on his coat sleeve. "It's flat burning up, ain't it?"

The group around the convertible was now joined by

others from inside the bar, including Jimmy Dean Styles. They stared at Marvin in dismay.

"Somebody put you up to this? Or you just a dumb white motherfucker want to commit suicide?" said a man with a nylon stocking crimped down on his head.

Marvin looked innocuously at a cloud, his eyebrows raised. "Most of y'all got born 'cause your mama dint have money for an abortion. That's why you call other people 'motherfucker' all the time. It's 'cause y'all know everybody in town got in your mother's drawers. So anytime you insult other folks with a bad name like that, it's on your own self. I ain't trying to hurt your feelings. It's just a psychological fact."

The tall man with rings in his eyebrows picked up his beer bottle from the oyster shells, tossed Marvin Oates's hat into the crowd, and smashed the bottle across Marvin's head. The crowd roared.

Marvin fell across his suitcase and took a kick in the ribs and another between his buttocks. He pushed himself up on the convertible's bumper, his coat powdered with white dust, his eyes closing, then opening, as though a piece of sharp metal was buried deep in his bowels.

He felt the back of his head and swallowed, then walked unsteadily on the shells and found his hat and knocked it clean of dust on his leg.

"You still ain't got the right to throw trash in old folks' yard," he said.

The crowd surged forward, but Jimmy Dean Styles stepped between Marvin and his adversaries and leaned over and retrieved the tow strap of Marvin's suitcase from the dust and placed it in his hand.

"Don't come around here no more," he said.

Marvin stared into Styles's eyes, as though looking for an answer to an ancient question about the nature of evil.

"Who are you?" Marvin asked.

"The man who know a nigger when he see one. You better hoof it, bro," Styles replied.

Helen and I were on our way back from an inter-agency law enforcement meeting in Jeanerette when we passed the situation in progress in front of the Boom Boom Room. We pulled to the side of the road and told Marvin to get in the backseat of the cruiser, behind the steel-mesh screen.

He threw his suitcase on the seat and pulled the coned brim of his hat down on his brow as we roared away, looking back through the window like a Pony Express rider who had been saved by friends from Indians.

"You crazy, Marvin?" Helen said, glancing in the rearview mirror.

"What's the name of that guy, the one in charge back there?" Marvin asked.

"Jimmy Dean Styles. Why do you ask?" I said.

"I just feel sorry for them people, that's all." He sprayed his mouth with an atomizer.

Helen and I dropped him off downtown, by the Shadows, his face freckled with the sunshine that fell through the oak limbs overhead.

"He seems to have people of color on the mind," I said.

"He should," Helen said.

"Pardon?"

"His mother took on all comers. I always heard Marvin's father was black," she said.

*   *   *

That same afternoon Clete Purcel drove to the motor court on the bayou, where he used to live, and knocked on Joe Zeroski's cottage door.

"What'd you want, Purcel?" one of Joe's men said. He was bald and wore slacks and a strap undershirt. Pieces of his sandwich were hanging from his mouth while he ate. A television set blared in the background.

"Where's Joe?" Clete asked.

"He ain't here."

Clete looked through oaks at the bayou, a tugboat passing, the sunlight breaking like glass on the water.

"You want to tell me what I already know, or you want to clean the dog food out of your mouth and answer my question?" he said.

Then Clete drove from the motor court, across the drawbridge, to a Catholic church on the other side of the bayou. He walked inside and saw Joe Zeroski seated in a pew, by a rack of burning candles, in an otherwise empty church. Clete went back outside and waited. Five minutes later Joe emerged in the sunlight, putting on his hat as he exited the vestibule. He stared at Clete.

"You following me?" Joe asked.

"I didn't know you went to church."

"I burn a candle for my daughter. Why you here, Purcel?"

Joe wore a gray suit and a gray and red tie, and the wind blew his tie over his shoulder.

"The sheriff's department is looking at a guy by the name of Legion Guidry for Linda's murder. I thought you ought to know that," Clete said.

"What, you owe me favors?"

"You were always straight up with me. So was Frankie

Dogs. Who knows, maybe Frankie Dogs was on to the guy. Maybe that's why Frankie got clipped."

Joe studied the trees along the bank of the bayou, popped a crick out of his neck, as though there were a thought behind his eyes he couldn't deal with.

"I had her cremated. There wasn't no way to fix her face for the funeral," he said.

"Guidry has a long history of violence against females, Joe. You said it yourself, how many guys like this are running around in one small town?"

"Say this guy's name again."

Late that evening Clete sat with me at the redwood table under the mimosa in my backyard and told me the story of his conversation with Joe Zeroski. When he finished, he took off his Marine Corps utility cap and refitted it on his head and looked at the purple light in the sky and the wind blowing across my neighbor's cane field, his green eyes red-rimmed with fatigue.

"I thought the drought was over. Two days of dry weather and it's the dust bowl again," he said.

"You bothered about taking Zeroski over the hurdles?" I asked.

"Joe will probably eat his gun one day. But he never tried to jam anybody who wasn't in the life. I guess if I could feel sorry for a gumball, I do for him," Clete said.

"We don't have any influence over these guys. Stop trying to orchestrate them, Clete."

"I think I ought to call him up," he said.

I squeezed Clete's bicep, hard, my fingers biting deep into the muscle. "Once and for all and forever, leave

Zeroski and especially Legion Guidry alone." I tightened my grasp when Clete tried to pull away from me.
"Did you hear me? Legion Guidry comes from someplace the rest of us don't. That's a theological statement."

"Sometimes I wish you didn't share all your thoughts,
big mon."

I awoke before sunrise on Tuesday and walked down the
slope through the oaks and pecan trees to the bait shop.
The fog was a bluish gray in the false dawn, then the sun
broke on the horizon and the fog turned the color of cotton candy and I could see snow egrets rising like confetti
above the cypress trees in the swamp.

Batist and I scrubbed down the spool tables, popped
opened the umbrellas above them, picked up beer cans
and bait cups from the boat ramp, and used a boat hook
to gather floating trash from the pilings under the dock.
All of this was done under the supervision of Tripod,
Alafair's fat, three-legged, silver-ringed pet coon. Then
Batist took a break and poured a cup of coffee for himself
from a drip pot on the gas burner and dropped a red
quarter into the jukebox and played Guitar Slim's "I
Done Got Over It." The haunting sounds of Slim's
music reverberated across the water and into the trees
like electronic echoes inside a stone pipe.

"Why'd you play that particular song?" I asked.

"The man talking about getting over it. You don't
never get ahead of it. You just get over it. I t'ink he figured out what it was all about."

"You think Tee Bobby Hulin murdered that white
girl?" I asked.

Batist picked up Tripod from a shelf, where he was

sniffing a glass jar filled with candy bars. Batist opened the screen and dropped him with a thump on the dock.

"That boy ain't no good, Dave. You don't believe I'm right, ax yourself who he hang around wit'. Jimmy Dean Styles say jump, Tee Bobby say 'How high?'"

Then, as irony would have it, just as I was about to go up to the house and change clothes for work, the phone on the counter rang. It was Sister Helen Bienvenu, the nun who gave art lessons at the public library.

"I did something I think I shouldn't have," she said.

"What's that, Sister?" I said.

"Rosebud Hulin did a lovely drawing of Amanda Boudreau with her parents. I think the photo was in the *Daily Iberian* about a week ago. When she finished it, she pressed it into my hands, as though she wanted me to give it to someone. There was a kind of sadness in her I can't adequately describe."

"I don't understand. What did you do that was improper?" I said.

"I gave the drawing to the Boudreau family. I didn't tell them who drew it, but last night Mrs. Boudreau was at the library and saw Rosebud in my drawing class. It was obvious she made the connection. I feel like I've exacerbated an already very bad situation."

"Did you ask Rosebud why she wanted to draw the Boudreau family?"

"Yes. She ran away from me. What are you going to do, Mr. Robicheaux?" she said.

"Did you tell anybody else about this?"

"No. But there was a black man who saw the drawing. He came to the class one night to drive Rosebud home. She wouldn't go with him. He owns a bar."

"Jimmy Dean Styles?"

"Yes, I think that's his name."

"Styles is a bad guy, Sister. Don't have anything to do with him."

"This upsets me, Mr. Robicheaux," she said.

"You didn't do anything wrong."

"Did Rosebud witness a murder? Please don't lie to me," she said.

I went up to the house and changed clothes and fixed coffee and a pan of hot milk and ate a bowl of Grape-Nuts and blueberries at the kitchen table. Bootsie came out of the bedroom in her terry-cloth bathrobe and took the medication that kept her lupus, what we called the red wolf, in abeyance. Then she sat down across from me and wrapped the inflatable tourniquet of her blood pressure monitor around her upper arm. She waited for the digital numerals to stop flashing on the monitor, then pushed the button on the air release valve and puffed out her cheeks, exasperated at not being able to change a condition that seemed both unfair and without origin.

"You've eaten salt and fried food every day of your life and your systolic is ten points above a cadaver's. What's your secret, Streak?" she said.

"*Picture of Dorian Gray* syndrome."

"Let me take your blood pressure," she said.

"I'd better get on the road."

"No, I want to see if my monitor's accurate," she said.

She wrapped my arm and pumped the rubber ball in her hand. She looked at the numbers on the monitor and punched the air release, her expression neutral.

"Your systolic is 165 over 90," she said.

I turned the page on the newspaper and tried to shine her on.

"That's almost forty points above your normal," she said.

"Maybe I'm off my feed this morning."

She put the monitor back in its box and began fixing cereal for herself at the drainboard. When she spoke again, her back was still turned to me.

"All my diet pills are gone. So is the aspirin. So are all the megavitamins I bought in Lafayette. What the hell are you doing, Dave?" she said.

I went to the office and tried to concentrate on a back-load of paperwork in my intake basket. A dozen messages were on my voice mail, a dozen more in my mailbox. A homeless man, who daily walked the length of the city with all his belongings rolled inside a yellow tent that he carried draped over his neck and shoulders like a gigantic cross, wandered in off the street and demanded to see me.

His eyes were filled with madness, his skin grimed almost black, his yellow hair glued together with his own body grease, his odor so offensive that people left the room with handkerchiefs over their mouths.

He said he had known me in Vietnam, that he'd been a medic who had loaded me with blood-expander and shot me up with morphine and pulled me onboard a slick and held me in his arms while the air frame rang with AK-47 rounds from the canopy sweeping by below us.

I looked into his seamed, wretched face and saw no one there I recognized.

"What was your outfit, Doc?" I asked.

"Who gives a shit?" he replied.

"I've got twenty bucks here. Sorry it's not more."

He balled his hand on the bill I gave him. His nails were as thick as tortoiseshell, gray through the tops with the amounts of dirt impacted under them.

"I had a rosary wrapped around my steel pot. I gave it to you. Don't let them get behind you, motherfucker," he said.

After he was gone we opened the windows and Wally the dispatcher had the janitor wipe down the chair the deranged man had sat in.

"You knew that guy?" Wally said.

"Maybe."

"You want me to have him picked up, take him to a shelter?"

"The war's over," I said, and went back to my office.

At ten o'clock my skin was coming off. I drank water at the cooler, chewed two packs of gum, went to Baron's Health Club and pounded the heavy bag, then returned to the office, sweating inside my clothes, burning with irritability.

I checked out a cruiser and drove out to the home of Amanda Boudreau's parents. I found Mr. Boudreau at the back of his property, under shade trees by the coulee, uncrating and assembling an irrigation pump. It was a large, expensive machine, the most sophisticated one on the market. But he had no well or water lines to attach it to, no network of ditches to carry the water it would draw from the aquifer.

He wore a white, short-sleeved shirt and new strap overalls, dark blue and still stiff from the box. His face was flushed, his knuckles skinned where his hand had slipped on a wrench.

"I ain't gonna get caught by drought again," he said. "Last year almost all my cane dried up. Ain't gonna allow it to happen again. No, sir."

"I think the drought is pretty well busted," I said, looking at a bank of black clouds in the south.

"I'm gonna be ready, me. That's the way my father always talked. 'I'm gonna be ready, me,'" he said.

I squatted down next to him.

"I know you and Mrs. Boudreau don't think well of me, but I lost both my mother and my wife, Annie, to violent people. I wanted to find those people and kill them. There's nothing wrong in feeling that way. But I don't want to see a good man like yourself take matters into his own hands. You're not going to do that, are you, sir?"

He clapped his broad hand on a mosquito that had landed on the back of his neck and looked at the bloody smear on his palm.

"Lou'sana's been drying up. Gonna dig me a well. Gonna have ditches and lines all through those fields. It can get dry as a brick in a stove, but I'm gonna have all the water I want," he said. He went back to his work, twisting a wrench on a nut, his meaty, skinned hand shining with sweat.

I stopped at a phone booth and called Clete's apartment.

"You still have flashbacks?" I asked.

"About 'Nam? Not much. Sometimes I dream about it. But not much."

"A guy came off the street today. He said he was the medic who took care of me when I was hit."

"Was he?"

"He was deranged. His hair was blond. The kid who got me to battalion aid was Italian, from Staten Island."

"So shit-can it."

"The homeless man had a New York accent. What's a New York street person doing around here?" I said.

"Where are you, big mon?"

I drove to Jimmy Dean Styles's New Iberia bar and was told by his bartender that Jimmy Dean was at his other club, the one he owned jointly with a bondsman in St. Martinville. I was there in twenty minutes. Styles was at the bar, reading a newspaper while he dipped cracklings into a bowl of red sauce and ate them, wiping his fingers on a moist towel, his eyes never leaving the page he was reading.

"You follow the market?" I asked.

"High-yield municipals, Lou'sana Chuck. Pay twenty-four hours a day, seven days a week. Like a girl got her groove with the right people, it always working, know what I'm sayin'? I can help you with something?" Styles replied.

"I don't know if you can or not, but hold that thought. Where's your rest room?" I said.

He nodded his head toward the rear of the building and dipped a crackling into his bowl and inserted it in his mouth, an amused light in his eyes.

His entourage of rappers and whores were at tables by the dance floor. They paid no attention to me as I passed. Inside the rest room I washed my face with cold water and looked in the mirror. I could hear a sound in my ears, like wind whistling inside a tin can, feel a pressure band along the side of my head, as though I were wearing a tight hat. A jukebox began playing by the dance floor, and I would have sworn the voice on the recording was Guitar Slim's.

I washed my face again. When I closed my eyes against the coldness of the water, I saw faces from my platoon, kids who had been out too long, their legs pocked with jungle ulcers, the smell of trench foot rising from their socks, scared shitless of night-trail toe-poppers and booby-trapped 105's, nobody in touch with who they used to be. A San Bernardino hot-rodder with a juju bag tied under his throat and a scalp lock to his rifle. A black kid from West Memphis, Arkansas, zoned on uppers and too many firefights, a green sweat towel draped over his head like a monk's cowl, the barrel of his blooker painted with tiger stripes. I could hear them marching, blade-faced, their uniforms stiff with salt, feeding off one another's anger, their boots thudding across a wooden bridge.

I spit in the lavatory and dried my face on my shirt rather than touch the cloth towel on the roller, then went out the door, the breeze from a fan suddenly cool on my skin, my heart racing.

Jimmy Dean Styles closed his newspaper and lifted a demitasse of coffee to his lips.

"Marse Charlie not wit' you today?" he said.

"You were at Rosebud Hulin's art class. That area is now off-limits for you. If she needs a ride, I'll provide one," I said.

"I don't know you, never brought you no grief, never given you no truck, but you always in my face and on my case. What is it wit' you, Chuck?"

"I don't think you're hearing me. Rosebud Hulin is out of your life. We're together on that, right?"

"You wrapped too tight for your job, man. I got a girl over there can take care of that for you, unzipper your problem, know what I'm sayin', but in the meantime don't be jabbing your finger at me."

"Just so you understand later why it all went south, you shouldn't call a guy 'Chuck,' not unless you've paid some dues, humped a sixty-pound pack for twenty klicks in the rain, had Sir Charles kick your ass, seen your friends blown into hamburger, that sort of thing. You reading me, partner?"

"You got a serious jones, Lou'sana Chuck. Now shake your cakes down the road, before I have you picked up," he said.

I caught him solidly on the jaw with a right cross, snapping his head sideways, slinging food out of his mouth, then hooked him in the eye and caught him with another right, this time in the throat, before he could get off the bar stool. He threw two fast punches at me, off balance, unable to draw his arms back for a full swing, and I slipped one of his punches, took the other on the ear, and then hit him with everything I had.

I put my whole weight into each blow, breaking his nose, splitting his mouth against his teeth, gashing open the skin above one eye. He managed to roll off the stool and right himself, even to get his guard up and catch me once, hard, in the chest, but I drove my fist into his rib cage, right under the heart, and saw his willpower leave him, his resistance drain from his face, like water bursting from the bottom of a balloon. I hooked him in the kidney, then in the stomach, doubling him over, forcing him to cling to the stool for support.

But I couldn't let go of it. I seized the back of his head

and drove his face down on the knurled edge of the bar, smashing it into the wood, over and over, while behind me women screamed and a tall black man with orange and purple hair and rings through his eyebrows tried to get his arms around me and put himself between me and Jimmy Dean Styles.

I pulled my .45 and barrel-stroked the man with orange and purple hair across the face, knocking him to the floor, then racked a round into the chamber and aimed the sight between his eyes, my hands streaked with Jimmy Sty's blood, shaking on the grips.

"I'll get out of town. I promise. Don't do it, man. Please," the man on the floor said, turning his face to one side.

A dark stain spread through his slacks.

I was arrested before I could get out of the parking lot. Ten minutes later I was escorted in cuffs inside the St. Martin Parish Jail, my shirt split down the back, and pushed inside the drunk tank. My skin felt dead to the touch, my muscles without texture or tone, as though I had just come off a two-day whiskey drunk. The voices of the inmates around me seemed muffled, filtered through wet cotton, even though some of them appeared to know me and were speaking directly in my face. In my mind's eye I saw a homeless man bent under a cross made of a rolled yellow tent stuffed with all his earthly belongings, and I knew that for all of us who had been there the war would never be over and the real enemy was not Jimmy Sty but a violent creature who rose with me in the morning and lived quietly inside my skin, waiting for the proper moment to vent his rage upon the world.

CHAPTER 17

When the Iberia sheriff arrived at the jail, I thought he would have me released. Instead, he had me moved out of the drunk tank to an empty holding cell, one with a drain hole and a urine-streaked, rusty grate in the center of a cement floor, graffiti and female breasts and male genitalia smoked on the ceiling with Bic lighters. I sat on a wooden bench, the sheriff in a chair on the other side of the bars, his eyes deep-set with his anger and disappointment. I felt light-headed and my hands were swollen and as thick as grapefruit when I tried to close them.

"Were you trying to kill him?" the sheriff asked.

"Maybe."

"Everyone in the bar says there was no provocation. They say Styles was just sitting on a stool and you went apeshit and started tearing him apart."

"He owns the bar. He owns most of the people in it. I'm a cop. What are they supposed to say?"

"You're being charged with felony assault."

"Thanks for passing on the news," I said.

"You just going to sit there and act like a wiseass?"

"Styles is a human toilet. Someone should have ripped out his spokes a long time ago," I said.

He rose from his chair and put on his Stetson hat and stared down at me, the light from a high window breaking around his head.

"You want me to call your wife, or can you handle that yourself?" he asked.

"You know, there is something you could do for me. I'd really appreciate a pack of gum from the machine out in the hall. That would really be nice," I replied.

I sat for twenty minutes, listening to all the sounds that are common to any jailhouse environment: steel doors clanging, toilets flushing, trusties dragging wash buckets down the corridor, Mariel felons yelling at one another in Spanish, a blaring television set tuned to a stock car race, a three-hundred-pound biker, wrapped in chains and stink, his hair like a lion's mane, deciding to make his captors earn their money when they tried to shove him inside a cell.

I took off my ruined shirt and rolled it into a ball for a pillow and lay down on the wooden bench and placed my arm over my eyes. Then I heard footsteps in the corridor again and, vain fool that all drunks are, thought it was the sheriff, my friend, returning to set things straight.

But the sheriff did not return, nor did anyone take me out of the holding cell or indicate when I might be arraigned.

The unpleasantness of jailhouse life has less to do

with confusion and the cacophony of noise that fills the inside of your head twenty-four hours a day than it does with your disconnection from the outside world and the fact that for you time stops when the cell door slams behind you.

You make no decisions for yourself. You are strip-searched by a bored turnkey who fits on polyethylene gloves before he pries your buttocks apart, then finger-printed, photographed, given a cleansing cream and a dirty rag to remove the ink from your hands, spoken to in a toneless voice by people who never address you as an individual or look into your face, as though eye contact would grant you a level of personal identity that you do not deserve.

Then you sit. Or lie on the floor. Or try to find any-place in a crowded cell away from the open toilet that eventually you will use in full view of everyone in the cell and anyone passing in the corridor. But most of the time you simply wait. No sexual encounters in the shower, no racial beefs with blacks or the Mariels from Castro's pris-ons whose space is rented for them by the G, no meet-ings with Damon Runyon street characters or O. Henry safecrackers. Most of the miscreants are hapless and stu-pid. Out-of-control hardcases are sedated, forced to shower, powdered with disinfectant, and transferred to hospitals. The screws are usually duffers worried about their prostates.

You wait in a vacuum, maybe in a large, colorless room, one more face among the faceless and uneducated and inept and self-pitying, convinced you are not like the others, that it is only bad luck that has put you here. After a while you wonder what it is you are waiting for, then realize you're thinking about your next meal, a chance to use the toilet or to stand a few moments at a window that looks out upon a tree. One morning you ask somebody which day of the week it is.

The life that used to be yours comes to you only in glimpses, perhaps through a letter, a visitor who sees you out of obligation, or financial notices of foreclosure and repossession. The noise, the ennui, the lack of uncomfortable comparisons inside the jail now become a means of forgetting the sense of loss that eats daily at your heart.

If there was ever a viable benchmark to indicate a person's life is unraveling around him, I know of none better than the day a person discovers himself inside the gray-bar hotel chain.

I called Bootsie, but no one was at home. When Alafair's recorded message ended and the machine beeped, I started to speak, then realized the inadequacy as well as harmful potential of the message I would have to leave. I replaced the receiver in the cradle and called Clete's apartment, but there was no answer. A half hour went by and I asked the turnkey for another visit to the phone.

"Maybe you won't need it. You got a visitor," he said. Then he shouted at the other cells, "Female on the gate!"

"Female?" I said.

Barbara Shanahan walked down the corridor in a pink suit and white blouse and heels, her perfume as strange and incongruous inside the jail as a flower inside a machine shop. She stood at the cell door, a tinge of pity in her eyes that made me look away.

"Clete told the locals he saw the fight. He got them to

go back to Styles's club and search the area where Styles was sitting. They found a switchblade knife under a table," she said.

"Switchblade knife, you say?" I said.

"Right." Her gaze wandered over my face. "Clete says he saw Styles pull it on you. But the arrest report makes no mention of a knife. I wonder why that is."

"I'm a little unsure of what happened, actually."

"I'm not going anywhere near this, but I made a couple of calls. A bondsman will be over here shortly. So will your lawyer."

"My lawyer? I don't have a lawyer."

"You do now. He's a prick, but he's the best at what he does."

"Why are you doing this?" I asked.

"You're a good cop and don't deserve this bullshit. Most people think you're nuts. The sheriff has washed his hands of you. You're totally self-destructive. I wish you'd killed Jimmy Dean Styles. Take your choice."

"Who's the lawyer?"

She winked at me. "Put a piece of ice on that eye, handsome," she said.

She walked back down the corridor, her scent lingering in the air, smiling slightly at the remarks made to her through the bars of the adjoining cells.

Ten minutes later Perry LaSalle came down the corridor with the turnkey.

"You know a song by Lazy Lester titled 'Don't Ever Write Your Name on the Jailhouse Wall'? Man, I love that song. By the way, Jimmy Dean Styles swallowed his bridge and had to have his stomach pumped. How's it hangin', Dave?" he said.

*   *   *

Cops call it a "drop" or sometimes a "throw-down." It can be a tear-gas pen, a toy pistol, or perhaps the real article, the serial numbers burned off with acid or on an emery wheel.

Or it can be a switchblade knife.

When a shooting goes bad and the suspect is on the ground with his dead hand open and a set of car keys falls from his palm rather than the pocket-size automatic you thought you saw, either you can tell the truth at an Internal Affairs inquiry and be hung out to dry on a meat hook, perhaps even do serious time in a mainline joint with the same people you put there, or you can untape the drop from your ankle, wipe it with a handkerchief, throw it on the corpse, and ask God to look in the other direction.

"Barbara must like you a lot," Perry said as we drove through a long tunnel of oaks toward New Iberia, the top of his Gazelle down, the air warm, the four-o'clocks blooming in the shade.

"Why's that?" I asked.

"She called me to get you out of the can. Normally she treats me like chewing gum on the bottom of a the-ater seat." He turned his head, his cheeks ruddy, his brownish-black hair blowing on his brow. "Purcel saw the fight but didn't try to stop it?"

"Better ask Clete about that."

"He wouldn't commit perjury for you, would he?"

"Clete?" I replied.

The next morning was Wednesday. I reported to work and walked down the corridor to my office as though nothing unusual had occurred the previous day. Wally the dispatcher gave me a thumbs-up and two uniformed deputies patted me on the shoulder as I passed. I didn't do as well with the sheriff.

"You're confined to desk duties until we clear up this mess in St. Martinville," he said, leaning in the door.

I nodded.

"Nothing to say?" he asked.

"Friends back their friends' play," I said.

"My department isn't going to be the O.K. Corral, either," he replied, and went back down the corridor, the heat rising in his face.

At noon I drove to Perry LaSalle's law office across from the Shadows, unaware I was about to have one of those experiences that teach you that your knowledge of human behavior will always be inadequate, that weakness and the capacity for self-abasement seem to reside in us all.

Perry asked me to write out what had happened in Jimmy Dean Styles's nightclub. While I wrote on a legal pad, he gazed down on the street, on the caladiums along his front walk, the live oaks under which Louisiana's boys in butternut retreated up the Teche in 1863, the columned homes on whose upstairs verandas people still served tea and highballs in the afternoon, regardless of the season or the historical events that might shake the rest of the world.

After I had finished a very short description of my attack on Jimmy Dean Styles, ending the account in the passive voice ("a switchblade knife was found under a nearby table by local officers"), I waited for Perry to detach himself from whatever he was watching down below.

"Sir?" I said.

"Oh, yes, sorry, Dave," he said, frowning as he read the legal pad.

"I didn't do a very good job?" I said.

"No, no, it's fine. There's someone here to see me."

Before he had finished his sentence, Legion Guidry stood in the doorway. His khakis were freshly ironed, stiff with starch, his eyes hard to see under the brim of his straw hat. But I could smell the maleness of his odor, a hint of sweat, onions and hamburger, diesel fuel perhaps splashed on his boots, grains of cigarette tobacco that he picked off his tongue.

"What *he* doin' here?" he asked.

"A little legal work. That's what I do for a living," Perry said, trying to ignore the insult.

"This son of a bitch spit in my food," Legion said.

"Have a seat downstairs, Legion. I'll be right with you," Perry said.

"What y'all doin', you? What's on that tablet there?"

"It has nothing to do with you. I give you my word on that," Perry said.

"Gimme that," Legion said.

"Mr. Dave and I have private business to conduct here. Legion, don't do that. This is my office. You need to respect that," Perry said.

"You got the man in your office called me a queer. He ain't no 'mister' to me," Legion said, his hand crimped on the legal pad, the paper creasing from the pressure of his thumb. "What this say?"

"Dave, do you mind waiting downstairs?" Perry said, his face reddening with embarrassment.

"I have to go back to the office. I'll see you later," I said.

I walked out of the air-conditioning into the midday sounds of the city, the heat suddenly more oppressive, the gasoline fumes from the street more offensive. I heard Perry open the door behind me and come down the walk, trying to smile, to reclaim what dignity he could from the situation.

"He's old and uneducated. He's frightened by what he doesn't understand. It's our fault. We denied these people opportunity and access at every turn. Now we have to pay for it," he said.

Wrong, Perry. Not *we*, I thought.

That evening I sat by myself for a long time in the backyard. The sky was purple, full of birds, the sun a molten red inside a bank of rain clouds. I felt Bootsie's hands on my shoulders.

"Perry LaSalle called. He says the assault charge probably won't hold up. Something about Clete seeing a knife," she said.

"Clete's testimony is a little bit of an ethical problem," I said.

"Why?"

"He wasn't there. He went in later and threw a switchblade under a table."

I felt her hands leave my shoulders.

"Dave, this seems to go from bad to worse," she said.

"Clete's a loyal friend. The sheriff isn't."

"He's an elected official. What's he supposed to do? Let you kick the shit out of anyone you don't like?" she said.

I got up from the picnic table and walked down the driveway to my truck. I heard her on the grass behind me, but I started the engine and backed onto the road, then shifted into first gear and drove away, her face slipping past the window like a pale balloon, her words lost in the wind.

The 7 P.M. Wednesday night AA meeting was held in the living room of a small gray house owned by the Episcopalian church, arbored by live oaks, across from the massive stone outline of old Iberia High. The neighborhood, with its firehouse, its ubiquitous trees, its streets glistening from a sun shower, its lawns and small porches on which a boy on a bicycle sailed the afternoon newspaper, the flashing signals dinging at an empty rail crossing, was an excursion into the America that perhaps all of us are nostalgic for, a country secure between its oceans and content with its working-class ambitions, somehow in my mind forever identified with an era when a minor league baseball game or an evening radio show was considered a special pleasure.

It was a Big Book meeting, one in which the participants read from the book that is the centerpiece of the fellowship known as Alcoholics Anonymous. But my purpose in being there was to do what AA members call a Fifth Step, or, more specifically, to admit the exact nature of my wrongs.

Most of the people there were from middle-class backgrounds and did not use profanity at meetings or discuss their sexual lives. By and large, they were the same people you would see at a PTA gathering. When it was my turn to speak, I realized that the world in which I lived and worked and looked upon as fairly normal was not one you shared with people whose worst legal sins might reach the level of a traffic ticket.

I told them all of it. How I had stolen and eaten my wife's diet pills for the amphetamine in them, then had kicked it up into high gear with white speed I had taken from an evidence locker. How I had bludgeoned Jimmy Dean Styles's face with my fists, breaking his nose and lips, knocking his bridge down his throat, grabbing his head and smashing it repeatedly on the bar, my hands slick with his blood and the sweat out of his hair, while an insatiable white worm ate a hole in the soft tissue of my brain and I ground my teeth together with a need that no amount of sex or violence or dope would relieve me of, that nothing other than whiskey and whiskey and whiskey would ever satisfy.

The room was silent when I finished. A well-dressed woman got up from her chair and went into the bathroom, and we could hear the water running in the lavatory while she kept clearing her throat behind the door.

The discussion leader that evening was a genial, silver-haired, retired train conductor from Mississippi.

"Well, you got it off your chest, Dave. At least you're not aiming to kill anybody now," he said, starting to smile. Then he looked at my face and dropped his eyes.

After the meeting adjourned, I sat by myself in the living room, the light failing in the trees. When I left, the parking area was deserted, the streets empty. I drove to a pool hall in St. Martinville and drank coffee at the bar and watched some old men playing bouree, the shadows from the blades of a ceiling fan breaking on their faces and hands with the rhythmic certainty of a clock that no one watched.

CHAPTER 18

During the night a 911 caller reported an assault with a deadly weapon in a black slum area off the Loreauville Road. A New Orleans man with orange and purple hair by the name of Antoine Patout had been asleep with his girlfriend in his aunt's house when an intruder climbed through a window, drew back the sheet from Patout's rump, and sliced him a half-inch deep across both buttocks.

While Patout screamed and his girlfriend wadded the sheet and tried to close his wound, the intruder calmly climbed back out the window into the darkness, at the same time folding his knife and slipping it into his back pocket. No one heard an automobile. The girlfriend told the first officer on the scene that she did not see the assailant's face, nor could she determine his race, but she thought he was one of the neighbors with whom Patout had quarreled over the rap music he played full-blast almost every night until 1 A.M.

Helen Soileau came into my office early Thursday morning.

"You know the name of the guy with the tie-dye hair, follows Jimmy Dean Styles around?" she asked.

"No."

"You don't know the name of the guy you hit across the face with a .45?"

"No, I didn't check it out."

"Isn't he the same guy who smashed a beer bottle on Marvin Oates's head?"

"Could be, Helen. I'm on the desk."

"Then get off it. While you're at it, pull the telephone pole out of your ass," she replied.

Just before noon I walked down to the sheriff's office. He was reading a fishing magazine and eating a ham-and-egg sandwich.

"Sorry to interrupt," I said.

He closed the magazine and brushed the crumbs off his mouth with the back of his wrist.

"What is it?" he said.

"I'm sorry about my conduct. It's not going to happen again."

"I'm glad to hear you take that position. But you're on the desk."

"We've got two open homicides. What's the harm if I help Helen?"

"You tell me. You've gone into St. Martin Parish twice now and thrown one black person in the bayou and stomped another one into jelly. We're lucky we don't have black people burning down the town. You leave me at a loss for words."

I could see the genuine bewilderment in his face, as though the simple fact that I worked under his supervision made him doubt his own sanity.

"I guess I dropped in at a bad time," I said.

"No, it's just you, Dave. What you've never understood is that you resent authority just like the people we lock up. *That's* your problem, podna, not all this bullshit you keep dragging into my office," he said.

"That doesn't leave a lot unsaid, does it?" I said.

"No, I don't guess it does," he replied. He picked up his magazine again, his cheeks blotched with color.

I signed out of the office and wrote the word "dentist" in the destination box. Then I drove my truck across the railway tracks to the shotgun cottage of Marvin Oates.

The yard was covered with trash—shrimp husks, spoiled food, used Q-Tips, disposable female items—that seemed to have been methodically sprinkled from the gallery out to the street. I knocked on the door, but no one answered. The air was hot and close and smelled like brass and distant rain. I walked around back and saw Marvin in a sweaty T-shirt, scuffed boots, and a beat-up cowboy hat, hacking dead banana trees out of the ground with a machete. A bolt of lightning popped across the bayou in City Park. He looked in the direction of the lightning bolt, as though it contained meaning directed specifically at him. He had not heard me walk up behind him, and he remained motionless, the machete dripping from his hand, listening, watching the stormclouds that creaked with thunder, the wind blowing leaves out of the trees.

"Who threw garbage all over your front yard?" I said.

He jumped at the sound of my voice. "Folks that belong on chain gangs, if you ask me," he said.

"You seem to be a pretty good student of Scripture, Marvin. Maybe you can help me with a question that's been bothering me. What does the Old Testament admonition about an eye for an eye actually mean?" I said.

He grinned. "That's easy. The punishment ain't s'posed to be greater than the crime. It's got to be in equal measure," he replied.

"So if you were a judge, what would you do to the people who raped and killed the Boudreau girl?"

"Send them to the Death House up at Angola."

"Cancel their whole ticket?"

"She never harmed nobody. Them men didn't have no right to do what they done."

"I see. This guy Antoine Patout, the one who hit you upside the head with a beer bottle?"

"Miss Helen was already out here. I ain't gonna talk no more about that fellow got his rear end slashed. Think what y'all want."

"I think his punishment fit the crime. He broke a bottle on your head and maybe he or some of his friends trashed your yard. So now he won't be sitting down for a while. But Frankie Dogs was a special case. You know, shoving your face into a toilet bowl like that while other people watched? Maybe he made fun of you while he did it, too. I heard he dumped your magazines and Bibles all over the bathroom floor. I figure a guy like that deserves to get smoked."

"You asked me a question about the Boudreau girl, but

you try to turn my words around and use them against me. People has been doing that to me my whole life, Mr. Robicheaux. I dint think you was that kind of man," he said.

"It's nothing personal."

"When folks treat you simple-minded, it's real personal."

He went back to his work, slashing the machete across the base of a banana tree that had already given fruit and whose stalk had gone mushy with rot. He pushed against the stalk until it snapped loose from the root system in a shower of loam, exposing the concentric circles of brown pulp inside.

"See, it's plumb eaten up with ants and cockroaches. You got to prune back the tree to free it of disease and give it new life. It's God's way," he said, and flung the stalk on a fire.

That afternoon, when I arrived home from work, I saw Perry LaSalle's Gazelle parked by the cement boat ramp and Perry leaning against the fender, one foot propped on the bumper, the top button of his sports shirt loosened. His relaxed posture made me think of a male model in an ad. But it was a poor disguise for the agitation he was obviously trying to hide.

"I've got a problem. Or maybe we both do. Yeah, I think your stamp is on this, Dave. Undoubtedly, it's got the Robicheaux mark," he said, nodding profoundly.

"On what?" I said.

"Let me run it by you. Actually, it all took place in one of your old haunts," he said, and told me of the incident that had occurred the previous night on a back road in the Atchafalaya Basin.

Two black women ran a crib next to a bar that had been built in the 1950s, deep inside a woods that admitted almost no light through the canopy, a landlocked elevated piece of swamp strung with air vines, layered with dead leaves and river trash and webbed algae. The people who drank in the bar were leftovers from another era, mostly men who still spoke French and did not shave for days, rarely traveled more than a few parishes from the place of their birth, and considered events in the outside world unimportant and unrelated to their lives.

It was a place where Legion Guidry drank. Either before or after he visited the crib next door.

The two men who sought him out were obviously not from the Atchafalaya Basin. They wore sports coats and open-necked shirts, and although they were dark-featured, their accents were not Cajun. They even seemed viscerally repelled by the litter on the ground, the rusted cars in the undergrowth, the smoldering pile of garbage behind the bar. When they entered the crib, which was actually a tar paper–and-board shack, with a woodstove for heat and a gasoline-powered generator for electricity, one of the black prostitutes rose from the cot she was resting on and stared mutely at them, waiting for one of them to produce a badge.

"Where's the guy belongs to that red truck out there?" one of the men asked. He didn't look at her when he spoke. He had touched a doorknob with his hand when he entered the shack, and he tore a square of paper towel from a roll on the table by the prostitute's cot and wiped his palm and fingers with it.

"That's Mr. Legion's truck," the woman said.

"I didn't ask you his name. I asked where he was," the man said, balling up the paper towel in his hand, looking for a place to throw it.

The black woman wore a halter and a pair of shorts but felt naked in front of the two white men. Their hair was cut short, lightly oiled, neatly combed, their clothes pressed, their shoes shined. They smelled of cologne and had shaved late in the day. They had no sexual interest in her at all, not even a mild curiosity.

"He ain't been here yet," she said.

"This is a waste of time," the second man said.

"He's not up at the bar and he's not here, but his truck is outside. Now, you want to tell me where he is or you want us to walk you out in the trees?" the first man said.

"Mr. Legion got a crab trap. He goes out in the bay and brings it back to the bar and boils up some crabs for his dinner sometimes," the prostitute replied.

"You never saw us, did you?" the first man said.

"I don't want no trouble, suh," she replied, then pulled at the bottom of her shorts to straighten her underwear and dropped her eyes in shame when she saw the looks the two men gave her.

The first man saw a bucket to throw the crumpled square of paper towel in. But he looked in the bucket first and was so revolted by the contents, he simply tossed the paper towel on the table and glanced around the room a last time.

"Y'all live here?" he said.

For the next hour the two men sat in the back of the bar, in the shadows, and played gin rummy and drank a diet soda each and kept their score in pencil on the back of a napkin. The drone of an outboard motor reverberated through a flooded woods outside, then they heard the aluminum bottom of a boat scrape up on land, and a moment later Legion Guidry came through the front door, a cage trap dripping with blue-point crabs suspended from his fist.

He did not notice the visitors in the back of the bar. He went directly behind the counter to a butane stove where a tall, stainless-steel cauldron was boiling and shook the crabs from the trap into the water. Then he hooked his hat on a wood peg and combed his hair in an oxidized mirror, lit an unfiltered cigarette, and sat down at a table by himself while a mulatto woman brought him a shot of whiskey and a beer on the side and a length of white boudin in a saucer.

"Go tell Cleo I'm gonna be over in a half hour. Tell her I want a fresh sheet, me," he said to the mulatto woman.

Then he turned and saw the two men in sports coats standing behind him.

"My name's Sonny Bilotti. Man in town wants to talk to you. We'll give you a ride," one of them said. He wore a tan coat and a black shirt and gold-rimmed glasses, and he adjusted the gold watchband on his wrist and smiled slightly when he spoke.

Legion drew in on his cigarette and exhaled the smoke into the dead air. The few people at the bar kept their faces averted, deliberately concentrating on their drinks or the water dripping down the sides of the stainless-steel cauldron into the butane flame. They glanced automatically at the screen door each time it opened, as though the person entering the room were a harbinger of change in their lives.

"I ain't seen no badge," Legion said.

"We don't need a badge for a friendly talk, do we?" said the man who called himself Sonny Bilotti.

"I don't like nobody bothering me when I eat my dinner. Them crabs is done near boiled. I'm fixing to eat now," Legion said.

"This guy's a beaut, isn't he? We met your girlfriend. She like crabs, too?" the second man said.

"What you talkin' about?" Legion asked.

"Get up," the second man said. He had removed his coat and hung it on the back of a chair. His arms were clean of tattoos, firm with the kind of muscle tone that came from working out on machines at a health club. He placed one hand under Legion's arm and sensed a power there he had underestimated, then for the first time he looked directly into Legion's eyes.

He released Legion's arm and reached for the automatic that was stuck down in the back of his slacks. Perhaps for just a moment he felt he had stepped into an improbable photograph that should have had nothing to do with his life, a frozen moment involving a primitive barroom with plank floors, ignorant people bent over their drinks, moonlit Spanish moss in the trees outside the windows, a swamp coated with a patina of algae that was dissected by the tracings of alligators and poisonous snakes.

The blackjack in Legion's hand crushed the cartilage in the man's nose and filled his head with a red-black rush of pain that was like shards of glass driven into the brain. He cupped his hands to the blood roaring from his flattened nose and saw his friend Sonny Bilotti try to back away, to raise a hand in protest, but Legion whipped the blackjack across Sonny's mouth, then swung it across his jaw, breaking bone, and down on the crown of his skull and across his neck and ears, until Sonny Bilotti was on his knees, whimpering, his forehead bent to the floor, his butt in the air like a child's.

Legion picked up the sports coat from the chair where the second man had hung it and wiped his black-jack on the cloth.

"This been fun. Tell Robicheaux to send me some more like y'all," he said.

Then he dragged each man by his collar to the screen door and shoved him with his boot into a pool of dirty water.

But those guys weren't cops, were they?" Perry said.

"Who knows? Maybe they're out of New Orleans," I said.

"They sound like greaseballs?"

"Could be," I replied, looking up the slope at my house among the trees, avoiding his stare.

"Why would greaseballs want to talk to Legion Guidry?"

"Ask him."

"I tried to. He was in my office this afternoon. He's convinced himself we're writing a book together and he's in it. He thinks you sent these guys to do him in and that maybe I helped you."

"That's the breaks," I said.

"Say again?"

"Who cares what he thinks? Why do you represent a cretin like that, anyway?" I said.

"You're a police officer I have to get out of jail on a felony assault and you call my other clients cretins?"

"Want to come in and have dinner?" I said.

"What's between you and Legion Guidry? Did you sic a couple of wiseguys on him?"

"Adios," I said.

"I think your pet hippo, that character Purcel, he's mixed up in this, too. Tell him I said that. While you're at it, tell him to keep his shit out of Barbara Shanahan's life," he said.

I picked the newspaper up off the lawn and walked through the deepening shade of the trees and up the steps of the gallery into my house. When I saw Bootsie at the sink, I kissed her on the back of the neck and touched her rump. She turned and threw a wet dish towel at my head.

The next day was Friday. I walked to Victor's Cafeteria on Main and ate lunch by myself. It was dark and cool under the high, stamped-tin ceiling, and I drank coffee and watched the lunch crowd thin out at one o'clock. The front door opened and inside the glare of white light from the street I saw the slightly stooped, simian silhouette of Joe Zeroski. He headed for my table, brushing past a customer and a waitress.

"I need to talk," he said.

"Go ahead."

"Not here. In my car."

"Nope."

"What, I got bad breath?"

"Is that a piece under your coat?"

"I got a permit. You believe that?"

"Sure, it's a great country. Come to my office," I replied.

He thought for a moment, his fingers working at his sides, his facial muscles like stone.

"So I'll find you another time," he said.

"Bad attitude, Joe," I said, but he was gone.

It was too fine a day to worry about Joe Zeroski. The air was sweet and balmy from a morning sun-shower. Leaves floated on the bayou and the floral bloom in the yards along East Main was absolutely beautiful. But Joe Zeroski bothered me and I knew why. Clete Purcel had wound up his clock and broken off the key, and even Clete now regretted it.

That evening I was counting receipts out of the cash register at the bait shop when I heard someone behind me. I turned and looked into Joe Zeroski's flat-plated face. He was dressed in dark blue jeans, a checkered sports shirt, a yellow cap, and new tennis shoes. He held a cheap rod and reel in his hand, the price tag still dangling from one of the eyelets.

"Your sign says guided fishing trips," he said.

Twenty minutes later I cut the gas feed on the outboard and we coasted out of a channel into an alcove of moss-strung cypress trees that were lacy with new leaf. The sun was a red cinder through the canopy, the wind down, the water so still inside the shelter of the trees you could hear the bream and goggle-eyed perch popping along the edges of the hyacinths. Joe cast his lure across the clearing, right into a tree trunk, hanging the treble hook deep in the bark.

"I'll row us over," I said.

"Forget it," he said, and broke off his line. "How many guys you heard I popped?"

"Nine?"

"It's closer to three or four. I never done it on a contract, either. They all come after me or a friend or the man I worked for first. Can you relate to that?"

I cast a Rapala deep between the trees, reeled the slack out of the line, and handed Joe the rod.

"Retrieve it in spurts, so the lure swims like a wounded minnow," I said.

"You were easier to talk with when you were a drunk. Are you hearing anything I say? Listen, I went out and talked to Mr. Boudreau."

"Amanda Boudreau's father?"

"That's right. He's a nice gentleman. He don't need to be told what it feels like to have your daughter killed by a degenerate. He says you belong to the same club."

"What?"

"He said some fuckheads killed your mother and your wife. I didn't know that."

"So now you do."

"Then you understand."

"It doesn't change anything, Joe."

"Yeah, it does. I don't know what's going on. I get a lead on some old guy by the name of Legion Guidry, a guy maybe you're looking at for Linda's murder. Now two of my best guys are in Iberia General. You looking at this guy or not? What's going on?"

"You got to dial it down, Joe."

"Don't tell me that."

"I apologize for what's happened to you in New Iberia. I think you deserve better."

Just then a largemouth bass struck Joe's lure, roiling the surface, taking the treble hook down with it, its firm body straining against the monofilament, then rising, bursting through the water's surface, like green and gold glassware breaking inside a shaft of sunlight, the lure rattling at the corner of its mouth, sprinkling the air with crystal.

Joe jerked his rod and tried to retrieve the slack in the line, but his fingers were like wood. The reel clanked once against the aluminum gunnel and the rod tipped downward toward the water, the cork handle flipping upward and out of Joe's fingers.

He watched the rod sink into the darkness, then stared uncomprehendingly at his lure floating uselessly in the middle of the pool.

"What happened? I had it under control. Right here between my hands. How'd it get away? I can't figure nothing out," he said.

His eyes searched mine, waiting for me to reply.

CHAPTER 19

Clete Purcel grew up in the Irish Channel in the days when white gangs fought with chains over the use of a street corner. His father was a drunken, superstitious, and sentimental man who delivered milk in the Garden District, made his children kneel on grains of rice for sassing a nun, and whipped Clete with a razor strop when he lost a fight. A gang of kids from the Iberville Project jumped Clete by St. Louis Cemetery and bashed his eye open with a steel pipe. Clete packed the wound with a cobweb, closed it with adhesive tape, and drove around all night in a stolen car until he caught the pipe wielder alone.

After New Orleans the Marine Corps was a breeze. Even Vietnam wasn't much of a challenge. Women were another matter.

His second wife, Lois, was driven by either her own neurosis or living with Clete to a Buddhist monastery in

Colorado. In the meantime Clete flowered as a vice cop. Unfortunately, he seemed to fit into the milieu too well. His girlfriends were addicts, strippers, compulsive gamblers, deep-fried cultists, or beautiful Italian girls with complexions and long hair like the bride of Dracula. The latter group usually turned out to be the sweethearts or relatives of criminals. When we were Homicide partners at NOPD, I often had to roll down all the windows in our car to blow out the odors Clete carried in his clothes from the previous night.

But one way or another he always got hurt. What neither his inept, uneducated father, sadistic brig chasers, nor even Victor Charles could do to him, Clete managed to do to himself.

He burned his kite at NOPD with pills and booze and by killing a government witness. He hired out as a mercenary in Central America and worked for the Mob in Reno and maybe engineered the crash of a gangster's seaplane in the Cabinet Mountains of western Montana. His P.I. license and his job as a hunter of bail skips for Nig Rosewater and Wee Willie Bimstine were the only elements of stability in his life. The effect of his arrival in any environment was like a junkyard falling down a stairs. Chaos was his logo, honor and loyalty and a vulnerable heart his undoing.

Now Clete was swinging into high gear again, this time with Battering Ram Shanahan.

Just after Joe Zeroski had driven away from my dock, Clete pulled into the driveway. He was wearing a summer tux, his sandy hair wet and parted neatly on the side, his cheeks glowing, a corsage in a plastic box by his thigh.

"How do I look?" he asked.

"Beautiful," I said.

He got out of the car and turned in a circle. A piece of toilet paper was stuck to a shaving cut on his chin. "The coat's not too tight? I feel like I'm wrapped in a sausage skin."

"You look fine."

"We're going to a dance at a country club. Barbara has to pay her dues with some political people. The last time I went dancing Big Tit Judy Lavelle and I did the dirty bop in Pat O'Brien's and got thrown out."

"Smile a lot. Leave early. Take it easy on the hooch," I said.

He blotted his forehead with his wrist and looked down the dirt road under the row of oaks that paralleled the bayou.

"On another subject, I just passed Joe Zeroski. What was he doing here?" he said.

"Legion Guidry scrambled a couple of his guys. One by the name of Sonny Bilotti. You know him?"

"He was a hitter for the Calucci brothers. He shanked a guy from the Aryan Brotherhood in Marion. Guidry cleaned his clock?"

"He put him in the hospital."

"That's hard to believe."

"Really?" I said.

He caught the look on my face. "Oh, like you're a pushover? The difference is you have parameters, Dave. A guy like Bilotti parks one in the brain pan and then checks to see if he got the right guy. That's the edge these guys have on us. I've got to work out a new strategy on Guidry."

I pulled the piece of toilet paper off the shaving cut on his chin and let it blow away in the breeze.

"Enjoy the dance," I said.

The dance at the country club in Lafayette was one of those insular events where the possession of power and money are celebrated in ways that never require the participants to acknowledge the secret chambers of the heart or perhaps, more accurately, the edges of the conscience.

The buffet tables and ice sculptures and silver bowls brimming with champagne and sherbet punch, the 1950s orchestra music, the flagstone patio overhung by electrically lit oak trees, the white-jacketed, sycophantic waiters, were a testament to an idea, a fusion of the antebellum South with twenty-first-century prosperity, a systemic exclusion of everything in the larger culture that seemed coarse and intellectually invasive and contrary to the ethos of free enterprise.

The celebrants were politicians and judges and attorneys and shopping-mall developers and realtors and executives from petrochemical industries. They greeted one another with a level of warmth and gaiety that seemed born of lifelong friendships, although few of them had any personal contact outside of their business dealings. They gave the sense that they all shared the same love of country and the same patriotic commitment to its governance. There was almost an innocence in the narcissistic pleasure purchased by their success and in their shared presumption that a great, green, rolling continent had been presented to them by a divine hand for their own use.

Clete ate his steak and lobster and drank wine

spritzers and said virtually nothing during the evening. In fact, two petroleum executives who had been fighter pilots in Vietnam kept hitting him on the shoulders and roaring at his jokes. But Barbara Shanahan became increasingly restless, her face ruddy with either alcohol or frustration, blowing her breath upward to clear her hair out of her eyes, crunching ice between her molars. Then a congressman who had changed his party affiliation the day after the balance of power shifted in the House of Representatives, receiving the chairmanship of a committee in the bargain, mounted the bandstand and told jokes about environmentalists.

He brought the house down.

"I can't take these assholes," Barbara said, and snapped her fingers at the waiter. "Clean these spritzers out of here and bring us a couple of depth charges."

"Depth charges, madam?" the waiter said.

"A shot and draft. Put it on Fuckhead's tab," she said, gesturing with her thumb at the congressman.

But the waiter, who had an Irish accent, was a piece of work. "Which fuckhead is that, madam?" he asked.

"Not bad. Have one yourself while you're at it," Barbara said.

"Maybe we ought to hit the road," Clete said.

"Not a chance," she said.

When the waiter returned, Barbara lowered a jigger of bourbon into a schooner of beer, then drank the schooner empty. She blew the hair out of her face, her eyes slightly out of focus.

"Wow," she said. "You gonna drink yours?"

"Absolutely," he said, putting his hand on the schooner before she could pick it up.

She waved at the waiter. "Hey, Irish, bring us a couple more," she called out.

Then they went out on the crowded dance floor. The band had gone into "One O'clock Jump," and Barbara danced in her stockinged feet, her arms flying in the air, her body caroming off the dancers around her.

"Oops, excuse me," she said to a woman she knocked into a table.

"My, but you're an energetic thing, aren't you?" the woman said, her glasses askew.

"Sorry. Don't I know you? Oh, you're the new federal judge. Hi, Your Honor," Barbara said, stopping, shutting her eyes, then opening them again. "Boy, am I shit-faced."

She walked unsteadily back to the table, then pulled off her corsage and threw it on her plate and leaned over and hooked her shoes in her fingers and almost fell when she tried to put them on. Clete put his arm around her shoulders.

"Guess who is seriously fucked up," she said.

"You're beautiful," Clete said.

"I know. But I think I'm going to throw up," she replied.

They drove back to New Iberia on the old highway that led past Spanish Lake. It started to rain and mist blew out of the trees, and a long Southern Pacific freight clicked by on the elevated grade, its whistle blowing down the line. Barbara pressed her fingers against her head as though she were awaking from a dream. Her skin looked green in the glow of the dashboard.

When he mentioned food, she made a sound like someone slipping into a whirlpool.

"I think you were great back there," he said.

"Good try," she said.

When they reached her apartment on Bayou Teche, he walked her upstairs and was about to say good night.

"No, come in. I'll try to stop acting like a basket case. Watch television while I take a shower. Then I'll fix you something to eat," she said, then sprained her ankle going through the bedroom door. She threw a shoe at the wall and closed the door behind her.

Clete could hear her pulling at zippers and snaps on her clothes. He folded the coat of his summer tux and pulled off his tie and sat on the couch and watched a boxing match on a sports channel. He tried not to think about Barbara Shanahan in the shower. When she came back out of the bedroom, she had put on faded jeans, a blue terry-cloth pullover, and Indian moccasins. Her hair was damp, her skin rosy from the heat of the shower. But her eyes were scorched with an early hangover, her voice husky, her speech clipped, as though she could not coordinate her thoughts with her words.

She started breaking eggs in a skillet.

"Is there something on your mind I could help you with?" he said behind her.

"I thought I might run for district attorney. You know, make a difference, put away more of the bad guys, stick it to the polluters, all that jazz. What a joke."

"No, it's not," he said.

She dropped an egg on the floor and looked at it wanly. "I'm sorry, Clete. I just don't feel very well," she said.

He used a dishrag to clean the floor, then squeezed it out in the sink and dropped the broken eggshells in a waste can. "I'd better get going," he said.

"You don't have to."

"I probably should."

"You don't need to," she said, her face averted, looking at the streetlights on the drawbridge.

Then, against all his instincts, all the warnings that told him not to take advantage, not to be a surrogate, he closed his arms around her, his biceps swelling into the girth of pressurized firehoses. He could smell the freshness of her clothes, the powder she had sprinkled on her shoulders, a touch of perfume behind her ears. He ran his big hand across the firmness of her back, the taper of her muscles along her hips.

"You're stand-up," he said.

"Not really," she said.

"You feel great, Barbara. Wow, do you feel great," he said, rubbing his cheek against her hair, petting her back, closing his eyes as he breathed in the fragrance and heat on her neck.

"So do you. But, Clete . . ." she said uncomfortably.

"What is it?" he asked, looking with alarm at her face.

"You're standing on my foot."

From her bedroom window he could look out across the veranda and see the tops of the banana trees below, the old gray convent across the bayou, and the moss in the oaks that grew above the convent's roof. He saw a milk truck drive by, one like his father had driven, and he tried to think of an explanation for the presence of a milk truck on a quiet, lamp-shadowed street at this time of night. For some reason he saw images out of his childhood: a razor strop, a thick-bodied child walking to school, bent down in the wind, a peanut butter sandwich and an apple in a paper bag for lunch. Clete blew out his breath and shook the image out of his head and tried to remember the number of drinks he'd had that evening, almost as a form of reassurance.

He felt awkward undressing in front of Barbara, conscious of his weight, the gold hair on his back and shoulders. She lay down on the far side of the bed and waited for him, her hair like points of fire on the pillow.

"Is something wrong, Clete?" she asked.

"No, not at all," he lied.

He lay down beside her and kissed her mouth, then touched her breasts and stomach and felt his sex harden against her thigh. But all his movements seemed heavy-handed, clumsy, his knees constantly hitting her, making her flinch.

"I jog and lift weights. I've cut down my beer intake to eleven or twelve cans a day. But I keep tubbing up," he said.

"I think you're a sweet man," she said.

He knew it should have been a compliment. In fact, he was convinced she was sincere. But he knew there were other words that women used in certain moments, words that were intimate, naked in their expression of vulnerability and love and surrender, words they used rarely in an entire lifetime and that marked a contract with a man that no wedding ceremony ever provided. But these were not the words he heard.

"I think you're a fine woman who's had a bad night. I think maybe the wrong guy shouldn't take advantage of the situation," he said.

She brushed at his hair with her hand, in almost a maternal way, then mounted him and cupped his sex in her palm and placed it inside her. There was a spray of strawberry freckles on her shoulders and arms and the tops of her breasts. He put her nipples in his mouth and ran his hands down her hips and over her rump, and then turned her sideways in the bed and reentered her, this time on top, and he saw her mouth open and her eyes close and felt her fingers dig tightly into his back.

When she came, her face grew small and pale, then he felt a long, sustained shudder commence inside her womb and a tightening in her thighs and a cry burst from her throat that was strangely more like need and unsatiated desire than it was satisfaction. But he could not sort out his thoughts from the nature of his own desire and the incredible loveliness of her face, the smallness of her mouth that in the dark looked like a purple flower, the caress and grace of her thighs, and the heat of her womb, the orgasm that broke inside him and rushed out of his body in a way he had never experienced before, like a burst of white light that had nothing to do with the self or the fear and hunger and sometimes rage that characterized his life.

He sat up on the side of the bed and kissed her hands and her forehead and traced her features with his fingers. Her arms lay by her sides now, the sheet pulled to her navel, her head turned toward him in a melancholy fashion.

"You doin' all right?" he said.

"You were fine, Clete."

But the answer did not fit the question he had asked, and he searched her eyes and found no explanation for the strange sense of disquiet he felt.

"Dave and I were always the odd pieces at NOPD. He got fired and I had to run for a plane to Guatemala. Both of us learned too late not to fight with the bastards," he said.

She covered his hand with hers. But her eyes were focused beyond him, over his shoulder, and she was not listening to his words now.

"Clete, a shadow just went across the screen," she said.

He pulled on his pants and walked shirtless and barefoot out on the veranda. He smelled cigarette smoke, then heard footsteps leave the stairs down below and head across a grassy area toward a side street that led to the drawbridge. But the person was not running, as though he had no fear of apprehension or sense of shame at being discovered in a voyeuristic act.

The lamps above the side street were haloed with humidity. He heard an automobile or truck engine fire up, then fade between the buildings as the driver turned into the Friday-night traffic crossing the drawbridge. A burning cigarette glowed in the grass next to the sidewalk. Clete picked it up gingerly with the balls of his fingers and looked at it. It was unfiltered, still wet on the unlit end with the smoker's saliva. He tossed it in a sewer grate, then wiped his fingers on his pants.

On his way upstairs Clete saw a Bible on the top step, barely visible in the shadows, a rose stem inserted under the cover.

"Did you see him?" Barbara said when he came back through the door of her apartment.

"No," he replied.

He put on his shirt and tucked it in his trousers, then stuffed his socks into his coat pocket and slipped on his shoes without tying them.

"What are you doing?" Barbara said.

"That kid with the mush-mouth accent, Marvin something or other? Where does he live?" he asked.

The next day, Saturday, Clete parked his car in my drive and walked across the road and down the boat ramp, where I had propped a ladder against one of the dock pilings and was painting termicide and tar on some of the wood that had started to rot. He sat down heavily in a moored outboard, in the dock's shade, and told me of the previous evening.

"You slapped Marvin Oates around?" I said.

"Yeah, I guess that's fair to say," he replied. He pulled on his nose and looked into space. "He told me he left the Bible earlier in the evening."

"I think you got the wrong guy. Marvin doesn't smoke."

"There was a pack of cigarettes on the dashboard of his car," Clete said.

"Unfiltered cigarettes?"

"No."

"You got the wrong guy, Clete. In more ways than one."

"Meaning?"

"Bad things seem to happen to people who hurt Marvin Oates."

"Why did I have all those weird feelings when I saw that milk truck passing by the convent?" he asked.

"Maybe you're like me. You wonder about where you've been and who you are now and what you'll eventually become. It has something to do with mortality."

"My old man could be a decent guy. He'd take me to ball games and out fishing for green trout. Then he'd get drunk and tell me the best part of me ran down my mother's leg."

"Time to cut loose from it, Cletus."

"You think Barbara and I could have a serious go at it? I mean, marriage, kids, stuff like that?"

He lifted his head and looked up at me from his seat on the boat, the water chucking against the aluminum hull in the silence, one of his eyes watery from a shaft of sunlight that fell through the slats in the dock.

Later that afternoon Alafair, Bootsie, and I went to Mass. After I took them back home I drove to Iberia General and asked at the reception desk for the room number of Sonny Bilotti. I bought a magazine in the gift shop and walked down the corridor to a double-occupancy room. Bilotti was in the room by himself, propped up against pillows, his jaws wired shut, his eyes raccooned, his lips black with stitches. The windowsill was lined with bouquets of carnations, roses, and hollyhocks, but they obviously did little to cheer the man in the bed, who had probably taken one of the worst beatings I had ever seen.

"Your friend already check out?" I asked.

He didn't answer, his eyes following me across the room as I pulled a chair up to his bedside.

"Here's an *Esquire* magazine in case you need something to read," I said. "My name is Dave Robicheaux. I'm a detective in the Iberia Parish Sheriff's Department."

Before he could speak, I heard someone behind me. I turned and saw Zerelda Calucci standing in the doorway, wearing white jeans, cowboy boots, and a black Harley-Davidson T-shirt cut off at the armpits.

"Shit," she said.

"This is official business, so please get out of here," I said.

"I have a bone to pick with Clete Purcel. Where is he?" she said.

"I don't think you're hearing me. You need to move yourself out of this immediate environment," I said.

She leaned against the doorjamb, her arms folded, chewing gum, her black hair hanging almost to her breasts. "Then hook me up, darlin'. I get wet just thinking about it," she said.

"You were a rumdum in the First District. You used to hang in Joe Burton's piano bar on Canal," Sonny Bilotti interjected himself, compressing his words flatly, his head motionless against the pillows.

"That's me, partner," I said. "The word is you shanked a guy from the Aryan Brotherhood in Marion. You've got to be stand-up to 'front the A.B., Sonny. Don't let a sack of shit like Legion Guidry get away with what he did. File against him and we'll bust his wheels."

Bilotti's head shifted slightly on the pillow so that he could look directly at me. His eyes possessed the luminosity of obsidian, but they were also marked by an uncertain glimmer, a conclusion or perhaps a new knowledge about himself that would plague him the rest of his days.

"You scared of this guy, Sonny?" I said.

His eyes went to Zerelda.

"You're done here," she said to me.

"If that's the way you want it," I said, and walked outside.

She followed me to the front door of the hospital,

then out into the parking lot under the trees. The air was warm, golden, smelling of smoke from Saturday-afternoon leaf fires.

"I did some checking on you. You were in this same hospital. Somebody made you count your bones. Maybe with a blackjack. I have a feeling it was Legion Guidry," she said.

"So?" I replied, my eyes focused across the street on the bayou.

"You didn't bring charges against him. You're trying to use Sonny to get even. Because you're too gutless to do it head-on," she said.

I turned from her and walked to my truck. But she wasn't finished with me yet. She stepped between me and the door.

"Guidry did something to you that makes you feel ashamed, didn't he?" she said.

"I'd appreciate your moving out of the way."

"I bet you would. Here's another flash. You got a beef with Legion Guidry, take it to Perry LaSalle. He got Guidry his job at the casino. Then ask yourself why Perry has influence at the casino."

"Is there any particular reason I've earned your anger?" I asked.

"Yeah, Sonny Bilotti is my cousin and you're an ass-hole," she replied.

CHAPTER 20

I awoke early Sunday morning and drove 241 miles to Houston, then got lost in a rainstorm somewhere around Hermann Park and Rice University. When I finally found the Texas Medical Center and the hospital where the sheriff's wife had just undergone a double mastectomy the previous week, the rain had flooded the streets and was thundering on the tops of cars that had pulled to the curb because their drivers could not see through the windshields. I parked in an elevated garage, then splashed across a street and entered the hospital soaking wet.

She was asleep. So was the sheriff, his body curled up on two chairs he had pushed together, a blanket pulled up to his chin. I walked back to the nurses' station. No one was there except for a physician in scrubs. He was a tall, graying man, and he was writing on a clipboard. I asked him if he knew how the sheriff's wife was doing.

"You a friend of the family?" he asked.

"Yes, sir."

"She's a sweetheart," he said, and let his eyes slip off mine so I could read no meaning in them.

"Is the flower shop open downstairs?" I asked.

"I believe it is," he said.

On the way out of the hospital I paid for a mixed bouquet and had it sent up to the sheriff's wife. I signed the card "Your friends in the department" and drove back to New Iberia.

The next morning, Monday, the sheriff and I were both back at work. I knocked on his office door and went inside.

"Got a minute?" I said.

He sat behind his desk in a pinstripe suit and turquoise western shirt, his eyes tired, trying not to yawn. "You sound like you have a cold," he said.

"Just some sniffles."

"You get caught in the rain?"

"Not really."

"What's up?" he asked.

I closed the door behind me.

"It was Legion Guidry who worked me over with a blackjack. When he finished, he held my head up by the hair and put his tongue in my mouth and called me his bitch," I said.

It was quiet in the room. The sheriff rubbed his fingers on the back of one hand.

"You were ashamed to tell me this?" he said.

"Maybe."

He nodded. "Write it up and get a warrant," he said.

"It won't stick. Not after all this time," I said.

"If it doesn't, it's because you tore up Jimmy Dean Styles."

"Run that by me again?"

"You do everything in your power to convince people you're a violent, unstable, and dangerous man. Get a warrant. Nobody assaults an officer in my department. I want that son of a bitch in custody."

I started to speak, then decided I'd said enough.

"I think you had another reason for not reporting this," the sheriff said. "I think you planned to pop Guidry yourself."

"I was never big on self-analysis."

"Right," he said.

I got up to leave.

"Hold on," the sheriff said.

"Sir?"

He touched the bald spot in the center of his head, then looked at me for what seemed to be a long time. "My wife and I appreciated the flowers," he said.

I paused in the doorway, my face blank.

"I saw you leaving the flower shop at the hospital. I'll never figure you out, Dave. That's not necessarily a compliment," he said.

I guess I should have felt liberated from the deceit I had practiced on the sheriff. In fact, it should have been a fine day. But I stayed restless, discontented, and irritable, without cause or remedy, and the five miles I jogged that evening and the push-ups and bench presses and sets of curls I did with free weights in my backyard did little to relieve the pressure band along one side of my head and the electricity that seemed to jump off the ends of my fingers. That night I thought I heard caterpillars eating inside a pile of wet mulberry leaves under the window, and I pressed the pillow down on my head so I would not have to hear the sound they made.

I dreamed I was teaching a class of police cadets at a community college in north Miami. In my dream I was part of an exchange program with NOPD and Florida law enforcement, and what should have been a vacation in the sun was for me a long drunk in the bars adjacent to Hialeah and Gulfstream Park racetracks. I entered the classroom stinking of cigarette smoke and booze, unshaved, my mouth like cotton, sure that somehow I could get through the hour, with no notes or lesson plan, then find a morning bar in Opa-Locka, where a vodka collins would sweep all the snakes back into their wicker baskets.

Then I realized, as I stood at the lectern, that I had become incoherent and foolish, an object of pity and shame, and the cadets, who had always treated me with respect, had dropped their eyes to the desks in embarrassment for me.

The dream wasn't a fabrication of the unconscious, just an accurate replication of what had actually taken place, and when I woke from it just before dawn, I could not shake the feeling that I was still drunk, still drinking, still caught in the alcoholic web that had made my nights and days a misery for years.

I showered and shaved and went to an early Mass at Sacred Heart, then stayed alone in the church and said the rosary. But when I came out into the daylight the sun and humidity were like a flame on my skin and I curled and uncurled my fists for no reason.

Legion Guidry bonded out of jail at 10 A.M. An hour later I saw him crossing Main Street to eat lunch at Victor's Cafeteria. For just a moment I could taste his tobacco and saliva in my mouth and smell the testosterone on his clothes. My palm ached to fold around the checkered grips of my .45, to feel the heavy, hard, cold weight and the perfect balance of the frame resting securely in my hand.

Zerelda Calucci had tried to find Clete Purcel for two days, then discovered he'd hooked up a bail skip to the D-ring inset in the back floor of his Cadillac and had driven back to New Orleans to deliver the bail skip to the bondsmen for whom he worked.

Zerelda tracked Marvin Oates down on a side street in New Iberia's old bordello district, where he had dragged his roller-skate-mounted suitcase to the porch of a wood-frame store and was eating from a paper plate filled with rice and beans and sausage in the shade of a spreading oak. A half-block away was a stucco crack house, also shaded by an oak tree, the yard filled with trash, the windows broken, the screens slashed and rusted-out and hanging from the frames. White and black crack whores sat on the porch, walking in turns down to the store for beer or food or cigarettes, but Marvin did not look up from his paper plate when they walked past him.

Zerelda pulled her pearl-white Mustang convertible onto the oyster shells and did not cut the engine.

"Throw your suitcase in the back, sweetie, and let's take a drive," she said.

"Where we going?" Marvin asked.

Her eyes roved over a barked area by his eye, a bruise on his chin. Her face became suffused with pity and anger.

"To straighten out somebody who thinks he's a swinging dick because he can knock around someone half his size. Now get in the car, Marvin," she replied.

"I dint want to cause no trouble, Miss Zerelda," Marvin said.

She opened the car door and started to get out.

"I'm coming," he said.

It was almost dusk when Zerelda crossed the Mississippi River and drove down Canal and into the French Quarter and parked around the corner from Clete's office and upstairs apartment on St. Ann Street. The doors were locked, but a note addressed to an infamous nuisance in the New Orleans underworld was stuck in the corner of a window. It read: "Dear No Duh, I'm over at Nig and Willie's—Clete."

The bail bond office of Wee Willie Bimstine and Nig Rosewater was located just off Basin, just inside the ragged edges of the Quarter, not far from St. Louis Cemetery and Louis Armstrong Park. Zerelda pulled to the curb and parked next to a cluster of overflowing garbage cans. Down the street and across Basin she could see the old redbrick buildings and the green wood porches of the Iberville Project, a community whose crack addicts and gangbangers and teenage prostitutes would not only mug tourists and roll johns in the adjacent cemetery but occasionally execute them out of pure meanness. In fact, the city had poured cement barricades across some of the streets leading into the Iberville so that tourists would not drive into it by mistake.

But Marvin Oates's attention was focused on the window of the bail bond office, where Clete was playing cards at a desk with a thin, nattily dressed, deeply tanned man who wore an oxblood fedora with a gray feather in the band and a mustache that looked like it had been grease-penciled on his upper lip.

Marvin's face was wind-burned from the trip to the city, and now he was sweating heavily in the dusk, pinching his mouth dryly in his hand.

"I'll wait out here," he said.

"Nobody's going to hurt you," Zerelda said, getting out of the car.

"That's 'cause I'm staying out here."

She walked around to his side of the convertible. "Comb your hair, sweetie. Then I'm going to take you out to dinner. Don't you ever be afraid. Not when you're with me," she said, and smoothed his hair back up on his head.

His face looked like a fawn's.

Then she went through the door of the bail bond office, her purse swinging heavily from a cloth strap wrapped around her wrist.

"Zerelda, what's the haps? Great coincidence. I wanted No Duh here to check out our man Marvin the Voyeur, see if he wasn't a guy No Duh ran across in central lockup," Clete said.

"Where the fuck do you get off knocking around an innocent boy like that?"

"He has a way of showing up in places where he has no business," Clete replied.

"Oh, yeah?" Zerelda said, and swung her purse with both hands at his head, the cloth bottom bulging with the weight of her .357 Magnum.

He caught the blow on his forearm, but she swung again, this time hitting him squarely across the back of the head.

"Come on, Zerelda, that hurts," Clete said.

"You tub of whale sperm, you thought you could just dump me and get it on with some pisspot at the D.A.'s office?" she said.

"Remember strolling off to the ice cream parlor with dick brain out there? I took that as a signal to get lost. So I got lost," Clete said.

"Well, lose this, you fat fuck," she said, and hit him again.

"What's going on?" No Duh Dolowitz said. "Hey, Nig, we got some people getting hurt out here!"

Nig Rosewater came out of the back office. His porcine neck was as wide as his head inside his starched collar, so his head looked like the crown of a white fire-plug mounted on his shoulders. Nig took one look at Zerelda and went back inside his office and closed and bolted the door.

"All right, I'll talk to him! Calm down!" Clete said, and rose from his chair.

"You ought to be ashamed of yourself," Zerelda said.

"That guy is a bullshitter, Zee," Clete said.

She took a step toward him, but he raised his hand in a placating gesture. "All right, we've got no problem here," he said, and went outside in the dusk, into the noise of the street, the smells of stagnant water and overripe produce and flowers blooming on the overhanging balconies, the air crisscrossed with birds.

Clete took a deep breath and looked down at Marvin. "If I falsely accused you of something you didn't do, I apologize," Clete said. "But that also means you keep that stupid face out of my life and you don't get anywhere near certain friends of mine. This is as much slack as you get, Jack. We clear on this?"

"The twelve disciples are my road signs. I ain't afraid of no bullies. There ain't no detours in heaven, either," Marvin said.

"What?" Clete said.

"I dint do nothing wrong. I think you was trying to seduce Miss Barbara and somebody messed it up for you. So you put it on me 'cause I give her a Bible."

"You listen, shit-for-brains—"

Marvin got out of the car and lifted his suitcase from the backseat, wrapping the pull strap around his wrist, blade-faced under the brim of his hat, a hot bead of anger buried in his eye.

"Come back, Marvin," Zerelda said from the doorway of the bail bond office.

But Marvin pulled his suitcase down the street between the rows of dilapidated cottages toward Basin, his rumpled pale blue sports coat and coned straw hat and cowboy boots almost lost in the mauve-colored thickness of the evening. Then he crossed Basin amid a blowing of horns and a screeching of tires and tugged his suitcase on its roller skate over the curb and into the bowels of the Iberville Project.

"You're mean through and through, Clete. I don't know what I ever saw in you," Zerelda said.

But Clete wasn't listening. No Duh was staring into the distance, into the glow of sodium lamps that rose in a dusty haze above the project.

"You know him?" Clete asked.

"Yeah, I definitely seen that guy before," No Duh said.

"You sure?" Clete said.

"No doubt about it. I don't forget a face. Particularly not no nutcase."

"Where did you see him, No Duh?" Clete asked, his exasperation growing.

"He used to sell vacuum cleaners to the coloreds for Fat Sammy Figorelli. It was a scam to get them to sign loans at twenty percent. What, you thought he was somebody else?" No Duh said.

He tilted his head curiously at Clete, his mustache like the extended wings of a tiny bird.

What did Marvin Oates mean by 'There ain't no detours in heaven'?" Clete asked the next day as he walked with me from the office to Victor's Cafeteria.

"Who knows? I think it's a line from a bluegrass song," I replied.

"Zerelda Calucci says I'm butt crust."

"How you doing with Barbara?" I said, trying to change the subject.

"Marvin dimed me with her, too. You think the Peeping Tom was Legion Guidry?"

"Yeah, I do," I said.

Clete chewed on a hangnail and spit it off his tongue. We were walking past the crumbling, whitewashed crypts of St. Peter's Cemetery now.

"I put flowers on my old man's grave when I was in

New Orleans. It was a funny feeling, out there in the cemetery, just me and him," he said.

"Yeah?" I said.

"That's all. He had a crummy life. It wasn't a big deal," he said. He took off his porkpie hat and refitted it on his head, turning his face away so I could not see the expression in his eyes.

That afternoon Perry LaSalle asked me to stop by his office. When I got there, he was just locking the doors. The gallery and lawn and flower beds were deep in shadow, and his face had a melancholy cast in the failing light.

"Oh, hello, Dave," he said. He sat down on the top step of the gallery and waited for me to join him. Through the window behind him I could see the glass-framed Confederate battle flag of the 8th Louisiana Vols that one of his ancestors had carried in northern Virginia, and I wondered if indeed Perry was one of those souls who belonged in another time, or if he was a deluded creature of his own manufacture, playing the role of a tragic scion who had to expiate the sins of his ancestors, when in fact he was simply the beneficiary of wealth that had been made on the backs of others.

"Fine evening," I said, looking across the street at the Shadows plantation house and the bamboo moving in the wind and the magnificent, lichen-encrusted, moss-hung canopy of the live oaks.

"I've got to cut you loose," Perry said.

"You're resigning as my lawyer?"

"Legion Guidry is my client, too. You've got him up on assault charges. I can't represent both of you."

I nodded and put a stick of gum in my mouth and didn't respond.

"No hard feelings?" he said.

"Nope."

"I'm glad you see it that way."

"What's this guy have on you?" I asked.

He rose from the steps and buttoned his coat, removed his sunglasses from their case, and blew dust off the lenses. He started to speak, then simply walked to his car and drove away into the sunlight that still filled the streets of the business district.

I parked my truck in the backyard and went into the kitchen, where Bootsie was fixing supper. I sat down at the table with a glass of iced tea.

"You're disappointed in Perry?" she said.

"He helped organize migrant farm workers in the Southwest. He was a volunteer worker at a Dorothy Day mission in the Bowery. Now he's the apologist for a man like Legion Guidry. His behavior is hard to respect."

She turned from the stove and set a bowl of étouffée on the table with a hot pad and blotted her face on her sleeve. I thought she was going to argue.

"You're better off without him," she said.

"How?"

"Perry might have taken a vacation from the realities of his life in his youth, but he's a LaSalle first, last, and always."

"Pretty hard-nosed, Boots."

"You just learning that?"

She stood behind me and mussed my hair and

pressed her stomach against my back. Then I felt her hands slip down my chest and her breasts against my head.

"We can put dinner in the oven," I said.

I felt her straighten up, her hands relax on my shoulders, then I realized she was looking through the hallway, out into the front yard.

"You have a visitor," she said.

CHAPTER 21

Tee Bobby Hulin had parked his gas-guzzler by the cement boat ramp and had walked up into the gloom of the trees. His autistic sister, Rosebud, sat in the passenger's seat, a safety belt locked across her chest, staring at an empty pirogue floating aimlessly on the bayou. The evening was warm, the string of lightbulbs above my dock glowing with humidity, but Tee Bobby wore a long-sleeved black shirt buttoned at the wrists. His armpits were damp with sweat, his lips dry and caked at the edges.

"I just cut a CD. It's got 'Jolie Blon's Bounce' on it. Nobody else seem to like it too much. Anyway, see what you think," he said.

"I appreciate it, Tee Bobby. You kind of warm in that shirt?" I said.

"You know how it is," he replied.

"I can get you into a treatment program."

He shook his head and kicked gingerly at a tree root.

"Your sister okay?" I asked.

"Ain't nothing okay."

"We're getting ready to eat dinner right now. Maybe we can talk later," I said.

"I just dropped by, that's all."

It was dark where we stood under the trees, the molded pecan husks and blackened leaves soft under our feet, the air tannic, like water that has stood for a long time in a wooden cistern. The dying light was gold on the tops of the cypresses in the swamp, and snow egrets were rising into the light, their wings feathering in the wind.

"Why are you here?" I asked.

"You busted up Jimmy Dean Styles real bad. You shamed him in front of other people. Jimmy Sty always square the score."

"Forget about Jimmy Sty. Tell the truth about what happened to Amanda Boudreau."

"The lie detector say I didn't do it. That's all that counts. I ain't raped or shot nobody. Got the proof."

"You were there."

He tried to stare me down, then his eyes watered and broke.

"I wish I ain't come here. The lie detector say I'm innocent. But ain't nobody listening," he said.

"That girl is going to live in your dreams. She'll stand by your deathbed. You'll never have any peace until you get honest on this, Tee Bobby."

"Oh, God, why you do this to me?" he said, and walked hurriedly down the incline, slightly off balance.

That night I listened to his CD down at the bait shop.

The rendition of his new composition, "Jolie Blon's Bounce," was the best Acadian rhythm and blues I had ever heard. But I had a feeling the larger world would never come to know the tormented musical talent of Tee Bobby Hulin.

The next morning the sheriff took me off the desk and sent me to New Orleans with Helen Soileau to pick up a prisoner. It was noon when we crossed the Mississippi and drove into the city. While she ate lunch, I went back across the river to Algiers and caught the end of a low-bottom AA meeting off an alley, next to a bar, in the back of a warehouse with painted-over windows.

But this was not an ordinary AA group.

The failed, the aberrant, the doubly addicted, and the totally brain-fried whose neurosis didn't even have a name found their way to the Work the Steps or Die, Motherfucker meeting: strippers from the Quarter, psychotic street people, twenty-dollar hookers, peckerwood fundamentalists, leather-clad, born-again bikers, women who breast-fed their infants in a sea of cigarette smoke, a couple of cops who had done federal time, male prostitutes dying of AIDS, parolees with a lean, hungry look who sought only a signature on an attendance slip for their P.O.'s, methheads who drank from fire extinguishers in the joint, and Vietnam vets who wore their military tattoos and black- or olive-colored 1st Cav. and airborne T-shirts and still heard the thropping of helicopter blades in their sleep.

When it was my turn to speak, I began to do another Fifth Step, confessing my use of speed, the injury I had done Jimmy Dean Styles, the abiding anger and violence that seemed to afflict my life. But as I looked out into the smoke at the seamed and unshaved and rouged faces of the people sitting around the long table strewn with AA pamphlets, my words seemed twice-told and melodramatic, removed from the problems of people who counted themselves fortunate if they had food to eat that evening or a place to sleep that night.

I took a breath and started over again.

"An evil man did me physical injury. I think I know to at least a degree what a woman must feel like after she's been raped. For this deed and others he has committed, I believe this man does not deserve to live. These are serious and not idle thoughts that I have. In the meantime, I'm possessed of an enormous desire to drink," I said.

The discussion leader was a gaunt-faced biker with sunglasses as dark as welders' goggles and long silver hair that looked freshly shampooed and blow-dried.

"I'd get a lot of gone between me and them kind of thoughts, Dave. In California I went down for twenty-five and did twelve flat because of a dude like that. When I got out, I married his wife. She wrecked my truck, give my P.O. the clap, and run off with my Harley. Tell me that dude wasn't laughing in his grave," he said.

Everybody howled.

Except me and a street person at the far end of the table, a man with the glint of genuine madness in his eyes, his blond hair like melted and recooled tallow.

When the meeting broke up, he caught me at the door, his fingers biting into my upper arm, the vinegary stench of his body welling out of his yellow raincoat.

"Remember me?" he said.

"Sure," I replied.

"Not from New Iberia. You remember me from 'Nam?"

"A guy has lots of memories from the war," I said.

"I killed a child," he said.

"Sir?"

"We got into a meat grinder. It was after you got hit. We burned the ville. I seen a little girl run out of a hooch. She come apart in the smoke."

There were lines like pieces of white thread in the dirt around the corners of his eyes. His breath was odorless, his face inches from mine. He waited, as though I held a key that could unlock doors that were welded shut in his life.

"You want something to eat?" I asked.

"No."

"Take a ride with me," I said.

"Where?"

"I'm not sure," I replied.

There was no place for him, really. He was trapped inside memories that no human being should have to bear, and he would do the time and carry the cross for those makers of foreign and military policy who long ago had written their memoirs and appeared on televised Sunday-morning book promotions and moved on in their careers.

I took him to a motel and put two nights' rent on my credit card and gave him thirty dollars from my wallet.

"There's a Wal-Mart down the street. Maybe you can get yourself a razor and some clothes and a couple of food items," I said.

He was sitting on the bed in his motel room, staring at the motes of dust in a column of sunlight. I studied his

face and his hair and eyes. I tried to remember the face of
the medic who had cradled me in his arms as the AK-47
rounds from the trees below whanged off the helicopter's
frame.

"How'd you get to New Orleans?" I asked.

"Rode a freight."

"The medic who saved my life was Italian. He was
from Staten Island. You from Staten Island, troop?" I
said.

"The trouble with killing somebody is it makes you
forget who you used to be. I get places mixed up," he
said. He rubbed his face on his sleeve. "You gonna pop
that guy you was talking about in the meeting?"

Huey Lagneaux, also known as Baby Huey, had been
hired as a bartender and bouncer at his uncle's club
because of his massive size, the deep black tone of his
skin, which gave him the ambience of a leviathan rising
from oceanic depths, and the fact he only needed to lay
one meaty arm over a troublemaker's shoulders in order
to walk him quietly to the door.

But the uncle had also given him the job out of pity.
Baby Huey had not been the same since he had been kidnapped by a collection of white men from New Orleans
and prodded at gunpoint through a cemetery, down to
the water's edge on Bayou Teche, and systematically tor-
tured with a stun gun.

The club was on a back road out by Bayou Benoit, an
area of deep-water bays, flooded cypress and willow and
gum trees that under the rising moon was dented with
what looked like rain rings from the night feeding of
bream and largemouth bass. On Friday nights the club

thundered with electronic sound, and the parking lot, layered from end to end with flattened beer cans, clattered like a tin roof under the hundreds of automobiles and pickup trucks driving across it.

Tee Bobby Hulin was behind the microphone, up on the bandstand, in black slacks and a sequined purple shirt, his fingers splayed on the keys of an accordion whose case had the bright, wet shine of a freshly sliced pomegranate. The air was gray with cigarette smoke, heavy with the smell of body powder and sweat and perfume and okra gumbo. Baby Huey wiped down the bar and began rinsing a tin sink full of dirty glasses. When he looked up again, he saw a sheep-sheared white man in a tailored suit and a tropical shirt walking toward him, oblivious to the stares around him or even to the people who stepped out of his way before they were knocked aside.

"You know me?" the white man asked.

"Hard to forget, Mr. Zeroski," Baby Huey answered. He bent over the sink and washed the dish soap from his hands and wrists.

"A white man named Legion Guidry just went to the service window. Then I lost him. I hear he's got a camp around here," Joe said.

Baby Huey's face remained impassive, his gaze focused on the bandstand, the dancers out on the floor.

"You hear me?" Joe asked.

"I knew your daughter. She was nice to people. If I knew who killed her, I'd tell you. That night on the bayou, you didn't have no right to hurt me like that."

"You should have said that on the bayou. Maybe it would have gone down different."

"You wasn't looking for the troot. You was looking to get even," Baby Huey said.

Joe scratched at his cheek with the balls of his fingers.

"You keep the wrong company, you pay dues. They ain't always fair," he said. He took a one-hundred-dollar bill from his wallet and creased it lengthwise and placed it on the bar like a miniature tent.

Baby Huey pushed it away and dried a glass. "I ain't axed you for nothing. In case you ain't noticed, you in the wrong part of town," he said.

"Yeah, I got that impression when I walked in. You want to earn that hunnerd bucks and another hunnerd like it, or keep blaming me 'cause you decided to be a pimp and sell crack?"

Baby Huey filled a bowl with gumbo and put a spoon in it and set it on a napkin in front of Joe.

"It's on me. I made it this afternoon," Baby Huey said. "You want a beer wit' it?"

"I don't mind," Joe said.

"You got bidness wit' the man people call Legion, huh?" Baby Huey said.

"What do you mean the man they 'call' Legion?"

"He ain't got a first name. He ain't got a last name. Just 'Legion.' That's all black people ever call him."

"He's hard on women?" Joe said.

"If they the right color," Baby Huey said, and put the one-hundred-dollar bill in his shirt pocket.

They drove in Joe Zeroski's car up on a levee that looked out on a wide bay fringed with flooded cypresses. A storm was kicking up out on the Gulf, and the wind was blowing hard from the south, wrinkling the bay, puffing leaves out of the adjacent woods. Joe turned off on a dirt track, dropping down into persimmon and pecan trees, palmettos, and landlocked pools that had the greasy shine of an oil slick. Baby Huey pointed to a shack in a clearing, a lantern burning whitely on a table inside. In back were a privy and a collapsed smokehouse and Legion Guidry's truck, parked next to an oak that was nailed with the scraped hides of raccoons.

One of the truck's rear tires was flat on the rim.

Joe cut the engine. Through the trees they could hear Tee Bobby's band belting out Clifton Chenier's "Hey, Tite Fille." They stepped out of the air-conditioned car into the darkness, the mosquitoes that boiled out of the trees, the wind that smelled of humus and beached fish.

"You stay where you are," Joe said, and pitched a cell phone to Baby Huey. "It goes south in there, you push the redial button and say 'Joe needs a hose crew.' Then you tell them where we're at and you take my car down the road and wait for whoever comes."

"That's Legion in there, Mr. Joe," Baby Huey said.

"I think you're a nice kid. I think you were sincere what you said about my daughter. But take the collard greens out of your mouth and tell me what you're trying to say. That's why you people are always gonna be cleaning toilets. You can't say what's on your mind."

Baby Huey shook his head. "Legion ain't no ordinary white man. He ain't no ordinary man of any kind."

Joe Zeroski opened the screen door of the shack and walked inside without knocking. While he and Baby Huey had talked outside, the tall, black-haired man in khaki clothes who sat at the table with a six-pack of beer and a bottle of bourbon in front of him had shown no curiosity about the headlights or the presence of others in his yard.

He knocked back a jigger of whiskey, took a sip of beer from a salted can, and picked up a burning cigarette from an inverted jar top. He drew in the smoke, the cigarette paper crackling in the silence.

"You busted up two of my men. But I'm letting that slide for now, 'cause maybe they were rude or maybe you didn't know who they were. But somebody beat my daughter to death and I'm gonna rip his ass. I hear you got a bad record with women," Joe said.

"Robicheaux send you?" Legion asked.

"Robicheaux?"

"You one of them dagos been staying in town, ain't you? Working for Dave Robicheaux."

"Are you nuts?" Joe said.

Then Joe heard a sound in a side room, behind a blanket that was hung with sliding hooks on a doorway. Joe pulled back the blanket and looked down at a black girl, probably not over eighteen, sitting on the side of a bed in shorts and a T-shirt razored off below her breasts, snorting a line off a broken mirror through a rolled five-dollar bill.

Joe took her by the arm and walked her barefoot and stoned to the front door.

"Go home. Or back to the nightclub. Or wherever you come from. But stay away from this man. Where's your father, anyway?" he said, and closed the door behind her. Then he turned around, his back feeling momentarily exposed, vulnerable.

Legion's face wore no expression, the skin white as a fish's belly, creased with vertical lines. He inhaled off his cigarette, the ash glowing red, crackling against the dryness of the paper.

"You just made a mistake," he said.

"Oh, yeah, how's that?" Joe asked.

"I paid forty dollars for her dope. So now you owe the debt."

"You're an ignorant and stupid man, but I'm gonna try to explain something to you as simply as I can. My daughter was Linda Zeroski. A degenerate piece of shit tied her to a chair not far from here and smashed every bone in her face with his fists."

Joe removed a .38 revolver with a two-inch barrel from the back of his belt. He flipped out the cylinder and dumped all six shells from the chambers into his palm.

"I'm gonna put two rounds back in the chambers and spin them around, then we're gonna—" he began.

That's when Legion Guidry slid a cut-down, double-barreled twelve-gauge shotgun from a scabbard nailed under the table and raised it so the barrels were suddenly pointed into Joe Zeroski's face.

"Who's stupid now?" Legion said. "You got nothing smart to say, you? Just gonna stand there wit' your li'l gun wit'out no bullets in it? Time you got down on your knees, dago."

"I look Italian? Zeroski is Polish, you moron. Poles ain't Italians," Joe said.

Legion rose from the table and walked to the screen door, where Baby Huey stood frozen, his eyes wide at the scene taking place in front of him.

"Come inside," Legion said.

Baby Huey opened the screen and stepped out of the darkness into the white radiance of the lantern on the table. The muscles in his back jumped when the screen swung back into the jamb behind him.

"On your knees, nigger," Legion said.

"My uncle owns the nightclub. He knows where we're at," Baby Huey said.

"That's good. He come here, I'll shoot me two niggers 'stead of one," Legion said.

Baby Huey bent slowly to the floor, his knees popping, sweat breaking on his brow now, his gaze sliding down the length of Legion's body.

Legion screwed the barrels of the shotgun into Baby Huey's neck and looked at Joe.

"T'row your li'l gun down and get on your knees, or I'm gonna blow the nigger's head off. Look into my eyes and tell me you don't t'ink I'll do it, no," he said.

Joe Zeroski let the .38 shells spill from his hand onto the floor, then tossed the revolver to one side and got to his knees.

Legion Guidry stood above him, his stomach and loins flat, his khaki shirt tucked tightly inside his western belt. He reached behind him and removed his straw hat from the back of a chair and fitted it on his head so that his face was now in shadow. He drank from his whiskey bottle and spread his feet slightly and cleared his throat.

"What you t'ink about to happen? Bet you didn't t'ink a day like this would ever come in your life, no," he said.

Then he unzipped his fly.

"How far you willing to go to keep a nigger alive?" he asked, pressing the shotgun harder into Baby Huey's neck, his eyes riveted on Joe's.

Joe felt himself swallow, his hands balling at his sides.

Legion's finger was wrapped tightly inside the trigger
guard on the shotgun. The back of his hand was spotted
with sun freckles, his cuff buttoned at the wrist, his veins
like pieces of green cord. Joe could smell the nicotine
ingrained in his skin, the boilermakers that still hung on
his breath, the raw odor of his manhood that seemed
ironed into his clothes.

Joe Zeroski felt his heart thundering, then a rage well
up in him that was like a fire blooming in his chest. His
face grew tight and his scalp seemed to shrink and shift
against his skull, his eyes bulge in their sockets, with
either adrenaline or fear, he would never know which.
"Go ahead and shoot, you worthless cocksucker. Me
first. 'Cause I get the chance, I'm gonna tear your throat
out," he said.

He heard Legion Guidry snort.

"You t'ink pretty high of yourself, you. I wouldn't
dirty my dick on a dago or a Pollack," Legion said, drawing his zipper back into place. "Give me your car keys."

"What?" Joe asked, staring up in disbelief at the mercurial nature of his tormentor.

"I'm taking your car to find my whore. I don't find my
whore, I'm gonna come after you for my forty dollars.
Next time you want to pretend like you a New Orleans
gangster, remember what you look like right now, on
your knees, next to a nigger, just about an inch from
sucking a man's dick. Tell yourself later you wouldn't do
it, no. Believe me, I wanted you to, you would, you," he
said.

Legion collected Joe's automobile keys and his .38
revolver and shells. Minutes later, Baby Huey and Joe
watched him drive away in Joe's automobile, the radio

playing, Legion's hat and tall frame silhouetted against the front window. Baby Huey could hear Joe breathing in the darkness.

"You saved my life, Mr. Joe. I cain't believe you told him to shoot. That's the bravest thing I ever seen anybody do," he said.

Joe waved his hand to indicate he did not want to hear about it. Baby Huey started to speak again.

"Hey, forget it," Joe said.

"What we gonna do now?" Baby Huey asked, looking up the dirt track through the woods.

"It wasn't him beat my daughter to death," Joe said.

"How you know?"

"He don't have no feeling about people. It wasn't him. The ones to be afraid of are the ones got feelings about you. That's a sad truth, kid, but that's the way it is," Joe said.

CHAPTER 22

But Baby Huey Lagneaux's encounter with Legion was not over. Toward closing time that night, after he had returned to his uncle's club, he glanced through a back window and saw Joe Zeroski's automobile parked at the café next door. He called a telephone number Joe had given him, but there was no answer. He went out the back door of the club and crossed the parking lot and looked through a side window of the café.

Legion was eating at a table by himself. At the next table was a group of shrimpers who had just come off the salt, hard-bitten men in rubber boots who hadn't shaved for weeks and who filled the air with cigarette smoke and drank mugs of beer while they ate platters of fried crabs with their fingers.

In his mind's eye Baby Huey saw himself confronting Legion, here, in public, demanding the keys to Joe Zeroski's car, somehow regaining a degree of the self-respect he'd lost when a shotgun was screwed into his neck and his bowels turned to water. He entered the café's side door and stared at Legion's back, at the untrimmed locks of hair on his neck, the power in his shoulders, the way the bones in his jaws stretched his skin while he chewed. But Baby Huey could not make his feet move any closer to Legion's table.

Then Tee Bobby Hulin came through the front door and sat at the counter, within earshot of the shrimpers, some of whom must have recognized him as the man about to go on trial for the rape and murder of Amanda Boudreau. At first they only looked at him and whispered among themselves; then they seemed to ignore him and concentrate on their food and beer and the burning cigarettes they left teetering on the edges of ashtrays. But willingly or not, their eyes began to drift back to Tee Bobby, as though he were a troublesome insect that someone should swat.

Finally one of the shrimpers turned in his chair and aimed his words at Tee Bobby's back: "You ain't got no bidness in here, buddy. Get what you need and carry it outside."

Tee Bobby stared at his menu, as though he were nearsighted and had lost his glasses, his hands clenched on the corners, his spine and shoulders rounded like a question mark.

The same shrimper, silver and black whiskers festooned on his jaws, made a soft whistling sound through his teeth. "Hey, outside, bud. Don't make me walk you there, no," he said.

Legion had set his knife and fork on the rim of his plate. He half-mooned one of his nails with a toothpick, his back hard as iron against his khaki shirt, his eyes studying Tee Bobby's profile. Then he rose from his chair and walked to the counter, the board floor creaking with his weight, the inside of his hands as yellow and rough as barrel wood under the overhead light.

"Get up," Legion said.

"What for?" Tee Bobby asked. His gaze lifted into Legion's, then his face twitched, as though he recognized a figure from a dream he had never defined in daylight.

"Don't you let them men talk down to you," Legion replied, and pulled Tee Bobby off the counter stool. "You stand up, you. Don't you never take shit from white trash."

The shrimpers looked blankly at both Tee Bobby and Legion, confused, unable to connect the indignation of the towering white man with a diminutive black musician who only a moment ago had been an object of contempt.

"Y'all looking at somet'ing? Y'all want to go outside wit' me? How 'bout you, yeah, big mouth there, the one telling him to carry his food outside?" Legion said.

"We ain't got no problem with you," one of the other shrimpers said.

"You better t'ank God you don't," Legion said.

He paid his bill in the silence of the café, put two half-dollars by his plate, and walked outside, into the darkness, into the flicker of heat lightning and the *tink* of raindrops on the tin roof of the café. He heard Tee Bobby come out the door behind him.

"You're him, ain't you?" Tee Bobby said.

"Depends on who you t'ink I am," Legion said.

"The overseer. From Poinciana Island. The one called Legion. The one who—"

"Who what, boy?"

"The overseer who slept wit' my grandmother. I'm Tee Bobby. Ladice Hulin is my gran'mama."

"You look like her. But you ain't as pretty."

"What you done inside the café, it's 'cause of what happened at the plantation, ain't it? It's 'cause maybe you're my—"

"Your what, boy?"

"My mama was half-white. Everybody on the plantation know that."

Legion laughed to himself and shook a cigarette out of his pack and fed it into the corner of his mouth.

"Your daddy didn't know how to use a rubber. That's how you got here, boy. That's how come other people try to wipe their shit on your face," he said.

Tee Bobby brushed a raindrop out of his eye and continued to stare at Legion, his sequined purple shirt puffing with air in the wind.

"I said you slept with my grandmother. That ain't true. You raped her. You pushed old man Julian around and you raped my gran'mama," he said.

"The white man gonna screw down whenever he got the chance. Nigger woman always gonna get what she can out of it. Which one gonna lie about it later?"

"My gran'mama don't never lie. You better not call her a nigger, either," Tee Bobby said.

Legion struck the flint on his lighter and cupped the flame in the wind, inhaling on his cigarette.

"I'm leaving now. Them shrimpers gonna be coming out of there. You better get your ass home, you," he said.

Legion got behind the wheel of Joe Zeroski's automobile and started the engine, his cigarette hanging from his mouth. But before he could back out and turn around, Tee Bobby picked up a piece of broken cement the size of a softball and smashed the driver's-side window with it.

Legion braked the car and got out, a huge hole in the window, his forehead bleeding, his cigarette still in his mouth.

"You got sand," he said.

"Fuck you," Tee Bobby said.

"Ax yourself where you got it. The parents who didn't want you? Be proud of the blood you got, boy," Legion replied.

He got back in Joe Zeroski's automobile, tossed his cigarette through the hole in the window, and drove away.

Late that night Baby Huey Lagneaux stole Joe Zeroski's automobile out of Legion's yard and was driving it back to New Iberia when he was stopped for speeding. Baby Huey sat in jail for suspicion of car theft until Monday morning. Before he went back on the street, I had a deputy bring him by my office.

"You were taking the car back to Joe?" I asked.

"Yes, suh."

"I don't get it. His men used a stun gun on you."

"Mr. Joe t'rew down his .38 and got on his knees to save my life. He don't even know me."

The chair he sat in groaned with the strain, his skin so black it had a purple sheen to it. He gazed out the window at the freight train clicking by on the rail crossing.

"See you around, Huey," I said.

"I can go?"

"Why'd you ever become a pimp?"

He shrugged his shoulders. "I ain't one now. Can I go?"

"You bet," I said. I leaned back in my chair, my fingers laced behind my head, and wondered at the complexities and contradictions that must have existed in the earth's original clay when God first scooped it up in His palm.

Twenty minutes later my desk phone rang.

"This kid Marvin Grits or whatever was handing out Bible pamphlets at the motor court this morning. But that ain't why he's here. He's got the hots for Zerelda. I want him picked up. Besides, he's drunk," the voice said.

"Joe?"

"You thought it was the pope?"

"Marvin Oates is drunk?"

"He looks like he got hit by a train. He smells like puke. Maybe he just come from First Baptist," Joe said.

"I'll see what I can do. Baby Huey Lagneaux just left my office. He told me about your run-in with Legion Guidry."

"Don't know what you're talking about."

"I always said you were a stand-up guy."

"Go soak your head," he said, and hung up.

I told Wally, our dispatcher, to have Marvin Oates picked up at the motor court.

Later, I walked downtown to eat lunch. When I came back to the department, Wally stopped me in the corridor. He was holding three pink message slips that he was about to put in my mailbox.

"This woman keeps calling and axing for you. How about getting her off my neck?" he said.

He put the message slips in my hand. The telephone number was in St. Mary Parish, the caller's name one I didn't immediately recognize.

"Who is she?" I asked.

"Hillary Clinton, in coonass disguise. How do I know, Dave? By the way, Marvin Oates wasn't at the motor court when the cruiser got there," he answered.

The woman's name was Marie Guilbeau. I returned her call from my office phone. When she picked up, I suddenly remembered the face of the cleaning woman who had claimed a man in a rubber mask, wearing leather gloves, had invaded her house and molested her.

"The priest tole me I got to tell you somet'ing," she said.

"What's that, Ms. Guilbeau?" I asked.

There was no response.

"I'm a little busy right now, but if you like, I can drive out to your house again," I said.

"I clean at the motel out on the fo'-lane," she said. "They was a nice-looking fellow staying there. I kind of flirted wit' him. Maybe I give him the wrong idea," she said.

"Was he a white or black man?" I asked.

"He was white. I t'ink he t'ought I was a prostitute from the truck stop. I tole him to get away from me. I was ashamed to tell you about that when you come out to my house."

"You think the man in the rubber mask was the guy from the motel?"

"I don't know, suh. I don't want to talk about this no more," she replied. The line went dead.

*   *   *

What do you say to sexual assault victims?

Answer: You're going to catch the guys who hurt them and bury them in a maximum-security prison from which they will never be paroled, and with good luck they'll cell with predators who are twice their size and ten times more vicious.

Except it's usually a lie on every level. More often than not the victims get torn apart on the stand by defense attorneys and ultimately exit the process disbelieved, discredited, and accused of being either delusional or opportunistic.

I once heard an elderly recidivist say, "Jailing ain't the same no more. Folks just ain't rearing criminals like they used to." Any old-time lawman, if he's honest, will probably tell you he's sickened by the class of contemporary criminals he's forced to deal with. As bad as the criminals of the Great Depression were, many of them possessed the virtues Americans admire. Most of them came from midwestern farm families and were not sexual predators or serial killers. Usually their crimes were against banks and the government, and at least in their own minds they were not out to harm individuals. Even their most vehement antagonists, usually Texas Rangers and FBI agents, granted that they were brave and died game and asked for no quarter and pleaded no excuse for their misdeeds.

Clyde Barrow was beaten unmercifully with the black Betty in Eastham State Prison and made to run two miles to work in the cotton fields and two miles back to the lockup every workday of his sentence. He swore that one day he would not only get even for the brutality he suffered and witnessed there, but he would return to Eastham a free man and break out every inmate he could. Sure enough, after he was paroled, he and Bonnie Parker shot their way into the prison, then shot their way back out with five convicts in tow, whom they packed into a stolen car and successfully escaped with.

Doc Barker and four others got over the wall at Alcatraz Island and were almost home free, a rubber boat waiting for them in the shoals, when one man sprained his ankle on the rocks. The other four went back for him, got caught in the searchlights, and were blown apart by automatic-weapons fire. Oddly, the prison authorities named the stretch of rocky sand where they died Barker Beach.

Lester Gillis, also known as Baby Face Nelson, declared war on the FBI and hunted federal agents as though he was the offended party, not they, carrying their photos and names and license tag numbers in his automobile, on the last day of his life actually making a U-turn and pursuing two of them down a road, forcing them into a ditch and a firefight that lasted over an hour and left Gillis with seventeen bullet holes in his body.

He managed to drive away and receive the church's last rites.

Helen opened the door of my office without knocking and came inside. "Lost in thought?" she said.

"What's up?"

"The bartender at the Boom Boom Room says Marvin Oates is stoking up the neighborhood. The skipper wants a net over him," she said.

"Send a uniform," I said.

"Marvin got into it with Jimmy Dean Styles."

A drop of rain struck the window glass.

"Let me get my hat," I said.

We signed out a cruiser and drove out past the city limits, crossed a drawbridge spanning the Teche, next to a leafy pecan orchard, and entered the black slum community where Jimmy Sty operated the Boom Boom Room. When Helen got out of the cruiser, she slipped her baton into the ring on her gun belt.

Styles was inside, behind the bar, his face still swollen from the beating I had given him. The room was dark except for the lit beer signs on the wall and the glow of a jukebox in the corner. Two black women sat at the end of the bar, their mouths thick with lipstick, their hair in disarray, glasses of bulk synthetic wine in front of them.

"Hey, my man Lou'sana Chuck, I hear you lucking out. My charge against you being dropped," Styles said.

"News to me," I said.

"My lawyer got the word. Marse Purcel say he saw me pull a switchblade knife. Funny how a big fat pig like that can see a knife when he wasn't even there."

"Marvin Oates been giving you a bad time?" I said.

"Passing out religious tracts in a bar? Trying to hide the boner in his pants at the same time? You tell me, Lou'sana Chuck."

"Watch your language," Helen said.

"Where is he?" I asked.

"Think he met a girlfriend. He be converting her now," Styles said. He reached into the cooler behind him and unscrewed the cap on a bottle of chocolate milk. In the light of the beer sign above his head, his gold-textured face seemed grotesque, a blood knot on the ridge of his nose, the skin puckered where it had been stitched. He drank until the bottle was half empty, then rested his hands on the bar and lowered his head and belched.

"Can you give us a minute?" I said to Helen.

"No problem. I just hate to give up the *eau de caca* coming from the bathroom," she said, fitting on her sunglasses, stepping out the front door into the hazy midday glare, her baton at a stiff angle on her left side.

Styles looked at me curiously.

"I think you're a sorry sack of shit, Jimmy. But I didn't have the right to take you down the way I did. I also think you're getting a lousy deal with the St. Martin D.A.'s office. But you know the rules. Cops take care of their own. Anyway, I apologize for busting you up," I said.

"Lookie here, Chuck, you want to feel good about yourself, go somewhere else to do it. You want to shut my bidness down, come back wit' a court order. In the meantime, get the fuck out of my life."

"You helped Tee Bobby get on the spike, Jimmy. How's it feel to ruin one of the greatest musicians ever to come out of Louisiana?" I said.

"Had about all this I can stand," he replied. He walked to the front door and called outside. "Gots a problem in here!"

Helen came through the door, pulling off her sunglasses, letting her eyes adjust to the darkness.

"What's the trouble?" she said.

"I hear you a dyke who's straight up and don't take

shit from nobody. 'Preciate you being a witness if Chuck here decides to assault me again," Styles said.

"Say again?" Helen said.

Styles blew out his breath and made an exasperated face. "Lady, I ain't give you the reputation. You walked in here wit' it. Yesterday, in the McDonald's on Main, male cops was laughing about you. I ain't lying. Ax Chuck here they don't do it."

Styles upended his bottle of chocolate milk. He had worked the hook in deep, with a good chance of getting away with it. Except he let his eyes light on Helen's while a smile tugged at the corner of his mouth. Helen pulled her baton from the loop on her belt and swung it back-handed across his face. The bottle shattered in Styles's hand, speckling his face with chocolate milk and fragments of glass.

She placed her business card on the bar.

"Have a nice day. Call me if you need any more assistance," she said.

We drove through the neighborhood, past shacks with rusted screen galleries that were still hung with Christmas lights, and crossed a coulee that was shaded by pecan trees and whose banks were green and raked clean and sprinkled with periwinkles. Then, back among the trees, we saw a pale yellow shotgun house and Marvin's suitcase on the porch. Music came from the windows, and, incongruously, a bright red Coca-Cola machine sat in the carport, the refrigeration unit vibrating, the exterior beaded with fat drops of moisture.

We pulled into the yard and walked up on the porch. The inside door was open and a heady, autumnal odor, like wet leaves burning, drifted through the screen. I knocked, but no one answered.

Helen stayed in front and I walked around to the rear door. Then, through the screen, I witnessed one of those scenes that makes us wish we knew less about the human family's potential for deceit and the manipulation of those who are weaker than ourselves.

Marvin Oates sat at a bare kitchen table, his shirt off, his eyes pinched shut, his balled fists trembling with anxiety or perhaps visions that only he saw on the backs of his eyelids. His forehead was barked and there was a bruise along his jawbone like the discoloration in an overripe banana. A pair of marijuana roach clips sat in an ashtray, smoldering at the tips.

A young black woman, her short hair curled and peroxided at the ends, stood over him, kneading his shoulders, letting her breasts touch his head, her loins rub against his back, blowing her breath in his ear. She wore white shorts rolled up into her genitalia, a denim shirt embroidered with flowers, a rose tattooed on her throat, bracelets that jangled on her ankles, and pink tennis shoes, like a little girl might wear.

"Leona got what you want, honey. But I got to have a li'l more money than what you give me. That ain't hardly enough to cover Jimmy Sty's end of things. Girl got to have some money for rent. Got to pay for the liquor you drunk, the dope you smoked, too, darlin'. Don't make me go down the road and get another date. You a cute t'ing . . ."

She traced her hands down his chest and touched his sex. His chin lifted and his face seemed to sharpen, to blade with color and the heated energies he could barely control. He opened his eyes, like a man waking from a dream.

His voice was a rusty clot, a mixture of desire and guilt and need. "There's more money in my britches," he said.

The woman reached over to remove his wallet from his back pocket. When she did, I saw Marvin's naked back and the pockmarks on it that ran all the way down to his beltline.

I opened the screen door and stepped into the kitchen.

"Sorry to bother you, Leona, but Marvin has an appointment at the sheriff's department," I said.

At first her face jerked with surprise. Then she grinned and straightened her shoulders and pushed back her hair.

"Dave Robicheaux come to see me? I love you, dar-lin', and would run off wit' you in a minute, but I'm all tied up right now," she said.

"I realize that, Leona. But how about returning the money you were holding for Marvin so we can be on our way?" I said.

"He want me to have it. Tole me so wit' his hand on his heart," she said, rubbing the top of Marvin's head.

Helen came through the front of the house, whirled Leona against the table, and kicked her feet apart. She pulled a sheaf of bills from Leona's pocket. "You take anything else from him?" she said.

"No, ma'am," Leona said.

"Where'd you get the rock?" Helen said, holding up a two-inch plastic vial with a tiny cork in the top.

"Don't know where that come from," Leona said.

"Is that your baby in the other room?" Helen said.

"Yes, ma'am. He's eighteen months now," Leona said.

"Then go take care of him. I catch you turning tricks again, I'm going to roust Jimmy Sty and tell him you dimed him," Helen said.

"Can I have the rock back?" Leona said.

"Get out of here," Helen said. She picked up Marvin's shirt and draped it on his shoulders and put his hat on his head.

"Let's go, cowboy," she said, and pushed him ahead of her toward the front door.

It had started to rain. The trees were blowing on the bayou, and the air was cool and smelled like dust and fish spawning.

Marvin began putting on his shirt, drawing it over the network of scars on his back.

"Who did that to you, partner?" I asked.

"I don't know," he replied. "Sometimes I almost remember. Then I go inside in my head and don't come out for a long time. It's like I ain't s'pposed to remember some things."

Helen looked at me. I picked up Marvin's suitcase and placed it in the trunk of the cruiser, then shut the hatch and opened the back door for him.

"Why'd you get drunk?" I asked.

"No reason. I got beat up in the Iberville Project. I looked all over for Miss Zerelda, but she was gone. I dint know where she went," he replied.

"Think you can stay out of this part of town for a while?" I asked.

"I ain't gonna drink no more. No, sir, you got my word on that," he said. He shook his head profoundly.

Helen and I got in front. She started the engine, then

turned and looked back through the wire-mesh screen that separated us from Marvin Oates. Lightning splintered the sky on the other side of the pecan trees that lined the coulee.

"Marvin, have you ever noticed you never answer a question directly? Can you tell us why that is?" she said.

"The Bible is my road map. The children of Israel used it, too. They crossed the Red Sea of destruction and God done seen them safely through. That's all I can say," he replied.

"That's very illuminating. Thanks for sharing that," she said, and shifted the cruiser into gear.

Fifteen minutes later we dropped him in front of his house. He hefted his suitcase out of the trunk and ran through the rain, his straw hat clamped on his head, his hand-tooled cowboy boots splashing on the edge of the puddles in his tiny yard, his shirt flapping in the wind.

"You think those scars on his back are from hot cigarettes?" Helen asked.

"That'd be my guess."

"It's a great life, huh?" she said.

I'm sure I knew a glib reply to her remark, which she had obviously intended to hide her feelings, but the image of a child being systematically burned, probably by a parent or stepparent, was just too awful to talk about.

Through the window I saw a man walk against the red light at the intersection, a heavy piece of rolled canvas draped over his shoulders, like a cross, his unlaced work boots sloshing through the water.

"Let's take that fellow to the shelter," I said.

"You know him?" Helen said.

"He was a medic in my outfit. I saw him in New Orleans. He must have hopped a freight back to New Iberia."

She turned in the seat and looked into my face. "Run that by me again."

"When I was hit, he carried me piggyback into the slick and kept me alive until we got to battalion aid," I said.

"I'm a little worried about you, Pops," she said.

CHAPTER 23

I rose before dawn the next morning and walked down to the dock to help Batist open up. I fixed chicory coffee and hot milk and heated an egg sandwich and ate breakfast by an open window above the water and listened to the moisture dripping out of the trees in the swamp and the popping of bluegill that were feeding along the edge of the hyacinths. Then the stars went out of the sky and the wind dropped and the stands of flooded cypresses turned as gray as winter smoke. A moment later the sun broke above the rim of the earth, like someone firing a furnace on the far side of the swamp, and suddenly the tree trunks were brown and without mystery, streaked with night damp, their limbs ridged with fern and lichen, the water that had been layered with fog only moments ago now alive with insects, dissected by the V-shaped wakes of cottonmouths and young alligators.

I washed my dishes in the tin sink and was about to

walk back up to the house when I heard a car with a blown muffler coming down the road. A moment later Clete Purcel came through the bait shop door, wearing new running shoes, elastic-waisted, neon-purple shorts that bagged to his knees, a tie-dye strap undershirt that looked like chemically stained cheesecloth on his massive torso, and his Marine Corps utility cap turned sideways on his head.

"What d'you got for eats?" he asked.

"Whatever you see," I replied.

He went behind the counter and began assembling what he considered a healthy breakfast: four jelly doughnuts, a quart of chocolate milk, a cold pork-chop sandwich he found in the icebox, and two links of microwave boudin. He glanced at his watch, then sat on a counter stool and began eating.

"I'm jogging three miles with Barbara this morning," he said.

"Three miles? Maybe you should pack another sandwich."

"What's that supposed to mean?" he asked.

"Nothing," I replied, my face blank.

"I've done some more checking on our playboy lawyer LaSalle. If I were you, I'd take a closer look at this guy."

"Would you?"

"Big Tit Judy Lavelle says he's got a half-dozen regular pumps in the Quarter alone. She says his flopper not only has eyes, it's got X-ray vision. A female walks by and it pokes its way out of his fly."

"So what?" I said.

"So he's hinky. Sex predators can have college

degrees, too. He uses people, then throws them over the gunnel. He got it on with both Barbara and Zerelda, then treated them like yesterday's ice cream. His whole family made their money on other people's backs. You see a pattern here?"

"You're saying you don't like him?"

"Talk to Big Tit Judy. She used the term 'inexhaustible needs.' Gee, I wonder what she means by that."

"I'd better get to work. How are things going with you and Barbara?"

He crumpled up a paper napkin and dropped it on his plate. He started to speak, then shrugged his shoulders, his face chagrined.

"My feelings seem a little naked?" he said.

"I wouldn't say that."

"You're sure a bum liar."

I walked with him to his car, then watched him drive down the dirt road, his convertible top down, a Smiley Lewis tape blaring from his loudspeakers, determined not to let mortality and the exigencies of his own battered soul hold sway in his life.

I went to the office, but I couldn't quite shake a thought Clete had planted in my head. His thinking and behavior were eccentric, his physical appetites legendary, his periodic excursions into mayhem of epic proportions, but under it all Clete was still the most intelligent and perceptive police officer I had ever known. He not only understood criminals, he understood the society that produced them.

When he was a patrolman in the Garden District, he busted a choleric, obnoxious United States congressman for D.W.I. and hit-and-run and had the congressman's car towed to the pound. When the congressman and his girlfriend tried to walk off to a bar on the corner of St. Charles and Napoleon, Clete handcuffed him to a fireplug.

Charges against the congressman were dropped, and one week later Clete found himself reassigned to a program called Neighborhood Outreach. He spent the next year ducking bullets and bricks or garbage cans weighted with water and thrown from roofs at the Desire, Iberville, and St. Thomas projects.

Even though Clete made constant derogatory allusions to the population of petty miscreants and meltdowns that cycles itself daily through the bail bond offices, courts, and jails of every city in America, in reality he viewed most of them as defective rather than evil and treated them with a kind of sardonic respect.

Drug dealers, pimps, sexual predators, jackrollers, and armed robbers were another matter. So were slumlords and politicians on the pad and cops who did scut work for the Mob. But Clete's real disdain was directed at a state of mind rather than at individuals. He looked upon public displays of charity and morality as the stuff of sideshows. He never trusted people in groups and was convinced that inside every reformer there was a glandular, lascivious, and sweaty creature aching for release.

After Clete made plainclothes, he worked a case involving a Garden District doyenne whose philandering husband went missing on a fishing trip down in Barataria. The husband's outboard was found floating upside down in the swamp immediately after a storm, the rods, tackle boxes, ice chest, and life preservers washed into the trees. His disappearance was written off as an accidental drowning.

But Clete learned the husband hated to drive an automobile and regularly hired taxicabs to take him around New Orleans. Clete searched through hundreds of taxi logs until he found an entry for a pickup at the husband's residence on the day he went fishing. The destination was the husband's new downtown office building. Clete also questioned a security guard at the office building and was told the wife had been installing new shelves in the basement very early on the Saturday morning her husband had disappeared.

Clete obtained a blueprint of the building and got a search warrant and discovered that behind the shelves a brick wall had been recently mortared across an alcove that was meant to serve as a storage space.

He and three uniformed patrolmen sledgehammered a hole in the bricks and were suddenly struck by an odor that caused one of them to vomit in his hands. The doyenne had not only walled up her husband in his own office building, she had hosted a dance, with a hired orchestra, right above the alcove that evening. The coroner said the husband was alive for the whole show.

Clete busted an infamous gay millionaire on Bayou St. John who fed his abusive mother to a pet alligator, helped wiretap a Louisiana insurance commissioner who went to prison for bribery, and eventually caught up with the United States congressman who had been instrumental in shipping Clete off to Neighborhood Outreach.

During Mardi Gras someone had flung a beer bottle from a French Quarter hotel window into the passing parade and had seriously hurt one of New Orleans's most famous trumpet players. Clete went down a third-floor corridor, knocking on doors, trying to approximate the probable location of the room from which the bottle had been thrown.

Then he reached the door of a large suite, marched off the distance to the end of the corridor, comparing it with the distance he had measured between the suspect window and the edge of the building outside. When he and the hotel detective were refused entrance to the suite, Clete kicked the doors open and saw the congressman amid a group of naked revelers, their Mardi Gras masks pushed up on their heads, spitting whiskey and soda on one another.

This time Clete made a call to a police reporter at the *Times-Picayune* right after busting the whole room.

"You think Perry LaSalle may be a sex predator?" Bootsie said that afternoon.

"I didn't say that. But Perry always gives you the feeling he's Prometheus on the bayou. Jesuit seminarian, friend of the migrants, professional good guy at a Catholic Worker mission. Except he represents Legion Guidry and has a way of involving himself with working-class girls who all think they're going to be his main squeeze."

We were in our bedroom and Bootsie was putting on eyeliner in the dresser mirror. She had just had her bath and was wearing a pink slip. Through the window I could see Alafair pouring fresh water in Tripod's bowl on top of his hutch.

"Dave?" Bootsie said.

"Yes?"

"You need to get your grits off the stove."

"I need to talk to Perry."

"About what?" she said, no longer able to suppress her irritation.

"I think he's being blackmailed by Legion Guidry. How's that for starters?"

"Are we going out to dinner?"

"Yeah, sure," I replied.

"Thanks for confirming that," she said, her eyes out of focus in the mirror.

A few minutes later we walked out on the gallery. The yard was already in shadow, and on the wind I could smell an odor like cornsilk in a field at the end of the day. It should have been a fine evening, but I knew the white worm eating inside of me was about to ruin it.

"I've got to go to a meeting," I said.

"This isn't Wednesday night," she replied.

"I'll drive to Lafayette," I said.

She turned and walked back into the bedroom and began changing out of her dress into a pair of blue jeans and a work shirt.

When I came home late that night, she had made a bed on the couch and was asleep with her face turned toward the wall.

The next morning I drove to Perry LaSalle's office on Main Street.

"He's not in right now. He went out to Mr. Sookie's camp," Perry's secretary said.

"Sookie? Sookie Motrie?" I said.

"Why, yes, sir," she replied, then saw the look on my face and dropped her eyes.

I drove deep down into Vermilion Parish, where the

wetlands of southern Louisiana bleed into the Gulf of Mexico, passing through rice and cattle acreage, then crossing canals and bayous into long stretches of green marshland, where cranes and blue herons stood in the rain ditches, as motionless as lawn ornaments. I turned onto a winding road that led back through gum trees and a brackish swamp, past a paintless, wood-frame church house whose roof had been crushed by a fallen persimmon tree.

But it wasn't the ruined building that caught my eye. A glass-covered sign in the yard, unblemished except for road dust and a single crack down the center, read, "Twelve Disciples Assembly—Services at 7 P.M. Wednesday and 10 A.M. Sunday. Welcome."

I stopped the cruiser and backed up, then turned onto the church property. A dirt lane led back to an empty house, now packed to the eaves with bales of hay. A sawhorse with an old Detour sign on it lay sideways in the middle of the lane. Road maintenance equipment and a tree shredder used by parish work crews were parked in a three-sided tin shed, surrounded by water oaks and slash pine. Just past the shed was a railed hog lot that gave onto a thick woods and a dead lake. The hogs in the lot were indescribably filthy, their bristles matted with feces, their snouts glazed with what looked like chicken guts.

I tried to remember the lyrics of the song Marvin Oates was always quoting from but they escaped me. Maybe Bootsie was right, I told myself. Maybe I was so deep in my own head that I saw a dark portent in virtually everyone who had been vaguely connected with the lives of Amanda Boudreau and Linda Zeroski, even to the extent that I had actually begun to think Perry LaSalle, who had represented Linda in court, might bear examination.

I continued on down the paved road and turned onto a grassy knoll and drove through an arbor of oak and pecan and persimmon trees to an old duck-hunting camp that Sookie Motrie had acquired by appointing himself the executor of an elderly lady's estate.

He was a slight man who kept an equestrian posture and dressed like a horseman, in two-tone cowboy boots and tweed jackets with suede shoulders, to compensate for his lack of physical stature and a chin that receded abruptly into his throat. He wore a mustache and deliberately kept his hair long, combing it back over the collar in a rustic fashion, which gave him an unconventional and cavalier appearance and distracted others from the avarice in his eyes.

He had recently moved his houseboat from Pecan Island to his camp, chainsawing down twenty-five yards of cypresses along the bank to create an instant berth for his boat. Rather than haul his garbage away, he piled it in the center of the knoll and burned it, creating a black sculpture of melted and scorched aluminum wrap, Styrofoam, tin cans, and plastic.

Perry LaSalle stood under shade trees by his parked Gazelle, watching Sookie Motrie, stripped to the waist, bust skeet with a double-barreled Parker twelve-gauge over the water. The popping of the shotgun was almost lost in the wind, and neither man heard me walk up behind them. Sookie triggered the skeet trap with his foot, raised the shotgun to his shoulder, and blew the skeet into a pink mist against the sky.

Then he turned and saw me, the way an animal might when it is alone with its prey and wishes no intrusion into its domain.

"Hello, Dave!" he called, breaking open the breech of his gun, never letting his eyes leave mine, as though he were genuinely glad to see me.

"How do you do, sir?" I said. "I didn't mean to disturb y'all. I just need a minute or two of Perry's time."

"We're gonna have lunch. I got any kind of food you want," Sookie said.

"Thanks just the same," I said.

"You want to shoot?" he said, offering me the shotgun. I shook my head.

"Well, I'm gonna let you gentlemen talk. It's probably over my head, anyway. Right, Dave?" he said, and winked, inferring an insult that had not been made, casting himself in the role of victim while he kept others off balance. He slipped his shotgun into a sheepskin-lined case and propped it against the back rail of his houseboat, then opened a green bottle of Heineken in the galley and drank it on the deck, his skin healthy and tan in the salt breeze that blew off the Gulf.

"What are you doing with a shitpot like that?" I asked Perry.

"What's your objection to Sookie?"

"He fronts points for the casinos," I said.

"He's a lobbyist. That's his job."

"They victimize ignorant and compulsive and poor people."

"Maybe they provide a few jobs, too," he said.

"You know better. Why do you always have to act like a douche bag, Perry?"

"You want to tell me why you're out here?" he asked, feigning patience. But his eyes wouldn't hold and they started to slip off mine.

"You're in with them, aren't you?" I said.

"With whom?"

"The casinos, the people in Vegas and Chicago who run them. Both Barbara and Zerelda tried to tell me that. I just wasn't listening."

"I think you're losing it, Dave."

"Legion Guidry blackmailed your grandfather. Now he's turning dials on you. How's it feel to do scut work for a rapist?"

He looked at me for a long time, the skin trembling under one eye. Then he turned and walked down the grassy bank to the stern of Sookie's houseboat and lifted the shotgun from the deck railing. He walked back up the incline toward me, unzipping the case, his eyes fastened on my face. He let the case slip to the ground and cracked open the breech.

"Make another remark about my family," he said.

"Go screw yourself," I said.

He took two shotgun shells from his shirt pocket and plopped them into the chambers, then snapped the breech shut.

"Hey, Perry, what's going on?" Sookie called from the stern of his boat.

"Nothing is going on," Perry replied. "Dave just has to make a choice about what he wants to do. Right, Dave? You want to shoot? Here, it's ready to rock. Or do you just want to flap your mouth? Go ahead, take it."

He pressed the shotgun into my hands, his eyes blazing now. "You want to shoot me, Dave? Do you want to roll all your personal misery and unhappiness and failure into a tight little ball and set a match to it and blow somebody else away? Because I'm on the edge of reaching down your throat and tearing out your vocal cords. I can't tell you how much I'd love to do that."

I opened the breech on the shotgun and tossed the shells into the grass, then threw the shotgun spinning in a long arc, past the bow of Sookie's houseboat, the sun glinting on the blue steel and polished wood. It splashed into water that was at least twenty feet deep and sank out of sight.

"You ought to go out to L.A. and get a card in the Screen Actors Guild, Perry. No, I take that back. You've got a great acting career right here. Enjoy your lunch with Sookie," I said.

"Are you crazy? That's my Parker. Are you guys crazy?" I heard Sookie shouting as I walked back up the knoll to the cruiser.

But any pleasure I might have taken from sticking it to Perry LaSalle and Sookie Motrie was short-lived. When I arrived home that afternoon, Alafair was waiting for me in the driveway, pacing up and down, the bone ridging in one jaw, her hair tied up on her head, her fists on her hips.

"How you doin'?" I said.

"Guess."

"What's the problem?" I asked.

"Not much. My father is acting like an asshole because he thinks he's the only person in the world with a problem. Outside of that, everything's fine."

"Bootsie told you about my breaking off our dinner plans last night?"

"She didn't have to. I heard you. If you want to drink, Dave, just go do it. Stop laying your grief on your family."

"Maybe you don't know what you're talking about, Alafair."

"Bootsie told me what that man, what's his name, Legion, did to you. You want to kill him? I wish you would. Then we'd know who's really important to you."

"Pardon?" I said.

"Go kill this man. Then we'd know once and for all his death means much more to you than taking care of your own family. We're a little sick of it, Dave. Just thought you should know," she said, her voice starting to break, her eyes glistening now.

I tried to clear an obstruction out of my throat. A battered car passed on the road, the windows down, a denim-shirted man behind the wheel, the backseat filled with children and fishing rods. The driver and the children were all laughing at something.

"I'm sorry, kiddo," I said.

"You should be," she said.

That night I lay in the dark, sleepless, the trees outside swelling with wind, the canopy in the swamp trembling with a ghostly white light from the lightning in the south. I had never felt more alone in my life. Once again, I burned, in almost a sexual fashion, to wrap my fingers around the grips and inside the steel guard of a heavy, high-caliber pistol, to smell the acrid odor of cordite, to tear loose from all the restraints that bound my life and squeezed the breath from my lungs.

And I knew what I had to do.

CHAPTER 24

Later the same night I drove past a deserted sugar mill in the rain and parked my truck on a dead-end paved street in a rural part of St. Mary Parish. I jumped across a ditch running with brown water and cut through a hedge to the stoop of a small house with a tin roof set up on cinder blocks. I slipped a screwdriver around the edge of the door and prized the door away from the jamb, stressing the hinges back against the screws until a piece of wood splintered inside and fell on the linoleum and the lock popped free. I froze in the darkness, expecting to hear movement inside the house, but there was no sound except the rain tinking on the roof and a locomotive rumbling on railway tracks out by the highway.

I pushed back the door and walked through the kitchen and into the bedroom of Legion Guidry.

He was sleeping on his back, in a brass bed, the breeze from an oscillating fan ruffling his hair, dimpling the sheet that covered his body. Even though the air outside was cool and sweet smelling from the rain, the air in the bedroom was close and thick with the odor of moldy clothes, unwashed hair, re-breathed whiskey fumes, and a salty, gray smell that had dried into the sheets and mattress.

A blue-black .38 revolver lay on the nightstand. I picked it up quietly and went into the bathroom, then came back out and sat in a chair by the side of the bed. Legion's jaws were unshaved, but even in sleep his hair was combed and the flesh on his face kept its shape and didn't sag against the bone. I placed the muzzle of my .45 against his jawbone.

"I suspect you know what this is, Legion. I suspect you know what it can do to the inside of your head, too," I said.

A slight crease formed across his forehead, but otherwise he showed no recognition of my presence. His eyelids remained closed, his bare chest rising and falling with no irregularity, his hands folded passively on top of the sheet.

"Did you hear me?" I asked.

"Yes," he said.

But he used the word "yes," not "yeah," as would be the custom of a Cajun man with no education, and I would have sworn there was no accent in his pronunciation.

"Don't bother looking for your .38," I said, and opened my left hand and sprinkled the six rounds from the cylinder of his revolver on his chest. "I put your piece in the toilet bowl. I notice you don't flush after you take a dump."

He opened his eyes but kept them on the ceiling and did not look at me.

"You don't know who I am, do you?" he asked.

My skin shrunk against my face. His voice sounded like a guttural echo rising through a chunk of sewer pipe, the Cajun accent completely gone.

I started to speak, then felt the words seize in my throat. I pushed the .45 harder into his jaw and caught my breath and tried again. But he cut me off.

"Ask me my name," he said.

"Your name?" I said dumbly.

"Yes, my name," he said.

"All right," I heard myself say, as though I had stepped inside a scenario that someone other than I had written. "What's your name?"

"My name is Legion," he replied.

"Really?" I said, my eyes blinking, my heart racing. "I'm glad we've gotten that out of the way."

But my rhetoric was bravado and I felt my palm sweating on the grips of the .45. I cleared my throat and widened my eyes, like a man trying to stretch sleep out of his face. "Here it is, Legion," I said. "I'm a recovering drunk. That means I can't hold resentments against people, even a piece of human flotsam like you, no matter what they've done to me. This may seem like I'm pulling a mind-fuck on you, but what I'm telling you is straight up. You're going down, as deep in the shitter as I can put you, but it'll be by the numbers."

I blew air out of my nostrils and wiped the sweat off my forehead with the back of my wrist.

"Afraid?" he said.

"Not of you."

"Yes, you are. Inside you're a very frightened man. That's why you're a drunk."

"Watch and see," I said.

I removed the muzzle of the .45 from his jawbone and started to release the magazine. There was a small red circle where the steel had been pressed against his skin.

Suddenly he sat up and dropped his legs over the side of the mattress and pulled the sheet off his body. He was naked, his thighs and torso ridged with hair, like soft strips of monkey fur, his phallus in a state of erection.

"I can still put a hollow-point between your eyes," I said.

But he didn't try to rise from the mattress. He tilted his head back and his mouth parted. A long, moist hiss emanated from his throat. His breath covered my face like a soiled, wet handkerchief.

I backed out of the bedroom, the .45 still pointed at Legion, then hurried through the kitchen and out into the night.

I started the truck and roared away toward a street-light burning inside a vortex of rain, my hand shaking violently on the gearshift knob.

The next morning I ate breakfast at the kitchen table with Bootsie. Outside, the sky was a washed-out blue, the trees a deep green from last night's rain. Through the side window I saw Alafair lead her Appaloosa, whose name was Tex, out of the horse lot and begin brushing him down under a pecan tree.

"You get enough sleep?" Bootsie said.

"Sure."

"Where'd you go last night, Dave?" she asked, her eyes not quite meeting mine.

"I broke into Legion Guidry's house. I held a gun to the side of his face," I said.

There was a long silence. She set her spoon down on the plate under her cereal bowl and touched her coffee cup but did not pick it up.

"Why?" she said.

"I haven't been working the program. I've been fueling my resentment against this guy and thinking of ways to drill one through his brisket. The consequence is, I want to drink or use. So I thought I'd do a Ninth Step with him, make amends, and let go of my anger."

"You don't make amends with rabid animals."

"Maybe not," I said.

"What happened?" she asked.

"Not much."

"Look at me," she said.

"I threw his piece in the toilet and left. Did Alafair hear something from Reed College yesterday? I thought I saw an envelope on the couch."

"Don't change the subject."

"The guy's got another voice. One with no accent. Like words floating up from a basement. He's got somebody else living inside him. What's it called, dissociative behavior or personality disorder or something like that?"

"You're not making any sense."

"Nothing happened, Boots. It's a new day. Evil always consumes itself. People like us live in the sunshine, right?"

"God, I can't believe I'm having this conversation. It's like talking to a cryptologist."

"I'm coming home for lunch. See you then," I said,

and went out the door before she could say anything else.

I started the truck, then looked through the windshield at Alafair grooming her horse under the pecan tree. We had not spoken since she had taken me to task the previous afternoon, either out of mutual embarrassment or the fact that, as far as she knew, I had done nothing to rectify the problems I had caused in my home. I turned off the ignition and walked across the yard, through the dappled shade and the unraked leaves that had pooled in rain puddles and dried in serpentine lines. I know she saw me, but she pretended she did not. She smoothed down a quilted pad on Tex's back, then started to lift his saddle off the fence rail.

"I've got it," I said, and swung the saddle into place on Tex's back and lifted the hand-carved wood stirrup from the pommel and straightened it on his right side.

"You look nice," she said.

"Thank you," I replied.

"Where'd you go last night?" she asked.

"To set some things straight."

She nodded.

"Why do you ask?" I said.

"I thought maybe you'd gone to a bar. I thought maybe I'd caused you to do that," she replied.

"You would never do that, Alf. It's not in your nature."

She rested her arm across Tex's withers and looked down the slope at the bait shop.

"I think going away to school isn't a good idea," she said.

"Why not?"

"We can't afford it," she replied.

"Sure we can," I lied.

She inserted a booted foot in the left stirrup and swung up in the saddle. She looked down at me, then tousled my hair with her fingers.

"You're a cute guy for a dad," she said.

I popped Tex on the flank so that he spooked sideways. But Alafair, as always, was not to be outdone by the manipulations of others. She kicked her heels into Tex's ribs and bolted through the yard, ducking under branches, thundering across the wooden bridge over our coulee and out into our neighbor's sugarcane field, her Indian-black hair flying in the wind, her jeans and cactus-embroidered shirt stitched to her hard, young body.

I told myself I would not allow Legion Guidry and the evil he represented to hold any more claim on my life. In the damp, sun-spangled enclosure among the trees, I was convinced no force on earth could cause me to break my resolution.

Later, at the office, Wally walked down the corridor from the dispatcher's cage and opened my door and leaned inside.

"That soldier, the nutjob, the one who claimed he knew you in Vietnam?" he said.

"What about him?" I asked.

"He's hanging around New Iberia High. They've got summer-school classes in session now. One of the teachers called and says they want him out of there."

"What'd he do?"

"She said he's got all his junk piled up on the sidewalk and he tries to make conversation with the kids when they walk by."

"I think he's harmless," I said.

"Could be," Wally replied. His hair was a coppery-reddish color, his sideburns neatly defined. His eyes were bright with an unspoken statement.

"What is it?" I asked.

"You check your mail this morning?"

"No."

"If you had, you might have seen a note I put in there late yesterday. We got a complaint he was bothering a couple of hookers over on Railroad. On the same corner where Linda Zeroski used to work."

"Thanks, Wally," I said.

"Any time. Wish I could be a detective. You guys got all the smarts and stay on top of everything while us grunts clean the toilets. You think I could sharpen up my smarts if I went to night school?" he said.

I checked out a cruiser and drove to the high school. I saw the ex-soldier sitting in a shady spot on his rolled-up tent, his back propped against a fence, watching the traffic roar by. His face was clean-shaved, his hair washed and cut, and he wore a pair of new jeans and an oversize T-shirt emblazoned front and back with an American flag.

I pulled the cruiser to the curb.

"How about coffee and a doughnut, Doc?" I said.

He squinted up at a palm tree, then watched a helicopter thropping across the sky.

"I don't mind," he said.

We packed his duffel bag, his rolled-up tent, and a plastic clothes basket filled with cook gear, magazines, and canned goods into the backseat of the cruiser, then drove to the center of town and crossed the train tracks to a doughnut shop.

"Wait here. I'll get it to go," I said.

"You don't want to go inside?" he asked, his face vaguely hurt.

"It's a nice day. Let's eat it in the park," I replied.

I went inside the store and bought pastry and two paper cups of hot coffee, then drove across the draw-bridge into City Park and stopped by one of the tin-roofed picnic shelters next to Bayou Teche.

He sat at the plank table, his coffee and a doughnut on a napkin in front of him, gazing through the live oaks at the children swimming in the public pool.

"You ever been in trouble?" I asked.

"I been in jail."

"What for?" I asked.

"For whatever they wanted to make up."

"You're looking copacetic, Doc."

"I went to the Catholic men's shelter in Lafayette. They give me new clothes and a haircut. They're nice people."

"What were you doing over on Railroad Avenue yesterday?"

His face colored. He bit a large piece out of his doughnut and drank from his coffee and fixed his atten-tion on the gardens in the backyard of the Shadows, across the bayou.

"You don't have a girlfriend on Railroad, do you?" I said, and smiled at him.

"The woman didn't have no cigarettes. So I went in the store and bought some for her."

"Yeah?" I said.

"She took the cigarettes, then I asked her why she didn't change her life."

I kept my eyes averted, my expression flat. "I see. What happened then?" I said.

"She and the other broad laughed at me. They laughed for a long time, real loud."

"The report says you threw a rock at them."

"I kicked a rock. It hit their pimp's car. Take me back where you found me. Or put me in that shit bucket you call a jail. You want a lesson, Loot? Everybody does time. It just depends on where you do it. I do my fucking time wherever I am." He pointed a stiffened index finger into the side of his head. "I got stuff in here worse than anything you motherfuckers could ever do to me."

"I believe you," I said.

In seconds his face had gone from pity to rage. Then, just as quickly, he seemed to disconnect from his own rhetoric and fix his attention on a butterfly that had just come to rest on a camellia leaf, its pink and gray wings gathered together, its purchase on the leaf tenuous and unsteady.

When the breeze came up, the butterfly fell to the ground, among red ants that had nested below the camellia bush. The ex-soldier, who in my encounters with him had given me three different Italian names, got down on all fours and lifted the butterfly up on a twig and walked it down to the bayou, protecting it from the wind with his cupped hand. He stooped and set it inside a hollow cypress on a mound of moss.

I cleaned up our trash and wedged three fingers inside his paper cup and placed it inside the cardboard box containing the rest of our doughnuts. After I dropped him off on Main, I drove out to the crime lab by the airport and asked one of our forensic chemists to lift the latents on the cup and run them through AFIS, the Automated Fingerprint Identification System.

"We got any kind of priority?" he said.

"Tell them it's part of a homicide investigation," I replied.

That afternoon Clete Purcel picked up Barbara Shanahan after work, and the two of them drove to a western store, located on the south end of town among strip malls and huge discount outlets whose parking lots were blown with trash. Clete sat in his convertible and listened to the radio while Barbara went inside and bought a western shirt and a silver belt buckle as a birthday gift for her uncle. While the clerk processed her credit card, she felt a sense of uneasiness that she could not explain, a tiny twitch in her back, a puff of fouled air on her neck, although the front door of the store was closed and no one stood behind her.

Then she smelled cigarette smoke, even though the store was supposedly a smoke-free environment. She turned and looked down an aisle lined with racks of cowboy boots and hand-tooled leather purses and saw a tall, sinewy man, with vertical furrows in his face, wearing a snap-button, long-sleeved maroon shirt, a Panama hat at a jaunty angle, starched khaki trousers, and a chrome belt buckle with a rearing brass horse on it.

The man was smoking a nonfiltered cigarette with two fingers that were yellow with nicotine. His eyes moved over her face, her breasts and stomach, her hips and thighs. Inside the shadow of his hat brim, a smile wrinkled at the corner of his mouth.

For some reason her credit card did not clear. The clerk started to excuse himself.

"Where are you going?" she asked.

"The line's down. I don't know what's wrong. I have to use a separate line," he replied.

"I can pay cash," she said.

"That's all right, ma'am. I'll be right back," he said, and walked away.

She looked straight ahead, examining a row of antique firearms on the wall. Then she smelled an odor behind her, like sweat and unrinsed soap detergent ironed into someone's clothes. No, that wasn't it. It was far worse, raw and dead smelling, like a rat buried inside a wall.

She turned and stared into Legion Guidry's face, only inches from her own. He took a puff off his cigarette and averted his face and blew his smoke at an upward angle.

"Is there something I can help you with?" she said.

"I seen you. Both you and him," he said. He nodded toward the parking lot, where Clete sat in his car, reading a magazine.

"You saw me? What are you talking about?" she said.

"What you t'ink? T'rew your window. You must be hard up, you. To let some shithog like that one out yonder put his dick in you."

She tried to step back from his words, from the smell that seemed auraed on his body. She felt the edge of the glass counter knock into her back.

He laughed under his breath and spit a grain of tobacco off his tongue and started to walk away. Her hand went into her purse.

"Wait," she said.

He dropped his cigarette to the wood floor and twisted his shoe on it, then turned.

"What you want, bitch?" he said.

Her hand closed around her car and house and office keys. They were mounted on a ring, and the ring was mounted on a stainless-steel handle. She pulled the keys out of her purse and swung them, like a sock filled with scrap iron, across his face.

"You ever look through my window again, you pathetic fuck, I'll blow your goddamn liver out," she said.

A narrow welt, needle-pointed with blood, appeared just below his eye. He touched it with the balls of his fingers, then rubbed them against his thumb. He reached out and clenched her hand in his, squeezing, cupping the bones behind the knuckles into a circle of pain, blowing his breath into her face, touching her hair with it, tracing her eyes and mouth with it, causing her to push her free hand against his chest like a child.

"I know where that shithog live. Y'all gonna be seeing a lot more of me. You gonna like it, you," he said.

Then he walked toward the rear of the store, past customers who stepped back from him, stunned and open-mouthed. He pushed through the back door, and the interior of the store was filled with a hot light like the sun leaping off a heliograph. Then Legion Guidry was gone.

Clete opened the front door and walked into the air-conditioning, his face puzzled.

"Anything wrong? What's that smell?" he said.

That evening, just at sunset, I ran four miles on the dirt road that wound past my house. The moss was blowing

in the trees along the road, and I could smell water sprin-
klers twirling on my neighbors' lawns and the heavy,
fecund odor of the bayou. The sugarcane and cattle
acreage and distant clumps of pecan trees behind the
houses had already fallen into shadow, but the summer
light still filled the sky, as though somehow it had a life of
its own and was not affected by the setting of the sun.
Then a huge flock of birds rose out of the swamp and
freckled the perfection of the sky directly overhead, and
for some reason I thought of a painting by Van Gogh, a
cornfield suddenly invaded by black crows.

A gas-guzzler passed me, with two figures in the front
seat, then stopped at a bend in the road, the muffler rattling against the frame. The driver cut the engine and
got out and stood with one arm propped across the top
of the door, waiting. He wore a pink shirt unbuttoned on
his chest and black trousers, stitched with silver thread,
that hung down below his navel. His throat and chest ran
with sweat.

I slowed and wiped my face with a bandanna, then
tied it around my forehead. "Just taking a drive?" I said.

"I'll go into that treatment program you was talking
about," Tee Bobby said.

"What changed your mind?"

"I cain't take it no more."

I leaned down slightly, below the top of the car door.
"How you doin', Rosebud?" I asked.

His sister smiled lazily, in a private and self-indulgent
way, then her eyes closed and opened vacantly and
looked at nothing.

"Your trial is in a couple of weeks," I said to Tee
Bobby.

"If I'm in a treatment program, I can get it postponed. See, a guy got to be able to hep with his own defense."

"Talk to Mr. Perry. You can't scam the court."

"Ain't no scam. I'm sick. Perry LaSalle ain't worried about me. He worried about his family, his pink ass, his Confederate flags and portraits he got all over the walls."

"Know what's bothered me from the jump on this deal, Tee Bobby? It's the fact you've got everything else in the world on your mind except the death of that girl. Yourself, your habit, your music, your troubles with Jimmy Sty and Perry LaSalle, a kind of general discontent with the entire universe. But that poor girl's murder never seems to enter your thought processes."

"Don't say that," he said.

"Amanda Boudreau. That was her name. Amanda Boudreau. It's never going to go away. Amanda Boudreau. You knew her. She was your friend. You saw her die. Don't tell me you didn't, Tee Bobby. Say her name and look me in the eye and tell me you're not responsible in any way for her death. Say her name, Tee Bobby. Amanda Boudreau."

Rosebud twisted against her seat strap and began to keen and slap the seat and the dashboard, her face round with fear, the corners of her mouth flecked with slobber.

"See what you done? I hate you, you white motherfucker. I hate Perry LaSalle and I hate every drop of white blood I got in my veins. I hate y'all in ways y'all cain't even think about," Tee Bobby said, and smashed his fists into the window glass of the back door, again and again, the glass flying into the interior, his knuckles flaying against the broken edges.

I stared at him stupidly, only now realizing some of the complexities that drove Tee Bobby's soul.

"Perry should plead you out, but he's not. He's feeding you to the lions, isn't he? Perry's connected in some way to Amanda's death," I said.

But Tee Bobby had gotten behind the wheel of his car again and started the engine, the backs of his hands slick with blood. He floored his car down the road while his sister screamed insanely out the window.

CHAPTER 25

The next morning was Friday. I awoke early, rested, my mind free of dreams and nocturnal worries, the trees outside filled with birdsong. Wednesday night I had broken into the home of Legion Guidry and had probably experienced the most bizarre behavior I had ever witnessed in a human being, namely, the revelation of what I believed to be an enormous evil presence living inside a man who looked little different than the rest of us. But nonetheless, because I had been able to tell him I would pursue no personal vendetta against him, I felt freed of Legion Guidry and the violation he had committed against my person.

The white worm was gone. I didn't feel the need to drink and use.

Bootsie's body was warm with sleep under the sheet, the breeze from the window fan ruffling her hair on the pillow. I kissed the back of her neck and began making breakfast, then noticed an unopened envelope from Reed College under the toaster, the same envelope I had seen two days earlier on the couch. It was addressed to Alafair, and the fact that she had not opened it told me what the contents were. Ever since she and I had gone on a backpacking trip up the Columbia River Gorge, she had longed to return to the Oregon coast and to major in English and creative writing at Reed. She had applied for a scholarship, then had realized that even with a grant we would still have to pay several thousand more in fees than we would if she chose to commute to the University of Louisiana at Lafayette.

I sliced open the envelope and read the letter of congratulations awarding her most of her tuition for her first year. I went into the living room and wrote out a two-thousand-dollar check to be applied against her registration and dormitory fees for her first semester, placed a stamp on the return envelope, and walked out to the road and stuck it in the mailbox, then flipped up the red flag for the postman.

When I came back inside, Alafair was seated at the kitchen table, drinking coffee. She had put on makeup and a powder-blue dress and earrings. Through the back screen door I could see Tripod eating out of a bowl on the steps, his ringed tail damp with dew.

"Where you headed?" I asked.

"Over to UL. I'm going to enroll, get things started," she replied.

"Hear anything from Reed?"

"Not exactly. I've decided against it, anyway. I can learn as much here as I can out there."

"You look pretty, Alafair. When I grow up, I'm going to marry you," I said.

"Thank you, thank you, thank you," she said.

"You're going to Reed."

"No, it was a bad idea. I wasn't using my head."

"It's a done deal, kid. Your scholarship came through. I sent them a check for your fees."

Her eyes were a dark brown, her hair like black water on her cheeks. She was quiet a long time.

"You did that?" she asked.

"Sure. What did you think I'd do, Alf?"

"I love you, Dave."

The best moments in life are not the kind many historians record.

I went to the office, then signed out at ten o'clock and drove south toward Poinciana Island, crossing the freshwater bay that separated the island from the rest of the parish. At the far end of the bridge the security guard came out of the little wooden booth he used as an office and flagged me down. He wore a gray uniform and a holstered revolver, an American flag sewn to his shirtsleeve. His face was young and sincere under his cap. He held a clipboard in one hand and bent down toward my window.

"You're here to see somebody, sir?" he said.

"My name's Dave Robicheaux. I'm a police officer. Otherwise I probably wouldn't be driving a sheriff's cruiser," I replied, and took off my sunglasses and grinned at him.

"You're Mr. Robicheaux?" He glanced down at his clipboard. He cleared his throat and looked away nervously. "Mr. Robicheaux, I ain't supposed to let you on the island."

"Why not?"

"Mr. Perry just says there's some folks ain't supposed to come on the island."

"You did your job. But now you need to get on the phone and call Mr. Perry and tell him I just drove across your bridge on official business. Our conversation on this is over, okay?"

"Yes, sir."

"Thank you," I said, and drove onto the island, out of the sun's white glare into the damp coolness of trees and shade-blooming four-o'clocks and the thick stands of water-beaded elephant ears that grew along the water's edge.

I followed the winding road to the log-and-brick house where Ladice Hulin lived, directly across from the scorched stucco shell of Julian LaSalle's home. She came to the door on her cane, wearing a print dress, her thick gray hair pinned up on her head with a costume-jewelry comb, her gold chain and religious medal bright on her throat.

"I knowed you was coming," she said through the screen.

"How?"

" 'Cause I cain't hide the troot no more," she said, and stepped out on the gallery. "I'd ax you in, but Rosebud's sleeping. She come in last night, moaning and crying and hiding in the closet. She's got terrible t'ings locked up in her head. Some of this is on me, Mr. Dave."

She sat down in her wicker chair and gazed across the road at the peacocks that wandered lumpily through the shade trees arching over the ruins of Julian LaSalle's home.

"How is it on you, Miss Ladice?" I asked.

"Lies I tole," she replied.

"People always thought your daughter was fathered by Mr. Julian. But I think the father was actually Legion Guidry. He raped you, didn't he? I suspect on a repeated basis."

"People didn't call it rape back then. The overseer just took any black woman he wanted. Go to the sheriff, go to the city po-lice, they'd listen while you talked, not saying nothing, maybe writing on a piece of paper, then when you was gone they'd call up the man who had raped you and tell him everything you'd said."

"When did Tee Bobby learn his grandfather is Legion Guidry?" I asked.

I saw her knuckles tighten on the handle of her cane. She studied the scene across the road, the peacocks picking in Julian LaSalle's yard, a scattering of poppies, like drops of blood, around a rusted metal roadside cross put there by a friend of Mrs. LaSalle's.

"I always tole Tee Bobby his granddaddy was Mr. Julian," she replied. "I t'ought it was better he didn't know the blood of a man like Legion was in his veins. But this spring Tee Bobby wanted money to go out to California and make a record. He went to see Perry LaSalle."

"To blackmail him?"

"No, he t'ought he deserved the money. He t'ought Perry LaSalle was gonna be proud Tee Bobby was gonna make a record. He t'ought they was in the same family." She shook her head. "It was me who put that lie in his life, that made him the po' li'l innocent boy he is."

"Perry told him Legion is his grandfather?"

"When Tee Bobby come back to the house, he t'rew t'ings against the wall. He put Rosebud in his car and said he was gonna meet Jimmy Dean Styles and fix it so he could take Rosebud out to California, away from Lou'sana and the t'ings white people done to our family."

"I see. That was the day Amanda Boudreau died?"

"That was the day. Oh, Lord, this all started 'cause I t'ought I could seduce Mr. Julian and go to college. Tee Bobby and that white girl got to pay for my sin," she said.

"You didn't choose the world you were born into. Why don't you give yourself a break?" I said.

She started to get up, then her arm shook on her cane and she fell back heavily into her chair, dust ballooning out from her dress, her face riven with disbelief at what age and time and circumstance and the unrequited longings of her heart had done to her life.

I went back to the department and called Perry LaSalle at his office. His head secretary, who was an older woman, robin-breasted and blue-haired and educated at Millsaps College, told me he wasn't in.

"Is this Mr. Robicheaux?" she said.

"Yes," I said, expecting her to tell me where he was. But she didn't.

"Do you expect him soon?" I asked.

"I'm not quite sure," she replied.

"Is he in court today?" I asked.

"I really don't know."

"Does it seem peculiar when a lawyer doesn't tell his secretary where he is or when he will be back in his office?" I said.

"I'll make a note of your observation, Mr. Robicheaux, and pass it on to Mr. Perry. By the way, has anyone ever told you how charming your manner can be?" she said, and hung up.

After lunch the forensic chemist with whom I had left the ex-soldier's paper coffee cup dropped by my office. He was an ascetic, lean man by the name of Mack Bertrand who wore seersucker slacks and bow ties and white shirts and bore a pleasant fragrance of pipe tobacco. He was a good crime scene investigator and seldom, if ever, made mistakes.

"Those latents off the paper cup?" he said.

"Yeah, what did you come up with?" I said expectantly.

"Zero," he replied.

"You mean my man has no criminal record?"

"No record at all," he said.

"Wait a minute, the guy who drank out of this cup was in the service. In Vietnam. Probably in a hospital as well. The V.A. must have something on him."

"The cup was handled by three unknown persons. I assume it came from a takeout café or convenience store. We didn't get a match on any of the latents I sent through the pod. I don't know how else to put it. Sorry."

He closed the door and walked away, his pipe stem crimped upside down in his mouth. I went after him and caught him at the end of the corridor.

"Run it through again, Mack. It's a glitch," I said.

"I already did. Simmer down. Take a couple of aspirin. Go fishing more often," he said. He started to grin, then gave it up and walked outside.

I called Perry LaSalle's office again.

"Has Perry come back?" I asked.

"He's in a conference right now. Would you like for me to leave him another message?" his secretary said.

"Don't bother. I'll catch him another time," I said.

Then I signed out a cruiser and drove directly to Perry's office before he could get away from me. I sat on a sofa under his glass-encased Confederate battle flag and read a magazine for a half hour, then heard footsteps coming down the carpeted stairs and looked up into the faces of Sookie Motrie and two well-known operators of dockside casinos in New Orleans and Lake Charles.

The two gamblers looked like a Mutt and Jeff team. One was big, lantern-jawed, stolid, with coarse skin and knuckles the size of quarters, whereas his friend was sawed-off, porcine, with a stomach that hung down like a curtain of wet cement, his voice loud, his Jersey accent like a sliver of glass in the ear.

"That's the man who t'rew my shotgun in the water," Sookie said, and pointed at me. "Honest to God, t'rew it in the water. Like a drunk person."

I rested my magazine across my knee and stared back at the three of them.

"Word of caution about Sookie," I said. "About ten years ago he had to be pried out of a car wreck with the jaws of life. Three surgeons at Iberia General worked on him all night and saved his life. When he got the bill, he refused to pay it. A lawyer called him up and tried to appeal to his conscience. Sookie told him, 'I ain't worth ten thousand dollars and I ain't paying it.' It was the only time anyone around here remembered Sookie telling the truth about anything."

"You're a police officer?" the shorter gambler said.

"Sookie told you that?" I said, and laughed, then raised my magazine and began reading it again.

But as I watched the three of them walk outside, all of them gazing with the innocuous interest of tourists at the trees and antebellum homes along the street, I knew that being clever with the emissaries of greed and profit was a poor form of Valium for the political reality of the state where I was born, namely, that absolutely everything around us was for sale.

I went up the stairs to Perry's office.

"You trying to bring casinos into Iberia Parish?" I said.

"No, people here have voted it down," Perry answered from behind his desk.

"Then why are those two characters in town?"

"If it's any of your business, there are people in Lafayette who believe gaming revenues shouldn't go only to the parishes on the Texas border," he replied.

"Gaming? That's a great word. You don't have any bottom, Perry. I was out to Ladice Hulin's place this morning. The same day Amanda Boudreau was murdered, you told Tee Bobby that Legion Guidry was his grandfather. He came home in a rage, put his sister in the car, then went to find Jimmy Dean Styles. But you knew all this from the jump. You're going to let Tee Bobby take the needle rather than see your family's dirty bedsheets hung on the wash line."

He sat very still in the deep softness of his black leather chair. He wore a cream-colored suit and a sky-blue shirt, opened casually at the collar. His mouth was puckered, as though he had sucked the moisture out of it, the folds of flesh in his throat pronounced, his hands cupped slightly on his desk blotter, the heated intensity of his eyes focused no more than six inches in front of him.

When he spoke, his vocal cords were a phlegmy knot.

"For one reason or another, you seem to have a need to demean me whenever we meet," he said. "Obviously I can't discuss the case of a client with you, but since you've chosen to attack me personally on this gambling stuff, maybe I can offer you an explanation that will allow you to think better of me. Most of the hot-sauce companies use foreign imports now. We don't. We've never laid off an employee or evicted a tenant. That's our choice. But it's an expensive one."

He looked up at me, his hands folded now, his posture and demeanor suggestive of the cleric he had once studied to be.

"I don't have it all figured out yet, Perry. But I think the story is a lot dirtier than you're letting on," I said.

He clicked the edges of a pad of Post-its across his thumb. Then he pitched the pad in the air and let it bounce on his desk. "You'd better go take care of your own and not worry so much about me," he said.

"You want to take the corn bread out of your mouth?"

"Your friend, the Elephant Man, Purcel, is it? He pulled Legion Guidry off a counter stool in Franklin this morning and threw him through a glass window. A seventy-four-year-old man. You two make quite a pair, Dave," he said.

I went back to the office and called the jail in St. Mary Parish and was told by a sheriff's deputy that Clete Purcel was in custody for disturbing the peace and destroying private property and would appear in court that afternoon.

"No assault charges?" I asked.

"The guy he tossed through a window didn't want to press charges," the deputy replied.

"Did the guy give an explanation?"

"He said it was a private argument. It wasn't no big deal," said the deputy.

No big deal. Right.

After work I drove to Clete's apartment. From the parking lot I saw him up on his balcony, above the swimming pool, in a Hawaiian shirt and faded jeans that bagged in the seat, grilling a steak, a can of beer balanced on the railing.

"How's it hangin', noble mon?" he called, grinning through the smoke.

I didn't reply. I went up the stairs two at a time and through his front door and across his living room toward the sliding glass doors that gave onto the balcony. He drank from his beer, his green eyes looking at me over the top of the can.

"There's a problem?" he said.

"You threw Legion Guidry through a window?"

"He's lucky I didn't feed it to him."

"He's going to come after you."

"Good. I'll finish what I started this morning. You know what he did to Barbara in the western store?"

"No, I don't."

He told me about the scene in the store, Legion Guidry blowing his breath in Barbara's face while he crushed the bones in her hand.

"He's setting you up, Clete. That's why he didn't file against you," I said.

He forked his steak off the grill and slapped it on a

plate. "I don't want to talk about it anymore. Get some bread and a Dr Pepper out of the icebox," he said.

"What's eating you?"

"Nothing. The world. My weight problem. What difference does it make?"

"Clete?"

"Barbara's shitcanning me. She says we're not a match. She says I deserve more than she can give me. I can't believe it. That's the same line I used when I broke it off with Big Tit Judy Lavelle."

"When did she tell you this?"

"A little while ago."

"After you got out of jail for defending her?"

"It's not her fault. My ex said I always smelled like dope and whores. The only person who won't accept what I am is me."

He went into the kitchen with his steak and took a bottle of whiskey from the cabinet and poured three fingers in a glass. He glanced at me, then opened the icebox and tossed me a can of Dr Pepper.

"Get that look off your face. Everything is under control," he said.

"You going to get drunk?" I asked.

"Who knows? The evening is young."

I blew out my breath. "You're going to try to make up with Zerelda Calucci, aren't you?"

He drank his whiskey in one long swallow, his eyes watering slightly from the hit his stomach took.

"Wow, the old giant killer never lets you down," he said.

That night I helped Batist in the bait shop, but I couldn't let go of Perry LaSalle's smug complacency. I picked up the phone and called him at his home on Poinciana Island.

"Just a footnote to our conversation this afternoon," I said. "Legion Guidry physically abused Barbara Shanahan in public. He called her a bitch and almost broke her hand. This is the woman you supposedly care about. In the meantime, you denigrate Clete Purcel for going after the guy who hurt her. In this case the guy is your client."

"I didn't know this."

My hand was squeezed tight around the phone receiver, another heated response already forming in my throat. But suddenly I was robbed of my anger.

"You didn't know?" I said.

"Legion did that to Barbara?" he said.

"Yes, he did."

He didn't reply and I thought the line had gone dead.

"Perry?"

"I apologize for saying what I did about Purcel. Is Barbara all right? I can't believe Legion did that. That rotten son of a bitch," he said.

On Saturday morning I called Clete's apartment, but there was no answer and his machine was turned off. I tried again Sunday morning, with the same result. That afternoon I hitched my outboard and trailer to the pickup and headed toward Bayou Benoit and stopped at Clete's apartment on the way. He was lying in a recliner by the pool like a beached whale, his body glowing with lotion and sunburn, a bottle of vodka and a tall glass filled with crushed ice and cherries by his elbow.

"Where have you been?" I asked.

"Me? Just messing around. You know how it is," he said.

"You look very content. Relaxed. Free of tension."

"Must be the weather," he said, smiling behind his sunglasses.

"How's Zerelda?"

"She said to tell you hello," he said.

"I think you're about to run over a land mine."

"I had a feeling you might say that." He slipped his sunglasses up on his head and gazed at my truck and boat in the parking lot. "We going fishing?"

A half hour later I cut the engine on the outboard and we floated into a quiet stretch of cypress-dotted water on Bayou Benoit, our wake sliding through the tree trunks into the shore. There were stormheads in the south, but the sky was brassy overhead, the wind hot and smelling of salt and dead vegetation inside the trees. I clipped a rubber worm on my line and made a long, looping cast into a cove that was rimmed with floating algae.

On the ride out to the landing Clete had tried to sustain his insouciant facade, refusing to be serious, his eyes crinkling whenever I showed concern about his reckless and self-destructive behavior. But now, in the dappled light of the trees, the thunder banging in the south, I could see shadows steal across his eyes when he thought I wasn't looking.

"I'm right, you and Zerelda are an item again?" I said.

"Yeah, you could call it that."

"But you don't feel too good about it?"

"Everything's copacetic there. That kid, Marvin Oates, was around yesterday, but Zerelda told him to take a hike."

"What?" I said.

"She finally got tired of wet-nursing him. She spent a whole day looking for him in the Iberville Project, then he showed up at the motor court drunk. So yesterday she told him he should spend more time on his criminal justice studies or find some friends more his age."

"You've got something on your mind, Cletus."

"This character Legion Guidry," he said. Unconsciously he wiped his palms on his pants when he said the name. "When I dragged him off that counter stool, I could smell an odor on him. It was awful. It was like shit and burnt matches. I had to wash it off my hands."

I reeled in my artificial worm and cast it against a hollow cypress trunk and let it sink through the algae to the bottom of the cove. He waited for me to say something, but I didn't.

"What, I sound like I've finally become a wetbrain?" he said.

I started to tell him about my experience breaking into Legion's house, but instead I opened the ice chest and took out two fried-oyster po'-boy sandwiches and handed one to him.

"This is guaranteed to help you lose weight and make you younger at the same time," I said.

"I smelled it, Dave. I swear. I wasn't drunk or hungover. This guy really bothers me," he said, his face conflicted with thoughts he couldn't resolve.

CHAPTER 26

Monday morning the sky was black, veined with lightning over the Gulf. Right after I checked into the department I went to see Barbara Shanahan in the prosecutor's office. She was dressed in a gray suit and white blouse, her face defensive and vaguely angry.

"If you're here to talk about something of a personal nature, I'd rather we do that after business hours," she said.

"I'm here about Amanda Boudreau."

"Oh," she said, her face coloring slightly.

"I want to pick up both Tee Bobby Hulin and Jimmy Dean Styles," I said.

"What for?"

"I think we can find out once and for all what happened to Amanda. But we have to keep Perry LaSalle away from Tee Bobby."

She was standing behind her desk. She pushed a couple of pieces of paper around on her desk blotter with the ends of her fingers.

"This office won't be party to any form of procedural illegality," she said.

"You want the truth about what happened to that girl or not?" I asked.

"You heard what I said."

"Yeah, I did. It sounds a little self-serving, too." I saw the anger sharpen in her face and I changed my tone. "You need to be in the vicinity when Tee Bobby and Styles are interviewed."

"All right," she replied. She stared out the window. The wind was blowing hard, bending the trees along the railway tracks, bouncing garbage cans through the streets. "You pissed off at me about Clete?"

"He went to jail for you and you eighty-sixed him," I said.

"He was talking about 'clipping' Legion Guidry. You think I want to see him in Angola over me? Why don't you give me a little goddamn credit?" she said.

"Clete is hurt more easily and deeply than people think," I said.

"Actually, I like you, Dave. You probably don't believe that, but I do. Why are you so cruel?"

Her eyes were moist, the whites a light pink, as though they had been touched by iodine.

Way to go, Robicheaux, I thought.

I went back to my office and called the number of the Boom Boom Room.

"Is Jimmy Sty there?" I said.

"He'll be here in a half hour. Who want to know?" a man's voice said.

"It's okay. Tell him I'll see him tonight," I said.

"Who see him tonight?" the voice asked.

"He'll know," I said, and hung up.

Then I called Ladice Hulin's number on Poinciana Island.

"It's Dave Robicheaux, Ladice. Is Tee Bobby home?" I said.

"He's still sleeping," she replied.

"I'll talk with him later. Don't worry about it," I said.

"Somet'ing going on?" she said.

"I'll get back to you," I said, and eased the receiver down.

I went down the corridor to the office of Kevin Dartez, the department plainclothes who worked Narcotics exclusively and bore a legendary grudge against pimps and dope dealers for the death of his sister.

When I opened his office door, he was tilted back in his chair, talking on the phone while he squeezed a hand exerciser in his palm.

"Maybe if you pulled your head out of your cheeks and did your job, we wouldn't be having this conversation," he said into the receiver, then quietly hung up. He had narrow bones in his face and jet-black hair that he oiled and combed straight back. His needle-nose cowboy boots and pencil-line mustache and wide red tie, a tiny pair of silver handcuffs pinned in the center, made me think of an early-twentieth-century lawman or perhaps a Los Vegas cardplayer of the kind you didn't cross.

"You doin' okay, Dave?" he asked.

"I want to flip Tee Bobby Hulin and I could use your help," I said.

"I'm a little jammed up right now," he replied.

"I skated on an assault beef against Jimmy Dean Styles in St. Martin Parish. I'd like you to bring him in and tell him you need some information for an Internal Affairs investigation. In other words, the department would still like to hang me out to dry."

"Jimmy Sty again, huh? He's not one of my fans. Maybe you ought to use somebody he trusts," Dartez said.

"You're straight up, Kev. Street people respect you."

"You wouldn't try to twist my dials, would you?"

"Not a chance." I opened a notebook to a page on which I had written down several tentative questions for Kevin Dartez to ask Styles and set the notebook on Dartez's desk. "It really doesn't matter what you specifically say to Styles. Just get him to talk about me and make sure it's on tape. Also bring up Helen Soileau."

"Why Helen?" Dartez asked.

"Styles called her a dyke to her face. I don't think he's quite forgotten the reaction he got," I said.

Dartez squeezed the hand exerciser in his palm. "When you want him in here?" he asked.

"How about as soon as possible?" I replied.

A few minutes later Helen Soileau and I got into a cruiser and drove toward Poinciana Island.

"A bad storm building," she said, looking over the steering wheel at the blackness in the sky, the cane thrashing in the fields. When I didn't reply, she looked across the seat at me. "You listening?"

"I took Tee Bobby's grandmother over the hurdles," I said.

"She raised him. Maybe she should sit in her own shit for a change."

"That's rough," I said.

"No, Amanda Boudreau staring into the barrel of a shotgun is rough. There's a big difference between vics and perps, Streak. The victim is the victim. I wouldn't get the two confused."

Helen always kept the lines simple.

We crossed the freshwater bay onto the island. Waves were capping in the bay and hitting hard against the pilings under the bridge, slapping the shoreline and sliding up into the elephant ears along the shore. We rolled down the windows in the cruiser, and the light was cool and green inside the tunnel of trees as we drove toward Ladice's house. A tree limb cracked like a rifle shot overhead and spun crazily into the road ahead of us. Helen swerved around it.

"I never liked this place," she said.

"Why not?" I asked.

Helen looked out the window at a black man trying to catch a horse that was running through a field of pepper plants while lightning forked the sky above the treeline.

"If the LaSalles' ancestors had won the Civil War, I think the rest of us would be picking cotton for a living," she said.

We parked in Ladice's yard and knocked on the door. Leaves were puffing out of the trees and blowing across the gallery and flattening against the screens. Inside, I could see Tee Bobby watching television in an overstuffed chair, his chest caved in, his mouth open, his chin peppered with stubble. His grandmother came out of the kitchen and stood in silhouette behind his chair.

"What you want?" she asked.

"Need to take Tee Bobby into town and clarify a few things," I said.

"What t'ings?" she asked.

"We're looking at somebody else in the murder of Amanda Boudreau. Maybe it's time Tee Bobby did himself a good deed and starting cooperating with us," I said.

Tee Bobby got up from his overstuffed chair and walked to the door, his long-sleeved shirt unbuttoned on his stomach, an unwashed odor wafting through the screen.

"You looking at who?" he said.

"This isn't a good place to talk. Call Mr. Perry and ask him what he wants you to do," I said, my face blank.

"I ain't got to ax permission from Perry LaSalle to do nothing. I'll be back in a li'l while, Gran'mama. Right? Y'all gonna drive me back?" Tee Bobby said.

"Right as rain," Helen said.

That's the way you do it sometimes. Then you try to forget your own capacity for deceit.

On the way back to the department Tee Bobby lazed against the backseat and watched the country go by, his eyes half shut. He woke with a start and looked around as though unsure of his whereabouts. Then he grinned for no reason and stared vacuously into space.

"You all right back there?" Helen said, looking into the rearview mirror.

"Sure," he said. "It was the lie detector test got y'all looking at somebody else?"

"Lots of things, Tee Bobby," she said.

" 'Cause I ain't raped or shot nobody," he said.

I turned in the seat and searched his face.

"Why you staring at me like that?" he asked.

"I get a little perplexed about your choice of words."

"What you talkin' 'bout, man? These are the only words I got." His brow furrowed, as though his own statement held a meaning he had not yet sorted through. "I need to stop and use the bat'room somewhere. I ought to wash up, too. Maybe get some candy bars."

"We'll get you some from the machine at the office," Helen said.

Tee Bobby stared silently out the window for the rest of the way into town, his face twitching as last night's dope and booze wore off and he realized the day waited for him like a hungry tiger.

We parked the cruiser and walked him straight into an interview room and closed the door behind us.

Around the corner, in the convivial atmosphere of his office, Kevin Dartez was talking to Jimmy Dean Styles. Styles was sitting in a chair, his knees slightly spread, squeezing his scrotum, enjoying his role as participant in the process. Dartez had started the tape recorder on his desk and was reviewing his notebook as Styles talked, nodding respectfully, sometimes making a small penciled notation.

"So without provocation, Dave Robicheaux, of the Iberia Parish Sheriff's Department, attacked you in your place of business, known as the Carousel?" Dartez said.

"You got it, man," Styles said. Through the venetian blinds he watched a black woman in an orange jumpsuit being led in handcuffs down the corridor. He grinned and touched at some mucus in the corner of his mouth and pulled a Kleenex from a box on Dartez's desk and wiped his fingers.

"And you say Detective Helen Soileau hit you with a baton?"

"That's the way it went down. That bitch got shit in her blood."

"That's a serious allegation against Detective Soileau. You're sure that's the way it happened? You made an idle remark and she swung a baton in your face? This could do a lot of damage to her career, Jimmy. You want to be sure what you're telling me is correct."

"I ain't gonna say it again. Put it down in your report or leave it out. It don't matter to me. But you got an out-of-control bull dyke on your hands."

Dartez nodded agreeably and wrote in his notebook.

"Doesn't Tee Bobby Hulin play at the Carousel sometimes?" he asked.

"I try to throw him some work. But Tee Bobby hard to hep, know what I mean?" Styles said.

"Look, this is not related, but you know what nobody around here can understand?" Dartez said. "Why's a kid with so much talent get in all this trouble? How come he never made it in Los Angeles or New York? I don't know anything about music, but—"

"I don't want to speak bad of a guy that's on third base, okay? But Tee Bobby's a hype and a ragnose. Ain't nobody can talk to him. He got a thing for white cooze, too. Which mean he don't respect himself." Styles glanced at his watch. "Say, man, I ain't s'pposed to be gone from my bar too long. My bartender get a li'l generous pouring to the ladies, know what I'm sayin'?"

"Got you," Dartez said, dropping his eyes to his notebook again. "Okay, so you didn't in any way put your hand on the person of Detective Robicheaux? You committed no form of assault or what could be interpreted as such, no threatening gesture?"

"No, man, I tole you, he's a sick, violent motherfucker been beating up people around here for years. He done it, just like some crazy person been wanting to hurt somebody a long time. Hey, you ax me if I'm bothered about that cunt, what's her name, Helen Soileau? Anything happen to her, man, she deserve. Now, that good enough? 'Cause I got a bidness to run."

"Thanks a lot, Jimmy. I need to go to the rest room a minute. Stay cool and I'll be back to check a couple of fine points with you, then you'll be on your way," Dartez said.

He popped the cassette tape out of the recorder and walked around the corner to the interview room and tapped on the door. When I opened it a crack, he wagged the cassette in the air and winked.

Tee Bobby sat at the interview table, leaning forward on his forearms, his hands balling and unballing, a twitch at the corner of one eye. He peeled a candy bar we had bought him from the machine by the courthouse entrance and began eating it, his eyes busy with thoughts that he did not share.

"You want another cup of coffee?" Helen asked.

"I got to use the bat'room," he said.

"You just went," she said.

"I ain't feeling too good. You said I was s'pposed to identify somebody."

"Be patient, Tee Bobby. Come on, I'll walk you down to the rest room," Helen said.

While they were gone, I went to my mailbox, picked up the cassette tape that Kevin Dartez had placed there, and walked down to my office, where Mack Bertrand, from the crime lab, waited for me.

Dartez's interview with Styles was not a long one. We listened to it in a few minutes, and it was easy to isolate the material that I thought would be most helpful to Helen and me.

"Can you excerpt those few lines and get them on another tape without too much trouble?" I said.

"No problem," he said, his pipe inverted in his teeth.

"I'll go back to the interview room. When you've got it, just bang on the door, okay?"

"Call me up later in the day and tell me how all this came out," he said.

"Sure," I said.

"Whenever I run into Amanda Boudreau's parents I feel guilty. Our twins are going to graduate next year. Every day of our lives is a pleasure. The Boudreaus did all the things good parents are supposed to do, but their daughter is dead and they'll probably wake up miserable every morning for the rest of their lives. Just because some bastard wanted to get his rocks off."

"Thanks for your help, Mack. I'll call you later," I said.

I went into the rest room and washed my hands and face and blew out my breath in the mirror. I could feel the adrenaline pumping in my veins now, in the same way a hunter feels it when a large animal, one with a heart and nerve endings and mental processes not unlike his own, suddenly comes into focus inside a telescopic sight.

I dried my hands and face with a paper towel and went back to the interview room. Tee Bobby was drinking coffee from a paper cup, the soles of his shoes tapping nervously on the floor.

"You going to make it?" I asked.

"Make it? What you mean 'make it'?"

I pulled up a chair across from him. "Remember back there in the cruiser, you told me you didn't 'shoot' anyone?" I said.

"Yeah, that's what I said."

"You used the word 'shoot,'" I said.

"Yeah, I said I ain't shot nobody. Is that hard to understand?"

"You didn't say you didn't 'kill' anybody."

"This is bullshit, man. I want to go back home," he said.

"Why do you avoid using the word 'kill,' Tee Bobby?" I asked.

"I ain't playing no word games wit' you." His eyes fluttered toward the ceiling, where he examined an air duct as though it were of great complexity.

"You want another candy bar?" I said.

"I want to go. I ain't sure this is a good idea no more."

There was a tap on the door. I opened it and Mack Bertrand handed me a cassette recorder. He was wearing a raincoat and a hat, and his ascetic face looked hard-edged and dark under the brim of his hat. He walked away without speaking.

"Who's that?" Tee Bobby asked.

"There's been a development here, Tee Bobby. I think it's only fair you know everything that's going on. Walk around the corner with me," I said, getting up from the chair.

"What's he doin', Miss Helen?" Tee Bobby asked.

"Time you knew your enemy, Tee Bobby," she replied.

"My enemy?" he said.

I opened the door and slipped my hand under his arm. The muscles in his arm were flaccid, without tone, like soft rubber.

"Where we goin'?" he asked.

We walked to the glass window that gave onto the interior of Kevin Dartez's office. Tee Bobby's eyes bulged in his head when he saw Jimmy Dean Styles sitting in front of Dartez's desk, rolling his shoulders, rotating a crick out of his neck, the profile and down-hooked nose like a sheep's.

"Why's *he* here?" Tee Bobby said.

"Jimmy Dean just made a statement. You know how he operates, Tee Bobby. Jimmy Dean's not about to take somebody else's bounce," I said.

"Statement 'bout what?"

"The shit's in the fire, partner. You want to go down for this guy?"

"You saying he—" Tee Bobby stopped and squeezed his mouth with his hand as though he were about to be sick.

"Let's go back to the interview room," I said, draping my arm over his shoulders. "Listen to this tape I have, then tell us what you want to do. You can be in the driver's seat on this."

Tee Bobby was breathing hard now, the pulse jumping in his neck.

"What he tole you, man?" he said, looking backward over his shoulder at Dartez's office. "What that son of a bitch tole you?"

I closed the door to the interview room behind us and pulled out a chair for Tee Bobby. I placed my hand on his shoulder. His shirt was damp, his collarbone as hard as a broomstick.

"Calm down, kid. Eat another candy bar," Helen said. "It's not as bad as you think. You've got choices. Everybody knows Jimmy Sty is a liar and a pimp. Just don't take his weight."

I pressed the Play button on the recorder. The voice of Jimmy Dean Styles seemed to leap from the speaker: "Tee Bobby's a hype and a ragnose. He got a thing for white cooze, too."

"You committed no form of assault or what could be interpreted as such?" the voice of Kevin Dartez said.

"Man, I tole you, he's a sick, violent motherfucker. He done it, just like some crazy person been wanting to hurt somebody a long time. Hey, you ax me if I'm bothered about that cunt? Anything happen to her, man, she deserve," Styles's voice said.

I snapped off the recorder. The sound of Tee Bobby's breathing filled the silence. Sweat had popped on his forehead. His tongue looked like a gray biscuit in his mouth.

"Is what he says correct?" I asked.

"I cain't believe it. Jimmy Dean put it on me? Man, that lying— How I got in this? If they just hadn't been there. If they had been anyplace else. If we'd gone to drink beer at the drive-in instead of by the coulee. I cain't believe this is happening, man." He squeezed his hands in his lap and rocked in the chair.

"You heard what Miss Helen said, Tee Bobby. Don't take Jimmy Dean's weight. Time to lay down your burden, partner," I said.

"You got that right. I'm gonna cook his hash, man. You want to know how it went down? Push on your recorder. Get that videotape machine going. Jimmy Dean call it cooling out a white broad. That's the kind of dude he is, all 'cause they was making too much noise."

"Yeah, too much noise. That can be a real problem," Helen said, a look of unrelieved sadness in her eyes.

There are stories no one wants to hear. This was one of them.

CHAPTER 27

Tee Bobby had loaded Rosebud in the car and roared across the bridge that separated Poinciana Island from the rest of Iberia Parish, his anger burning in his chest, the words of Perry LaSalle like a dirty presence in his ears.

"Let's see if I understand this correctly, Tee Bobby. You want money to go to California? To make a record?" Perry had said. He had been stripped to the waist, combing his hair in a mirror by his wet bar, his gaze wandering through the sliding doors to the bass pond, where a woman in shorts and a halter was fly-casting on the water's surface.

"Yes, suh. I got a shot with a recording company in West Hollywood. But I got to have money to go out there, stay at a hotel for a week, maybe, buy meals, front a few dol'ars wit' this agent setting up the gig," Tee Bobby said.

"You sure this agent isn't throwing you a slider?" Perry said, his eyes watching the woman in the mirror.

"No, suh. It's just the way they do things out there."

"It sounds interesting, Tee Bobby, but if you're looking for a loan, my income is a little down right now. Maybe another time."

"Suh?"

"I'm short of cash, podna," Perry said, and grinned at him in the mirror.

"I ain't never made no claim on the estate," Tee Bobby said.

"You haven't what?"

"Never claimed no kind of inheritance. Neither my mother or my gran'mama, either. We ain't never axed money from your family."

"You think you're owed something by my family, do you?"

"Everybody know old man Julian was sleeping wit' my gran'mama."

"Ah, I get your drift now. We both share the same grandfather? Is that correct?" Perry said.

Tee Bobby shrugged and looked at the woman by the pond. She was lovely to watch, her skin unblemished by the sun or physical work, her body firm and graceful as she whipped the popping-bug over her head.

"You shouldn't refer to my grandfather as 'old man Julian,' Tee Bobby. That said, the child your grandmother had out of wedlock was not his. Mr. Julian had been dead over a year when Miss Ladice's baby was born. There was an overseer here named Legion Guidry. He did things he shouldn't have. But that was the nature of the times."

"The man people call 'Legion' is my grandfather?"

"Better talk to Miss Ladice," Perry said, slipping his comb into his back pocket and drawing the sleeve of a silk shirt up his arm.

Then Perry, with a grin on his face, still tucking his shirt in his slacks, opened the sliding doors and walked down to the bass pond to join his companion.

In the neon-lit darkness of the Boom Boom Room, Tee Bobby and Jimmy Dean smoked some high-octane Afghan skunk and snorted up a half-dozen lines of Colombian pink from Jimmy's private stock, so pure and unstepped on it roared up Tee Bobby's nostril with the white brilliance of a train engine inside a tunnel.

"Tell me that ain't righteous, my man. It put the snap in yo' whip, don't it? Forget that cracker on Poinciana Island. I'll introduce you to a lady down the road make you fall in love," Jimmy Dean said.

"I got Rosebud out front. Can you give me the money to go to California, Jimmy Dean?"

"If we talking about recording contracts, I got to have my lawyer draw up some papers, make sure you protected. Let's take a ride, drink some beer, make a house call on a couple of bidness associates later. It gonna be all right, man. The Sty got yo' ass covered, bro. Hey, go a li'l easy on my stuff. You slam a gram and you fry yo' Spam. You heard it first from Jimmy Style. Come on in back wit' me a minute."

Tee Bobby followed Jimmy Dean into the back room of the bar, where Jimmy Dean knelt down in front of a cabinet with a burlap bag spread by his foot.

"What you doing wit' that shotgun and them watch caps?" Tee Bobby asked.

"Sometimes you got to put a li'l scare into people. A couple of my artists think they gonna dump me for some Los Angeles niggers got more gold chains than brains. It ain't gonna happen."

"I ain't up for no guns," Tee Bobby said.

Jimmy Dean rested on one haunch, the barrel of a cut-down, pistol-grip pump shotgun propped at an angle on his shoulder, a box of twelve-gauge double-ought buckshot by his foot.

"Ain't nobody gonna get hurt, Tee Bobby. It's all show. But you want me to back your play, you got to back mine. Tell me what you want to do. Tell me now," he said, his eyes burrowing into Tee Bobby's face.

A few minutes later they drove across the bridge over the Teche and stopped at a convenience store that sold gas. They bought a twelve-pack of beer and a bucket of microwave fried chicken and a soda for Rosebud, who sat belted in the backseat, staring at the pecan orchards, the dust blowing out of the cane acreage, the carrion birds circling in a hot, brassy sky that gave no promise of rain, a truck filled with oil-field workers at the gas pumps.

"You gonna take Rosebud to California?" Jimmy Dean asked, glancing at the oil-field workers. He had tied a black silk scarf on his head, and the tails of the scarf hung from the knot down the back of his neck.

"Yeah," Tee Bobby replied.

"You doin' the right thing, man. I mean, getting out of here."

But while he spoke Jimmy Dean continued to stare at the oil-field workers, who were now lounging by the gas pumps, throwing a child's football to each other. They were all grease-stained, sweaty, tobacco-chewing white

men, with crewcuts and hillbilly sideburns and faces that
were red with sunburn. Their truck bore a Mississippi
license plate. Jimmy Dean's eyes were close-set, a lump
of cartilage working in his jaw. He sniffed and rubbed his
nose with the back of his wrist, then bit down on a
matchstick. "Let's get out of here," he said.

"Something wrong?" Tee Bobby asked.

"Yeah."

"What?" Tee Bobby asked.

"There ain't no open season on crackers."

They drove on up the state highway toward St.
Martinville, chugging beers, throwing chicken bones
out the window. The new cane in the fields was dry and
pale green, the air crackling with electricity. The wind
began gusting, buffeting the car, kicking dust out of the
fields.

"I got to take a leak. Pull down by that coulee," Jimmy
Dean said.

Tee Bobby turned off the highway onto a dirt road
that led past a black man's house. He stopped by a clump
of bushes downstream from a wooden bridge and a grove
of gum trees, and Jimmy Dean got out and urinated into
the coulee. The coulee was almost dry, the mud at the
bottom spiderwebbed with cracks, and the odor of a dead
armadillo rose into Jimmy Dean's face, causing him to
wrinkle his nose and grimace while he shook off his
penis. A four-wheeler roared across the field behind
them, a teenage boy at the handlebars, a girl with long
black hair clinging to his waist.

Jimmy Dean got back in the front seat and began
rolling a joint. The four-wheeler turned in circles, the
driver gunning the engine, scouring a cloud of dust in

the air that drifted back through the car's windows. Jimmy Dean opened his mouth and flexed his jaws to pop the noise out of his ears.

"There's a white boy need a slap upside the head. Here, blow the horn," he said, and reached across the seat to press down on the horn button.

"That's Amanda Boudreau. Let it go, Jimmy," Tee Bobby said.

"That high school girl you been scoping out?"

"Not no more. She say I'm too old."

"Too old? What she mean is too black. You let her talk shit like that and get away wit' it?"

Tee Bobby didn't answer. The noise of the four-wheeler was like a chainsaw cutting through a chunk of angle iron. Amanda's arms were wrapped tightly around the boy's stomach, the side of her face pressed into his back.

Jimmy Dean slapped his hand on the horn and held it down for almost ten seconds. When the driver of the four-wheeler turned around, Jimmy Dean shot him the finger over the top of the car.

The driver shot him the finger back, then rumbled across the wooden bridge into another cane field.

"You see what that motherfucker just did?" Jimmy Dean said.

Tee Bobby looked straight ahead, uncertain as to what he should say, grit blowing in his eyes, the humidity like steam on his skin.

"Let me ax you, Tee Bobby, how much shit you willing to take in one day?" Jimmy Dean said. "Perry LaSalle do everything except put his dick in your mouth and a li'l white pissant give us the bone in front of the girl who tole you she ain't getting it on wit' no raggedy-ass plantation nigger from Poinciana Island. 'Cause that's what it is, man."

"I ain't saying you wrong," Tee Bobby said.

"Then do something about it," Jimmy Dean said, handing Tee Bobby the joint.

Tee Bobby put the joint loosely in his mouth and shotgunned it, huffing air and smoke along the paper until it burned almost to his lips, holding each hit deep down in his lungs. But he made no reply to Jimmy Dean's challenge.

"How 'bout it, Tee Bobby? You don't stand up in Los Angeles, they'll use you to wipe their ass. If I'm putting out my bread, you got to show me ain't nobody shoving you around," Jimmy Dean said.

Tee Bobby gave the joint back to Jimmy Dean, his hand trembling slightly. He started the engine and heard the transmission clank loudly and reverberate through the floorboards when he dropped the gearshift into drive, almost like he had begun a mechanical process that would take on a life of its own. For just a moment, as the car inched forward toward the wooden bridge, he saw Rosebud in the rearview mirror, her face drowsy in the heat, a strand of hair stuck damply to her forehead.

"Go back to sleep, Rosebud. I'm going to talk to a smart-ass white boy a minute, then we be back on the highway," Tee Bobby said.

He was surprised by the resolution in his own words. When he looked across the seat at Jimmy Dean, he saw an approval in Jimmy Dean's face he had never seen there before. Maybe Jimmy Dean was right. A day came when you stopped taking people's shit.

Amanda and her boyfriend had pulled the four-wheeler to a stop in a dusty space between the cane field and a grove of gum trees next to a humped cluster of blackberry bushes. Amanda and the boy were watching a hot-air balloon drifting high in the sky to the west, the engine of the four-wheeler idling loudly, and they did not hear Tee Bobby's car approach them. Jimmy Dean reached inside the gunnysack at his feet and removed the two watch caps he had placed inside it with the cut-down twelve-gauge and a box of shells.

"Put it on, my man. Let's see if Chuckie want to stick his finger up in the air again," Jimmy Dean said.

"Just shake 'em up, right? That's all we doing, huh, Jimmy Dean?" Tee Bobby said.

"It's their call, man. Watch me and go wit' the flow," Jimmy Dean replied. He pulled a pair of leather gloves on his hands, then got out of the car, his watch cap stretched tightly over his face, the pistol-grip shotgun held at an upward angle.

"Hey, motherfucker, you just shot the bone at the wrong nigger!" he yelled, and jacked a round into the chamber.

Tee Bobby hurriedly pulled his watch cap over his face, his heart exploding in his chest. What was Jimmy Dean doing?

But the answer was simple: Jimmy Dean had just forced Amanda and her boyfriend to get on the ground, inside the hot shade of the sweet gums, a child's jump rope hanging from his left hand. He threw the jump rope in the boy's face.

"Tie her wrists to that tree," Jimmy Dean said.

"I don't want to," the boy said.

"What makes you think you got a choice?" Jimmy Dean said, and kicked the boy in the ribs.

"Okay," the boy said, raising his hands, his face jerking with the blow.

Jimmy Dean looked back at the road, then at the hot-air balloon drifting across the sun, his palms opening and closing on the shotgun. When the boy had finished looping the rope around Amanda's wrists, knotting it behind the tree trunk, Jimmy Dean leaned down and tested the tension.

"Now you gonna take a walk wit' me, make up your mind if you want to live or be a smart-ass some more," Jimmy Dean said. "You heard me, cracker, move! And take off your belt while you at it."

The boy walked ahead of Jimmy Dean, his skin almost jumping off his back each time Jimmy Dean touched him with the shotgun's barrel.

Tee Bobby stared down at Amanda through the weave of his watch cap. She wore elastic-waisted jeans and red tennis shoes with dusty socks and a purple blouse that was printed with little rabbits. Her cheeks were hollowed with shadow, her lips dry, caked on the edges, but there was no fear in her eyes, only anger and contempt. The skin on her wrists was crimped, her veins like green string under the tightness of the jump rope. He knelt down and tried to rotate the rope to a narrower place on her wrists, but instead he only managed to bunch and pinch the skin even worse.

"You filthy scum, get your hands off me!" she said, and reared her forehead into his cheek.

He felt the blow all the way to the bone. He started to cry out but clenched his teeth so she would not hear and recognize his voice. Then he lost his balance and fell against her, accidentally hitting her breast with his elbow.

He looked down at her, propped up on his arms now, wanting to apologize, conscious of his own stink, the foulness in his breath, the sweat that crawled like ants inside his cap. Then he saw the level of loathing and disgust in her eyes, just a moment before she gathered all the spittle in her mouth and spat it into his face.

He rose to his feet, stunned, her spittle soaking through the thread in his cap, touching his skin like a badge of disgrace. He hooked his thumb under his cap and pulled it above his eyes, then whirled away from her and the shocked recognition he saw in her expression.

Suddenly he was staring at Jimmy Dean, who had just walked back through the trees from the coulee, where he had tied up the boy with the boy's T-shirt and belt.

"You done it now," Jimmy Dean said.

"No, she ain't seen nothing," Tee Bobby said, pulling his cap back over his face.

"We'll talk about that in a minute. But right now it's show time," Jimmy Dean said, and unzipped his pants, the tails of his scarf fluttering on his neck. "You up for it or not?"

"I ain't signed on for this."

"She dissed you 'cause you black."

"Don't do it, Jimmy Dean."

"You're hopeless, man. Go back to the car 'cause that's where you left your brains at."

Tee Bobby walked away, out of the shade into the sunlight and the dust devils spinning out of the cane field. The wind tasted like salt, like stagnant water and diesel fumes from the state highway and a dead animal in the bottom of a dry coulee. He heard Amanda cry out, then Jimmy Dean's labored breathing inside the trees, followed by a grinding noise that built in Jimmy Dean's throat and burst suddenly from his mouth as though he had passed a kidney stone.

It was quiet inside the gum trees now, but Tee Bobby stood in front of his gas-guzzler, looking at Rosebud in the backseat, both of his palms pressed against his ears, knowing it was not over, that the worst moment still waited for him.

The shotgun's report was muffled, not as loud as he thought it would be, but maybe that was because he had pressed his hands so tightly against his ears. Or maybe something had gone wrong and the gun had misfired, he told himself.

He turned and saw Jimmy Dean walk out of the trees, the shotgun smoking, blood splattered on his shirt.

"She fought. She kicked the barrel. I only had one round. Get the shells," he said.

"What?" Tee Bobby said.

"Snap out of it. She's still alive. Get the fucking shells."

Tee Bobby opened the passenger door and removed the box of twelve-gauge double-oughts from the gunnysack, his hands trembling, and started to give it to Jimmy Dean. But Jimmy Dean was already walking back toward the gum trees, and Tee Bobby, for reasons he would never be able to explain to himself, followed him, without even being commanded. Jimmy Dean stooped and picked up the spent casing he had ejected from his gun, then fished two shells from the box in Tee Bobby's hands and thumbed them into the gun's magazine.

"Stand back, 'less you want to get splattered," Jimmy Dean said.

Amanda's eyes glanced at Tee Bobby for only a second, but the expression of loss and sadness and betrayal in them would live in his dreams the rest of his life.

He whirled around and ran directly into his sister, who was staring wide-eyed at the scene taking place in the trees. When the shotgun discharged, Rosebud pulled at her clothes and beat at the air with her fists, as though she were being attacked, then ran out into the cane field, keening like a wounded bird.

CHAPTER 28

That afternoon Tee Bobby stood in wrist and leg chains on the levee at Henderson Swamp with me and Helen while two scuba divers went over the side of a state powerboat and began hunting in the darkness twelve feet down. The sky was black, the wind driving hard across the tops of the willow and cypress trees, the air clean smelling and unseasonably cool, peppered with rain off the Gulf. Tee Bobby's face was wan, his jaw slack.

"You call my gran'mama?" he asked.

"That's not my job, Tee Bobby," I replied.

One of the scuba divers broke the surface of the water, a dollop of mud on his cheek, the pistol-grip shotgun raised above his head.

"Call my gran'mama and tell her I ain't gonna be back home for a while, will you? Not till I get my bail re-set, work out some kind of deal wit' Barbara Shanahan," Tee Bobby said.

I stared at him. "Bail re-set?" I said.

"Yeah, friend of the court, right? Jimmy Dean gonna be the one to ride the needle. He gonna stay in custody, too. Cain't hurt us no more. I'm gonna see if I can get in one of them diversion programs, too, you know, like you talked about," Tee Bobby said.

The diver who had recovered the shotgun waded up on the bank and handed it to me. He had heard what Tee Bobby said.

"Is that guy for real?" he asked.

Later, back at the department, while the thunder banged outside and pieces of newspaper whirled high in the air and a freight train groaned down the tracks that were now shiny with rain, I called Ladice and told her what had happened to Tee Bobby and where she could visit him that evening. I thought I would feel guilt about having deceived her, but in truth I didn't feel anything. Tee Bobby's story had left me numb, and had convinced me once again the worst deeds human beings commit are precipitated by a happenstance meeting of individuals and events, who and which, if they were rearranged only slightly, would never leave a bump in our history.

I took off early that afternoon and drove home in a strange green light that seemed to rise from the darkness of the trees and fields into the sky. Just as it began to rain, I took Bootsie and Alafair for supper at the Patio in Loreauville and did not mention the events of the day.

It's never over.

Tuesday morning, while rain flooded the streets, Perry LaSalle parked his Gazelle in a no-parking zone and sprinted up the walk into the courthouse. He didn't bother to knock when he came into my office, either.

"You entrapped Tee Bobby," he said.

"It's good of you to drop by, Perry. I'll get the sheriff in here and maybe a newspaper reporter or two, so everyone can have the benefit of your observations," I said.

"Be cute all you want. You didn't Mirandize my client and you denied him access to his attorney."

"Wrong and wrong. He was already Mirandized and I told him to call you up before we brought him in. In front of witnesses, including his grandmother."

I saw the certainty go out of his eyes.

"It doesn't matter. You tricked a frightened kid," he said.

"Listen to what Tee Bobby has to say on the videotape. Then come back and tell me how your stomach feels. By the way, he says he came to you for financial help the day of the murder and you blew him off. He says you also told him Legion was his grandfather."

"So I'm responsible for Amanda Boudreau's death?"

"No, you're not a noun, just an adverb, Perry. Maybe that's reassuring to you," I said.

"You really know how to say it," he replied.

"Adios," I said.

I picked some papers off my desk and read them until he was gone.

But later my own sardonic remark began to bother me. Perhaps "adverb" was too soft a term, I thought. Perry was a master at convincing others he was a victim, never the perpetrator. I got out the case file I had assembled on Legion Guidry and looked back at the notes I had made concerning the 1966 shooting by Legion of a New York freelance writer named William O'Reilly. The Morgan City newspaper had said that O'Reilly had drawn a pistol in a bar and been shot when Legion tried to disarm him. However, Ladice Hulin claimed a black man in the kitchen saw Legion take the gun from under the bar and literally execute O'Reilly in the parking lot, the gun muzzle so close that flame rose from O'Reilly's coat.

I called the reference librarian at the Iberia Parish Library on Main and asked if she could find any bibliographic or biographical information on William O'Reilly. A half hour later she called me back.

"I couldn't find much you don't already know. He published two pulp-fiction novels. You want their titles?" she said.

"Yeah, that'd be fine. Do you have the publisher's name?"

"Pocket Books," she said.

"Anything else?" I said.

"The obituary gives the names of some of the survivors."

"You found the obituary? You mean in the Morgan City paper?" I said.

"No, in Brooklyn. That's where he was originally from. You want me to fax it over to you?" she said.

God bless all reference librarians everywhere, I thought.

The fax came through our machine a few minutes later. Listed among the family survivors of William O'Reilly was the name of a sister, Mrs. Harriet Stetson. I dialed Brooklyn information and was prepared to hang up when the automatic response gave me a phone number. I called the number and left two messages on the machine, then went to lunch. When I came back to the office, the phone on my desk was ringing.

"I'm Harriet Stetson. You wanted to talk about my brother?" an elderly voice said.

I didn't know where to begin. I repeated who I was and told her I did not believe her brother had drawn a weapon in a Morgan City bar. I told her I thought that he had been followed outside and murdered in the parking lot and that the witnesses to his death had lied.

She was silent a long time.

"I can't tell you how much this call means to me, Mr. Robicheaux," she said. "My brother had his problems with alcohol, but he was a gentle man. He was a volunteer at the Catholic Worker mission in the Bowery. He would never carry a firearm."

"The Dorothy Day mission?" I asked.

"It was founded by Dorothy Day. But it's called the St. Joseph House, on East First Street. How did you know?"

My head was pounding now.

"Why was your brother down here? What was he working on?" I asked.

"A book about a famous family there. They lived on an island. They owned canneries, I think. Why?" she replied.

I signed out a cruiser and went looking for Perry LaSalle. I ran up the walk to his office on Main Street, a newspaper over my head, and closed the door hurriedly against the rain. When I wiped the water out of my eyes,

I saw the secretary sitting very stiffly behind her type-writer, an angry bead in her eyes, her face averted from the man in khaki clothes who sat on a divan, his hat next to him, crown down, the smoke from an unfiltered ciga-rette curling through his fingers.

Legion Guidry's gaze shifted from the secretary to me. I looked away from him.

"Is Perry here, Miss Eula?" I asked.

Her full name was Eula Landry. Her hair was dyed almost blue, and her robin-breasted posture and Millsaps College manner were almost like part of the decor in Perry's office. Except it was obvious that her glacial detachment from the ebb and flow of the world was being sorely tested.

"No, he's not," she replied.

"Can I ask where he is?"

"I don't know," she said irritably.

She got up from her chair and walked primly into a small kitchen in back and poured herself a cup of coffee. I followed her inside. Her back was to me, but I could see her cup trembling on the saucer.

"What's going on, Miss Eula?" I asked.

"I'm not supposed to tell that man out there where Mr. Perry is. His name is Legion. He frightens me."

"I'll get him out of here," I said.

"No, he'll know I told you."

"Where's Perry?" I asked.

"At Victor's Cafeteria. With Barbara Shanahan." Then her eyes went past me and widened with apprehension.

Legion stood in the kitchen doorway, listening.

"You tell Robicheaux where Perry LaSalle's at, but not me?" he said.

"I'm sorry," she said.

"You sorry, all right," he said, then walked back in the waiting area and stood in the middle of the room, biting a hangnail on his thumb.

He picked up his hat and put it on his head, then slipped his raincoat over his shoulders. Miss Eula poured her coffee down the sink and began rinsing her cup and saucer under the faucet, her face burning. I heard glass breaking in the waiting area.

Legion had picked up a globular paperweight, one with a winter landscape and drifting snow inside it, and smashed the glass case on the wall and removed the Confederate battle flag that had been carried by Perry's ancestor at Manassas Junction and Gettysburg and Antietam.

Legion bunched up the sun-faded and bullet-rent cloth in his hand and blew his nose in it, then wiped his nostrils and upper lip carefully and threw the flag to the floor. When he left, he closed the door behind him and lit a cigarette on the gallery before running through the rain for his truck.

I got in the cruiser and drove up the street to Victor's and went inside. Perry LaSalle and Barbara Shanahan were having coffee and pie at a table against the side wall. A half-dozen city cops, both male and female, were drinking coffee a short distance away. Perry set down his fork and looked up at me.

"I'm not interested in whatever it is you have to say," he said.

"Try this. I just talked to William O'Reilly's sister in New York. Legion Guidry murdered her brother in 1966. O'Reilly was writing a book about your family.

Legion's not too smart, but he knew a book that revealed the LaSalles' family secrets would end his career as a blackmailer. So he killed this poor fellow from New York outside a Morgan City bar."

"You have an obsession, Dave. It seems to be an obvious one to everyone except yourself," Perry said.

"Why don't you join us and give this a rest for a while?" Barbara said, and placed her hand on the back of an empty chair.

"You knew Legion murdered this man, Perry. And you knew why, too," I said.

"You're mistaken," Perry said.

"After you left the Jesuit seminary, you were a volunteer at a Catholic Worker mission in the Bowery. It's the same mission William O'Reilly used to work in. I think you were trying to do penance for your family's sins. Why not just own up to it? It's not the worst admission in the world."

Perry rose to his feet. "You want it in here or out in the street?" he said.

"I'm the least of your problems. I just left your law office. Legion Guidry not only terrified your secretary, he literally blew his nose on your Confederate battle flag."

I turned and started to walk away from him. He grabbed my arm and whirled me around, swinging his fist at the same time. I caught the blow on my forearm and felt it graze the side of my head. I could have walked away, but I didn't. Instead, I let the old enemy have its way and I hooked him in the jaw and knocked him through the chairs onto the floor.

The entire cafeteria was suddenly quiet. Barbara

Shanahan knelt beside Perry, who was trying to push himself up on one elbow, his eyes glazed.

"I know where Clete gets it now. You're unbelievable. You belong in front of a cave with a club in your hand," Barbara said to me.

"Don't listen to her! Way to go, Robicheaux!" one of the city cops yelled. Then the other cops applauded.

I went back to the department and soaked my hand in cold water, then ate two aspirin at my desk and pressed my fists against my temples, my face still burning with embarrassment, wondering when I would ever learn not to push people into corners, particularly a tormented man like Perry LaSalle, who had every characteristic of an untreated sexaholic, psychologically incapable of either personal honesty or emotional intimacy with another human being.

Three deputies in a row opened my door and gave me a thumbs-up for decking Perry. I nodded appreciatively and ate another aspirin and tried to bury myself in my work.

I pulled out my file drawer and began going through some of the open cases I had been neglecting since the murders of Amanda Boudreau and Linda Zeroski. Many of these cases involved crimes committed by what I call members of the Pool, that army of petty miscreants whom nothing short of frontal lobotomies or massive electroshock will ever change. Some of the cases were a delight.

For six months the department had been looking for a burglar we named the Easter Bunny, because witnesses who had seen him said he was an albino with pink eyes and silver hair. But it was not only his appearance that was unusual. His attitude and methods of operation were so outrageous we had no precedent for dealing with him.

In one home he left a handwritten note on the refrigerator door that read:

> Dear Folks Who Own This House,
>   I rob homes in this neighborhood only because most people who live hereabouts try to keep up decent standards. But after breaking into your house I think you should consider moving to a lower rent neighborhood. You don't have cable TV, no beer or snacks in the icebox, and most of your furniture is not worth stealing.
>   In other words, it really sucks when I spend a whole day casing a house only to discover the people who live in it take no pride in themselves. It is people like you who make life hard on guys like me.
>   Sincerely,
>   A guy who doesn't need these kinds of problems

He took a shower and shaved in one home, ordered delivery pizza in another, and sometimes answered the telephone and wrote down phone messages for the home owners.

Two nights ago he robbed a city councilman's house, a short distance from City Park. Evidently the councilman had locked his pet poodle in a pantry by mistake and the poodle was dying to go to the bathroom. The Easter Bunny leashed him up and took him for a walk along the bayou, then returned him to the house and filled his bowls with fresh water and dog food.

The phone on my desk rang.

"What are you doing, Streak?" Bootsie said.

"Looking for the Easter Bunny," I replied.

"If that's a joke, it's not funny. I just heard you punched out Perry LaSalle in Victor's Cafeteria."

"I guess that's fair to say," I replied.

I expected a rejoinder, but in the silence I realized she had called for another reason.

"The homeless man, the ex-soldier you told me about, he's down at the bait shop," she said.

"What's he want?"

"He said he thought you usually came home for lunch. He wanted to talk to you."

"What's he doing now?"

"Reading the newspaper. Is he dangerous, Dave?"

"I'm not sure. Is Batist there?"

"Yes."

"I'll call the shop, then ring you back," I said.

The phone at the bait shop was busy. Five minutes later Batist picked up the receiver.

"That homeless fellow in the shop? He's a couple of quarts down. Everything okay there?" I said.

"All our boats is full of water. That's about it," he replied.

"Give me a call if you need to."

"Ain't no problem here, Dave," he said.

After I hung up I called Bootsie back, then began replacing the case folders I had removed from my file cabinet. A piece of lined yellow paper on which I had scribbled several notations with a felt pen became unstuck from the outside of a manila folder and floated to the floor.

The notations had to do with the telephone call I had received from Marie Guilbeau, the cleaning lady in St. Mary Parish who had been molested by an intruder at her house and had felt obliged to tell me she had flirted the same day with a guest at the motel where she worked.

It took about ten minutes to create what is called a photo lineup, in this case six mug shots that I pulled from the department's files. Actually, her identifying the man at the motel would do little to make a case against the intruder, but the report she had filed had been treated casually by the authorities in St. Mary Parish and by me as well, and perhaps now was an opportunity to make it right. I called Marie Guilbeau's home and was told by a niece that her aunt was at the motel on the four-lane where she worked.

But I didn't drive directly to the motel. First I called Batist at the bait shop.

"Is that fellow still there?" I asked.

"It's raining too hard for him to go nowhere. I'll give him a ride to town later on," Batist replied.

"Tell him to stay there. I'll be along in a few minutes," I said.

When I got to the bait shop, the swamp looked colorless and stricken in the rain, except for the canopy of cypresses, which was a dull green against an infinite gray sky. Most of the concrete boat ramp was under water and a flock of mallards and pintails had taken shelter under the dock. I opened an umbrella over my head and ran for the bait shop.

The man who claimed to have been a medic from my outfit was looking out the window at the rain dancing on the bayou. He was dressed in clean denims, his short sleeves turned up in cuffs, steel-toed oil-field boots laced on his feet.

"Take a ride with me down to St. Mary Parish, Doc," I said.

"What for?" he asked.

"Nothing in particular. You got anything else to do?" I said.

"Nope," he said.

We walked up the dock together, under the umbrella, while lightning banged and flashed around us and thunder peeled across the sky like incoming mail from a distant war.

The motel out on the four-lane was a run-down two-story building that had once belonged to a chain but was now operated by the owner of the truck stop next door. I parked the cruiser by a walkway and asked my friend, the ex-soldier, to wait for me. I found Marie Guilbeau in a laundry room, stuffing sheets into a washing machine. Her dark hair was pinned on the back of her head, her maid's uniform stretched tight against the thickness of her body when she bent over the machine.

"I'd like for you to look at a man for me, Ms. Guilbeau," I said.

"The one who was staying at the motel?" she said, her face stark.

"Let's find out," I replied. "Take a walk with me to the cruiser."

She hesitated, then set down her laundry and followed me through an alcove to the outside walkway. I stepped out into the rain and held my umbrella over the passenger's door and tapped on the glass.

"Hey, Doc, I want you to meet someone," I said, making a rotating motion with my finger.

He rolled down the window and looked at me.

"This is a friend of mine, Ms. Guilbeau," I said.

"Hi," he said.

She folded her hands and lowered her eyes and said nothing in reply.

The ex-soldier glanced at me, unsure of what was happening.

"I'll be with you in a minute, Doc," I said, then stepped back into the alcove with Marie Guilbeau.

"You know that fellow?" I asked.

"Yeah, why you bringing him here?"

"He's the man who made an inappropriate remark to you?"

"No. He's a homeless person. He walks all over New Iberia. Carrying his t'ings on his back. I seen him there," she replied.

"Okay, take a look at these pictures," I said, and removed a piece of mounting board from a manila envelope. Six mug shots were slipped into viewing slots in two rows of threes, one on top of the other.

It didn't take her five seconds to place her finger on one photo in particular.

"That's the one," she said. "He was nice at first. Then he got the wrong idea and said somet'ing fresh. Like he t'ought I was a prostitute." Maybe it was simply the light, but the memory of the incident seemed to climb in her face like a bruise.

"You're sure this is the guy?" I asked.

"That's the guy. You better believe that's the guy," she said, tapping the picture again, her eyes angry now. "What's his name?"

"Marvin Oates. He sells Bibles," I said.

"I'm gonna remember his name. I'm gonna remember his name a long time. It was him broke in my house, wasn't it?" she said.

"I don't know."

"I t'ink you do," she replied.

I turned the cruiser around in the parking lot and headed back toward New Iberia. The broken frond from a palm tree spun crazily out of the sky and bounced off my windshield.

As we drove under the oaks at the city limits sign outside New Iberia, I glanced across the seat at the ex-soldier. His face looked reflective, philosophical, a pocket of air in one cheek.

"You never told me what you wanted to talk about," I said.

"Getting a job. I can do lots of different things. Run a forklift, clerk, fry-cook, swamp out your bait shop," he said.

"I suspect we can work out something."

"I sold the rest of the downers I been taking. I probably should have thrown them away, but I needed the money."

"The V.A. has no record on you. How do you explain that?"

"Some of my records were burnt up in a fire. That's what the V.A. says, anyway."

"You're a man of mystery, Doc."

"No, I ain't. If I live right, I get time off from the stuff that's in my head. For some people that's as good as it gets," he said.

He cracked a piece of peppermint in his jaw and smiled for the first time since I had seen him in New Iberia.

He had no place to stay. I drove home and gave him the room in the back of the bait shop. It contained a bunk, a table with a lamp, a chest of drawers, and a shower inside a tin stall, and I put fresh linen on the bunk and soap and a towel in the shower. When I left the bait shop, he was sound asleep, with all his clothes on, a sheet drawn up to his chin.

I walked up the dock to the house, the wind almost ripping the umbrella from my hand.

CHAPTER 29

In the morning the rain had slackened when I arrived at work. I walked down to the sheriff's office and knocked on the door. He looked up from some papers on his desk, his face darkening. He had on a pinstripe coat and a silver cowboy shirt unbuttoned at the collar. His Stetson hung on a rack, spotted with raindrops.

"Real good of you to check in," he said.

"Sir?" I said.

"You decked Perry LaSalle?"

"He swung on me."

"Thanks for letting me know that. He's called twice. I also just got off the phone with Joe Zeroski. I want this stuff cleaned up. I'm sick of my department being dragged into a soap opera."

"What stuff?" I said.

"LaSalle says Legion Guidry intends to do serious

harm to Barbara Shanahan and your friend Purcel. At least as far as I could make out. In the meantime, Joe Zeroski says Marvin Oates is bothering his niece again. What the hell is going on there?"

"Zerelda Calucci deep-sixed Marvin. I think he's a dangerous man, skipper. Maybe more dangerous than Legion Guidry."

"Marvin Oates?"

"I think he broke into a woman's house in St. Mary Parish and molested her. I think he should be our primary suspect in the murder of Linda Zeroski."

I told the sheriff the story of Marie Guilbeau. He leaned back and tapped the heels of his hands on the arms of his chair. He was thinking about the case now and I could see his irritation with me slipping out of his eyes.

"I don't buy it. Oates is simpleminded. He doesn't have any history of violence," he said.

"None we know about. I want to get a warrant and take his place apart."

"Do it," the sheriff said. "Are you going to talk to Perry LaSalle?"

"What did Legion say exactly?" I asked.

"I never got it straight. LaSalle doesn't sound rational. He says this guy Guidry isn't human. What's he talking about?"

Helen Soileau went to work on the warrant while I called Perry at his office. Outside the window I could see a round blue place in the sky and birds trapped inside it.

Perry's secretary said he had not come to the office yet. I called his number on Poinciana Island.

"Legion threatened Clete and Barbara?" I said.

"Yeah, on the phone, late last night. He threatened me, too. He thinks I'm writing a book about him," he replied. I could hear him breathing into the receiver.

"You told Barbara?"

"Yeah, she said she has a pistol and she's looking forward to parking one in his buckwheats."

"Did you warn Clete?" I asked.

"No."

"Why not?" I asked.

"I just didn't."

Because he's of no value to you, I thought.

"What did you say?" he asked.

"Nothing. You told the sheriff Legion wasn't human. What did you mean?"

His voice make an audible click in the phone.

"He can speak in what sounds like an ancient or dead language. He did it last night," he said.

"It's probably just bad French," I said, and quietly hung up.

I looked at the phone, my ears popping, and wondered how Perry enjoyed being lied to for a change, particularly when he was frightened to death.

I called Clete twice and got his answering machine. I left messages both times. By late that afternoon Helen and I had a warrant to search Marvin Oates's shotgun house on St. Peter Street. Marvin was not at home, but we called the landlord and got him to open the house. It had stopped raining and the sky overhead was blue and ribbed with pink clouds, but out over the Gulf another storm was building and the thunder reverberated dully through Marvin's tin roof as we dumped out all his drawers, pulled his clothes off hangers, flipped his mattress upside down, raked all the cookware out of his kitchen cabinets, and generally wreaked havoc on the inside of his house.

But we found nothing that was of any value to us.

Except five strips of pipe tape hanging loose from an empty niche in the back of the dresser, tape that was strong enough to hold a handgun in place against the wood.

"I bet that's where he hid the nine-millimeter he used to kill Frankie Dogs," I said.

"It's still hard for me to make that guy for anything except a meltdown, Dave," Helen said.

"I knew an old-time moonshiner who once told me the man who kills you will be at your throat before you ever know it," I said.

"Yeah? I don't get it," she said.

"What kind of guy could get close enough to cap Frankie Dogs?" I said.

Before I went home that evening I drove to Clete's apartment, but his blinds were closed and his car was gone. I slipped a note under his door, asking him to call me.

When I got home, the sky was maroon-colored, full of birds, the thunderheads over the Gulf banked in a long black line just above the horizon. One of Alafair's friends was spending the night and had blocked the driveway with her automobile, and I parked my truck by the boat ramp and walked up to the house. A few minutes later I looked through the front window and saw my friend, the ex-soldier, hosing down the truck, then scrubbing the camping shell in back with a long-handled push broom.

I walked back down the slope.

"There's another storm coming. Maybe you should wait on washing the truck," I said.

"That's okay. I just want to get the mud off. Then later I can just run the hose over it," he said.

"How you getting along?" I asked.

"I had a little trouble sleeping. The sound of your refrigeration equipment comes through the walls. When I put the pillow over my head, I don't hear it so much."

"You want to join us for supper?"

"That's all right, Loot. I went into town with Batist and bought some groceries," he said.

I turned to walk back to the house.

"There was an old guy here in a red pickup truck," he said. "He asked if somebody in a purple Cadillac convertible had been around. A guy named Purcel."

"What'd this guy look like?" I asked.

"Tall, with deep lines in his face. I told him I didn't know anybody named Purcel." The ex-soldier scratched his cheek and looked quizzically into space.

"What is it?" I said.

"He told me to go inside and ask the nigger. That's the word he used, just like everybody did. I told him he should watch what he called other people. He didn't like it."

"His name is Legion Guidry, Doc. He's one of those we don't let get behind us."

"Who is he?"

"I wish I knew, partner," I said.

* * *

After supper I walked out on the gallery and tried to read the newspaper, but I couldn't concentrate. The sky began to darken, and a flock of egrets rose out of the swamp and scattered like white rose petals over the top of my house, then the wind kicked up again and I heard rain clicking in the trees. I folded the newspaper and went back inside. Bootsie was reading a novel by Steve Yarbrough under a floor lamp. She closed her book, using her thumb to mark her place, her eyes veiled.

"Do you think your friend, the war vet out there, is a hundred percent?" she said.

"Probably not. But he's harmless," I replied.

"How do you know?"

"Good people don't change. Sometimes bad ones do. But good people don't."

"You're incurably romantic, Dave."

"Think so?"

She laughed loudly, then went back to her book. I walked into the kitchen, hoping she did not detect my real mood. Because the truth was my skin was crawling with anxiety, the same kind I'd experienced during my flirtation with amphetamines. But this time the cause wasn't the white worm; it was an abiding sense that my loyal friend Clete Purcel was skating on the edge of another calamity.

"Where you going?" Bootsie said.

"To Clete's. I'll be back in a few minutes," I said.

"You worried about him?"

"I've left him several messages. Clete always calls me as soon as he gets the message."

"Maybe he's in New Orleans."

"Legion Guidry was at the bait shop today. He wanted to know if Clete had been around."

Her book fell off her knee. Her reading glasses were full of light when she looked at me.

I drove to his apartment on the Loreauville Road. The underwater lights were on in the swimming pool, and the apartment manager, an elderly Jewish man who had been a teenager in the Bergen-Belsen concentration camp, was stacking the poolside furniture under a sheltered walkway.

"Have you seen Clete Purcel, Mr. Lemand?" I asked.

"Early this morning. He was putting his fishing things in the back of his car. A young woman was with him," he replied.

"Did he say when he might be back?"

"No, he didn't. I'm sorry," Mr. Lemand said. He was a bald, wizened man, with brown eyes and delicate hands. He always wore a tie and a starched shirt and was never seen at a dinner table without his coat on. "You're the second person who asked me about Mr. Purcel today."

"Oh?"

"A man in a red truck was here. He sat for a long time in the parking lot, under the trees, smoking cigarettes. Maybe because of your line of work you know this man," Mr. Lemand said.

"How do you mean?"

He inverted a plastic chair and placed it on a table.

"In my childhood I saw eyes like his. That was in Germany, in times quite different from our own. He wanted to know if Mr. Purcel was with Ms. Shanahan.

You know, Ms. Shanahan, who works in the district attorney's office? I didn't tell him."

"Good for you."

"Do you think he'll come back, this man in the truck?"

"Call me if he does. Here, I'll put my home number on the back of my business card," I said, and handed it to him.

"This man had an odor. At first I thought I was imagining it. But I wasn't. It was vile," he said.

His eyes searched my face for an explanation. But I had none to give him. The pool was a brilliant, clear green against the glow of the underwater lights, the surface chained with rain rings. I walked out into the darkness, into the parking lot, and started my truck.

Who else would go fishing in an electric storm or ignore the danger represented by a man like Legion Guidry? I asked myself. But that was Clete's nature, defiant of all authority and rules, uneducable, grinning his way through the cannon smoke, convinced he could live through anything.

Evidently, James Jones and Ernest Hemingway bore each other a high degree of enmity. Ironically, they both described the evolution of the combat soldier in a similar fashion. Each author said the most dangerous stage in a soldier's life is the second one, immediately after he has survived his initial experience in combat, because he feels anointed by a divine hand and convinces himself he would not have been spared in one battle only to die in another.

Clete had never evolved out of that second stage in a

combat soldier's career. His great strength lay in his courage and his uncanny knowledge of his enemy. But his weakness was in direct proportion to his strength, and it lay in his inability to foresee or appreciate the consequence of his actions, or, more simply said, the fact that a cable-strung wrecking ball is designed to swing both ways.

I drove back up the Loreauville Road and crossed the drawbridge in the center of town and turned onto Burke Street, then walked up the steps to Barbara Shanahan's apartment overlooking the Teche. A lamp was on in the living room, but no one answered the bell. I hammered on the door, but there was no movement inside. I stuck a note in the doorjamb, asking her to call the house when she returned.

I drove to the motor court where Joe Zeroski and Zerelda Calucci were staying. Zerelda was not in her cottage, but Joe was, dressed in pajama bottoms, a T-shirt, and slippers, holding the door open for me, the rain blowing in his face.

"Just the guy I wanted to see," he said.

"Me?" I said.

"Yeah, this whole town ought to be napalmed. I called the sheriff at his house. He told me to talk to him during business hours. Hey, crazoids don't keep business hours. That includes Blimpo."

"Blimpo is Clete?"

"No, Nancy Reagan. Who do you think I mean?"

"You're going too fast for me, Joe." I closed the door behind me. His television set was on, a glass of milk and a sandwich on a table by an overstuffed chair.

"Purcel took my niece fishing. He didn't say where,

either, which means he wants to boink her without me being around. In the meantime Marvin Dipshit is knocking on her door, with roses in his hand and this puke-pot look on his face," he said.

"When?" I asked.

"Two hours ago."

"Where is Oates now?" I asked.

"I'm supposed to know that? No wonder you people got a crime wave. Get out of here," he said.

"Joe, I think Marvin may have murdered your daughter," I said.

"Say that again."

"Marvin Oates may have molested a woman in St. Mary Parish. He keeps showing up in places he has no business at."

"When'd you start looking at this guy?" Joe said.

"He's been an unofficial suspect for some time."

"*Unofficial?* You got a way with words."

"I'm here now, Joe, because I'm concerned about both Clete and Zerelda. If you can help me in any way, I'll be in your debt."

An angry thought went out of his eyes.

"I don't know where they're at. But I'll make some calls," he said.

"No cowboy stuff. Oates is a suspect. That's all," I said.

"You figure him for the hit on Frankie?" he said.

"Maybe."

"How could a watermelon picker like that take out Frankie Dogs? A guy who wears boots that look like they come off a Puerto Rican faggot. You ever seen anybody besides an elf or a fruit wear red and green boots?"

"When did you see him in these boots?"

"Tonight. Why?"

I went back home. I tried to imagine where Clete might have gone, but I was at a loss. I called his apartment again and got the answering machine, but this time I just hung up.

"Clete always lands on his feet," Bootsie said.

"I wouldn't say that," I replied.

"You can't live his life, Dave," she said.

I went out on the gallery and sat in a chair, with the light off, and watched the rain fall on the swamp. I thought about the biblical passage describing how God makes the sun to shine and the rain to fall on both the good and the wicked. A few miles away Jimmy Dean Styles and Tee Bobby Hulin were both housed in the parish prison, held without bond, in twenty-three-hour lockdown. I wondered if Tee Bobby had finally accepted his fate, if he looked out at the drenched sugarcane fields surrounding the stockade and saw his future there, either as a lifetime convict laborer on Angola Farm or as a hump of sod in the prison cemetery at Lookout Point, with no identification on his grave marker except a number.

I even wondered if Jimmy Dean Styles still doubted his fate. I could not imagine a worse death than being confined in a cage, knowing the exact date, hour, minute, and second you will die at the hands of others. To me it was always miraculous that the condemned did not go insane before the day of their execution.

But an old-time warden at Parchman Penitentiary in Mississippi confided to me an observation of his own that I've never forgotten. He said that no matter how pathological or evil the condemned might be, they do not believe the state will carry out its sentence. An army of correctional officers, prison psychologists, physicians, hospital attendants, prison administrators, and chaplains is assigned to the care and well-being of those on death row. They're fed, given every form of medical care, nursed back to health if they try to kill themselves, and sometimes punished, as children would be, for possessing a stinger or a jar of prune-o.

Would these same representatives of the state strap down a defenseless individual and fill his veins with lethal chemicals or create an electrical arc from his skull to the soles of his feet? My friend the warden believed the contradictions were such that no sane person could quite assimilate them.

On the far side of the swamp a bolt of lightning leaped from the earth and quivered whitely in a pool of clouds at the top of the sky. I felt the day's events wash through me in a wave of fatigue. Then the phone rang in the living room and I went inside to answer it.

It was Mr. Lemand, the manager of Clete's apartment complex.

"I'm sorry to call so late," he said.

"It's all right. Can I help you?" I said.

"A lady named Mrs. LeBlanc lives next door to Mr. Purcel. After you left, her toilet became clogged and I had to go up and fix it. Since I knew you were concerned about Mr. Purcel, I asked if she had seen him. She said he'd told her he had rented a camp at Bayou Benoit."

"Do you know where exactly?"

"No, I asked her that."

"Thanks very much, Mr. Lemand," I said.

"I'm afraid that's not all. She said a man had been looking into Mr. Purcel's window. She was disturbed at first, then she recognized the man as a Bible salesman she knew. He told her he was delivering a Bible to Mr. Purcel but hadn't been able to find him. So she told him where Mr. Purcel was."

"What you've told me is very helpful, Mr. Lemand," I said.

"Unfortunately, there's more. When she looked out her window, she saw a red pickup truck follow the Bible salesman out of the parking lot. Then she noticed the man driving the truck didn't turn on his lights until he was out on the road. She had seen this man earlier. He had a pair of binoculars. She's quite concerned she put either Mr. Purcel or the salesman in harm's way."

"She and you have done all the right things, Mr. Lemand. Tell her not to worry," I said.

"I think that will be a great relief to her," he said.

I hung up the receiver and tried to think. My own thoughts made my head hurt. Linda Zeroski had been murdered on Bayou Benoit. The nightclub where Baby Huey Lagneaux worked was on Bayou Benoit, as was Legion Guidry's camp. Of all the places Clete could choose for a tryst, it would have to be there.

I went into the bedroom and removed my army-issue .45 automatic from the dresser drawer. I dropped an extra magazine, loaded with hollow-points, and a sap and a pair of handcuffs in the pockets of my raincoat and told Bootsie I did not know when I would be back home, then walked down the slope to my truck and started the engine.

I didn't realize, until I was over a mile down the road, that I had a passenger with me.

CHAPTER 30

I looked into the rearview mirror and saw the face of the ex-soldier staring at me through the back window. I swerved to the side of the road and got out. He climbed out of the camper shell, bare-chested, a crucifix and a G.I. can opener hung around his neck.

"What are you doing in there?" I asked.

"The motor on your refrigerator kept me awake. I got in your camper to sleep," he said.

"Bad night for it, Doc," I said.

"I'll walk back. No big deal," he replied.

He reached inside the shell and retrieved a pillow and his shirt. His face was beaded with raindrops.

"Hop in front. Let's take a ride upcountry," I said.

He thought about it a moment, his mouth screwed into a button, his eyes clear of both dope and madness, his expression almost childlike. "I don't mind," he said.

We drove up Bayou Teche, through Loreauville and

waving fields of sugarcane that flickered with lightning. We turned off the state road and passed scattered farmhouses and clumps of trees inside cattle acreage and a bait shop and a filling station that were dark inside. Then I saw the nightclub where Baby Huey bartended, the neon beer signs glowing in the rain, the empty parking lot lit by floodlamps.

I left the ex-soldier in the truck and went inside. The front and back doors of the club were open to air it out. Baby Huey was at the end of the bar, on the phone, his back to me. His hair was wet, his pink shirt spotted with raindrops. When he hung up and saw me standing behind him, he looked back at the phone, as though reviewing the conversation he'd just had.

"You want to tell me something?" I asked.

"Not necessarily," he replied.

"You wouldn't have been talking to Joe Zeroski, would you?" I said.

"You never can tell." He picked up a clean white cloth and began wiping the bar, although there was no water or drink residue on it.

"Lose the routine, Huey. I'm looking for Joe Zeroski's niece and a friend of mine named Clete Purcel. I think you are, too. You lie to me, you're going to be sharing accommodations with Tee Bobby Hulin."

He bit his lip and bunched the bar cloth in his huge hand.

"Use your head, partner. We're on the same side," I said.

"Mr. Joe called earlier. He thought his niece and her boyfriend had probably rented a camp somewhere. He axed me if I knowed who rented camps herebouts. I called a friend of mine runs the bait shop back up the road. He said a guy wit' a Cadillac convertible like the one Mr. Joe described was in there this afternoon. My friend said this guy and the woman wit' him was staying in a camp just the other side of the levee. So I drove on down there."

"So?" I said.

"You ain't gonna want to hear this."

"I don't mean to offend you, Huey, but you're starting to seriously piss me off," I said.

"The guy who lives next door to the cabin where your friend was at? He's been inside twice. He ain't the kind of guy got a real good relationship with the law or dials 911 a lot, know what I mean? He said a big white guy in swim trunks and a Marine Corps cap was cleaning fish on the porch in back when a guy dressed like a cowboy drove into the yard. He said the guy in swim trunks was talking loud and shaking his fish knife at the cowboy, but my friend couldn't see it too good 'cause the house was in the way."

"What happened?" I asked.

Baby Huey raised his eyebrows. "A few minutes later the woman drove away wit' the cowboy. The woman was driving, and the big guy in swim trunks wasn't nowhere around."

"What do you mean he wasn't anywhere around?"

Baby Huey's eyes went away from me, then came back again.

"My friend thought he might have been in the trunk of the car. A red pickup was parked down the road from the camp. It followed the Cadillac over the levee. My friend thought it look just like the pickup Legion drive," he said.

"Your friend didn't bother to tell anyone this until you asked him?" I said.

"That's the way it go sometimes," Baby Huey replied.

I pushed a napkin and my ballpoint pen across the bar to Huey.

"Write down your friend's name so I can thank him personally," I said.

I used the pay phone in the corner and called Helen Soileau at her house. She dropped the receiver when she answered, then scraped it up again. I described all the events that had occurred since I had seen her late that afternoon.

"Marvin was wearing red and green cowboy boots? Same color as the cowboy in the bar where Frankie Dogs got hit?" she said.

"That's right," I replied.

"Why did Legion pick today to go after Clete?"

"He thinks Clete is with Barbara. Barbara stood up to him in the western store. He wants to get them both at one time," I said.

"I'm still asleep. I can't think clearly. What do you want me to do?"

"Nothing right now. Look, when I went to see Perry LaSalle at Sookie Motrie's duck hunting camp down by Pecan Island, I saw an abandoned church that reminded me of the lyrics in a song Marvin Oates is always quoting from. The church has a sign on it that says Twelve Disciples Assembly. Is that just a coincidence?"

"Marvin used to stay with a preacher there when his mother was on a bender. I think the preacher was the only person who ever treated him decent."

"I'm going to head down there," I said.

"You sound a little strung out. Let it go till sunlight. There's a good chance Baby Huey's source is full of shit."

"No, the details are too specific," I said.

There was a pause on the line.

"You're not having the wrong kind of thoughts, are you?" she asked.

"No, everything's copacetic here," I said.

"Streak?"

"I'm telling you the truth. I'm fine," I said.

But when I hung up, my hands were tingling with fatigue, my mouth dry, my hair damp with sweat, as though my old courtship with the malarial mosquito had taken new life in my blood. I turned around and almost collided with Baby Huey, who was mopping down a table five feet behind me.

"What do you think you just heard?" I said.

"I was listening to the jukebox. That's Tee Bobby's new song. Boy got a million-dollar voice. Ain't been nobody like him since Guitar Slim," he said.

I was burning up inside my raincoat, and I took it off before I got back into the truck and put my sap, hand-cuffs, and extra magazine on the seat, beside my holstered .45. Then I turned the truck around and headed south, toward Pecan Island, down in Vermilion Parish.

"I don't have time to take you back home," I said to the ex-soldier.

"It's all right. I've been taking a nap," he said. He had put his shirt back on but had left it unbuttoned, and the crucifix on his chest shone in the dashboard light.

"What's your real name, Doc?" I said.

"Sal Angelo."

"You sure about that?" I said.

"Pretty sure," he said.

"You're okay, Sal," I said.

He grinned sleepily, then rested his head on his pillow and closed his eyes. I drove into Abbeville, past the old redbrick cathedral and the graveyard that was full of Confederate dead, then continued on south, into the wetlands and wind blowing across sawgrass and clumps of gum trees and swamp maples. My face felt hot to the touch, my jaws like emery paper. I thought I could hear the drone of mosquitoes, but none settled on my skin and I couldn't see any on the windshield or dashboard, where they usually clustered when they got inside the truck. When I swallowed, my spit tasted like battery acid.

My holstered .45 vibrated on the seat beside me. I touched it with my right hand, felt the coolness of the steel, the checkered hardness of the grips against my skin. It was the finest handgun I had ever owned, purchased for twenty-five dollars among a row of cribs in Saigon's Bring Cash Alley. I popped the strap loose with my thumb and slipped the heaviness of the frame into my hand and held it like an old friend against my thigh, although I could not explain the reason why I did so.

It wasn't far to the deserted church now. The rain had slackened and a crack of veiled moonlight shone among the clouds, like a dirty green vapor that had been sucked out of the Gulf during the storm. I rubbed the back of my wrist into my eye sockets and saw red rings recede into my brain, then I experienced a disturbing sense of clarity I had not felt all day, as though all my thought patterns for weeks, my prayers, my personal resolutions and soliloquies at AA meetings, were being made null and void because they were no longer useful to me.

Sigmund Freud was once quoted as saying, "Ah, thank you for showing me all of mankind's lofty ideals. Now let me introduce you to the basement."

I could feel myself descending into that subterranean place in the mind where the gargoyles frolic. The case against Marvin Oates for the murder of Linda Zeroski was tenuous and speculative, without even circumstantial evidence to support it, I told myself. Even if Marvin had harmed Clete and Zerelda and was in possession of the nine-millimeter that had killed Frankie Dogs, the right defense attorney could put him and his scarred back and his hush-puppy accent on the stand and have a jury of daytime soap-opera fans touching tears from their cheeks.

That's what I told myself about the future of Marvin Oates. But my real thoughts were on Legion Guidry and the women he had molested and raped and the methodical beating he had given me. In my mind's eye I once again saw his face lean down into my vision, his hand gripping my hair, his lips fastening on mine, his tongue probing my mouth. Then I swear I could taste the tobacco in his saliva and the tiny strings of decayed meat impacted in his teeth.

I felt my stomach constrict. I rolled down the window and cleared my throat and spit into the darkness. When I rolled up the window and wiped my mouth, I realized the ex-soldier who called himself Sal Angelo was awake, watching me.

"That guy who hurt you is down here, ain't he?" he said.

"Which guy?" I asked.

"We both know which guy, Loot."

"Can't ever tell," I said.

"Remember what I told you about making yourself the executioner? It's like your soul travels out of your body, then it can't find its way back. That's when you forget who you are."

"I may have to drop you off, Sal, and pick you up on my way out," I said.

"Hate to hear you say that, Loot."

"Why?" I asked.

"Our story is already written. You can't change it," he said.

I hit a deep rut and a curtain of gray water splashed across the windshield. I looked across the seat and saw him raise his head off his chest and open his eyes, as though awakening from a deep sleep.

"What did you just say?" I asked.

"I didn't say nothing. I was knocked out. Where are we, anyway?" he replied.

CHAPTER 31

While Zerelda drove the Cadillac, Marvin sat hunched forward in the passenger seat, wired to the eyes, sweating, licking his lips, breathing through his nose like a frightened child, she thought, with a nine-millimeter Beretta resting on his thigh.

"You didn't use your turn indicator back there. You use your turn indicator, Zerelda," he said.

She watched the country slip by them, the cows bunched in the coulees, a tree of lightning pulsing in the clouds. She felt Clete's weight shift in the trunk. It was the first time he had moved since Marvin had forced him to sit in the trunk, then had picked up a thick piece of steel pipe.

"I need to use the rest room," she said.

"There's time for that later," Marvin said.

She heard a clunking sound in the trunk. She clicked on the radio.

"I'm worried about this storm," she said.

He turned the radio off. "Don't do that," he said.

"Do what?"

He took a ragged breath of air and looked hard at the side of her face, his eyes narrowing. Then, for no apparent reason, he reached across the seat and fastened his fingers on the back of her neck, sinking them deep into the tendons.

"You make me mad," he said.

He lifted his fingers from her neck and touched her hair. Then he put both his hands and the Beretta between his legs and sat very still, his chest rising and falling.

"Marvin, no one meant to hurt you."

"Don't talk down to me. Not ever again. 'Cause that's what you been doing since the beginning. I don't like that."

"Then maybe you should get a life and stop feeling sorry for yourself."

Too late, she knew it was the wrong thing to say. She heard him make a grinding sound in his throat, then he struck her across the mouth with the back of his hand.

He grabbed the wheel and hit her again.

"Now, you steer the car and don't make me do what I'm thinking," he said, his voice starting to break.

Her hand was trembling when she touched the cut on her mouth.

"My uncle is Joe Zeroski. Can that fit in your head? What do you think he's going to do when he gets his hands on you, you nasty little pissant?" she said.

She thought he was about to hit her again. But he was hunched forward once more, looking at the road in the headlights, listening.

"Pull over," he said.

"What for?"

"Don't ask," he said.

She took her foot off the accelerator and felt the weight of the Cadillac slow, a tire touch on the shoulder of the road. She heard Clete kick solidly against the hatch. Marvin waited until a pickup truck passed, then flung open the door and walked to the rear of the vehicle.

"Shut up in there!" he said.

Through the backseat she heard Clete's voice: "Tell you what, pinhead. Pop the hatch and I'll take you in without scrubbing out the toilet with your face, the way Frankie Dogs did."

"Suck on this," Marvin said, and stepped back from the vehicle and fired a round into the hatch, the muzzle flash sparking into the darkness.

His hat was peaked in the crown, and rain slid off the brim when he got back in the front seat and pulled the door shut behind him. It was quiet in the back of the Cadillac.

"You motherfucker," she said.

Marvin's eyes closed, then opened, as though he were experiencing a sexual moment. "Drive the car, Zerelda," he said.

He rested the Beretta on the edge of his scrotum, the butterfly safety off, the red firing dot exposed. Minutes later Zerelda glanced in the rearview mirror and saw a vehicle click on its lights and pull out behind them, keeping a respectful distance in the rain. Was that the pickup truck that had just passed them? she asked herself.

*   *   *

Legion Guidry watched the Cadillac float into the curves ahead of him, the rain blowing in a vapor off the rear wheels. He put a fresh cigarette in his mouth and removed the lighter from the dashboard and pressed the red coils against the tobacco. He could hear the crisp sound of the paper burning as he inhaled. The smell of something burning on hot metal gave him a vague sense of satisfaction, one he could not quite define, but it traveled pleasantly down into his loins. He smiled to himself when the rear end of the Cadillac swung heavily on its springs as it went into the curves, and he wondered what that smart-ass Purcel was feeling now, his head bashed with a pipe, trussed like a three-hundred-pound hog in the trunk of his own car.

He hadn't figured out the connection between the kid in the cowboy hat and Purcel and the woman yet. He had seen the kid clearly in his binoculars for perhaps thirty seconds, just enough to recognize him as the salesman who drug a suitcase on a roller skate through black neighborhoods in St. Mary Parish. He had never gotten his binoculars adequately on the woman, but he knew she had to be that slut Barbara Shanahan, who walked around town with a pissed-off look on her face, like her shit didn't stink, whom he'd watched through her window while she mounted Purcel and stroked his sex like a whore before she put it inside her.

His blackjack and S&W .38 were in his glove compartment. He popped it open and removed the .38 and laid it on the passenger seat, where it vibrated with the motion of the truck. After Robicheaux had thrown it in his unflushed toilet bowl, he'd had to wash it with a garden hose outside, then take it apart and soak it in gasoline overnight, before reassembling and oiling the parts. But the gasoline had softened the blueing, which came off on his cleaning rag and streaked and dulled the uniform blue-steel shine that had defined the pistol he had always been proud to own.

But Robicheaux gonna have his day, too, he told himself. Maybe Perry LaSalle, too, who Legion had convinced himself was writing a book exposing Legion as a blackmailer and molester of Negro field women and the murderer of a New York journalist. Because he had convinced himself that the educated, the well-traveled, the technologically sophisticated, all belonged to the same club, one that had excluded him for a lifetime, treating him little differently from the Negroes, serving him his food in their backyards, on tin plates and in jelly jars that were kept in a special cabinet for people of color and white trash.

But no one could say he hadn't gotten even. He could not count the field women whom he had sexually degraded and demoralized and in whom he had left his seed so their bastard children would be a daily visual reminder of what a plantation white man could do to a plantation black woman whenever he wanted, nor could he count the black men whom he had made fear his blackjack as they would fear Satan himself, making each of them a lifetime enemy of all white people.

He mashed out his cigarette in the ashtray and took a six-pack of hot beer off the floor and ripped the tab off a can and drank it half empty, the foam curling down his wrist and forearm. Up ahead, the lavender Cadillac roared through a red light.

I bet that cowboy hitting on you now, bitch, he

thought. But that's just the previews. You cain't even guess what it gonna be like tonight. You gonna see, you.

He finished his beer and tossed the can out the window. He looked in the wide-angle mirror and watched the can bounce crazily in the middle of the road.

Zerelda drove where Marvin pointed, in this instance down a winding road bordered with ditches that were brimming with rainwater, to a dirt driveway that led past a church whose roof was embedded with a fallen persimmon tree. They passed a house that was stacked inside with baled hay, and Marvin told her to park behind the house, in a stand of slash pines and water oaks, and to cut the ignition and the headlights.

The hood of the Cadillac smoked in the rain, the engine ticking in the silence. There was no sound at all from the trunk.

"I got a place fixed up for us in the house. Food and soda, bedrolls, mosquito repellent, a Coleman lantern, paper towels, a mess of board games. I dint forget anything, I don't think," Marvin said, his lips pursed.

"Board games? We're gonna play board games here?" she said.

"Yeah, or anything you want to do. Till I can get rid of him." He nodded toward the trunk. "I'm gonna hide the Cadillac in a barn back in them trees. I'll borrow a car for us till I can buy us one in Texas. We'll cross into Mexico on the other side of Laredo."

"You think I'm staying with you? That's the plan? After you shot Clete and beat the shit out of me?" she said.

"What did you expect? You wouldn't do anything I tole you. I think it was the way you was brought up,

Zerelda. I'd like to have kids with you, but you're gonna have to change your attitude about a lot of things."

"Are you insane? I wouldn't let you touch the parings from my toenails."

"See? That's what I mean. It's being around them Sicilian criminals all your life. They give you that potty mouth," he said.

He pulled the keys out of the ignition and stepped out into the drizzle, the Beretta hanging from his right hand. He walked around the front of the car and opened the door for her. She could smell the odor of ozone and humus and evaporated salt in the air and the drenched earth out in the sugarcane fields, a fecund heaviness she had always associated with life and birth, then the wind changed and an execrable stench struck her face like a fist.

"God, what is that?" she said.

"It's them pigs. They shouldn't be penned up like that. The germs gets in the groundwater, too. This state don't have no environmental direction. Fact is, I'm gonna turn them poor critters out right now," he said.

He walked to the hog pen and kicked down the rails on one side, then threw dirt clods at the hogs to spook them into the woods. But they milled in circles, grunting, and stayed inside the confines of the pen. He watched them, perplexed, and sprayed an atomizer of breath freshener into his mouth.

"That's some dumb animals," he said, then saw Zerelda walking toward the road.

She felt his hand clench her under the arm and turn her back toward the house.

"You're a handful, woman. I'm gonna need to keep an eye on you," he said.

She looked at his chiseled profile, the smoothness of his complexion, his country-boy good looks and the vacuous serenity in his eyes, and she wondered, almost desperately, who lived inside his skin, whom she should address herself to.

But she realized his attention was diverted now, that he was staring at a pickup truck that had stopped on the road and was backing up to the small wooden bridge over the rain ditch. He chewed on his lip, hesitating only a moment, then pushed the Beretta inside her blouse, flat against her back, and began walking with her toward the truck.

"The man who taught me sales always said 'A good salesman is a good listener. The customer will always tell you what he wants if you'll just listen,'" Marvin whispered in her ear. "Just smile at this fellow while he talks. We'll tell him what he needs to hear and he'll go on about his bidness. There ain't nothing to it."

She watched a man in a straw hat and khaki shirt and trousers get out of the truck, a lit cigarette hanging from the corner of his mouth. He looked up and down the road, as though lost, then approached them, his boots hollow sounding on the wooden bridge that spanned the rain ditch. He nodded his head deferentially.

"I got lost on the turn-off to Pecan Island, me," he said.

"Just go a half mile back. This road here don't go nowhere except down to the bay," Marvin said.

The man in the straw hat puffed on his cigarette and looked down the road, bemused.

"You could have fooled me. I t'ought this went to Abbeville," he said.

"No, sir, it don't go nowhere," Marvin said.

"Y'all been fucking?" the man said.

"What?" Marvin said.

"I ain't caught y'all fucking, huh?" he said.

Both Marvin and Zerelda looked at the man, stupefied.

"You t'ink you bad, you?" the man said to Marvin.

He reached out, his cigarette still in his mouth, and grabbed Marvin by his shirt and ripped him away from Zerelda, the Beretta tangling under her blouse, falling to the ground. Almost simultaneously the man removed a blackjack from his side pocket and whipped it down between Marvin's eyes, then across the side and back of his skull as though he were driving nails in wood.

Marvin was unconscious before he hit the ground.

Zerelda's mouth hung open.

"You with Vermilion Parish? The sheriff's department?" she said.

"Ain't none of your bidness who I am, bitch. Where's Barbara Shanahan at?"

"Shanahan?" she said.

His fist seemed to explode in the center of her face.

The rain had stopped altogether when I came around the curve and saw the wood-frame church, the boughs of the persimmon tree, still in leaf, protruding from its crushed roof. I parked on the side of the road and cut the headlights. There were no vehicles in the yard or out in the trees, at least none that I could see, but the wooden bridge over the rain ditch was stenciled with fresh tire tracks.

I rolled down the window and listened.

"What's that noise?" Sal, the ex-soldier, asked.

"I don't know," I replied.

It was an irregular, cacophonous sound, like a tractor-mower idling and misfiring, perhaps without a muffler.

I slipped my .45 out of its holster and opened the door of my truck.

"What you gonna do, Loot?" Sal asked.

"I'll be back in a few minutes," I said.

"That don't sound too good. I think I'd better come along," he said.

"Wrong," I said.

He got out of the truck and grinned. "You gonna arrest me?" he said.

"I might," I said.

But he wasn't impressed with my attempt at sternness, and we crossed the bridge and saw two sets of vehicle tracks, one overlapping the other, both leading past the frame house filled with baled hay. Sal stooped down and picked up a Beretta nine-millimeter lying by a puddle of water. He tapped the mud out of the barrel and used his shirttail to wipe the mud off the grips and hammer and trigger guard, then pulled the slide far back enough to see the bright brass glint of a round already seated in the chamber.

I extended my hand for him to give me the gun, but he only grinned again and shook his head.

The moon looked like a piece of burnt pewter inside the clouds now, and in the pale light it gave off I could see hogs rooting at the edge of a flooded woods. I walked on ahead of Sal, past the church and the house where the preacher must have once lived, the sound of a gasoline- or diesel-powered engine growing louder. On the far side of a three-sided tin shed, someone turned on a lantern of some kind, one that exuded a dull white luminescence.

Out in the trees I could see Clete's Cadillac convertible and Legion's red pickup truck. The hatch to the Cadillac was open, gaping, the trunk empty. I bent down, the .45 gripped in two hands, and got closer to the shed and looked through the back window at the collection of tar cookers and road graders and bulldozers that had been stored there by a parish maintenance crew. A battery-powered Coleman lantern burned on the ground, the humidity in the air almost iridescent in the glow of the neon tubing.

Legion Guidry was filling a bucket from a water tap. Marvin Oates lay unconscious on the ground, his hair matted with straw and mud. Close by, Zerelda sat against a wood post. Her wrists were bound behind the post with electrician's tape. But it was Clete Purcel who was obviously in the most serious jeopardy. He was slumped over by the lantern, his head hanging down, his eyes half shut with trauma and blood loss, the back of his shirt a dark red.

A tree-shredding machine idled on the outer edge of the shed, the ejection funnel aimed out into the darkness, the entry chute that fed into the blades pointed back at Clete.

Legion turned off the tap and threw the bucket of water into Marvin's face.

"Get up, boy. You fixing to hep me make some pig food, you," he said.

Marvin blew water out of his nostrils and mouth and pushed himself up on his hands. Legion shoved him in the shoulder with his boot.

"Don't make me tell you twice, no," he said.

"I dint hear you," Marvin said.

"Pick up the other side of that shithog. He going in the grinder. You be good, maybe you won't end up there, too," Legion said.

Marvin glanced at Zerelda.

"What about her?" he asked.

"She lay down wit' the wrong dog. She got his fleas," Legion said.

Marvin rose to his feet, his face dazed, his eyes looking back at Zerelda.

"You'll let me go?" he said, the register of his voice falling. Then the skin on his face seemed to shrink when he heard the fear and cowardice in his own words.

I started to stand up straight, to move around the edge of the shed, where I could have a clear shot at Legion. But I felt an open handcuff come down on my right wrist, the steel tongue ratcheting into the lock. Sal locked the other end of the cuffs on a water pipe that elbowed out of the shed into the ground.

My handcuff key was in my right pocket and I couldn't reach it with my left hand. I tried to grab his arm as he walked away from me, but he only turned and grinned, lifting a finger to his lips.

Sal rounded the corner of the shed and aimed the Beretta with both hands at Legion's chest.

Legion released Clete's arm, his eyes focusing on Sal, as though recognizing an old enemy.

"Where you come from, you?" Legion said.

"Looks like you been causing folks a lot of grief," Sal said.

"I ain't got no quarrel wit' you."

"Time for you to check out, Jack. I don't mean boogie on down the road, either," Sal said.

Legion stepped backward, tripping over the water bucket, his .38 revolver pushed down in his belt, a loud hiss rising from his throat. Then he bolted for the woods.

Sal began shooting, the recoil of the Beretta jerking against his wrists, sparks flying from the barrel. I had worked my right pants pocket inside out with my left hand now, and I inserted my handcuff key into the lock on my wrist and ran around the corner of the shed with my .45.

I could see Legion running through the woods toward the bay, hogs scattering around him, while Sal fired all ten rounds from the Beretta. A bolt of lightning struck the bay or the woods, I couldn't tell which, and I saw Legion's silhouette in the illumination, like a piece of scorched tin. Then the woods were dark again, and I saw Clete looking up at me in the glow of the Coleman lantern, his face white, a smile at the corner of his mouth.

"Better hook up the pinhead, big mon," he said.

I cuffed Marvin Oates and put him on the ground, then knelt down and used my pocketknife to cut the tape on Zerelda's wrists. A pair of headlights bounced across the wooden bridge over the rain ditch, levering up and down as the car came too fast across the ground. Then Joe Zeroski's Chrysler braked by the shed and Joe and Baby Huey got out on each side. Joe wore a pair of tight slacks and a formfitting strap undershirt, his flat chest rising and falling, his vascular arms pumped. He studied his niece's battered face and stroked her hair.

Then he looked down at Marvin Oates. A small

chrome-plated automatic pistol protruded from his pocket.

"This is the man who beat my daughter to death?" he said.

"We going to have a problem here, Joe?" I said.

"I asked you if this is the piece of shit who killed my Linda."

"Yes, sir, I think he probably is," I said.

Joe stared at Marvin a long time, the nails of his right hand cutting into his palm. His nostrils whitened around the rims and his hand floated toward his pants pocket.

"Joe—" I began.

He removed a handkerchief from his back pocket and reached down to Marvin's face with it.

"He's got a runny nose. It ain't nice to look at. You ought to wipe it for him," Joe said. When he finished, he threw the handkerchief on the ground.

Twenty minutes later Helen Soileau and I watched the paramedics load Clete and Zerelda into an ambulance and take them to an emergency receiving room in Abbeville. The sky was still churning with black clouds, the air loud with crickets and the sound of tree frogs. I looked for the ex-soldier named Sal Angelo but found him nowhere. The last I had seen him, he had walked into the trees, but I could not remember seeing him come out. The coroner and several Vermilion Parish deputies were deep in the woods, almost to the bay, their flashlights bouncing off the trees and scrub brush.

"He locked you up with your own cuffs?" Helen said.

"Yeah, I'd left them on the truck seat," I said.

"Why'd he want to cap Guidry?"

"He knew I was going to do it," I replied.

"I didn't hear you say that."

She watched the coroner and three Vermilion Parish sheriff's deputies come out of the woods with a zipped body bag. The bag looked heavy, sagging in the center, and the deputies had trouble holding on to the corners.

"Did you talk to the coroner?" Helen asked.

"No," I replied.

"Your friend must have been the worst shot in the U.S. Army," she said.

"What do you mean?"

"There were no wounds in Guidry's body. It looks like he was hit by lightning. His boots were blown off his feet," she said.

"Lightning?" I said.

"Anyway, he didn't go out alone. He was floating around with a bunch of dead pigs. Buy me coffee, Pops?" she said.

EPILOGUE

It's winter now, and Clete Purcel and I hunt ducks out on Whiskey Bay like two duffers who have no need to share their war stories anymore and are more interested in the sunrise than the number of birds they knock out of the sky. Barbara Shanahan left town with Perry LaSalle, bound for the Pacific Rim, where cheap labor is called outsourcing and Perry plans to start up a half-dozen new canneries. Whenever Barbara's name is mentioned in conversation, Clete's eyes crinkle fondly, and no one ever guesses the nature of the thorn that was left in his heart.

In November, the same month Jimmy Dean Styles was sentenced to death and Tee Bobby Hulin to life, the Easter Bunny returned to New Iberia and creeped the mayor's house. Then he robbed a pet store in Lafayette and took two huge blue-and-yellow-and-red-flecked parrots with him. The next night he robbed the home of a notorious ex-Klansman and candidate for the U.S. Senate on Lake Pontchartrain while the ex-Klansman was promoting his most recent anti-Semitic book in Russia.

A week later the ex-Klansman's bank statements and record of receipts from his donors were mailed to the IRS and the FBI. The Easter Bunny left the stolen parrots in the house and the following day reported his own crime. The cops who investigated the break-in said the house was layered end-to-end with bird shit.

Marvin Oates was convicted of kidnapping, felony assault, and second-degree homicide in the death of Frankie Dogs. But he skated on the murder of Linda Zeroski and perhaps the murder of Ruby Gravano, the prostitute in St. Mary Parish. Helen Soileau and I and two ADAs from the prosecutor's office gave up trying to manipulate him into a confession. Whenever pressed about his crimes, he sang the lyrics from "I'm Using My Bible for a Road Map" and stared back at us with eyes that seemed incapable of guile or even momentary retention of violent thoughts.

Our psychiatrist said Marvin was sane. A fundamentalist preacher and a half-dozen church people testified as to his character. As I watched him on the stand, I was bothered by the nagging speculation that has troubled me since I became a police officer, namely, that no matter how heinous the crime or evil the deed, human beings feel at the time they commit the act that they are doing exactly what they are supposed to be doing.

I never again saw the ex-soldier who called himself Sal Angelo. I didn't want to think any more about his coming to New Iberia, virtually out of nowhere, dressed in rags and madness, or his claim that it was he who had carried me on his back out of the elephant grass and loaded me onto a helicopter bound for battalion aid. What did it matter who he was? I told myself. Legion Guidry was dead and I was glad. Let my friend keep his tattered mystique and let Vietnam remain a decaying memory.

But eventually I put in an information request with the Veterans Administration.

A soldier named Sal Angelo, from Staten Island, New York, had indeed been a medic in my outfit and had served in the same area as I in late 1964 and early 1965. But one month after I was hit, he had been killed ten miles from the Laotian border.

In the fall Alafair went away to Reed College and returned to us at Christmastime. It's been a wet and foggy winter this year, good for the ducks and me and Clete and for dinners and parties at the house with Bootsie and Alafair and Alafair's reassembled high school friends.

But sometimes amid the gaiety in our living room and the tinkle of glass ornaments on the Christmas tree, I look out at the swamp in the failing light, the denuded cypresses and wisps of moss stark against the sky, and I think about a black field woman of years ago and old man Julian and the moments of weakness and need they shared, and I think about a bullet-rent and sun-faded battle flag encased in glass like the dried blood of a saint, and I wonder if there is any way to adequately describe the folly that causes us to undo all the great gifts of both Earth and Heaven.

But those concerns are fleeting ones now, and when they occur during my workday, I concentrate on hunting down the Easter Bunny, the trickster in our midst, the buffoon and miscreant who lives in us all and allows us to laugh at evil and ourselves.

I don't think it's a bad way to go.

ABOUT THE AUTHOR

JAMES LEE BURKE, a rare winner of two Edgar Awards and named Grand Master by the Mystery Writers of America, is the author of thirty-six novels and two short story collections, including numerous *New York Times* bestsellers, such as *Robicheaux*, *The Jealous Kind*, *Creole Belle*, and *Heaven's Prisoners*. He lives in Missoula, Montana.